Diamond Lilly

by

Henriette Daulton

Diamond Lilly

Cover Art by *Kristian Norris*

The Wild Rose Press, Inc.
PO Box 708
Adams Basin, NY 14410-0708
Visit us at www.thewildrosepress.com

Publishing History
First Mainstream Thriller Edition, 2019
Print ISBN 978-1-5092-2632-0
Digital ISBN 978-1-5092-2633-7

Published in the United States of America

Jessie raced to the wrecked car. Wrapped around the post, the front end had collapsed onto itself. Its side was riddled with bullet holes. Shattered glass from the windshield covered the dashboard. The airbags were deployed and as she approached the driver's side, she discerned the back of a woman's head, hair saturated with blood, her face and torso entangled in the remnants of the bag. With adrenaline pumping through her veins, Jessie pulled on the handle. The door was bent and it didn't budge. Using both hands, she yanked harder. Several attempts later it finally gave, and she was able to force it open part of the way. She reached in, checked the woman's pulse, and found no sign of life.

A glance in the back seat revealed the driver was alone in the car. Realizing she had left her cell phone in the cottage, Jessie was about to run back when she thought she heard a whimper. Suddenly hopeful, she peered at the driver, but the woman hadn't moved. She took her pulse again. Nothing. Mystified, she looked into the back seat once more. There was only a crumpled blanket and a bag on the floor. She turned and was only a few steps away when a soft cry arose from the car. She opened the back door. Curled up on the floor under the blanket, a child stared at her with terror-filled eyes. Jessie's heart took a leap.

"What is your name, sweetie?" she asked softly.

"Lilly."

Dedication

To Lee, Dominic, Pam, and Jenny

Chapter One

At precisely nine o'clock on Monday morning, August first, Anton Adler, alias Charles Brent, stood on the dock at the Port Newark Terminal, his eyes focused on a tugboat gently nudging the freighter *Rotterdam* toward the wharf. Stacked high with containers, the aging ship groaned under their weight. As soon as it came to rest against the berth, a group of longshoremen waiting nearby ambled over to its side.

A short distance away, another man witnessed the activity as well. His name was Nasir Hakim. His dark face reflected his growing impatience with this lengthy procedure. A glance in Adler's direction did nothing to improve his mood. He recalled the heated argument he had with the Imam about using the man as their courier. The cleric insisted, and he gave in. Nonetheless, his feelings remained the same. He didn't trust him then, nor did he trust him now.

He shifted his gaze back to the freighter. Ready to fasten the ship to the dock, crew members tossed mooring lines to the stevedores below. At the same time, an old man with thinning white hair, his face deeply etched by sun and sea, made his appearance on deck. He leaned on the railing, and Hakim recognized him as the captain of the *Rotterdam*. After tightening the last of the six lines onto the bollards, the dock workers rolled up the gangplank, and attached it to the freighter. Then, their job completed, they waved to the crew, and strode down the pier toward their next assignment.

When they were out of sight, the captain headed for the gangway. Hakim allowed himself a thin smile at the sight of the black briefcase he was carrying. After setting foot on the pier, the captain approached Adler, they exchanged a few words, he handed him the case, then returned to the ship. At that point, Adler walked toward the terminal, and Hakim followed him at a safe distance. Several cabs sat idling in front of the building, waiting for their next fare. Adler got in the first taxi in line, and the driver took off.

Hakim hopped into the next cab. Its driver, a middle-aged Sikh sporting a bushy black beard and a white turban, was shouting into his phone and paid him scant attention. Hakim leaned forward and rammed his fist into the man's shoulder. "Airport, now!"

A glance in the rearview mirror revealed dark eyes in an angry face. Promptly, the driver ended his conversation and pulled away from the curb. Not wanting to lose sight of Adler, Hakim tersely ordered him to speed up. The cabbie shook his head silently but accelerated nonetheless, and they arrived at the airport just in time to see the courier enter Terminal A.

Hakim tossed some cash at the driver, jumped out of the vehicle, and raced inside. Adler was gone. Guessing he'd headed to departures, Hakim rushed up the escalator, two steps at a time. The second floor was packed with travelers, luggage sprawled in every direction. He pushed his way through the crowd until he reached a less congested area. For a few minutes, he stood scanning the perimeter. There still was no sign of

Adler. Fury mounting in his chest, he took off to check the rest of the building. A half hour later, he had covered the full length of the terminal, top to bottom, with no success.

Could Adler have disregarded his instructions and continued to the gate without waiting for him? Of course, there was yet another possibility, one he didn't want to think about, but had to consider at this point. What if the courier took off with the briefcase, never intending to get on the plane in the first place? In that case, surely the man would realize he was signing his own death warrant.

Teeth clenched, Hakim stood near a crowded bar, debating his options when he spotted Adler sitting on a stool in a dark corner, wolfing down the remnants of a sandwich. The man turned in his direction, and their eyes met. He shoved the rest of the food in his mouth, and tipped his glass to get at the last few drops of his drink. Then, gripping the briefcase, he rushed past Hakim toward the departure gate.

Pushing his rage aside for the time being, Hakim followed him, making sure to stay a few paces behind, his gaze fixed on the man's bulky body and glistening bald scalp. As the courier approached the security check and metal detectors, Hakim tensed up, but Adler cleared both without a hitch. They were moving down the concourse at a fast clip when the courier came to an abrupt halt. He doubled over with a loud groan. Hakim stopped in his tracks.

Before he could decide whether to grab the briefcase, Adler straightened up and resumed his walk. Relieved, Hakim took a deep breath, all the while damning the fat fool for his gluttony. They reached the gate as the last few stragglers were boarding. Hakim waited until Adler cleared the jet way before getting on the plane. Slowly, he walked down the aisle, scanning each row until he laid eyes on him. The courier sat near the wing, his head tilted back against the seat rest, his face ashen, his eyes shut.

Hakim located his seat and slid in, nodding politely at the old woman next to him. She stared back at him with faded blue eyes, and started saying something. He glanced away to discourage any attempt at conversation.

As the plane rolled down the runway, he considered his next move. His car was parked at the Ft. Lauderdale Airport, a knife and a gun securely hidden under the spare-tire well in the trunk. For a moment he mulled over using one or the other. He sighed. As much as he would enjoy plunging the sharp blade into the fat man, it was too risky, too messy, and there was too much at play. No, he would shoot him, drive to a wooded area in Dania, and toss him in the canal. Quick and clean. A wave of excitement swept over him.

"*Inshallah*. God is great," he voiced, and smiled.

The time for revenge was near.

Chapter Two

Dariel Thomas was edgy. Two hours spent roaming the Ft. Lauderdale Airport, and still nothing to show for it. Scads of people lined up at the check-in counters and packed the terminals, but so far, he hadn't been able to snatch a purse or a single piece of luggage. Usually, with the confusion and large crowds, many travelers got careless and distracted, often leaving their baggage unattended. Not today. Somehow, they all watched their belongings like a bunch of damn hawks. If he didn't score soon, he would have to leave empty-handed in order to pick up Lilly from school.

Luck had not been on his side lately. Now the rent was due, and the landlord, a sorry old son of a bitch, wasn't about to give him a break, no matter what. He glanced at the arrival board. Two more planes had landed in the past few minutes, one from Detroit and another from Newark. His best luck was usually with the international flights. None of those were due to land anytime soon, so right now, these would have to do. Time to get busy. He rushed to the arrival gates. The conveyor belts would soon disgorge more luggage, and it was his chance to latch on to something. Passengers came out of the gates, and Dariel stepped away from the sidelines to walk along with them, taking them in. He glanced around, making sure no security uniforms were nearby. The coast was clear. Satisfied, he turned back to check out the crowd when he noticed her, a tall elegant woman wearing a long leather coat and beautiful shoes. A very expensive designer bag was draped carelessly over her shoulder, and he would almost bet she had a matching wallet tucked away inside. If he was really lucky, there would be a few hundred in cash, along with several credit cards he could quickly put to use before they were reported stolen. Dariel was already doing the math in his head. He stayed a few steps behind her, getting ready to make his move, bump and grab, when all at once, a bunch of kids appeared out of nowhere. At least a dozen of them, teenagers in soccer uniforms, laughing, chanting, "Detroit! Detroit!"

The plane had just disgorged a team from Michigan, most likely here to play a game with the locals. And his target, the woman who was going to be his meal ticket for the day, strolled toward the escalators, surrounded by the boys.

Dammit! He could forget it. This one was gone, and he had been so close.

He sighed. One last plane, one last chance.

"Come on, Newark, give me something. I can't go home empty-handed," he muttered to himself.

He stood to the side and waited for the next wave of passengers stepping out of the gates. Slowly, they appeared. A couple of wheelchairs with attendants doing the pushing, a mother with a toddler, a stroller loaded with two more kids. Families closed ranks around their progeny; a few elderlies struggled along with their meager belongings. Not one of them looked like a prospect so far. He was beginning to despair when a commotion rippled through the crowd. He turned to look. A few steps away, a bald, stocky man had collapsed in a heap on the floor, his face turned sideways, eyes staring off into space. Almost immediately, horrified passengers formed a circle around him, shouting conflicting advice. Someone announced he was a doctor. He pushed his way forward to get to the man on the floor, while the rest of the crowd closed ranks around him once again, out of curiosity or concern, maybe both.

While everybody's attention was directed at the fallen man, Dariel's trained eyes honed in on the briefcase laying on the floor just a couple of feet away. It took him less than a second to realize it belonged to the man on the ground, and right now, it was obvious he had no need for it. It was a no brainer. All Dariel had to do was to reach out and grab it. He got a hold of it, and was out of there.

"Hey!" someone yelled behind him.

He knew better than to stop. Instead, he sprinted away, weaving in and out of the crowds with the ease of an expert at the game, pushing people aside, racing down the stairs, only glancing over his shoulder once just before he was about to exit the building. When he did, he caught sight of a dark-skinned man, wearing a red shirt, chasing him. Dariel was surprised by how fast he was, but it didn't matter. He was pretty confident he could outpace him. Small, skinny, and quick on his feet, if there was anything he was really good at, it was running. Only thirty years old, he already had a lifetime of it behind him. Bursting out of the automated doors into the blast of the August heat, he dashed across the street, barely avoiding a collision with a bus. At the last minute, the driver brought it to a screeching halt, and its horrified passengers nearly flew out of their seats. Unruffled, Dariel kept going. He reached the parking garage, hurried up the stairs to the second floor, ran down the ramp, and squeezed his small frame between a van and an SUV. He sat on his heels against the wall, and willed his pounding heart to calm down.

It wasn't long before footsteps resonated on the stairway. When they stopped on the landing, Dariel didn't move, beads of sweat trickling down the sides of his face and under his collar. After a few seconds of silence, he couldn't bring himself to wait any longer. He had to look. From his hiding spot behind the van's front tire, he cautiously took a step forward.

Squeal. He stopped abruptly, held his breath and glanced at his sneakers, the source of the noise on the painted concrete floor. Terrified his pursuer might have heard it as well, he peered under the vehicle, then reared back like a snake, fear pulsing in his veins. Red Shirt was down in a crouching position, ready to pounce, his dark eyes carefully scanning the floor under the parked cars. Afraid he may have been spotted, Dariel kept still. Nothing happened, and shortly after, the man resumed his ascent. With a sigh of relief, Dariel waited a few more minutes, listening intently. A couple of cars drove by. No other sounds came from the stairway. The man chasing him must have gone on to the top. With the parking garage nearly full, there were lots of places to hide. Dariel decided it was time to make a run for it. He hurried down the ramp and dashed out of the building. With his newly acquired briefcase firmly tucked under his arm, he easily ran the mile to the overnight parking lot. Directly across the street, a two-story building, once home to an aircraft parts distributor, sat empty and neglected. The building was surrounded by a chain link fence, and the front gate was padlocked. The back entrance was unlocked. On his visits to the airport, Dariel usually parked his car behind the building, out of sight, and until now, no one had been the wiser. He ran to the back, opened the gate, cranked up his car, pulled into the alley, carefully closed the gate—no sense ruining a good thing by bringing attention to it—and drove off with the briefcase lodged behind his seat.

****

The "Olde Heidelberg" sign, so faded it was barely legible, hung off one post. The closed restaurant sat dark and vacant. Paint peeled off the white stucco, and weeds thrived in crater-sized cracks in the parking lot. He drove around the trash littering the ground, and found a measure of shade under a small scrub oak. He lifted the briefcase onto his lap and pressed the release buttons. Not surprisingly, it was locked. Reaching into the glove compartment, he pushed aside odds and ends until he found the tool he was looking for. Screwdriver in hand, he popped the lock in no time. With a sigh of satisfaction, he opened the case. Printed in some foreign language, French maybe, a batch of documents stared back at him. Disappointment ran through his mind. All this and for what, a damn stack of useless papers?

Slumped in his seat, he moped, feeling sorry for himself. Really, what did he expect? He should have known. After all, it was a briefcase. The man probably was on some kind of business trip. Angry and frustrated, Dariel scooped up the papers, ready to toss them out the window, but his hand stopped in midair. His mouth dropped open. Was this for real? Staring back at him, in a neat row, were bundles of new hundred-dollar bills. Throwing the papers on the floor, he gently picked up one of the bundles, brought it up to his nose, and inhaled deeply. No doubt about it, it had the scent of real money. Nice, crisp, new money. He started counting. One stack, fifty bills, five thousand dollars. Shaking his head in disbelief, he counted again. Yep, five thousand. Another look determined there was a total of twenty stacks. Almost tenderly, he took them out, one by one, and spread them in the passenger seat. With a silly grin on his face, he stared at his new-found fortune. One hundred thousand dollars, and every bit of it was now his.

When the fog of excitement lifted from his mind, he realized the briefcase still sat in his lap. He picked it up and noticed something strange. Although it was empty now, it still had some heft. He turned it over, tapped on it, and turned it over again. The muscles in his jaw tightened as he stared at it. He leaned closer. Was the bottom layer unusually thick? He tugged at the lining. It didn't budge. There had to be some other way to loosen it. His gaze landed on the discarded screwdriver still laying on the passenger floor.

He picked it up, drove it into the material until he had a small hole, then worked it back and forth until the opening was large enough to insert part of his hand. A grin spread on his face. A hidden partition; he wasn't about to stop now. He yanked at the fabric with renewed energy. It gave way with a ripping sound, leaving Dariel holding it in one hand, while his eyes were riveted on a blue velvet bag, nestled comfortably on the bottom of the case.

Curiosity tugged at his gut. He grabbed the bag and

held it in his hand. Whatever was inside had hard, uneven edges. A bag of rocks? A tight double knot held it shut. Impatiently, he tugged and pulled. Finally the bag fell open, and he nearly jumped back at the sight. A pile of glistening stones rested against the soft fabric. Dumbfounded, he sat transfixed. While he was no expert in gems, he was pretty certain these were diamonds, yet they were quite different than those he had seen in the past. Carefully, he emptied the bag into the case and counted a dozen, each one of them a fairly good size. Almost delicately, Dariel picked up a stone and held it up to the sunlight. It was colorless. He probed the recesses of his mind. If he remembered correctly, someone once told him it indicated quality. Could he really be this lucky? All that cash and diamonds, too?

He scanned the parking lot. Sitting here with a fortune in his lap was not wise. It was time to move on. He dropped the stones back into the bag, and stashed it under his seat, then gathered the cash and shoved it under the passenger seat. He drove up next to the old dumpster at the back of the lot and tossed in the briefcase. A glimpse at the documents from the case convinced him he had no use for them, and besides, they could prove to be incriminating if they were found in his possession. He threw them away as well.

He had to plan his next move with the diamonds. After contemplating a couple of options, he concluded there was only one person he could trust with this—Sal, the old jeweler in Sunrise. Over the years, the man had purchased numerous pieces of jewelry from him, always giving him a fair price without asking too many questions.

While driving north on University, Dariel wondered about the man with the briefcase. Who was he? And the other man, the one who chased him into the parking garage? Were they together? Could this be drug money? After all, who travelled with this much cash? And what about the gems?

Before he knew it, he was two blocks past Sal's place, but he wasn't going to get himself frustrated, no sirree, not today. So he just laughed and did a U-turn at the next intersection. Within minutes, he pulled into the small plaza at the corner of University and Oakland Park. The whole area had seen better days. Every one of the store fronts could have used a face lift, yet somehow Sal, along with the check-cashing store and the food mart next to him, managed to survive regardless. Dariel found a parking space in front of the jewelry store, and went in clutching what he hoped would finally bring him and his family the life he had always dreamed of.

The old man sat at his usual spot, a small work station facing the entrance so he could keep an eye on things. If anyone suspicious approached the store, he would lock the door from his post with the push of a button. He told Dariel it had cost him a bundle to install. Well worth it, according to him, considering the number of robberies these days. He glanced up when Dariel walked in, eyeing him curiously.

"*Vus Machs Da?* What's up?" he asked in Yiddish, scrutinizing the younger man's face. "If I didn't know any better, I would say you're the cat that swallowed the canary."

With a wide grin on his face, Dariel set the bag on the counter. "Sal, wait until you see this."

"Really. That good?" the old man asked, a note of skepticism in his voice.

"Yeah, no kidding."

"What is it then?"

Dariel shook his head. "I'm not telling, you have to see for yourself."

Sal sighed. "I hope it's worth me getting up, eh?"

Dariel nodded. "Oh, yes indeed, you're gonna agree it's well worth it."

Groaning from the effort, Sal rose slowly and limped over to the counter. Dariel opened the bag and carefully shook out a few stones onto the glass top. Not saying a word, the old man glanced at them, peered at Dariel with raised eyebrows then went back to looking at the gems. He continued scrutinizing them for a while before reaching for one and holding it up to the light. He examined it for a long time before putting it back down. Even his tired old eyes couldn't hide his surprise. "Where did you get these?"

Dariel shrugged. "You know, the usual place."

The old jeweler emptied the rest of the stones on the counter and ran his fingers over them, shaking his head. "I don't think so. This is not the usual stuff."

With renewed energy, he went to his work bench and brought back his loupe. Slowly, carefully, he examined each stone. When he was done, he stared at Dariel. "Wherever you got them, you hit a home run. I haven't seen anything like this in years."

Dariel nodded. "What are they worth?"

Sal stared at him over the rim of his glasses. "A whole lot of money. *Fershtay*? (Do you understand?)"

Dariel's face lit up. "So, let's make a deal."

Sal shook his head. "These are way out of my

league," he said, pointing at the gems. "You're talking close to a million here. Top grade diamonds, large and colorless. Not too many people can handle those."

Dariel's face dropped. He was in possession of a fortune in gems with no idea where to cash it in. "At least tell me what I can get for them."

The jeweler shrugged. "I don't know, maybe two hundred thousand. They're worth at least that much. Of course, you'll have to get new authenticity papers for them."

"What do you mean?"

"It's a certificate to show where they come from. Without them it's harder to sell diamonds legitimately."

Dariel nodded. "Whatever you say. Hey, how about you hook me up with a buyer? I'll cut you in."

"Sorry, my boy, can't help you there. The contacts I have, they're like me, little fish in a big pond. I heard Russians, down in Miami and Hollywood, deal in high end stuff, and this definitely qualifies. I understand they're pretty good with the certificates as well. If you want, I'll ask around. Come back in a few days, I'll see what I find out." Sal paused. "Before you go any further with this, there's something you should know. These people down there? They're bad."

"What do you mean?"

"I mean they're tied to the Russian Mob. They play by different rules. When you deal with them, you have to be aware of the danger."

Dariel nodded impatiently as he put the diamonds back in the bag.

"Yeah, okay, I'll keep that in mind. Just let me know what you find out."

He headed toward the door.

"Dariel?"

He stopped and turned back toward the old man. "What?"

"I don't think the people those stones belonged to will let them go that easy. You know what I mean? The word might already be out there."

Dariel shrugged, smiling. "I don't think you have to worry Sal. The owner? I'm pretty sure he's dead."

The old man shook his head. "Hope you know what you're doing, *meyn iung fraynd*. (My young friend)."

Dariel waved at him and left. His mind was still going a mile a minute as he walked to his car. He liked Sal, but the old man was afraid of his own shadow these days, telling him he should be leery of doing business with the Russians. If it meant getting top dollar, he wouldn't mind dealing with the devil himself. Heck, if he could get two hundred thousand for the stones, along with the hundred in cash, holy cow, he would be a rich man.

He glanced at his watch. Shit, he forgot about Lilly! His wife worked as a maid at the Motel 6. She didn't get off until seven o'clock and he was supposed to pick up their daughter from school. Here he was messing up again. How many times did Mandy say he needed to start being more responsible, more reliable? When she got pregnant with Lilly, he promised her he would get a real job and Lord knows, he tried several times. And he hated it, so he went back to his regular profession, hanging out at the airport and the malls, stealing purses and luggage for little money and a lot of risk. Yet he loved the adrenaline rush, the sense of victory it gave him. After all, he grew up in a household of thieves. He was picking pockets by the time he was ten years old. His father was in and out of jail most of his life. Then one day, he swindled the wrong guy and took a bullet between the eyes. His uncle Jack told him it was that outlaw blood in them, and you can't get away from it. But God, how he hated the disappointment in Mandy's eyes the last time he got arrested.

He left the parking lot and headed north. He never owned anything of value in his life. This was overwhelming. Hell, what was he was going to do with his good fortune?

The money part was easy. The very first thing he would do was to buy Mandy a car, a decent one with an air conditioner that worked and a good set of tires. And she could quit the shitty job at the motel. They would move to a nice place, close to the beach maybe, because his little girl loved the beach. Get out of the crappy dump where they lived now. For once he would take care of his family like a man should. What about the diamonds? What should he do right now? His heart pounded like a drum. All these decisions to make, their life would never be the same again. A sharp pain shot through his chest and he realized he had to calm down, get a grip on himself. He inhaled deeply, exhaled slowly. Did it a couple more times. There, that was better. He would wait for Sal to come up with some names. In the meantime, he would lie low with the stones, see if the theft made the papers. Yeah, that's what he'd do, stash the rocks some place and wait it out. He sighed in relief.

Lilly was standing on the sidewalk next to her teacher when he pulled into the empty school yard. A big smile took over her face as she came skipping over to the car. "Hi Daddy!" she sang.

Dariel grinned, always amazed on how much she resembled her mother, small and delicate, with clear blue eyes and curly blond hair. And her nose, he loved that little nose of hers. Heck, everything about his little girl was perfect. The only positive thing he ever was a part of, come to think of it.

"How is my little Bunny today?" he asked.

"Fiiiine."

He shot a glance at the woman standing rigidly behind the child.

"You're late again," she uttered with a disapproving frown.

He smiled sheepishly. "Sorry, Mrs. Poppel."

She was having none of it. "Mm," she scoffed, turning on her heels and stiffly walking away.

The child climbed into the back seat and Dariel grinned at her in the rear-view mirror.

"Okay, Bunny, how about we do something different today?" he asked her, raising his eyebrows suggestively.

She nodded, eyes wide with excitement.

"Good. Let's start by getting an ice cream at the Frozen Yogurt place."

Lilly's face grew concerned.

Dariel frowned. "What's wrong, Bunny?"

"Isn't Mommy going to be upset?"

"Why?"

Lilly hesitated. "She said we don't have money for ice cream."

He reached back behind the seat and tickled her foot. "Don't worry, today is special."

The child's face broadened into a smile. "Can I have two scoops then?"

Dariel laughed. "You bet! Any kind you want!"

Sitting on a bench at the front of the ice cream store, he waited patiently as Lilly finished the last of her cone.

"Now what, Daddy?" she asked.

Dariel gently wiped her chin with a paper napkin. "How about we go to the park?"

She jumped up. "Smalley Park?"

Dariel nodded. It was her favorite. "Sure, if that's where you want to go."

While driving to the park, he mulled over various options to find a good hiding place for the diamonds. As he pulled into the parking lot, he had an idea. While Lilly was getting out of the car, he rummaged through the trunk before finding what he wanted, a plastic grocery bag holding a few beach toys and a handful of sand leftover from the last trip to the beach. He dumped the toys in the trunk, shook out the sand, dropped the blue diamond bag into the plastic bag, and tied it into a neat little bundle. He shoved it into the pocket of his cargo shorts, then reached for Lilly's hand and led her into the park. It was deserted and Lilly had the playground all to herself. He pushed her on the swing set, then she went up and down the slide, shrieking in delight at the sight of a family of ducks waddling by. The tiny ducklings anxiously strove to keep pace with their fast-moving mother.

"How about a walk?" Dariel asked after a while.

The little girl nodded, and they strolled down a trail into the woods, stopping for a moment at an old wooden bridge overlooking a small stream where turtles sunned themselves on nearby rocks. They continued on the trail with scrub oaks providing an oasis of shade before emerging into an open area where dozens of colorful butterflies flitted gracefully among clusters of wild flowers. In the midst of it stood an old wooden gazebo. While the child was busy chasing the butterflies, Dariel slowly walked around the structure, checking it out. He smiled when he found what he wanted. A couple inches of wooden lattice covered the base of the gazebo. On the backside there was a small gap where several slats were missing. He dug a bit further down into the dirt with his hand, then pushed the bag of diamonds into the opening. After he nudged it behind the remaining lattice, he was satisfied. The bag was no longer visible from the outside.

"What are you doing, Daddy?"

Lilly was standing behind him, watching him curiously.

He grinned at her. "Do you know how to keep a secret?"

The child nodded eagerly.

"Okay. I'm hiding a treasure. It'll be for you and me and Mommy. Right now, we're leaving it here, and you have to promise me not to tell anyone, not even Mommy, because it's going to be a surprise for her."

"I won't tell, Daddy."

"Cross your heart?"

Ceremoniously, she made the sign of the cross over her chest with her small hand. "I cross my heart."

"Good girl."

He stood up, took another peek, then kneeled back down and brushed some pine needles over the area. "There, all done. Now we have to go."

And he took his little girl's hand as she skipped happily down the trail.

Chapter Three

Moments after Jessie stepped out of the *Broward News* building, a rivulet of sweat weaved a path down her back. Traffic was heavy. Car exhaust fumes mingled with the heat and trapped waves of suffocating air in the streets downtown. August in south Florida usually was a scorcher, with the temperatures hovering in the mid-nineties on most days. Today was even worse, with a record breaking ninety-nine degrees. The torrid combination of heat and humidity managed to wring every bit of energy out of even the toughest Floridians.

Jessie stood under the glaring sun for three long minutes before the light changed at Broward and Andrews Avenue, and the flow of cars finally came to a stop. She dashed across the street and ran into the parking garage. As soon as she got into her car, she cranked up the A/C, heaving a sigh of relief when the cold air gushed out of the vents. Her cell phone chirped while she was backing up. Glancing at it, she was surprised to see it was her ex boy-friend, John Baldwin. She hesitated for a moment, then answered as she drove down the ramp.

"Hey, John, what's up?"

"Hi, Jessie. How are you?"

"Good. Staying busy with work. How about you?"

"I'm doing all right. Had a couple of charters back

to back and have another one scheduled in a week," he said.

"That's great."

"Yeah, yeah, sure is. I've been thinking of you lately Jessie, and... Actually, since I'm in Ft Lauderdale for a few days, I was hoping we could get together for a chat, maybe have a drink or two."

"I would love to, but right now isn't a good time for me. I'm working on a piece about the involvement of the Russians in human trafficking. Unfortunately, it's turning out to be more and more frustrating. Every time I think I have a lead, it evaporates. So I have to keep on digging. Hopefully I'll hit pay dirt one of these days. Is there something you wanted to talk about?"

He paused and she sensed his uneasiness. "Kind of. I met someone."

"What do you mean? Like a girlfriend?"

He hesitated and Jessie laughed. "You're not sure?"

He chuckled, sounding embarrassed. "No, no, I'm sure. That's why I wanted to talk to you."

"John, what is there to talk about? It sounds like a good thing."

"You don't mind?" he asked.

Jessie braked and pulled into another parking space. "No, of course not."

"She's a nurse at Broward General. I met her when I went to see one of my old customers after his surgery. She was taking care of him and he introduced us. We hit it off and started dating. She loves sailing, Jessie. We're even talking about taking out a charter together, you know, to see how it goes."

"What's her name?"

"Karen, Karen Winslow."

"That's a nice name," she said.

He sounded relieved. "You'll like her. So call me when you get a chance... for that drink. I miss you, Jessie."

"I'll call you, I promise. Bye, John."

Jessie sat in her car for a while, an odd feeling lingering in her chest, memories flooding her mind. Three years earlier, they had sailed the Caribbean together for six months on John's charter boat, in an effort to rekindle the relationship they had at one time. But the shadow of a dead man, Franco Morales, stood between them at all times, invisible, yet overwhelming in his presence. Franco was the love of Jessie's life and they had planned on spending the rest of their life together. But fate, in its infinite cruelty, had another ending in mind. Franco was murdered by drug runners while the two of them were marooned on a deserted island.

Eventually she resumed her life, but nothing was the same, and despite her deep affection for John Baldwin, she soon realized things could never go back to the way they once were between them. About the time they split up, she was offered her dream job, the position of investigative reporter at the *Broward News*, and she promptly accepted. Having worked at the paper in the past, she was familiar with most of the staff and found it pretty easy to adapt to her new position.

However, after giving up her apartment prior to sailing with John, she moved in with her mother, Sophie, until she could find a new place to live. It turned out to be a bad decision, creating a stressful situation at best. After a few months, she was desperate and put everyone on alert she was looking for an apartment. Through a receptionist at the newspaper, she found out there was a place available near the beach. The rental consisted of a cottage situated on a large property. It immediately appealed to her. The owner, Nina Ponti, a middle-aged Italian woman, gave her a price. It was affordable and Jessie quickly agreed. And now, more than two years later, she still loved her small home.

As she left downtown and made a turn on US1, the five o'clock traffic was once again stuck at the 17th Street Causeway. The drawbridge was up, and a long string of yachts and sail boats floated by slowly on the Intracoastal. Jessie sighed. Okay, maybe she could do without these constant traffic snarls, but it was a price she was willing to pay to live near the ocean. The drawbridge went down at last, and cars started moving onto A1A and toward the beach front. The entrance to the Ponti property was just around the curb off the busy road. Since the gate was no longer functional, it stood open at all times. Nina had promised to get it fixed, but it was doubtful it would happen anytime soon.

Jessie pulled into the drive, and parked in her usual spot on the side of the cottage. She had barely stepped into her living room when she heard a noise coming from the patio. She peered out the back door. Nina sat at the table, sipping a martini. Her flushed cheeks suggested it wasn't her first one tonight.

"Come, keep me company, *Cara*." she said, patting the seat next to her.

"Sorry, I can't. My friend Doris Anderson is expecting me at the Wildlife Center in Davie."

Nina nodded. "Oh right, the widow who saves the

animals. She has two young boys, yes?"

Jessie laughed. "Actually, they're both young men now, Mike is 25 and Daniel is 23. They've been involved with the Center since day one. It was one of them who started it all by bringing home strays, and wounded wild life. Things just kind of grew from there."

"You are a good friend to go out there so much to help out," Nina said.

"I've known Doris for years and I really enjoy the work. You should come by sometime."

Nina made a face and Jessie smiled. Not her cup of tea, apparently.

She picked up a couple of books on wildlife she had bought for Doris, grabbed her purse and left. Nina's intrusions were annoying at times, but she realized the woman was lonely and besides, she wasn't about to move again. She loved it here. During cooler nights, she slept with her windows open, enjoying the breeze blowing in from the ocean.

When she got to the Wildlife Center, Doris greeted her with a smile and a hug.

"Thank God you're here. Daniel had a dinner date with Stella and her parents. Mike is home in bed with the flu and I couldn't get a hold of Margaret. I got some of the food ready, I'll work on the rest, and you can start feeding the birds."

Jessie grabbed a pail full of birdseed, and another with finely diced fruits. "I'm on it."

Widowed at a young age and now in her fifties, with short blond hair and vibrant blue eyes, Doris was a bundle of energy and ran the Wildlife Center in a no-nonsense way. She rescued strays, rehabilitating the ones she could and returning them to the wild, while others stayed on for the rest of their lives. The center housed a large variety of birds, raccoons, ducks, pigs and more. The property, sitting on three acres with an old, refurbished house, was a gift from a donor aiming for a tax break. During the rainy season they were often waterlogged. Nonetheless, they appreciated having their own place for the animals.

Housing developments had sprung up all around them yet they co-existed, a strange oasis in the midst of nonstop urbanization. The center had been part of Jessie's life for a number of years, and she treasured Doris' friendship as much as she enjoyed the work. After they finished feeding the animals, the two of them sat in the office contemplating their day.

"Any progress with your story?" Doris asked.

"Sam told me it'll be a miracle if I find anyone who is willing to talk about the Russians. More and more, I think he's right. Everybody is terrified of them," she sighed.

"Sam Perrone?"

"Yeah."

"How's he doing?"

"Great. His boy is starting college, and his daughter is an ace tennis player. Pretty sure she's going to turn pro soon."

When Jessie was abducted while investigating a political plot, Sam Perrone, a detective for the Broward Sheriff's Office, arrested the man responsible for her kidnapping. Their friendship evolved over the years, and she often relied on him for her articles.

"He's a good man," Jessie added.

"Speaking of good men, have you considered

dating again?"

Jessie gave her an exasperated look. "Please, Doris, not you, too. My mother is constantly harping at me about this. She still thinks John and I will get back together."

"Any chance of that happening?" Doris asked.

Jessie was silent for a brief moment. "It's funny, he called me today. He met someone, a nurse. Her name is Karen. He wanted to know if it was okay with me. Doris, why would he ask me this when we broke up ages ago?"

"My opinion? He still loves you. Wants to make sure he can't have you back before committing to a new relationship."

Jessie shook her head. "No, it's over. I care about him a lot, but we're just not meant for each other. I told him to be happy. As far as I'm concerned, I don't need another man in my life at this time."

Doris nodded. "It wouldn't hurt if the right guy came along, though, would it?"

Jessie got up. "If he comes along, you'll be the first to know. For now, I'm out of here."

They hugged and Jessie headed home. On the way, she mulled over their conversation. It was true she was lonely at times, and maybe there was someone else out there for her. But right now, she sure wasn't looking.

Chapter Four

Nasir Hakim stared at the cell phone lying on top of his desk. Two days had gone by, and he had yet to tell his uncle about the stolen briefcase. After Adler dropped dead at the airport, he didn't stick around. While his focus was to catch the thief, having to avoid alerting airport security slowed him down, and the son of a bitch got away. A taste of bile crept into his mouth. Although the imam, El-Amin, bore responsibility for this disaster, he was sure his uncle would put the blame on him. Deep in thought, he didn't even notice when one of his men walked in the office.

"Nasir?"

He glanced up at Abdul Malik standing in front of his desk. "What?"

"Is there anything you want me to do?"

Hakim shook his head. "Not right now. I talked to Jenna this morning. The Broward Sheriff's office has a video of the thief from airport security. When she finds out who he is, she'll call me. Then it's going to be a matter of getting to him before the cops do."

Abdul snickered. "How can she find out? She's not a detective."

Hakim shrugged. "She works there, so don't worry, she'll figure it out. Just be ready when I call you. We'll have to move fast."

He followed him through narrow eyes as Abdul

Malik walked away. He was his first recruit. The man who had been with him the longest. Yet he wasn't quite sure he could trust him. One day very soon, he would have to test him.

Then there was Jenna Morales. A first cousin to Mohamed Salem, his most loyal jihadist, she joined their ranks only recently. With a Lebanese mother and a Cuban father, she was a mixed bag. At first he was reluctant to take her on. However, once he found out she was an internet technology specialist at the Broward Sheriff's office, he realized she could be a vital source of information, and he changed his mind. Now he hoped she would come through with the thief's identity before it was too late. With a deep sigh, he picked up the phone and dialed. Five rings later he was talking to Haji Abboud.

"Did you get the briefcase?" the man asked, not wasting any time.

Reluctantly Hakim gave him the bad news. "Don't worry, Uncle. I have someone inside the police department and I'm about to find out who the thief is. As soon as I do, I'll take action."

Abboud didn't answer right away, and Hakim was worried. He knew his uncle did not tolerate blunders, especially since he went to great length to get the cash and arrange the diamond theft in Paris. When he spoke again, his voice was full of quiet rage. "This is unforgivable, Nasir. How could you let this happen?"

Making excuses would be futile at this point. Hakim swallowed hard. "I'm sorry, Uncle. I will get the money back as well as the diamonds. Everything will still be right on target," he insisted.

"My agreement for the delivery of the diamonds

includes a certain time frame. If you don't meet it, you will not get the needed supplies," Abboud warned.

He paused, and the silence weighed heavily between them.

"How are things with you?" Hakim asked at last.

"I will be leaving for Somalia shortly. We are moving all our operations to Africa where we are reestablishing our Caliphate. New alliances are being formed in Niger and Nigeria. We are also making headway in Egypt with new fighters joining our ranks every day. And we are stepping up our attacks on our enemies on their own soil. We will destroy them, Nasir."

He nodded in agreement. Like his new group of jihadists, Nasir Hakim was born in the United States. His Iranian parents had fled their country to start a new life. They wanted to be able to bring up their children in a free society. Instead, their oldest son grew up steeped in bitterness, alienated by a society he despised. While a senior in college, he started attending mosque every day and had long talks with the Imam. After several months of watching him closely, the cleric, Hanif El-Amin, mentioned he was in contact with Haji Abboud, an ISIS commander, who also happened to be Hakim's uncle. Nasir was stunned. His family had never even mentioned him. That night, at the dinner table, he casually brought up the man's name. His father, normally a mild-mannered man, became so incensed, he jumped up, violently knocking down his chair in the effort.

Hakim's mother, fright written on her face, rose as well, taking hold of her husband's arm to calm him down. "Issam, please don't get so upset. Nasir doesn't know what kind of man my brother is. We never told him. Don't be mad at him. Please?"

Issam Hakim nodded, picked up his chair, sat back down, then turned to his son, shaking his head sorrowfully. "Haji is a monster, my son. Because of him, thousands of Iraqis and Syrians are now dead. By joining ISIS, he became a killer and a traitor. If the government in this country gets wind of anyone in our family contacting him, we will be arrested, questioned, and probably end up in jail."

Hakim shrugged. "I don't know why. We haven't done anything."

His father leaned across the table and spoke softly. "Just the suspicion of having ties to a terrorist organization could have dire consequences for all of us. Is being deported or thrown in jail what you want for your mother and your sister, Nasir? Is it?"

Although Hakim remained silent, he was burning with rage. His mother and his sister were both staring at him.

His father continued, "I do not want to hear his name mentioned again in my house. I forbid you to contact him, do you hear me, son?"

Hakim shook his head, got up, and slammed the door on his way out. There was no doubt his father's mind was warped, poisoned against his own kind. From now on, he would let no one, not even his father, tell him what to do. Every day he spent hours surfing the internet, seeking information about ISIS. The more he read, the more determined he became. Soon not a shred of doubt remained in his mind—he had to join the jihad. It was time for him to be a part of the war on the infidels.

When he went to see the Imam with his decision, the man smiled, told him to buy a throw-away phone, and gave him a number to call. "Leave a message," he said. "Your uncle will get back to you." Sure enough, Abboud returned his call the very next day. Hakim's heart pounded with excitement at the sound of his voice. He shared with him his eagerness to join the fight. From then on, they had several more conversations and despite Hakim's impatience to join the ranks of the jihadists overseas, Abboud did not seem to be in such a hurry.

Then one day he surprised him. "Do you think you are ready, Nasir?"

"Whatever you ask of me, I will do," he answered unflinchingly.

"Good. I want you to set up a cell, four or five jihadists. The Imam will help you find them. We will proceed from there."

At first Hakim was disappointed. He yearned to go to the Middle East and be part of the action. Eventually, he realized Abboud had a bigger plan for him. The right kind of attack could cripple the U.S. once more. And who better to bring this devastation to the enemies of the Caliphate than him? Now, months later, Hakim recalled those early conversations with his uncle and he smiled. There was no doubt in his mind. He would be that man.

****

Jenna called at midday. She talked in a whisper and sounded out of breath.

"Where are you?" he asked.

"In the alley behind the building. It's where the smokers hang out. I ran downstairs, I didn't want to take the elevator. Too slow. Listen, you won't find the thief at his home. They arrested him last night, searched his house. They took him in for booking."

Hakim cursed under his breath. "Did they find the briefcase?"

"According to what I heard, they found nothing."

He breathed a sigh of relief. "Good, then we still have a chance. Anything else?"

"He has a wife and a kid. Maybe she knows something."

"What's his name and address?"

She gave him the information. "Are you going to his house?"

"Yeah, we'll have a look around. Maybe talk with his wife."

"Can I go with you?" she asked.

"No, not a good idea."

There was silence on the line. "Jenna?" he asked.

She was gone. He slammed his fist on the desk. The damn woman was aggressive, too much so. She grew up with the western ways, the evil ways, not under the law of Islam, as it should have been. He grinned maliciously. Soon she would find out, but not yet. He still needed her. Setting his thoughts aside for the moment, he called El-Amin and brought him up to date on the events. The cleric listened quietly before speaking in a soft controlled voice.

"I think I have a solution for our problem. Several of our brothers are incarcerated right now. One of them, Yasuf Fattah, is a trustee at the Pompano facility. To my knowledge, he has access to most of the jail. If this Thomas is held there, I am confident he can get to him. As his prayer leader, I am allowed regular meetings with him. I can arrange a visit for this afternoon and I will bring up our situation. I will let you know the results."

Hakim stressed they had very little time, and told him he would be waiting for his call. He knew the man El-Amin referred to. He had a reputation as a vicious thug in their neighborhood. A couple of years earlier, he finally got caught and tried for a trafficking charge, which garnered him ten years in prison. And now, the job of trustee allowed him once more to impose his rule of intimidation. Only this time it was over the inmate population. Hakim actually had little sympathy for the man's victims. On the contrary, he wished a hundred like him could join his cell. In the meantime, he could only hope the trustee would be able to get his hands on Thomas. If he did, he had no doubt the man would talk. He dialed Abdul's number and told him about the Imam's plan.

"In the meantime, we'll scope the area where he lives. See if it's an apartment or a house. We'll go tonight. I want to make sure the wife is home. If she knows where the briefcase is, we'll get her to talk, without any nosy neighbors sniffing around. Come to the store at eleven... and Abdul, bring your gun."

Chapter Five

A bright moon, surrounded by stars, hung low in the dark sky. Midnight came and went, and Jessie was still wide awake, sitting on her patio, gazing at the show of lights above. The beauty of nature never contrasted more with the starkness of life than at a moment like this.

The thought brought her back to the story she was working on. From the start, when she suggested it to her boss, Arthur Brown, the investigative editor, he was reluctant to give her the go ahead. He warned her it could be dangerous to probe into the Russian mob's influence on sex trafficking in South Florida. She told him she would be careful. It didn't take long before she ran up against the wall of fear and silence surrounding the Russians. It became even more evident when one of her sources abruptly disappeared, and the other one went into hiding after a frantic phone call, warning her to stay away from him.

So at this point, she had very little to go on, and was unsure about what to do next. She sighed and closed her eyes, enjoying the quiet. The traffic on A1A had subsided with only the sound of an occasional car driving past the stone wall behind the cottage.

Suddenly, the roar of engines exploded in the stillness. Jessie sat up, guessing cars were drag racing along the beach front, an event which happened quite often. Then, as they got closer, the unmistakable sound of gunfire erupted in the night.

Startled, she jumped up, dashed to the front of the cottage, down the path and out the gate in time to see two vehicles, one barely trailing the other, racing around the sharp curve at full speed. Instinctively, Jessie stepped back. The first vehicle jumped the curb, missing her by inches, then scraped the wall, the grating sound of metal lingering painfully, before it bounced off violently, and without ever slowing down, crashed into a cement light post head on. The second car, a white sedan, screeched to a halt next to it.

Under the dim glow of the street light a hundred feet away, Jessie got a glimpse of a man in the passenger seat. As she did, he turned and glanced back at her before the car sped away.

Jessie raced to the wrecked car. Wrapped around the post, the front end had collapsed onto itself. Its side was riddled with bullets holes. Shattered glass from the windshield covered the dashboard. The airbags were deployed and as she approached the driver's side, she discerned the back of a woman's head, hair saturated with blood, her face and torso entangled in the remnants of the bag. With adrenaline pumping through her veins, Jessie pulled on the handle. The door was bent and it didn't budge. Using both hands, she yanked harder. Several attempts later it finally gave, and she was able to force it open part of the way. She reached in, checked the woman's pulse, and found no sign of life.

A glance in the back seat revealed the driver was alone in the car. Realizing she had left her cell phone in the cottage, Jessie was about to run back when she thought she heard a whimper. Suddenly hopeful, she peered at the driver, but the woman hadn't moved. She took her pulse again. Nothing. Mystified, she looked into the back seat once more. There was only a crumpled blanket and a bag on the floor. She turned and was only a few steps away when a soft cry arose from the car. She opened the back door. Curled up on the floor under the blanket, a child stared at her with terror-filled eyes. Jessie's heart took a leap.

"What is your name, sweetie?" she asked softly.

"Lilly."

"Hi, Lilly, I'm Jessie. Don't be afraid, I'm not going to hurt you," she said, reaching out.

The child shrunk back, whimpering. "I want my mommy…"

"I know. But right now we have to hurry and get her an ambulance, okay?"

"Are the bad men gone?"

"Yes, they are gone. You're safe."

The child nodded, and hesitantly reached out a hand. Jessie lifted her off the floor and into her arms. She took hold of the blanket and wrapped it around the child. "Hold on, Lilly, my house is right here, we're going to get help."

She ran back to the cottage with the child clinging to her. In the living room she gently sat her on the couch, crouched down next to her, and pointed to the kitchen. "I have to make a phone call. I'll be right over there, okay?"

The child nodded. Jessie grabbed her cell phone, stepped away, and dialed 911. With her back to the child so she couldn't hear her, she gave the operator her address and the information. Afterwards, she sat beside Lilly and pulled her close. "In just a few minutes, the police will be here. When they do, I'll have to go back outside to talk to them. I won't be far, I promise. You can lie down right here and wait for me."

"Is Mommy going to be all right?"

Jessie's throat tightened. She rubbed Lilly's back and nodded. "There's an ambulance coming and they'll take her to the hospital."

Tears filled the child's eyes. "I want her to wake up and talk to me."

The deception gnawed at Jessie. "I know, baby, but she can't talk right now. What about your Daddy? Can we call him?"

Lilly shook her head. "The police came to the house and took him away."

"When was that?"

"Yesterday."

"Was your Mommy there?"

Lilly nodded. "She was crying, and Daddy was crying, too. He didn't want to go. They were mean to him and made him get in the police car."

"That other car, tonight, do you know if it was following you?" Jessie asked.

Lilly nodded.

"Were those the bad men you asked about?" Jessie said.

The child nodded again. "Mommy and me, we went to the police station to see if they would let Daddy come home. We waited there a long time, and Mommy talked to a lot of policemen. She asked if we could see him. They said no. When we got back to the house, it was really dark and the two men were standing at the front door. Mommy was afraid, she said they were bad. She drove away really fast, and they chased us. Then she told me to get down on the floor, so I did."

Jessie stroked her face and smiled. "You did the right thing. You're a good girl."

Soon, the distant blast of sirens resonated in the night. Jessie had Lilly lie down and pulled the child's blanket over her legs. "I have to go talk to the policeman for a little while, but I'll be back soon, all right?"

Lilly nodded.

Jessie went back outside. The first patrol car pulled up, followed closely by an ambulance. Two deputies got out of their vehicle and approached cautiously. Jessie introduced herself, then described the pursuit and shooting as calmly as she could. As she was talking, a couple of EMTs jumped out of the ambulance and rushed to the wrecked car. It didn't take them long to confirm what Jessie already knew. The woman was beyond help. They stood about briefly, in a moment of hopelessness, before repacking their gear.

In the next few minutes, several more Broward Sheriff's cars arrived, along with a medical examiner's van and a truck from the crime lab. Lights were brought in, yellow crime tape went up, technicians walked around gathering evidence. A tow truck parked nearby, waiting to haul away the vehicle once the techs and the police were done.

As the eerie scene unfolded, Jessie was overcome with sadness, thinking about the child who was now without a mother. She was ready to step back inside to check on Lilly when an unmarked police car pulled up. A plainclothes man got out, and immediately was joined by the other cops on the scene. They conferred for a while before glancing in her direction. The man nodded, then headed her way.

As he got closer, Jessie recognized Jim Boyd, a Broward Sheriff's office homicide detective. Short and thick through the middle, he had a square jaw and sported a crew cut, probably dating back to his military days. She had interviewed him several times while reporting on a crime a while back. His eyebrows shot up. "Jessie, what the heck are you doing here?"

She pointed to the driveway nearby. "I live there. I was sitting on my patio when I heard the shots. I ran out here and saw the car crash."

"So you called it in?"

Jessie nodded and described the accident once more. She told him about the little girl. Boyd frowned. "How is she doing?"

She shook her head. "She doesn't realize her mom is dead. She told me her father was picked up by the police yesterday. I think he may still be in jail."

Boyd sighed. "Do you think you could stay with her for a while? We don't want her out here with all this going on. When I'm done, we'll talk."

Jessie nodded and went back into the cottage. Lilly was curled up on the couch, dolefully staring at the ceiling. She smiled at her. "Somewhere in the kitchen I have some cookies. Would you like some with a glass of milk or juice?"

Lillie shook her head. "No, thank you. Can I see Mommy now?"

Jessie's stomach roiled. She peered into the child's innocent blue eyes and lied. "Right now is not a good time Lilly. They had to take her to the hospital."

The child's chin trembled. "I don't want to stay alone at the house."

"No, no, you won't have to," Jessie reassured her.

"Can I stay with you until Mommy's better?"

Jessie smiled at her. "I'm not sure if it's possible. We'll find out."

Oddly enough for the late hour, she found a children's movie on TV. It wasn't long before Lilly had her head on Jessie's lap and was fast asleep. Nearly an hour later, Boyd rapped softly on the door. After a glance at the sleeping child, he motioned for Jessie to step outside. She gently eased herself out from under Lilly and joined him, closing the door behind her.

"The young woman's name is Mandy Thomas. She suffered multiple gunshot wounds. Until the autopsy is done, we won't know for sure if they're the cause of death. The little girl is her child, Lilly Thomas. The father, Dariel Thomas, was arrested yesterday."

"So he is in jail. Lilly said so. What was he arrested for?" Jessie asked.

"Monday he was caught on camera stealing a briefcase at the airport, so they revoked his probation. There probably will be charges coming from the theft."

"Could there be a link between the theft and his wife's death?"

Boyd shrugged. "It's possible. There's no way to know right now."

Jessie sighed. "Poor child. She asked for her mom. What will happen to her now?"

"We don't have too many options. After we talk to her, we'll have to turn her over to social services," Boyd said quietly.

"Could she stay with me for the night? This is really an awful situation for her," Jessie asked.

"I wish I could say yes, but it's not up to me. In a

case concerning a minor child, we have to involve the Department of Children and Families."

"If I can't keep her here, can I at least bring her in myself?"

He thought for a moment before shrugging. "Why not? I'm calling the social worker now, so she can meet us at the station. I'll be ready to leave in another few minutes. I'll come and get you."

True to his word, Boyd was back in fifteen minutes. "Ready to go? You can just follow me."

Jessie nodded, got her keys and her bag, and gently scooped up Lilly. The child woke up, confused for a moment. "We're going to the police station to talk to the detective," Jessie explained.

"Will my Daddy be there?"

"Not tonight, Lilly. Maybe you'll get to see him later."

The child smiled and nodded. "Then we can get Mommy and go home."

As they were leaving, Jessie noticed the coroner's vehicle pulling out on its way to the morgue. She glanced in the rearview mirror and was thankful Lilly had dozed off again.

The sheriff's office building was deserted. When they walked by the desk sergeant, Jessie saw he had nodded off. Boyd led them down the hallway into a small room with a few chairs and a table.

"The social worker is on her way. We had to get her out of bed," Boyd explained.

He smiled at the little girl and in a surprisingly soft voice for such a big man, he asked her a few questions. "Lilly, can you tell me how many men were waiting at your house when you and Mommy got home?"

Lilly nodded. "Two."

"Did your Mommy know those men?"

She shrugged. "No. She just said we had to get away."

"Do you remember what they looked like?"

The child shook her head, frowning in concern

Boyd gave her a reassuring smile. "It's all right."

He turned to Jessie. "When we get Lilly situated, we'll go over your statement one more time. Make sure we didn't overlook anything... you know, with everything going on, it would be easy to do. Right now, won't you sit down? You must be tired. Can I can get you anything? I wouldn't recommend the coffee here. At this time of the night it's probably so thick you couldn't stir a spoon in it. You want water or a soda?"

She shook her head. Adrenaline had kept her going until now. Then all at once, the reality of the tragedy, costing a woman her life and leaving a little girl without a mother, left her numb. She glanced at the chairs. The sheen on the metal had worn off a long time ago. They looked cold and uninviting. But exhaustion won out, and she sat down, pulling Lilly into her lap. Fifteen minutes later, a slim black woman walked in. Smartly dressed in a cream-colored suit, she looked as if getting up in the middle of the night was a pretty common occurrence for her. She smiled at the detective, acknowledging they already knew each other. Boyd nodded at her, then turned to Jessie.

He cleared his throat. "Jessie Milner, meet Mary Gilmore. We have a situation right now, Mary, and we need a placement for this little girl."

The social worker focused her dark eyes on Lilly. "And who is this lovely young girl?"

43

Lilly eyed her apprehensively before burying her face in Jessie's chest.

"This is Lilly," Jessie said, gently patting the child's back, to reassure her.

"Can I talk to you for a little while, Lilly?" the woman asked softly.

The little girl hesitated a moment, then turned toward her.

"How old are you, Lilly?"

"Five."

"You're a big girl. Now, how about you and I go see a very nice lady who can't wait to meet you?" the social worker asked.

Lilly shook her head. "I want my Mommy!"

"We can't see Mommy right now. We'll talk about it tomorrow."

"Why can't I stay with Jessie?" the child whimpered.

"I wish you could. Maybe later."

Jessie raised her eyebrows, quietly mouthing the words. "Why not?"

The woman glanced at Boyd. He walked over, and reached for the child's hand. "You know what? I would love a candy bar right now. Only I don't know what kind I want. Maybe you can help me make a decision. Let's go check the machine and see what choices we have. Ladies, we'll be right back."

Surprisingly, Lilly didn't protest and let herself be guided away. Mary Gilmore waited until he walked out and closed the door behind him.

"This child is traumatized. She just lost her mother. Why can't she at least spend the night with me?" Jessie asked anxiously.

"No. Unfortunately, there are rules and regulations I cannot ignore, for your safety and the child's. On my way here, I called one of our foster moms who agreed to take her for the night. I understand the father is in jail. We'll have to talk to him, see if there are relatives in the area. Family is usually the best option if they qualify. We won't just let her stay with anyone without making sure they are able to care for her. I promise I will keep you posted."

Jessie shook her head. "How can you tell her about her mom? This is just so awful."

"We're not doing this now. What I can tell you for a fact is the home where Lilly will be staying tonight"—Mary Gilmore smiled reassuringly—"is where I would want my child to go, if she had to. Annabelle, the foster mom, is a wonderful, caring lady. Lilly will be fine there for tonight. Tomorrow we'll deal with the rest."

"What if there's no one else for her?"

The woman held up a hand. "Let's not go there right now." She hesitated slightly, then went on, "I don't like saying this, but it would be best if you weren't here when Detective Boyd comes back with Lilly. It will make it harder for her."

Jessie got ready to protest, then realized the woman was right. If she stayed, Lilly would want to go home with her. She was torn. She didn't want the child to think she abandoned her. Mary's eyes softened.

"Jessie, I will tell her you had to leave. It's for the best."

"All right," she agreed reluctantly.

Mary Gilmore reached over and squeezed her hand. "There's another room across the hall. I hope you don't mind waiting there until we're gone. I'll talk to you tomorrow."

Jessie nodded and walked away.

"Thanks for caring," the woman called after her.

Still upset, Jessie didn't answer. She went into another room painted stark gray, sat down, leaned her head against the wall, and closed her eyes. After she waited for what seemed like an eternity, Boyd finally appeared in the doorway.

"Let's go next door, it's a little less cramped," he said smiling awkwardly. The other room didn't seem any larger, but she was too tired to point it out.

"You sure I can't get you anything? Water, soda, a candy bar?"

Jessie shook her head somberly.

Boyd pointed to a couple of chairs and they sat down. "Let's get started. I'm sorry about Lilly. You formed a bond with the child, but you know bureaucracy. There's no way around it," he apologized.

"I'm tired, so let's do this," she sighed.

They went over everything once more, from the moment Jessie heard the first shot until she walked up to the wrecked car and found Lilly. He asked about the driver and the passenger of the other car. And again, she indicated she only had a brief glimpse of a dark-skinned passenger, none of the driver. As for the vehicle they were driving, she was pretty sure it was a white or cream-colored sedan.

The detective took copious notes, and she noticed his handwriting was neat and precise. When they were done, Jessie leaned forward in her seat. "You know I have to write this up for the paper, so you might as well tell me what you think right now."

Boyd shrugged. "Right now? It could be anything, including a carjacking that went wrong."

"Lilly said the men were standing at their front door when they pulled into the driveway. When the mother spotted them, she spooked and took off, and they chased her. Certainly doesn't sound like they were looking to steal a car. Also, it seems like an amazing coincidence the father was arrested yesterday for theft. I think maybe he had accomplices who wanted their share of the loot."

"You know how it goes. We have to investigate all angles before we jump to conclusions. Right now it's too early to tell." Boyd stood up and stretched. It was nearly three in the morning. "Let's call it a night. If you remember anything else, no matter how inconsequential it seems, you call me."

Jessie sighed. He gave her his card and led her out. This time, the officer at the front desk was awake, although barely. Broward Blvd. was a ghost town, and the darkness matched her mood. She drove home in a near trance. In bed she couldn't fall asleep, Lilly's face etched in her mind, her blue eyes drenched in sadness.

She said she wanted to take her home, keep her here with her. Realistically, how could she? She had no support network for babysitting, or school, or for any other needs a five-year-old required. Yet, knowing Lilly could grow up lost in a world not of her making tugged at her heart and wouldn't let go. She tried to convince herself there probably was a family member who cared about the child, and would be there for her. As dawn's first light filtered through the bedroom shade, Jessie finally dozed off.

Chapter Six

The alarm blared loudly at seven o'clock sharp. Jessie buried her head in her pillow, a deep moan of exhaustion rising from her chest. A mere two hours of sleep left her mind clouded in fog and her body aching with fatigue. A long hot shower brought some relief, although not nearly enough.

Now she sat at the kitchen table, sipping coffee while staring at her half-eaten cup of plain yogurt. Let's face it, there was nothing enticing about its taste. In an attempt at improving her eating habits, she had bought a half dozen of them and now, every time she opened the refrigerator door, they sat there, all nicely lined up in a row, reigniting the old guilt. Eventually she would eat them all, maybe even drop in some fresh fruit to improve their flavor.

Her thoughts went back to Lilly. Did she sleep? No doubt she would ask for her mom this morning. How does one tell a child she would never see her mother again without tearing her heart apart?

She sighed deeply, drank the rest of her coffee, and threw away the remains of the yogurt.

It was time to go.

In the lobby of the office building, she paused briefly before pushing the button to summon the elevator. She didn't like them, avoided them as much as possible. However, today, she was just too tired to attempt the stairs. Stepping off on the eighth floor, she spotted Lonnie McKenzie standing near his desk. He was talking to Sandy Herzog, the lifestyle editor and her former boss. Sandy had hired her at the newspaper fresh out of college, and although their relationship had not been a close one, she was more than supportive when Jessie applied for her new position.

But right now, Jessie wasn't willing to share the previous night's events with her. She stopped short of the glass door leading into the office.

Lonnie noticed her hesitation, and broke off his conversation with Sandy. He came out to meet her.

"What's wrong?" he asked, frowning in concern.

Tears welled in her eyes as she told him about the shooting, the car wreck and Lilly. Lonnie shook his head. "This is awful, Jess. She lost her mom, and her father is in jail. What will happen to her?"

"Right now she's in a foster home. The social worker assured me she would be well taken care of. This has been on my mind all morning, Lonnie. I want to go see her father, talk to him. I have to make sure there's somebody out there to take care of her."

"And if there isn't?" he asked.

She shook her head. "I don't know. Like you always tell me: one thing at a time, right?"

He motioned to her. "Come here."

Jessie stepped closer and he folded her in his arms and held her tight. "You're such a good soul."

Then he gently pulled her away and looked into her eyes. "If there is a way to help this little girl, you will find it. I'm sure of it. God only knows how persistent you can be. And if you need me, I'm right here."

His words brought a smile to her face. "Thanks,

Lonnie. Your support means a lot."

She smiled, watching him saunter back to his desk. Lonnie had been an entertainment reporter at the *Broward News* for quite some time when Jessie was first hired.

From the very first moment they met, he made her feel at ease, and better yet, knew how to make her laugh. At thirty-eight, he was short, a few pounds overweight, with blond curly hair, dark blue eyes, and an easy smile. He was also gay, and not afraid to let anyone know.

Feeling somewhat better, she took the stairs down to her floor to find her boss, Art Brown. He was in the break room, pouring himself a cup of coffee. Jessie stood behind him, looking over his shoulder, while he added several heaping spoons of sugar. He turned to look at her. "What is it?" he barked.

She shook her head. "No wonder you're borderline diabetic. Have you considered cutting back on that stuff?"

"None of your business," he said gruffly, and squeezed past her, carrying his mug.

With bushy eye brows, a full head of white hair, a wide girth, and no tolerance for nonsense, Art gave the impression of a grumpy old man. Some of his reporters were quite intimidated by him. Jessie, on the other hand, knew him well enough to realize he was really a softie at heart.

She followed him, noticing his pronounced limp. "What's wrong with your leg?"

He ignored her question and glanced at her over his shoulder. "What do you want?"

She made a face. "Geez, most men don't mind

when I follow them."

He eyed her suspiciously. "I mind because I know you're up to something, and I seriously doubt I'll like it."

They went into his office, walled off by glass on all sides and in full view of every desk on the floor. Everyone referred to it as the fish bowl. "All right, let's have it," he sighed. Lowering himself into his seat, he winced in pain.

Without waiting for an invitation, Jessie plopped down into the chair across from his desk. "Really, Art, you don't look so good. What's wrong?"

"Why do you have to be so damn nosy?" he complained.

"I'm a reporter, it's my job. Besides, I care about you whether you like it or not."

His demeanor softened somewhat, and he shrugged. "Yeah, well, it's old age. Arthritis. Gotta learn to live with it. You're young. You'll find out someday."

"Grammy Milner used a menthol salve for aches and pains. As a matter of fact, she used it for just about everything. She swore by it."

He waved it away, "Yeah, yeah, everybody has a solution, and none of them work. Tell me what you want."

She told him about the car chase, the shooting and her involvement.

"So where is this going?" he asked when she finished.

"I want to get an interview with Dariel Thomas at the jail."

Art snorted. "How the hell you gonna do that?"

"I don't know yet. I want to talk to him about his daughter Lilly. Also to find out why someone would want to kill his wife."

"Well, good luck. If you manage that, we'll have a story. So get busy."

Jessie was smiling when she left his office. A couple of years earlier, he had pushed hard to get her the investigative slot despite the paper's efforts to cut back drastically. Newspapers were bleeding money, and the *Broward News* was no exception. Although the additional digital format gave them more readership, it was an uphill fight for survival in this new world. Nonetheless, Art came through for her.

Back at her desk, Jessie called Sam Perrone. The detective sounded pleased to hear from her. "Jessie. What's going on?"

She filled him in on the events of the previous night and told him about Lilly.

"Yeah, I heard about it this morning. I didn't know you were the one who called it in. It's too bad about Mandy Thomas and the little girl. But if you're writing an article about it, you're better off talking to Boyd. He'll have all the details."

"Sam, this isn't directly about the story, so I wonder if you could help me."

"What do you need?"

"Is there any way I can get in to see Dariel Thomas?" she asked tentatively.

"Mm...I don't know if it's possible. Granting interviews with prisoners isn't exactly on top of a warden's list."

"Sam, I hate asking you for favors, but this is really important to me. This little girl just lost her mom.

Talking to her father might give me some insight on what I can do to help her."

Perrone paused for a moment. "Sure, Jessie, I'll check it out for you."

It was mid-morning when he called her back.

"Sorry about the wait. Boyd just came in a little while ago. He stopped by the jail earlier to see Thomas, told him about his wife's death. According to him, the man really took it hard. He insisted he had no idea who would want to kill her. Swears he always works alone. His criminal record seems to confirm that, leaving out any potential accomplices. On Monday, airport security identified him as the man who stole a briefcase from a passenger who collapsed and died at the airport."

"I know. Boyd told me," Jessie said.

"This whole business is fishy. A fingerprint search for the dead man came up with an Anton Adler, a German national with an arrest in New York for assault three years ago. The charges were dropped when the victim withdrew her complaint. According to the German police, he made frequent trips to the Middle East where he was observed having contact with suspected terrorists. This time he was travelling with a fake U.S. passport under the name of Charles Brent, a man long deceased. They ran down the address. It led them to an empty lot in Kansas City. There's a good possibility he was a drug courier."

Jessie nodded. "So maybe he had associates who were desperate to get back this briefcase, and with Thomas tucked away in jail, they decided to go after his wife."

Perrone shrugged. "Could be. So far, Thomas is not talking, and a search at his house didn't turn up anything."

"Did you find out if I can see him? Maybe he will talk to me."

"I'm waiting for a call back from the warden. I'll let you know as soon as I hear from him," Perrone said.

Fifteen minutes later he rang her back. "Thomas is detained at the Pompano Facility." He gave her the address. "The captain who's in charge of the prison is an old acquaintance. He agreed to your visit. If you have any problems just tell them to call me."

"Sam, what are his charges?"

"Hang on a minute I'll check." She heard him typing. "It's for violation of his probation terms."

"He was on probation?" Jessie asked.

"Yep. Just got out of jail six weeks ago. Then, of course, they will be charging him for the theft at the airport," Perrone added.

"What was his last conviction?"

The typing resumed. "Petty larceny. You know, shoplifting, purse snatching, etc. The man just can't clean up his act. Not only that, he keeps getting caught."

Jessie sighed. "Poor Lilly."

"Yeah... I don't think he'll get off easy this time around."

"How long will he be incarcerated?" Jessie asked.

"At least long enough to serve out his prior sentence."

"How long is that?" she asked anxiously.

"It doesn't look good for him, Jessie. Three to five years."

"Okay, thanks, Sam. I'll let you know if he decides to talk to me."

"Yeah, see if you can get him to tell you what he did with that damn briefcase," he said.

"Will do."

Chapter Seven

After punching the address into her GPS, Jessie hopped onto I-95 Northbound, got off at Hammondville Road, and turned on Twenty Seventh Avenue. Twenty minutes later she was at the jail. After she sat waiting in a dingy gray room for a short while, a glum-faced guard led her down a narrow corridor, past two thick metal doors with coded keypads, before entering another drab room painted a darker shade of gray. He pointed to a metal table in the middle of the room. It was bolted to the floor. Two gray plastic chairs sat across from each other. He told her to take a seat and wait for Thomas to be brought in. Then he left, closing the door behind him. It made an odd clicking sound and Jessie wondered if he had locked her in. Twenty minutes later she was getting rather impatient, when a door opened on the opposite wall. Wearing prison garb two sizes too big, a small framed man shuffled in, with long straggly blond hair clinging to his scalp. He stopped and gave Jessie a confused look. The guard behind him pushed him forward.

As he approached the table, Dariel's pant legs dragged on the floor with an odd swishing sound. The guard shoved him down into the chair across the table from Jessie, then went to stand against the wall, his arms folded in front of him, his face expressionless. Dariel slumped in his seat, eyeing her through red-rimmed eyes.

Jessie smiled at him. "Hi Dariel, my name is Jessie Milner. I'm a reporter for the *Broward News*."

"I don't have anything to say to you," he muttered in a voice so soft she could hardly hear him.

"I'm sorry about your wife Mandy."

He glanced away. "I already know about Mandy. The cops told me."

"Dariel, I was there. Last night, when it happened—"

He jerked his head back, his eyes suddenly widening.

"You were there? Do you know who did it? Who killed my Mandy?"

Jessie shook her head. "I'm afraid not. I live nearby and when I heard the shots, I ran outside. I only got a glimpse at the other car before it took off."

He muffled a sob and lowered his head to his chest, limp hair spilling over his pallid face. Jessie wanted to reach out and hold his hands, bring him some comfort. She glanced over at the guard. He was glaring at her and she kept her hands in front of her.

"Dariel, I got to meet your little girl, Lilly."

He looked up at her, a glimmer of hope in his eyes. "You know my Lilly? Is she okay?"

She smiled. "She's fine, Dariel."

His eyes glistened with tears. "They said she was in a foster home now."

Jessie nodded. "For the time being. Hopefully it won't be for long. She's a wonderful little girl."

A faint smile appeared on his lips. "I know. She's my Bunny."

"Dariel, do you have any family, anyone close to

you who can take care of Lilly until you are released?"

He hesitated, and Jessie sighed in frustration. "If there is someone, don't you think it would be better for her than a foster home?"

He shook his head. "We don't have anybody, except for my sister Emily. We haven't been in touch, though, for a long time. Last we talked, she lived in Minnesota."

"Can you contact her?" Jessie asked.

"I don't know. I lost her number."

Jessie took out her notebook and a pen. "What's her name?"

"Emily Newhart. Her husband Martin, he doesn't like me very much. Back when I first was arrested, he didn't want her talking to me anymore. I can't really blame him. He wanted Emily to have a better life. Our family... well, we weren't like a normal family, so he moved her away as far as he could from us. They have a boy, Benjamin. He's a lot older than Lilly. He's probably thirteen now. My sister never even met Mandy or Lilly"—he started crying again—"and now Mandy is dead. Emily will never get to know her, to know what a good person she was."

Jessie waited a few minutes, giving him time to compose himself. "Do you remember the town Emily lives in?" she asked softly.

He frowned, thinking about it. "I think it was Pine Island. Yeah, that's what it was, because at the time she told me, we were living in an apartment on Pine Island Road in Sunrise. Emily said it's kind of a small town." He leaned forward and gave her a weak smile. "Only one stoplight. Can you imagine? Their place is just outside the town, a farm, with a big house, cows and chickens. You know, like a real country place."

"Okay, I'll find her," Jessie assured him.

His eyes took on a new intensity. "I have to see Lilly. Will you please bring my little girl to see me?" he implored.

"I don't know if I can, Dariel."

He glanced over at the guard, making sure he was out of earshot. "I can pay you. I have lots of money," he whispered.

Jessie frowned. "Where did you get it?"

He hesitated then glanced away.

"Dariel, look at me."

She held his eyes across the table. "You have to level with me. The cops are really eager to get their hands on that briefcase you stole at the airport. They have a video. So there's no denying you took it. Is that where your money came from?"

He didn't answer. Jessie leaned forward, speaking softly. "Listen to me. If you don't cooperate, they will charge you. But if you turn the briefcase over to them, they might be willing to show some leniency. Think about it. Lilly needs you."

He shook his head. "I don't have it anymore."

"What? The briefcase? What did you do with it?"

He shrugged. "I threw it away."

"And what was inside, Dariel?"

He sighed. "Did the cops say they'll let me go if I give them the stuff from the briefcase?"

"No, not exactly. Here is what I think. Somehow they're very concerned about the man who died at the airport. He seems to be their main focus, not you. This is why it may be your chance to get out of here and be with Lilly."

He covered his face with both hands.

"Dariel, come on," Jessie insisted.

"Maybe that man killed Mandy," he said, his voice muffled.

Jessie shook her head. "Impossible, he died from a heart attack at the airport."

Dariel dropped his hands and shook his head irritably. "No, not him! The other guy. As soon as I grabbed the briefcase, he was on my tail."

"There was someone else with him at the airport?"

"Yeah. He chased me all the way into the parking garage before I ditched him."

"So you had the impression they were together?"

Dariel shrugged. "I don't know. When the briefcase guy dropped dead, everybody else stood staring at him. Not this guy. He was on me right away. And the way he did it, very quiet like, to me it meant he had no intention on drawing attention."

"Can you describe him?"

"Dark hair, dark skin."

"Black?" Jessie asked.

He shook his head. "No, no, Arab or Spanish maybe."

"Dariel, what was in the briefcase?"

He shifted in his seat. Frustrated, she pounded her fist on the table. Dariel reared back in the chair. The guard took a step forward. "If you do this again, this visit is over," he said glaring at her.

"I'm sorry, officer, really. Everything is okay, I just got carried away. It won't happen again," she promised, giving him a contrite look.

The man nodded sullenly and stepped back. She stared at Dariel,

"One last time, do you want to get out and get Lilly back?" she whispered.

He nodded.

"Then tell me everything, so we can try to get you released."

"I don't trust the cops, they lied to me before. I'll tell you. You will be my witness and they can't deny it later," he said.

"Sounds fair."

He glanced in the guard's direction. When he seemed satisfied the man was looking away, he leaned across the table, motioning for her to do the same.

She leaned in.

"In the briefcase...There was money, lots of money, and diamonds," he whispered.

Her eyes widened. "Money and diamonds?"

He nodded.

"How much money?" she asked.

He leaned in further and spoke softly. "One hundred thousand."

Jessie let out a long breath. "That's a lot of money."

He nodded again.

"And the diamonds? Do you know how much they're worth?" she asked.

He looked at her and smiled.

Jessie shrugged. "Are you even certain they were real diamonds? They could have been fake."

Dariel smirked. "They're real, for sure. I took them to Sal and he checked them out."

"Who's Sal?"

"He's a jeweler, a good one. He knows his stuff," he answered.

"And what did he say?"

This time Dariel sat up straight and grinned. "They're worth a shit load of money, that's what he said."

Jessie nodded thoughtfully. "Somebody is bound to want all of it back."

He slumped back down in his seat. "Why did they have to kill Mandy? It's all my fault."

"Blaming yourself now won't do any good. The important thing is to get you back with Lilly. The sooner, the better. We have to let the police know about all of this. Give them the money and the diamonds. Was there anything else in the case?"

"Just some paperwork in a foreign language. I don't know what it said. I threw it in a dumpster with the briefcase. I hid the money in the house."

"How come they didn't find it?" Jessie asked.

Dariel smirked. "Beats me. Guess they didn't do a very good job, did they?"

"And the diamonds?"

He shook his head. "They're not in the house. But I'm not giving them up until I get to see Lilly. If they agree to let me go—and I want it in writing—then I'll tell you where everything is."

Jessie nodded. "I don't think it'll be a problem if they're sure you're ready to talk."

Hope crept into his voice. "Can you come with her tomorrow?"

"If they agree to the deal, Dariel. This afternoon, I'll get the information about your sister so you can call her."

"If I get released, I won't need to call her."

"Probably not. It might be a good idea to talk to her

anyway. Mend some fences. Wouldn't it be nice for Lilly to get to know the rest of her family?"

"If something happened to me, do you think she will care for my baby?"

"Yes, of course," Jessie replied. "Lilly is her little niece."

Her encouraging words brought back a smile to his face. Jessie stood up. "There is lots to do, so I'd better get going now."

"I'll see you tomorrow, right?" he asked eagerly.

"As I said, if they agree."

"And Lilly?" he asked.

"I will do my best to get her here. I promise."

"Thank you."

The guard led him away and Jessie hoped she would be able to keep her promise. He might be a petty thief, but it she was certain he loved his child. Right now, she planned to do everything in her power to bring him and Lilly back together. It was the very least she could do for that little girl.

As she walked back to her car, Jessie checked her phone and found she had a message from Mary Gilmore. She rang back the social worker, who answered on the second ring. "How is Lilly?" Jessie asked anxiously.

"I talked to the foster mom this morning, and she's doing just fine. There are a couple of other little girls at the home about the same age, so there is no lack of playmates. I know you were concerned, so you can put your mind at ease."

"Thank you. I'm just leaving the prison. I met with Dariel Thomas and he's willing to make a deal with the police. First he wants to see Lilly, then he will tell them everything. I promised him I would try and bring her here tomorrow. Do you think it's possible?"

"I don't know—"

"By stealing that briefcase, Dariel may have put his life, and Lilly's life as well, in danger. I have a feeling the people looking for the briefcase won't hesitate to kill again in order to get it back. They already murdered Mandy. If I bring Lilly to see him tomorrow, and the police drop any new charges against him, he can give them the contents of the briefcase. Then he can leave the area with his child. The sooner, the better," Jessie said.

The woman didn't respond.

"Please, Ms. Gilmore. There has been enough tragedy in that family already. Can you do it?" Jessie pleaded.

"There is a lot of paperwork to be completed before I can entrust you with the child."

"I understand. You tell me what I have to do, and I'll do it. You can call Detective Sam Perrone and talk to him. He will vouch for me. If you need any other references, I'll be glad to give them to you."

"I'll call you back as soon as I can," the woman promised.

Jessie sighed. She understood the bureaucracy and safety measures were meant to protect the child, yet sometimes it seemed like they did more harm than good.

The drive back from Pompano to downtown Ft Lauderdale found her sitting in gridlock on I-95 for nearly a half hour. Finally, she reached the Broward exit. Twinges of hunger told her it was lunch time. She stopped at a small deli and waited in line for an additional ten minutes before being handed a tuna wrap and a bottle of water.

While eating in her car, she called Perrone and described her visit with Thomas and his request to see Lilly the next day. She also asked him to put in a good word with the social worker if she inquired about her. "Sam, do you think I can go back to see him tomorrow?"

He hesitated. "Here's the problem, Jessie. This is Boyd's case, and I can't just insert myself into his investigation. What I can do is tell him what you found out today. I'm pretty sure he'll be eager to talk to you about this, especially since he hasn't gotten anywhere with Thomas so far."

Jessie sighed. More red tape. "So what do I do in the meantime?"

Sam chuckled. "Sounds like you're eating, so why don't you finish your lunch first—whatever it is, just sit back and enjoy it, okay? I know you, you're chomping at the bit to get going with this. Be patient. Boyd is a good detective, he will call you back, and you can take it from there."

She agreed reluctantly. Despite Perrone's advice, she was unable to relax. On the way out of the parking lot, she tossed the rest of her food in the dumpster and headed back to the office. She dashed up the stairs, opened the door into the lobby, and immediately spotted Art sitting at her desk, hands folded across his ample stomach.

"Should I start looking for another job?" she asked, raising an eyebrow.

He grunted while repositioning his thick body in the chair and swirled around to face her. "Not yet, but if

I don't get that story about the human sex trade pretty soon, I might reconsider."

Jessie protested. "We've talked about this earlier, Art. For the next couple of days, I need to follow up on the Thomas story. Would you like to hear about the contents of the briefcase Dariel Thomas swiped at the Airport?" She tilted her head and waited.

Art snorted impatiently. "Well, are you going to tell me or what?"

"Glad to know you're interested after all. The briefcase was chuck full of precious diamonds and lots of money, like a hundred thousand dollars' worth in cash."

He shot her a doubtful glance. "How do you know?"

"Thomas and I had a nice visit at the jail today. If all goes according to plan, tomorrow he will tell me where to find this treasure trove."

"What is the police's role in this little arrangement?" he said, looking less than persuaded.

Jessie went over the plan she hatched with Dariel. She'd bring Lilly to see him, in exchange for giving the contents of the briefcase to the police and having the charges dropped.

Art narrowed his eyes. "This all sounds too easy. What if he backs out?"

She shook her head. "No way. He really loves his child, and will do anything to be with her. By tomorrow I'll have all the details."

"We can't wait until tomorrow. I need something on it now, before the competition gets a hold of it and beats us to the punchline."

"I don't have the full story yet, Art. Let's just

report the car chase and the shooting. Let me work on the rest. I'll write it up now."

He held up a hand in objection. "You know you can't. You're a witness. Have Susan write the article."

Jessie hesitated. Although she knew he was right, and Susan Blandish, the News' crime reporter was a colleague, she was still reluctant to let go. Finally, she nodded in agreement. "Okay, but when I get the full story behind this, I want the byline."

He shifted again, then pulled himself out of the chair with a groan. Jessie wasn't very tall, but Art was quite short and they practically stood eye to eye. "All right, you've got a couple of days to work on it. If you're wrong, it'll cost you," he warned, pointing a stubby finger at her with a wink.

"Thanks, Art, you're a real mensch," Jessie replied sarcastically as he walked away.

It was three o'clock when she got a call from Jim Boyd. "Hey Jessie, sorry I didn't get back to you earlier. I had a lot going on here. Perrone filled me in on your encounter with Thomas. It's quite a tale he told you about diamonds and cash. The question is, how much of it is true?"

"I think all of it is true. The man is devastated by his wife's murder, and he desperately wants to be reunited with his little girl."

"Then he should start by telling us where to find the briefcase," Boyd retorted.

"Well, here's the problem: because of past dealings, and he didn't say any of it involved you, he has somewhat of a trust issue with the police. He wants to see Lilly tomorrow, and if you can offer him a deal, he will tell you everything."

"We don't make deals with criminals, Jessie."

"Come on, Detective, have a heart. We're just talking about releasing him back on probation. Besides, think about what it would mean for your investigation."

"We searched his house and came up empty handed. I don't know if he's playing you or what."

"I don't believe so. He told me he tossed the briefcase and some paperwork. He kept the cash, a hundred thousand dollars, in the house. He stashed the diamonds somewhere else for safe keeping. He knows they're worth a bundle because he first took them to a jeweler who told him so. Don't you think it's suspicious no one has come forward to claim this briefcase?"

There was silence on the line.

"Detective?" she asked after a while.

"I'll see what I can do."

Jessie took a deep breath. "Great. I talked to the social worker but she hasn't gotten back to me yet. Maybe you can call her, remind her how important this is for Lilly."

He sighed. "I'll give her a ring, see if you can pick up the child tomorrow. I'll call you back in a bit."

"A bit" took a couple more hours.

"She said the paperwork is still going to take a few more days. So here's the plan. In the morning Mary will pick up Lilly at the foster home and we'll all meet at the jail. You can take Lilly in to see her father, then he has to give me the information."

Jessie thought about it for a moment. "What about the deal? He won't talk if there's no deal."

"If his story pans out, there won't be any charges."

"Will you give him your word?"

"Unofficially."

"What do you mean?" she asked.

"Off the record."

Jessie paused for a moment. "He wanted it in writing,"

"Nope. We're not going down that path. He'll just have to trust us."

"Okay, I hope this works out. For Lilly's sake," she said apprehensively.

They agreed to meet at ten o'clock. She remembered telling Dariel she would get the information about his sister Emily. She decided to hold off until after the meeting.

As she got ready to leave, Susan Blandish walked off the elevator. Although a lot of the older reporters didn't like the tall, thin woman's blunt manner, Jessie found her refreshing. She knew firsthand that being a crime reporter and hanging around with cops and criminals for a living required a special toughness.

"Hey Susan!" she shouted, waving at her.

The woman came over and sat on the corner of the desk. "How's it going, Jessie?"

She filled her in on the car chase and told her she had already emailed her all of the details.

"Sounds like you had quite a night," Susan stated.

"Yeah, I'm going back tomorrow to see the father in jail."

"Okay, so you'll be doing the follow up story on this?"

"Yes, but Art wants you to do the article for the shooting. It has to be in by the deadline today," Jessie said.

If Susan was upset by the fact she would only get the first article, she didn't say. "Got it. See you later."

Jessie gathered her notes and headed out. Driving home, she had a sudden pang of guilt and changed directions. Just moments after she set foot in her mother's condo, she was already regretting her decision. Sophie Milner wasted no time complaining about the rarity of her visits.

"Mom, I'm here now, so let's not go over this again," Jessie protested.

The aroma of fresh baked apples wafted through the air. Jessie took a deep breath. "Something smells good."

"Apple pie, and I made a chicken pot pie earlier. I hope you'll stay for dinner."

"I don't know, I've got paperwork to do. I should head home."

Sophie made a face. "You're always in a rush. What's wrong with eating with me for a change?"

Jessie relented. "We'll have dinner together. You happy now?"

"Of course I am. When my only child pays me a visit, I'm always happy. Sit down, I'll get you a plate."

They sat across from each other at the dining room table. "This is really good," Jessie said, between hearty bites of the pot pie.

Sophie shrugged. "I've been making it all my life. Your father liked it, too. Remember? He wasn't a big eater, but he always asked for seconds when I made the pot pie."

They shared of moment of silence before Jessie spoke again. "John called me yesterday."

Her mother sat up eagerly. "Oh good, what did he have to say?"

"He told me he met somebody. Someone he likes."

Sophie frowned. "And you don't mind?"

"Mom, once again, it's over between us. We're friends now. I care about him and I want him to be happy. He deserves someone he can love and who will love him back."

The old woman shook her head. "Someday, you'll be sorry you let him get away."

Jessie leaned across the table. "Let it be, Mom. If I am sorry, it'll be my fault, no one else's."

When she left the condo, there was half a pot pie and a large piece of apple pie in her trunk. And as usual, a visit with her mother left her drained. Why did they always have such a hard time relating to one another? She realized how much she missed her father. A mild-mannered man, he somehow managed to keep the peace between the two women in his life before a heart attack took him away in his sleep. Jessie smiled sadly. Even dying, he avoided making a fuss.

Back at the cottage Jessie changed into shorts and a tank top, grabbed her sandals, and walked out. As she got to the beach, the sun was setting. Streaks of purple meshed with deep shades of pink, creating the illusion of a mountain range across the horizon. A lone white pelican glided in the sky along the shoreline. Small, industrious sandpipers scurried on the sand, back and forth, following the constant movement of the waves in a pattern set in eternity. A gentle breeze brought relief from the fading heat of the day, and she sat leaning against a palm, enjoying the sight of the vast ocean in front of her.

She closed her eyes and saw Franco's face. The memories of the wonderful times they shared, nestled in each other arms, suddenly flooded her mind. More than three years had gone by since he was killed, but she had never stopped longing for him. Eyes brimming with tears, she looked up at the fading light. No one ever said heartbreak would be easy.

Chapter Eight

His stomach rumbled. After barely touching his dinner of dried up beans, a hardened lump of rice and chunks of pork swimming in a greasy dark sauce, he was now starving. Jail fare was the pits. After talking with the woman reporter today, Dariel hoped he would soon be out of here. His heart ached for Mandy, but she was gone and it was all his fault.

His eyes started watering and he stifled a sob. Now Lilly didn't have her mommy anymore, all because he was such a screw up. He had thought about it long and hard since he was arrested and Mandy was killed. When he got out, he would start over, make a clean slate of it. Get on a bus with Lilly and head to Minnesota. Hopefully Emily would give him one more chance. This time he would convince her husband he meant it, he would be going straight from now on. He didn't know anything about farming, but what the hell, it couldn't be so difficult, and he was willing to learn. Lilly would be happy there. They were bound to have a dog on a farm, and he recalled how many times she had begged for one. With Mandy being allergic to them, they had to deny her that simple pleasure.

He wiped his eyes and lay down on his cot, stared at the ceiling, and waited for the lights to dim. At least he was lucky in one respect. He didn't have a cellmate to bother him when he just wanted to be left alone. The lights went out and Dariel dozed off, jarred awake a couple of times when one inmate or another cried out or sobbed loudly. Finally, quiet settled in and he fell into a deep sleep.

Suddenly his head was twisted sideways and his eyes opened wide with alarm. His shoulders were pinned to the cot, and a foul-smelling cloth was shoved down his throat until he nearly gagged. His reflexes took over. He fought back, arms flailing in an attempt to throw punches, legs kicking into the darkness. None of it mattered. There were two attackers and they were much stronger than him. One man grabbed his arms, another took hold of his legs and they whisked him out of his cell, carrying him down the cell block to the muffled sound of his screams. No one heard him, or if they did, they kept quiet. Snitches usually died a violent death, and inmates learned rather quickly to turn a blind eye to violent acts committed within their sight. See nothing and hear nothing was the rule if you wanted to stay alive.

After they stopped at last, the two men tossed him on the floor. His head bounced on the cold, wet tile floor, and he cried out in pain. In the dim light of a nearby bulb, he realized they were in the showers. Both men stood over him now, glaring at him hatefully. Dariel recognized one of them, a trustee who worked in admission when he was being processed. He believed his name was Fattah. As his terrified eyes darted from one man to the other, his heart took a leap at the sight of the shiv in Fattah's hand.

"Any sound out of you and you're dead, understand?" the trustee warned as he yanked the cloth from his mouth.

Dariel nodded. He shivered, paralyzed with fear. Something was very wrong. "What did I do?" he whimpered.

The men exchanged looks and smirked. "You tangled with the wrong people, Thomas, don't you know that yet?" Fattah sneered.

Dariel sensed there would be no compassion from him. He turned toward the other prisoner. "Tell me what you want. Whatever it is, if I have it, I'll give it to you."

The man ignored his plea and Fattah leaned down close enough for his foul breath to assault Dariel's nostrils. Nausea nearly overwhelmed him.

"I thought you might say that. Where is the briefcase?"

"What briefcase?" Dariel asked.

The shiv came down, fast and furious, slashing his arms, his face, his legs. Dariel threw up his hands in a vain attempt to block the assault.

"No, stop, please, please stop," he begged.

Panting from his efforts, Fattah stepped back to wipe his brow. Curled up, with every part of him on fire, Dariel kept his eyes tightly shut and prayed the attack was over at last. His respite was short lived. Screeching with laughter, Fattah's accomplice landed vicious kicks on every part of his body. The young man made a frantic effort to crawl away, slipping and falling in the puddles of his own blood. His screams bounced off the walls.

"Please stop! I'll tell you where it is," he pleaded, his voice quivering.

Fattah waved the other man away. "So far we've treated you gently, Thomas. Any more nonsense out of your mouth, and you'll find out what real pain is. And then you'll die."

Dariel nodded. He ran his trembling fingers over his face and realized his lips and nose were numb.

Fattah nudged him with his foot. "Where is the briefcase?"

"In my house, behind the living room couch. You just move it out, it's right there."

The trustee glared at him. "If you're lying, you're a dead man," he threatened.

Dariel was beyond caring now. Somehow his mind, mired in a thick fog, had detached itself from his body and a cold numbness overtook the pain.

The two men exchanged a quick glance, then the trustee stepped away and pulled out a cell phone. His conversation was brief, just a few words in Arabic and he was done. A short moment later, the convicts turned back to him. Through his blurry eyes Dariel saw his death written on their faces.

"It's time to say goodnight," the trustee said as they closed in on him once more. Punches rained down, crushing every bone in his body, until, growing impatient, Yasuf Fattah thrust the shiv deep into Dariel's chest, twisting it several times for good measure. For one last lucid moment, Dariel's mind drifted to Lilly's delightful laughter, the sweet scent of her hair, her unequivocal love, and a faint smile spread over what remained of his face before his world dissipated into darkness.

****

It was time to quit. For well over an hour now, they had been working in the dark, with a couple of small flash lights, with no luck in finding the diamonds.

Earlier that night, armed with the Imam's information, they went to the Thomas house. Hakim remembered it as a quiet working-class neighborhood with small houses and small yards. With only a sliver of moon hidden behind clusters of clouds, the neighborhood sat in darkness.

Hakim drove to the end of the street before making a U-turn, driving nice and slow, then parked in front of a vacant lot, just south of their target. The dim light of a solitary street lamp, some distance away, was shrouded in haze.

This time they approached the house from a different angle, and Hakim noticed a chain link fence and a side door they'd missed the other night. Entry from that direction would have enabled them to get in the house. Lie in wait for the Thomas woman. Too late now.

A simple latch held the gate shut. There was no one around. They stopped for a moment to put on gloves, then quickly stepped into the back yard and followed a narrow gravel path bordered by high weeds and grass.

Suddenly the furious bark of a dog shattered the silence, and they froze. It stopped as quickly as it started, no lights came on in any of the surrounding houses, and soon, it was quiet again. A few seconds later, Abdul was jimmying the lock on the side door and next they were standing in a cramped kitchen. It was barely big enough to hold a small table and a couple of chairs. Dishes with half eaten food still sat on the table, revealing a hurried departure. A narrow hallway led into the living room.

With his flashlight, Hakim made a quick sweep over the meager furnishings, a worn leather recliner, and an aging television sitting on top of a small stand. The light landed on a faded brown couch, and he stopped, let it linger there for a moment, then he told Abdul to grab one side as he took hold of the other. Together, they pulled it away from its resting spot against the wall. The motion caused a few dust bunnies to float into space before settling back on the bare wooden floor.

Abdul frowned. "I thought it was supposed to be behind the couch?"

Hakim was quietly eyeing the couch. "Let's turn it over," he ordered.

They flipped it over, and stood looking at a dark woven liner attached to the wood frame with a mixture of nails and staples. Hakim slowly ran his flashlight back and forth over the liner.

"Now what?" Abdul asked, getting impatient.

Hakim didn't answer, his attention focused on the fasteners holding the fabric in place.

"You see something?" Abdul asked.

Hakim motioned him closer. "See this? Here we have staples"—he pointed to the other side of the couch—"and on this side, we have tacks. They look pretty new to me."

Abdul nodded. Hakim handed him his flashlight, pulled the switchblade from his pocket. It made a gentle hiss when he flipped it open and he drove its sharp blade into the material, making a deep gash. With his other hand, he yanked at the fabric. Worn by time, it gave without resistance. Hakim tossed it aside and had Abdul direct his flashlight into the opening. Jammed high up between the springs was a plastic bag. Abdul leaned in.

"Shit!" he exclaimed.

Hakim pushed him out of the way and got down on the floor in order to reach into the narrow space. Twisting his arm sideways, he got a grip on the bag. The way it was wedged, it wouldn't budge. He gritted his teeth and pulled harder. The bag ripped open and bundles of hundred-dollar bills rained down. Abdul whooped and Hakim gave him a nasty look.

"Shut the hell up," he growled, "you're going to wake the damn neighbors."

Abdul stepped back, a miffed expression on his face. Hakim went back to scrutinizing the inside of the sofa. Pieces of the bag and a few stubborn bills remained trapped in the springs. He had to fish them out one by one. He got the rest of the bag and tossed it in Abdul's direction. As he yanked on the last bundle, one of the bills became impaled on a broken piece of spring. After some more maneuvering, he finally got a hold of it and wrenched it free. A small corner was missing, but he didn't give a damn. He sat up and smiled at Abdul, then it dawned on him. The diamonds were not in the bag. He ran the flashlight back and forth inside the couch once more. Nothing. His grin turned into an angry scowl. He looked at Abdul.

"That son of a bitch! There's no way he could have pawned the stones so quickly. Not those gems. They have to be somewhere in this dump. Don't just stand there, get busy. We have to find them."

They slashed mattresses, shredded pillows, groped in corners of cabinets and inside closets, searched through a couple of old suitcases, even gutted a teddy bear, before finally giving up. After more than an hour searching, Hakim came to the conclusion that Thomas knew the two convicts were going to kill him, and decided to cheat them out of the gems.

They tossed the money in an old gym bag they found in the hall closet, then waited a couple more minutes, listening and checking the street, before going out the front door. Rain, sharp as needles, pelted them as they dashed to the car.

Driving away, Hakim couldn't stop brooding. It was one bad turn after another. It started with that damn courier dropping dead at the airport, then Thomas' woman led them on a wild chase ending in her death. Sure, they had the money, but the stones were missing and he had no idea where to search for them.

The rain didn't let up all the way back to his computer repair shop. The parking lot had ankle-deep water. He drove to the rear of the building, parked near the back door and made a dash for it.

A flip of a switch lit up a windowless room furnished with an old metal desk, a couple of worn office chairs and two file cabinets. Abdul remained by the door, dripping water on the linoleum floor, holding the bag of money with an undecided look.

"Where do you want this?" he asked.

"Put it on the desk," Hakim said over his shoulder as he stepped into the adjacent room. A work bench, piled with phones and laptops, loomed like a dark monster. He made his way past computer equipment and a multitude of parts shoved along the wall, and entered the reception area. Leaning against the elevated glass desk, he peered into the darkness.

Thick sheets of rain pounded the shop window. Visibility was less than a foot. He could barely make out the sidewalk, much less the other stores. Reassured the shopping plaza was deserted, he went back to the office.

"Man, don't you have any towels?" Abdul inquired, squeezing water out of his T-shirt.

Hakim glanced down at his own drenched clothes and scoffed. "Towels? What do you think this is? A Turkish bath?"

He sat down at the desk, impatiently shoved aside a stack of paper, unzipped the gym bag and dumped its contents. Despite his anger at the turn of events, the sight of the pile of cash brought a small measure of satisfaction. He motioned to the other man. "Sit down, start counting."

Abdul shrugged and dragged the other chair up to the table. Hakim ignored his show of annoyance. He split up the bundles and pushed half of them across the table. They tallied the money, ending up just short of a hundred thousand. Hakim assumed Thomas more than likely helped himself to some of it.

Still, he shook his head, fuming. "It's not enough. We need those damn diamonds."

Abdul's eyes widened. "It's a lot of money, man."

"You have no idea, do you? It takes a load of cash for the operation we have planned. Without the diamonds, we come up short."

"The reason I don't know is because you won't tell me anything. Don't you think you should start filling me in on the details?" Abdul retorted.

"You're right. I will, as soon as I get the go-ahead from Abboud. It should be soon now."

"So what are you gonna do about the diamonds?"

Hakim gazed at the wall for a moment before answering. "He had to hide them someplace else. We went over that house with a fine-toothed comb. The stones aren't there. That's a fact."

"And what if he sold them?" Abdul asked.

Hakim scoffed. "Then the money would have been in the couch with the other cash. Besides, you don't just get rid of a million dollars' worth of stones just like that."

Abdul nodded. "So, now what?"

"I'm going to talk to Jenna. See what else she can find out at the police station."

Abdul gave him a skeptical look. "I don't know how you think she'll have access to their investigation."

Hakim glared at him. "She got us the name of the thief, didn't she? Besides, it's the only thing I can think of right now. Let's get out of here."

He shoved the money back into the bag, swung it over his shoulder and headed out the door. Tomorrow, he would start the hunt for the diamonds and he was determined. Nothing would stand in his way.

Chapter Nine

She was stepping out of the shower when the phone rang. She grabbed a towel and ran to answer it. It was Jim Boyd. "Jessie…"

She sensed something was wrong.

The detective continued, "We won't be meeting with Dariel Thomas today."

She frowned. "Why not?"

"He's dead."

She closed her eyes, lowered herself into a kitchen chair.

"What happened?" she asked weakly.

"He was murdered."

Somehow she could barely think. "How could this be? He was locked away in jail."

"Someone got to him last night. Took him out of his cell, stabbed him and beat him to death in the showers."

She was stunned. "I don't understand. Aren't the prisoners under watch at all times?"

"Apparently there was a lapse in security. It's being investigated right now."

"Do you think he was tortured?"

"From the looks of it, I would say yes." Boyd said glumly.

A chill crept up her spine. "This can't be a coincidence. It's about the briefcase. What other reason would there be for him to be tortured?"

"Now, Jessie, you can't jump to conclusions."

"Do they know who did this to him?" she asked bitterly.

"Not yet. But you can be assured we'll do everything we can to find out."

Jessie's chest tightened. "Oh my God, Lilly! First she loses her mom and now her dad."

"I know, it's pretty sad for the child. We're trying to find a relative," Boyd said.

"As far as I know, Dariel only has one relative, his sister Emily."

"How do you know?" he asked.

"We talked about it yesterday. I told him I would find her phone number."

"Do you have the information?" he asked.

"The last name is Newhart. Emily Newhart. Dariel said she last lived in Pine Island, Minnesota. I haven't checked yet for an address or a phone number. I was waiting to see when he would be released."

Boyd paused for a moment. "I'll get a hold of her. I have some questions and we need to find out about arrangements for both Dariel and his wife."

"Does Lilly know yet?" she asked.

"No. I talked to Mary Gilmore earlier and she wants to hold off."

"Can I go see Lilly?"

"You'll have to ask Mary. I don't see why not. But of course, it's not my decision," Boyd said.

"Will you let me know if you find out any more about Dariel's death?" Jessie asked.

"It won't be today, Jessie, that I can tell you. But I will call you whenever we find out."

"Thank you, Detective."

Jessie sat on the edge of her bed and thought about Dariel. And the more she thought about it, the more she was certain he was murdered by someone who was after the contents of the briefcase. Someone powerful enough to get to him in a jail cell. Someone dangerous. With her stomach still tied in knots, she skipped breakfast, got ready and left for work. Art looked at her questioningly when she walked in his office. "Who dressed you today?"

She glanced down at her clothes and realized she had pulled on an old Rolling Stones T-shirt and a pair of faded jeans. She shrugged. "I wasn't paying attention. I had other things on my mind."

His eyebrows shot up as she told him about Dariel's death. She could see his face changing.

"So you think his murder is linked to the briefcase?"

Jessie nodded. "I'm sure it is. Dariel was a small-time crook. He did whatever it took to survive, and that included keeping a low profile. This wasn't just a jail house fight resulting in his death. This was cold-blooded torture and murder. An act of desperation by very bad people. Remember what Dariel told me, Art. The briefcase held lots of money and priceless diamonds. The thought had to enter their mind that Dariel might make a deal with the cops, and then they would be out of luck."

The old man stared at her soberly. "Now the guy is gone. What if these people suspect that he told someone else about all this?"

Jessie realized what he was suggesting. "How would they know I talked to him?"

"Jessie, if you can get a man killed in jail, you can certainly find out who his visitors were during his short stay."

She hadn't considered this until now.

"I want you to be careful, you hear? We don't know who we're dealing with here," Art warned.

"Does this mean you'll give me more time to work on this?" she asked.

He gave her a stern look, pointing his finger at her. "I don't want my reporter killed in order to get this story. So proceed with caution, young lady."

"One of these days, I'm taking that finger away from you," she warned, suppressing a smile.

"Out!" he growled.

"Okay, okay," she said, throwing up her arms in mock defeat before walking away.

Right before lunch, the elevator doors opened and Boyd got off. Jessie saw him as he walked through the office double glass doors toward her desk.

"Anything new, Detective?"

"Is there somewhere we can talk in private?" he asked.

"There's the break room. I don't think anyone is using it right now." Jessie led him to the small room. It was empty and they pulled up a couple of chairs and sat down at the table.

"Were you able to get a hold of Dariel's sister?" Jessie asked.

Boyd nodded. "I did. We had a long conversation. She seems like a nice lady. Hasn't talked to her brother for a number of years. I guess her husband and Thomas didn't get along. She was in shock when I told her he had a child."

"So what now?"

"She wants to come and get her niece. The trouble is, her husband is scheduled to have major heart surgery in a couple of days, so it will be about two weeks before she can make the trip."

"What happens to Lilly in the meantime?" Jessie asked.

"Mary Gilmore can tell you more about it than I can," the detective said.

"Did the sister make arrangements for her brother and sister-in-law?"

"After the autopsy on Dariel is completed, they'll both stay in the morgue until she gets here." He hesitated.

"Anything else you want to tell me?" she inquired.

"We went back to the house, checked everything this morning. We're pretty sure we know where Dariel hid the money."

"You got it?" Jessie asked leaning forward in anticipation.

"We found out where it was hidden prior to being retrieved."

Jessie frowned. "It's gone?"

Boyd nodded.

"Where was it?" Jessie asked.

"The couch in the living room was tipped over and the bottom liner ripped off. Inside was the corner of a new hundred-dollar bill caught on a spring."

Jessie's eyes widened. "And they didn't see this during the previous search?"

Boyd's face turned red. "The search warrant didn't allow us to destroy his furniture, Jessie. Looks like Dariel removed the material covering the bottom of the couch, stashed the money inside, then stapled or nailed it back shut."

"And you think someone beat the information out of him before he was killed?"

Boyd nodded. "More likely."

"I wonder if he gave them the location of the diamonds," Jessie pondered.

"From the extent of damage inside the house, we think it was more than one person searching for them. Maybe they found them."

Jessie shook her head. "No, Dariel made it very clear to me the diamonds were not in the house, and I believed him. He had no reason to lie about it."

The detective drummed his fingers on the table. "All right. Then let's say he didn't reveal where the diamonds are. Only disclosed the location of the money, knowing they could find it anyway. Led them to think the gems were there as well."

Jessie considered it for a moment. "Maybe he was clinging to the notion he would survive the attack. To lose the money and the diamonds could end his chances of making a deal and get Lilly back. Regardless, we don't know where the diamonds are, either, do we?"

The detective nodded. "If we went over his conversation with you once more, in detail, maybe it would help."

Jessie shrugged. "I'm telling you, he was not going to talk until his charges were dropped."

"Let's do it anyway," he insisted.

"Okay," she agreed with a sigh.

They went back over everything for fifteen minutes with nothing new surfacing. After he left, Jessie considered her next move. If Art was right, maybe she should be worried the men wanting the diamonds might come after her. Hopefully they didn't know about her.

Engrossed in her thoughts, she nearly jumped out of her chair when Lonnie tapped her on the shoulder and asked her to lunch. They walked a couple of blocks to the Cheese Cake factory, and Jessie scanned the menu absentmindedly before settling on a salad. Lonnie ordered a burger with everything. He eyed her suspiciously as the waiter walked away.

"Don't tell me you're on a diet again. You're way too skinny already."

"No, I'm just not hungry, too many things going through my mind."

"Like what?"

She told him about Dariel.

"That poor kid. Did you talk to the sister?" Lonnie asked.

"Not yet. I have to check with Mary Gilmore to see if Lilly will stay at the same foster home. They can't ferry her around different places on top of everything else. It would be too hard on her."

Lonnie gave her an inquiring look. "Have you considered playing mom for a while?"

Jessie nodded. "I wanted to keep her that first night. They wouldn't let me. You have to be vetted. It involves an investigation and background check. They don't entrust a child to just anyone, which is a good thing. I guess. Lonnie, even if I could take her, what about my job? And I don't know how to take care of a five-year-old. I've never been a parent. What about school and lunches and all that other stuff?"

Lonnie laughed. "There's always a first time to be a parent. People don't go to school for it, they learn on the job. Although I must admit, it would be a good idea to make people take parenting classes before they even have a child. Take my parents, for example. If they had been told there was a possibility their child could be born gay, I'm certain they would have opted out. Not everyone is equipped to handle what they may consider to be outside the norm."

"Do you think you and Tom will ever adopt a child?"

Lonnie waved his fork at her menacingly. "Girl, don't you dare bring that up. I like our lives just the way they are. Besides, being a pilot keeps him away from home way too much. I would not want to handle parenthood on my own, no thank you."

"Then you see, raising a child is not so easy after all," Jessie pointed out.

****

She sat at her desk going back over her information. According to Boyd, the men who ransacked the Thomas home left no fingerprints or DNA. So much for that. If they didn't get their hands on the diamonds, and she was pretty sure they didn't, most certainly they wouldn't stop there. And having already committed two murders, it was obvious they would go to any length to get them back. At this point the question remained, who were these people?

Deep in thought, she almost missed her cell phone chirping. She grabbed it at the last minute. It was Sam Perrone.

"Hey Jessie, got a minute?"

"Yes, of course. What's up, Sam?"

"You talked to Boyd about the Thomas case?"

"He came by earlier. I couldn't help him," she

sighed.

"That's why I'm calling you."

Jessie sat up fully alert now. "What did you find out?"

"I got a call from a friend of mine who's an Interpol Agent. It seems there was a diamond heist in France last month."

"Really? I didn't read anything about it."

"According to my friend, a man was mugged and beaten in Paris' business district. On the way to the hospital, he told the ambulance driver he was transporting valuable diamonds when he was robbed. A couple of hours later, when he was questioned by the police, he changed his story. He said the EMTs misunderstood him, he only carried a minimal amount of cash and some paperwork."

"Mm…That's strange."

"After further questioning, they found out he worked for a company specializing in precious stones. And oddly enough, he was attacked after returning from a trip to the Central African Republic, a well-known source of conflict diamonds," Perrone said.

"What are conflict diamonds?"

"Do you remember the stories about blood diamonds in the nineties?"

Jessie nodded. "Yes sure, there was even a movie about them."

"Unfortunately, the smuggling never stopped, only now they call them conflict diamonds," Perrone stated.

"So you think Dariel's diamonds could have come from that heist?"

"It's a possibility."

"A case of a thief stealing from thieves."

He chuckled. "One way of putting it."

"Does Boyd already know this?" Jessie asked.

"I told him."

"And he knows you're telling me?"

"Yep."

Jessie hesitated. "You're my friend, Sam, and I appreciate every bit of information you can give me. I must say I'm a bit puzzled why you're sharing this with me now."

Perrone paused. "I have to ask you to hold off printing anything about this story until we get a better handle on who we're dealing with."

"Do you have any idea who this might be?" she asked.

"Right now, it's not something we can disclose... yet."

"You will let me know, as soon as you can?"

"You're in. You have my word."

"It's a deal then."

After talking to Perrone, Jessie thought it was clear the police had some type of lead they were unwilling to reveal. She turned to her laptop and googled a search for conflict diamonds. There was no lack of information.

Once the world became aware African diamonds were being used to fund civil wars resulting in thousands of deaths, a system called the Kimberley Process was established. Its purpose was to create "passports" for rough, uncut diamonds. Although the new procedure slowed down the smuggling of conflict diamonds, it did not stop it entirely. Continuing in that vein, she pulled up a different article, explaining that the value of diamonds was based on carat weight, clarity, color and quality of their cut. Colorless ones were usually considered among the most prized. Dariel had insisted the diamonds he had in his possession were indeed priceless. If that was correct, no wonder some individuals were eager to get their hands on them.

She glanced up to see if Art was at his desk. He stood nearby talking to one of the other reporters. As she got up, he took off toward the exit door and Jessie picked up the pace. She caught up with him as he was getting on the elevator.

"Wait, wait," she shouted.

Art sighed and held the door for her. "This better be good. It's late, I haven't had lunch yet, and I'm famished," he warned.

Jessie hesitated. "Do you want to take the stairs? It's good exercise."

Art stared at her as if she was crazy. "What? No! Are you getting on or not?"

Reluctantly, she stepped into the elevator. They were alone and she quickly relayed her talk with Perrone.

"Did you agree to hold the story?" he asked.

She shrugged. "I had to if I want them to keep me in the loop."

He looked unconvinced. "I don't know. I trust them about as far as I can throw them. In my present state of starvation, it wouldn't be very far at all."

Jessie persisted. "Art, what if some precious diamonds stolen in France ended up in Dariel's possession? Think about it. An international jewelry heist involving thieves and killers. It could be a huge story. We've got to keep at it."

The elevator stopped and the doors opened. They

were on the ground floor, and Art took off in a rush. Jessie followed, not willing to let him get away. Suddenly he stopped and she almost ran into him. He sighed and shook his head.

"Go ahead, do it. Now, leave me alone," he growled. Jessie barely hid a smile of triumph as Art dashed into his favorite deli across the street.

Chapter Ten

The house, a pink two-story with green shutters, faced a cul-de-sac. Visible in the fenced backyard was a swing set, and a child sized doll house. No one was outdoors. Jessie rechecked the address Mary Gilmore gave her, then pulled into the driveway. She killed the engine and waited. A few minutes later, the social worker pulled in behind her and walked up to her car smiling apologetically.

"Sorry, I got caught in the traffic. It's a real bear getting across town this time of day. Are you ready?"

Jessie nodded and got out. "So I've been approved?" she asked.

The woman sighed. "Well...sort of...Nothing moves too fast when it involves the government, you know," she explained. "However, I was able to get you some visitations for the short term."

"Meaning I can take her places?"

Mary paused, then smiled reassuringly. "You can. At least for a few hours."

"What about her parents? Does Lilly know yet?"

The woman shook her head. "Not yet, Jessie. I'm waiting until the aunt from Minnesota gets here next week. It's going to be painful for her no matter how we do it."

They went up a short flight of stairs to the front door. The sound of children's laughter resonated throughout the house. Mary rang the doorbell and they stood waiting. A plump middle-aged woman appeared at the door, a little girl peering shyly at them from behind her skirt.

"Hello, Mary. Come on in," the woman said with a welcoming grin. She turned to Jessie. "And you must be Ms. Milner."

"Please call me Jessie."

"I'm Annabelle," the woman answered. She gently prodded the little girl to come out in full view. "And this young lady is Laura."

They stepped into a spacious living room where Lilly sat on the floor, playing a board game with another other little girl about the same age. Her face lit up when she saw Jessie. She got up, ran up to her, and hugged her hips.

"You came to see me!"

They embraced and Annabelle invited them to sit down. Lilly climbed on Jessie's lap, laying her head on her chest.

"Can you take me to see my mommy and daddy now?" she asked anxiously.

Jessie held her breath. The woman leaned over and stroked the child's head gently.

"Not yet, Lilly. Listen, I have good news—you get to spend time with Jessie this afternoon."

Lilly sat up. "Where are we gonna go?"

Jessie raised her eyebrows and asked, "Do you like animals?"

The little girl nodded excitingly.

"Well, you'll love this place. There are birds, pigs, geese, rabbits and all kinds of other critters. You'll see."

Annabelle looked surprised. "Where is this?"

"The Wildlife Center where I volunteer," Jessie said, then explained their rescue and rehabilitation program. "My friend Doris Anderson runs the Center. Thanks to her, lots of wounded animals get a second chance at life. If they can be healed successfully, most of them go back into the wild. Those who can't make it on their own have a permanent home with us."

The child clapped her hands in glee and Annabelle took her upstairs to change clothes.

Mary Gilmore stood up. "It's time for me to go. I'm sure you and Lilly will have a great time together."

Jessie got up and they hugged. "I know you had to pull some strings to make this possible, Mary, so thank you again."

Lilly reappeared dressed in shorts and a sparkly top, her blonde curls combed neatly, her blue eyes bright with anticipation. She waved to the other little girls, who looked somewhat dejected. Jessie had a pang of guilt about leaving them behind. As she walked out the front door with Lilly, she overheard Annabelle promise them an outing at the movies. They cheered wildly, everything else already forgotten.

Lilly seemed to enjoy the ride to the Wildlife Center, checking out the sights on the way, pointing out landmarks. Jessie was amazed at her sense of direction. As soon as they pulled up at the Center, Doris came dashing out of the building carrying a blanket. "Come on you two, we gotta go."

She headed to a 1970's era Volkswagen bus, its roof a mass of rust, its original paint color, once a vibrant blue, now barely recognizable.

"My truck is getting new tires, so Margaret is

letting me borrow this pile of junk. Guess I better drive carefully. If anything happens to it, it'll be hell to pay. We have a fawn in distress. You must be Lilly," she said, smiling at the child as she jumped in.

Jessie opened the back door. Bags of feed, packages of paper towels and gallon containers of water were shoved against the driver seat. The passenger seats were missing.

"Doris, there are no back seats in this thing."

The woman waved at her impatiently. "I know, I know. Just sit anywhere back there, it's not far."

Reluctantly, Jessie had Lilly get in and sat next to her on the floor of the bus.

It took several tries to get the vehicle started and when it finally did, Doris turned to back up and grinned at the child. "I'm sorry about the rush, Lilly, we have a little baby deer needing our help."

The child nodded. "Is it okay?"

"I think so. According to the man who called, the mommy deer was run over by a car while crossing the road in front of their house. We're going to bring the baby here and make sure it's all right."

As they exited the Center, Doris turned left instead of taking the right, the usual way to get to Highway 84. Jessie craned her neck to peek out.

"Where are we going?"

"This is a shortcut. It comes out at Flamingo Road, so we don't have to worry about the no-seatbelt thing," Doris said, flying down the dirt road, a dust cloud trailing behind them.

Before Jessie had a chance to turn her attention back to Lilly, Doris suddenly swerved to get past a white sedan parked in the middle of the narrow road.

"Hey, you stupid jerk, what's wrong with you!" she shouted out the window. She glanced at Jessie in the rear-view mirror and shook her head. "Can you believe this guy?"

Jessie got a quick glimpse at the vehicle as Doris drove away. "Why on earth would he park out here?" she asked.

"I don't know. It's a good thing no one uses this road or they could end up in the ditch trying to get around him," Doris said.

As she had indicated, the dirt lane ended at Flamingo Road and a couple of miles later, she made a sharp turn onto a side street leading to a residential area. They drove past well-kept older homes on large lots until they reached a house where an older couple stood waiting on the sidewalk.

"Thank goodness you're here. The little guy is in the garage," the woman said anxiously.

They followed the couple to the house with the old man shaking his head the whole time. "People use this street as a short cut, and they drive like they're on a raceway. A lot of times, wildlife tries to get from the woods on the north to the preserve behind our house. We've already had several raccoons and foxes who were killed while trying to cross. I've begged the county to lower the speed limit and put up some speed bumps. So far, nada. I guess they want to wait until they have a human casualty to do something about it."

They went into the garage. A tiny fawn was backed into a corner, bleating, eyes open wide with shock.

"Do you have an old towel we could use?" Doris asked.

The woman nodded, took a towel out of a stack on

a shelf, and handed it to her. "This is clean. We keep them out here to dry off the car after we wash it."

"Thanks. I'm going to cover his head to keep him from getting more nervous while we take him back to the Center."

"Will you be able to release him when he's bigger?" the woman asked.

"I think so. At that point he should be ready to mate and start a family of his own. In the meantime, why don't you come and visit him?" Doris suggested.

The couple nodded eagerly. Jessie gave them directions to the Wildlife Center. Doris gently covered the small fawn's head with the towel and wrapped it in the blanket. It didn't resist. Jessie got in the bus and Lilly climbed in next to her. The little girl's eyes lit up when Doris handed her the fawn. She cradled it with care, and it didn't move.

"What should we name the baby, Lilly?" Doris asked her on their way back.

"Can we call him Andy?"

"Andy is a great name. How old do you think he is, Doris?" Jessie asked.

"Maybe three weeks, not much more. Remember when we had that little deer a year ago?"

Jessie smiled. "Baby Doe, I remember. We gave her goat's milk."

"Yeah, we'll have to get some. We still have a pretty good supply of baby bottles we can use," Doris said.

As they drove back on the dirt road, Jessie reminded Doris to watch out for the white vehicle. This time there was no sign of it, and she quickly forgot about it. Margaret stood on the front porch of the house, hands on hips when they pulled in the courtyard.

Well into her eighties, the tough old woman was a true Florida cracker, born and raised in a cabin at the edge of the Everglades where she still lived. Cackling with delight, she loved to describe how she lost a leg to a nasty old gator in the pond near her home. In the end, she managed to get away and she swore the beast died of indigestion shortly after. With her peg leg, her wide-breasted body, and wild white hair flying every which way, she was a sight to behold. For years now, she spent nearly every day at the Center, and despite her somewhat prickly nature, it was obvious Doris had a great deal of affection for her.

"You didn't speed, did you?" she asked Doris, eyeing her suspiciously.

"Of course not," Doris assured her, shooting a silent warning at Jessie, who quickly glanced away.

Margaret affectionately patted her dilapidated vehicle. "You have to treat her gently. She's an ole gal, like me. I don't ever push her over thirty-five. And that's why I don't usually let anyone else drive her."

Doris nodded in agreement. "I was probably only doing twenty-five."

The old woman's eyes narrowed. "I don't know, Doris, seems like you were going awfully fast when you pulled in."

Jessie decided it was time to change the subject. "Margaret, meet Lilly and our new little house guest, Andy." She handed the fawn to the old woman.

"Lilly and I are heading to the store to get some goat milk for our little buddy here. Okay?"

When they came back, Jessie heated the milk, filled the baby bottle and gave it to the child. "Here, you can be the first one to feed him."

Jessie showed her how to hold the bottle while the fawn stood up to nurse.

"The mommy would be standing up while the baby nurses. Very gently you can push and pull the bottle back and forth."

The little fawn emptied the bottle and Lilly smiled. "He's going to be okay, even though his mommy is dead, isn't he, Jessie?"

"Yes, he is. Everybody here at the Center will make sure he grows up healthy, and gets to go back to the wild the way he's supposed to."

When they were done, they carried Andy to an empty pen, and he quickly fell asleep. Jessie then took Lilly to meet the other animals. She shrieked in delight at the sight of the raccoons, possums, squirrels and all the colorful birds. She held baby rabbits in her arms, petted goats, and talked softly to a nervous young ferret. A couple of egrets eyed the child carefully from a safe distance, while a curious pig walked up to her and nudged her with its cold snout as she erupted in laughter.

Lilly helped with the feeding and wielded a broom to sweep the cages. Later Doris called them in for lunch. They sat on the porch, ate turkey sandwiches, and drank lemonade. Before Jessie left to take Lilly home, Doris took her aside.

"You're really getting attached to this little girl, aren't you?"

Jessie smiled. "How can you tell?"

"It's hard to miss. Just remember, she will be leaving soon," Doris warned.

Jessie nodded without answering. Her friend was

right. It would be tough to see Lilly move away. Driving back to the foster home, she glanced in the rear-view mirror. The little girl had dozed off, her blond locks falling over her cheeks, rosy from a day spent outdoors, and a sudden sadness gripped Jessie's heart. As if Lilly had sensed her thoughts, she woke up and their eyes met.

"I love you, Jessie," the child said.

"And I love you, Lilly," Jessie whispered back with a warm smile. And she realized no matter what the future held, she would always cherish this moment.

****

Leaning against the kitchen counter, she listened to the buzz of the microwave while it zapped a lasagna TV dinner. A knock on her patio door was barely audible over the sound of the appliance. Jessie peered outside. Nina grinned back at her, brandishing a bottle of wine. "Chateau Pontet Canet 2011," she exclaimed.

Jessie was duly impressed. "Sounds expensive."

The woman shrugged. "Only a few bottles left in the wine cellar. This one I saved for you and me, *Cara.*"

"I don't think my dinner is worthy of such a fine vintage," Jessie sighed.

Nina laughed. "On the contrary, it will make it taste like a gourmet dinner."

"In that case, let me grab a corkscrew and some glasses," Jessie said.

They sat on the patio. Jessie ate her dinner and they savored glasses of the fine wine while the sun was setting in a flamboyant show of colors. A gentle breeze rustled through the palms in the courtyard. Traffic noise from A1A had dimmed, and they enjoyed the moment.

Nina nodded. "You had a visitor today."

"Really? Anybody I know?"

Nina smiled. "Very official, nice suit, nice tie. Handsome man, lots of muscle. Drove a big black car. I could like such a man."

"Did he leave a card or a phone number?"

"No. He said he would try again later."

"When did he come by?"

"After lunch, maybe two o'clock."

Jessie frowned. "Odd. I can't imagine who would come here to see me. Not too many people have this address."

Nina refilled their glasses. "He came to the house."

"Did you tell him I live in the cottage?"

Nina gave her a guilty look. "Maybe not a good idea?"

Jessie shrugged it off. "No, don't worry about it."

"You're not mad at me?" Nina asked sheepishly.

"Of course not. It's no secret I live here."

After Nina went home, Jessie briefly wondered about the stranger, then decided it wasn't important.

Chapter Eleven

Seven am on Sunday, the phone rang. "Ms. Milner?"

"Yes," she answered, her voice still hoarse from sleep.

"This is FBI Special Agent Bruce Williams. I'm sorry if I woke you."

Jessie frowned. "What can I do for you?"

"I'm parked nearby. We need to talk."

Jessie hesitated. "Can you tell me what this is about?"

"I would rather have this conversation in person."

She sighed. "Give me a few minutes. I take it you know where I live?"

"I'll be there in ten."

While getting ready, she wondered if her probe into the Russian mob's involvement in the human slave trade had somehow drawn the FBI's attention. After all, she had called just about every government agency trying to get information. And so far, she had very limited success.

Special Agent Bruce Williams was right on time. When Jessie opened the door, she had to glance up. Dark skinned and sporting a short afro, the man stood at least six feet five. Jessie decided Nina's description was quite accurate. He was handsome and dressed impeccably.

He introduced himself once more and produced his badge. Jessie invited him in and offered him a cup of coffee. He politely declined.

"Ms. Milner, I am here about the Thomas case."

Jessie frowned in surprise. "Dariel Thomas?"

Williams nodded. "I understand you witnessed Mrs. Thomas's car crash. You also paid a visit to her husband in jail."

"Correct."

"Any particular reason?"

"Yes. Dariel Thomas was arrested for stealing a briefcase at the airport. Because of his prior dealings with the law, he refused to talk to them about it. The police were very keen on getting it back, and I attempted to broker some sort of agreement between them."

"Why was that?" the agent asked.

"So the charges could be dropped and Dariel could be reunited with his little girl."

The man nodded. "You know the child?"

"Her name is Lilly. I met her the night Mandy Thomas died. She was in the car with her mom. Thankfully, Mandy had her get down on the floor in the back of the car. It saved her life. She's only five years old."

"So you rescued the child."

Jessie nodded. "Lilly lost her mother and now, she's lost her father as well. Dariel would have done anything to be with her again."

"What did he tell you about the briefcase?"

"There was money, and according to him, some very valuable diamonds."

"And what did he do with the briefcase?" Williams

asked.

"He tossed it. Said he hid the money inside the house, and the diamonds elsewhere."

"So he didn't reveal their location?"

Jessie shook her head. "He wanted all charges dropped in exchange for that information. After my initial visit with him, we had an arrangement. Lilly and I would come to see him at the jail the next day—" She stopped suddenly. "May I ask why the FBI is involved in this?"

"We will get there in a minute. Did you see who was chasing Mandy Thomas?"

"I'm afraid not. The car stopped only briefly when it pulled up next to the wrecked car. I got a quick glimpse of the passenger, but it was very dark. I think he saw me and they took off."

"Were there two men in the vehicle?"

Jessie shrugged. "Two persons for sure, the driver, of course, and a passenger. There could have been someone else in the back seat. Like I said, it was dark and they left quickly."

"Do you think you could identify the passenger if you saw him again?"

"I can tell you he had dark hair. Going as far as actually recognizing him? I couldn't really make out his features. So no, I don't think so."

He nodded somberly. "I see."

Jessie stared at him. "You already knew all this, didn't you?"

"I had a talk with Detective Boyd."

"Then why are we going over everything again?" she protested.

"I needed to ask you these questions myself. Find

out if Thomas gave you any kind of hint or indication where he stashed the briefcase."

Jessie shook her head. "As I said, he threw it away. I believe the thugs who had him beaten and killed in jail got their hands on the money."

"And the diamonds?"

"I don't think Dariel gave them the location of the diamonds."

"What makes you think so?" he asked.

"This was his get-out-of-jail card. His only chance to get Lilly back. There's no way he would have given it up. Now, please tell me why the FBI is so interested in Dariel Thomas."

"We are investigating certain individuals who may be involved in this theft."

Jessie was taken aback. "You know who they are?"

"Some of them."

"Like the man who died at the airport?" she asked.

"I can't tell you any more right now, Ms. Milner, except this concerns national security. You are a reporter. Am I correct?"

Jessie scoffed. "You already know the answer to that question."

The man's face remained impassive. "None of this information can be published at this time. Do you understand?"

"If not now, when can it be published?"

Williams shook his head. "Frankly, I can't tell you right now. I hope you realize any attempt on your part to compromise our investigation can lead to your arrest. And, yes, you will be prosecuted to the full extent of the law."

Jessie leaned forward, eyeing him curiously.

"These days, when national security is mentioned, it usually involves terrorism. Is this what we're talking about here?"

"I can't answer that. You just have to take my word," he warned.

"I get it. Tell me when the time is right. I want to be the one who breaks this story," Jessie insisted.

The agent didn't answer. He got up and handed her his business card. "If you acquire any additional information about Mr. Thomas, or remember anything else, please call me."

Jessie nodded and he left. After he was gone, she made a cup of coffee, then sat in the kitchen going over their conversation. Although he revealed very little, it was enough to set off her internal antenna. If in fact the diamonds and the money were linked to a group involved in terrorism, it would put a whole new perspective on the heist. In that instance, from the moment Dariel Thomas stole the briefcase, he never had a chance. And neither did Mandy.

****

After calling Lilly's foster mom to confirm she would be picking up the child before lunch, she made a couple of peanut butter and jelly sandwiches. She dropped them into a beach bag along with some grapes, beach towels, sun tan lotion and bottles of water. Satisfied she had everything, she changed into a bathing suit, pulled on a T-shirt and shorts, and was searching through her closet to find a suitable hat for Lilly to wear at the beach, when there was a knock on the front door. Nina hardly ever got up before noon, so maybe it was the FBI agent again. With an exasperated sigh, she threw open the door and stood facing a man with deep green eyes and reddish blond hair long enough to rest on his collar. Wearing a Jimmy Buffett T-shirt, cargo shorts and deck shoes, he gave her a crooked grin. "Ms. Milner?"

"That would be me."

"My name is Liam Donovan. I'm a private investigator. Could I have a few moments of your time?" he inquired.

"I'm in a bit of a rush. What is this about?"

"Dariel Thomas."

Jessie sighed. "It seems a lot of people are suddenly interested in him."

"I won't take long, I promise," he persisted.

After a moment of hesitation, she asked for an ID. He handed her a business card. She read it, stepped outside and closed the door behind her. She headed for the stone path on the side of the cottage and motioned for him to follow. "Let's go around this way. We can talk out here."

She led him to the table in the courtyard and they took a seat. A couple of robins sauntered in the small grassy area, feasting on insects. Masses of purple bougainvillea blooms hugged the wall flanking the patio.

He glanced around. "You have a nice place here."

"I like it. Now tell me, what is it we need to talk about?" she said impatiently.

He smiled, revealing a nice set of white teeth. "I'll get right to the point. There's this French insurance company by the name of Courtel. Among their clients there is a business that specializes in buying and selling gold and precious stones. Last month there was a diamond heist in Paris... Did you hear about it?"

"Someone mentioned it to me."

He nodded. "That theft led to a substantial loss for this company. Needless to say, since Courtel is their insurer, they are expected to cover the loss. So, as you can guess, they are rather eager to get back these stolen gems."

Jessie knew where this was going. "And what does Dariel Thomas have to do with this theft?"

"According to our information, he ended up with the stolen diamonds."

Jessie made a face. "How do you know they're the same ones?"

"Good question. Recently, the French police arrested two Algerian nationals with known connections to ISIS. The courier who was transporting the gems identified them as his attackers. With a little friendly persuasion from the gendarmes, one of them admitted travelling to the Netherlands. At that point, he met with the captain of a Dutch freighter, and gave him a briefcase containing diamonds and cash."

Jessie frowned. "And how did it end up here?" she asked.

He nodded. "I'm getting there. The name of his ship was the *Rotterdam* and their destination was the Port of Newark in New Jersey."

"Did anyone question this captain?"

Liam shook his head. "Not yet. The Rotterdam is still on its way back to Europe and so far, the captain has made himself unavailable to authorities. It just so happened the ship docked in Newark the same morning a certain Alton Adler flew in from Florida. He immediately headed for the port. Some of the blanks still have to be filled in by our elusive captain. The fact is, Adler flew back just hours later. And according to my source, this time he carried a black briefcase."

"And soon after, he collapsed and died of a heart attack at the Ft Lauderdale airport," Jessie said.

"Exactly. Then your man, Dariel Thomas, took the opportunity offered to him by circumstances—"

"Dariel was not 'my man'," Jessie interrupted bluntly, "and unfortunately, he paid dearly for what he did. It was a terrible misfortune for him and his family."

"You're right," he apologized, "it's a tragedy both he and his wife lost their lives over this."

"Mr. Donovan—"

"Please call me Liam," he interrupted.

"Okay. Liam, were the stolen gems conflict diamonds?"

He frowned. "Conflict diamonds?"

"I read about them. They're similar to blood diamonds. They're mined in war zones in Africa, and the money is used to fund warlords."

He shook his head. "No, I assure you, this isn't the case. Those stones were acquired legally and all necessary documents were completed. There is a paper trail, part of a procedure called the Kimberley Process."

Jessie nodded. "Right. A passport for diamonds to legitimize their purchase. I don't understand why the man who was robbed, and his employer, denied he was transporting diamonds."

"I agree it sounds confusing. It's actually quite simple. Their reluctance to make it public stems from the fact that moving gems around the world is an extremely risky business. It's not like you can send a Brinks truck from Africa to Europe. Bringing attention to the way they do it could encourage more robbery attempts. In this instance, the poor guy was attacked and severely beaten, so you can understand their reasoning," Liam explained.

Jessie nodded. "Okay, I get it. What is your role in all this?"

"Normally, Courtel uses their own investigators. However, they are located in France, and since now it appears the diamonds are here, they hired me to track them down."

"No offense to you, but why aren't they working with Interpol or the local police instead of a private investigator?" Jessie asked.

He smiled. "Courtel is cooperating with Interpol, and I've already touched base with the local police department. Mostly, my job consists of keeping them in the loop for any progress in the investigation, and if possible, to help with the recovery of the diamonds."

Jessie sighed. "Well, Liam, I don't want to be the bearer of bad news. I was just informed this morning these gems are now part of an FBI investigation. So, just getting any kind of information could prove to be rather difficult. And then there's this little tiny fact, not to be overlooked… "

Jessie paused and Liam raised his eyebrows, waiting.

"Dariel hid the diamonds, and no one has any idea where they may be."

"No one?" he asked, looking at her uncertainly.

She shook her head. "No one."

"You talked to Thomas before—"

"Before he was murdered? Yes, I did. He didn't tell me their location. If he had, I would have passed on the information to the police." She glanced at her watch and stood up. "Now, I have to go. I'm sorry I was no help. I wish you luck in your search."

Liam got up. "Okay, thanks for your time."

He started walking away then turned around, "Can I ask you one more thing?"

Jessie sighed.

"Would you consider going to dinner with me sometime?"

"Oh!" she said, taken by surprise.

He smiled crookedly. "I won't bring up the diamonds, I promise."

She laughed. "Okay, why not? Give me a call."

He took her number before strolling out. She stood on the patio for a while longer, watching him walk away.

Chapter Twelve

Lots of colorful umbrellas dotted the sand as a Goodyear Blimp slowly glided through the cloudless blue sky. Wearing dark shades and sitting on the low wall bordering the beach, Nasir Hakim followed the movements of an attractive young woman in a small red bikini, while she lathered sun tan lotion on a fair-skinned little girl. When she was done, she planted a hat on the child's blonde head, and she dashed off to join other youngsters playing nearby.

He stayed focused on the woman. The first time he laid eyes on her was the night she appeared on the sidewalk on A1A, right after Thomas's wife crashed her car into the cement pole. The next day, he read an article about the chase and found out her name was Jessie Milner. According to the story, she was a reporter for the *Broward News*. As of right now, he was fairly certain she didn't get a good look at him that night. It was very dark when Abdul stopped next to the wrecked car, and they sped away almost immediately.

That whole night turned out badly. He bitterly remembered standing on the stoop in front of the Thomas house with Abdul, when Mandy Thomas pulled up and spotted them. One glance at them, her eyes widened in fear, and she took off at full speed, tires squealing. The two men exchanged a look and Hakim nodded.

They ran down the steps and dashed back to the car. As soon as they jumped in, Hakim opened the glove box and retrieved his gun. Seconds later, with Abdul at the wheel, they barreled down the street just as the other car disappeared around a corner.

"Hurry, dammit!" Hakim shouted.

They flew past several side streets with no sign of the other vehicle. There were only two more turn-offs in the residential area before the street came to a dead end.

"There she is!" Hakim yelled as they were halfway past the first turn. Abdul slapped on the brakes, veered to the right, ran over the sidewalk, and barely missed the corner of a building. As he accelerated once more, the woman picked up speed as well, weaving in and out of the neighborhood, nearly losing him once when she took off down a dark alley and exited on another street. But the rough sound of her engine, reverberating in the quiet of the night, gave her away, and he caught up with her just as she made a turn south onto Federal Highway. Despite the late hour, traffic was still fairly heavy on the busy road, forcing Abdul to come to a stop.

"Go! Go!" Hakim snapped.

Abdul gave him an exasperated look. He pulled out in front of a van to the screech of burning brakes and the sound of an angry horn. He gave the driver the finger, raced around a few more cars, scraping a fender along the way, and barely avoided another collision.

"There!" Hakim shouted, pointing ahead.

It was the woman, tearing across three lanes of traffic before speeding through the intersection onto Seventeenth Street. Reacting quickly, Abdul followed her daring move, and somehow squeezed through the red light. He was now directly behind her. The smile of triumph forming on his lips disappeared as they neared the drawbridge. The ominous sound of the bell announced it was going up, and the woman showed no sign of slowing. Abdul glanced at Hakim.

"Go!" Hakim yelled.

Abdul floored the accelerator and both cars flew over the widening gap across the Causeway, just inches apart, landing with rough thuds on the other side right next to each other. She slowed down for a split second, then took off once again at full speed. Abdul surged forward and struck her bumper with such force that her car careened sideways. Somehow she righted the vehicle and drove on. He caught up with her once more, pulled up beside her, and violently rammed her driver side door. Hakim recalled seeing her eyes fill with panic as she struggled to retain control of the car.

As they neared A1A, he took several shots at her tires. He missed. Realizing she was not going to stop, he aimed his gun at her and fired more shots. In a last-ditch effort to get away, or maybe because she was hit, she picked up speed going into the curve and lost control. Her car swerved onto the sidewalk, squealing as it scraped the wall, tearing off the passenger side mirror, and lurched back onto the road before crashing into a light pole head on. Abdul slammed on the brakes, and pulled up next to her. The front end of her car was wrapped around the pole. The driver's head was buried in the deployed air bag.

"I don't think she'll be talking to us," Abdul scoffed.

Hakim lowered the passenger window to get a better look. In the faint reflection of the light post, he saw a dark stain spreading on the airbag around the woman's head. *Blood.* At the same moment he spotted another woman running toward them on the sidewalk. He hollered at Abdul to get out of there, and they raced away. His muscles tightened in anger. His only remaining option had been to question Thomas' wife. But now if she was dead and she knew where the diamonds were, she took the secret with her. Once again, they were back to square one.

Later, when he told Jenna about the chase, she informed him the reporter who witnessed the crash paid Thomas a visit in jail prior to his murder.

"And you tell me this now?" he barked into the phone.

"I didn't know until a while ago. They had a meeting. I was next door and I heard them talking about the case. So I stayed, pretending to have more work to do on the hard drive. Then they brought up the reporter's name… You know, I'm taking a lot of chances for you, and I resent it when you don't appreciate it," she retorted.

He backed off. "Sorry, I'm just frustrated. We need those diamonds. Call me if you find out anything else."

Still seething, he threw the phone on his desk. He had to find a way to get back those diamonds. If Thomas talked to this woman, maybe she knew something. So, with no other leads, he decided to keep an eye on her, and hoped she could lead him to the gems.

The night of the chase, she'd run out of a property along A1A. Jenna checked and confirmed it was indeed her address. Despite making several sweeps past the place, he could only see a driveway bordered by lush greenery. There was no visible sign of a house. Surprisingly, the access gate stood open every time he went by. He decided to get a closer look. One evening shortly after dusk, he parked a block away and set out for the property on foot. As before, the gate stood open. He hesitated, almost went in, and then thought it was too risky.

Standing on the sidewalk, he stared at the eight-foot wall facing the road and wondered if it ran around the whole estate. He waited nearby until it was darker, then followed the outline of the wall, keeping a cautious eye on the neighboring houses. He needn't have worried; there wasn't a soul around. After twenty minutes, he had covered the whole distance and was back on the sidewalk on A1A. Now he knew, with some satisfaction, that the wall ran around the whole property and the only access was through the open front gate. He went back to his car, then slowly drove up and down the streets in the area until he found the perfect spot to set up his surveillance. As luck would have it, there were only two houses on a nearby dead-end street. One of them looked unoccupied and the other was still under construction, so there was no one to get nosy about a strange car sitting on their street. Plus, by parking at the right angle, he had a direct view of the access gate. Now he could observe all comings and goings from the property.

When the reporter left her house the next morning, he was there waiting. He followed her downtown, where she pulled into the parking garage across from the *Broward News* building. Hakim slowly drove on past the entrance, pleased to note access was automated. There was no guard to worry about. After following her for a few days without any results, he decided this took too much of his time. He purchased a small GPS tracking device, and while her car was in the parking garage, he attached it under her rear tire well. Next he installed an app on his phone, alerting him every time the vehicle was on the move. Depending on her destination, he could easily catch up with her. If she went to a restaurant at lunch time, he usually chose to ignore it, unless she took a different route afterwards.

So far, the woman seemed oblivious to his tail, but to err on the side of caution, he often switched vehicles. Most of the time, he alternated between Abdul's dark blue Ford Taurus and his own white Honda Civic. On occasion, he borrowed an aging Toyota belonging to Jamal, another of his men, although he hated that car. It was a piece of shit with a noisy air conditioner that blew only hot air. He was careful at all times, always staying a few car lengths behind. This is how he found out she often went west to a place called the Wildlife Center. Usually she remained there for several hours, and he assumed she did some kind of volunteer work. Once or twice, he was almost tempted to go in and casually inquire about the place, see her eye to eye. Maybe even find out if she would recognize him. Then he realized it would be foolish on his part. After all, if she did, he would be forced to take action right then and there, and obviously she wasn't alone. There seemed to be at least one or two other women and a couple of men working there at all times.

The reporter didn't seem to deviate much from her usual routine. There were a couple of surprises along the way as well as a close call or two. One time, she weaved through a residential area, and about the time he was ready to call it quits, she pulled into a driveway, went into a nice house, and came out minutes later with a little girl in tow. Hakim couldn't believe his eyes. He recognized her from her picture on the newscast after the chase. It was Thomas' daughter. Now it seemed like they were best friends, hugging and kissing.

He followed them. After she drove straight to the Wildlife Center, he kept going, past the entrance and onto a dirt path. It was riddled with potholes, vegetation closing in on one side, with a steep drop into a ditch on the opposite side. Assuming it was a dead end, he thought it safe to wait there. Then shortly after the reporter's arrival, along came an old Volkswagen bus pulling out of the Center, a wild-eyed woman at the wheel, flying directly toward him. With his car practically parked in the middle of the path, it was too late to move over. As the driver veered to avoid hitting him, he noticed the reporter peering out the back window. He quickly slumped down into his seat. As soon as they were out of sight, he took off, wondering if he was just wasting time following the reporter.

So far there had been no sign she knew anything at all. Maybe he did it partially because he was attracted to her, not sure if his feelings were triggered by animal lust or something deeper. Somedays, he couldn't wait to see her. Often at night, wide awake in his bed, he imagined stroking her dark hair, his hands tracing the curves of her slender body, before taking her and making her his.

But there was no time for relationships in his life and furthermore, this woman was an infidel, an American, an enemy of the Islamic State. He had to stop thinking about her, and concentrate on finding the diamonds in order to continue with their plan, which meant everything to him.

Hakim brought his mind back to the present. The reporter and the child were gathering their belongings, taking down the umbrella and getting ready to leave. At one point, the woman turned, gazed his way briefly then continued packing her gear. He walked back to his car and waited.

Shortly after leaving the beach, Jessie pulled in at an ice cream shop. Seated in his car, directly in front of the store's plate glass window, he had a clear view of the child excitedly making her selection. With no seats available indoors, the two of them came outside and sat at a small table to eat their ice cream. Hakim noticed how the young woman affectionately looked on as the little girl enjoyed her treat.

Suddenly he stiffened, the reporter was looking straight at him. Did she see him on the beach? Maybe he made a mistake parking so close to the store. Then she turned her attention back to the child. He sighed in relief. When they left, he followed them once more. After she dropped off the child and headed for home, Hakim's frustration mounted. Once again, he would walk away empty handed.

Chapter Thirteen

Jessie pulled into her driveway and found a jeep blocking the way. Annoyed, she parked behind the vehicle and walked to the driver's window. Liam Donovan glanced back at her with a sheepish grin.

"Did you forget something?" she asked.

"I did. I wanted to ask you out to dinner, but you weren't answering your phone."

"So you just show up?" she asked.

He nodded. "I'm sorry, it was kind of rude of me. I forget my manners when I'm under the spell of a beautiful woman."

Her eyes widened. "A spell? We spent all of what, five minutes together? Aren't you getting a little carried away here?"

He held up a hand in surrender. "Wow! Wait a minute! Too many questions at once. Can I just answer them one at a time—" he hesitated, then quickly added, "—over dinner?"

She sighed. "You are persistent, aren't you?"

"Oops, another question. I'm going to have to jot them down."

Finally, she laughed. "I just got back from the beach. I need to take a shower, so if you still want to have dinner, come back later."

They agreed on seven o'clock, then he maneuvered around her car and left.

Seven on the dot he was back, wearing dark blue slacks and a blue and white checked shirt. His eyes reflected his appreciation when she stepped out of the cottage in a white sleeveless linen dress and sandals. She took note of his new outfit. "You look different."

He grinned. "Yeah, believe it or not, I clean up occasionally. In my line of work, it's preferable to go unnoticed, so shorts and T-shirts are common; I blend in better." Then he added, "You however, would never just blend in. You look fantastic."

He drove north, following the shoreline as the setting sun turned the sky into a palette of vibrant colors ranging from soft purple to pale yellow.

"I'm curious. How did you find out about me?" Jessie asked.

He glanced at her with a raised eyebrow. "I'm a private investigator, remember?"

She eyed him skeptically and he grinned.

"It just so happens my contacts at the police department throw me a few scraps of information here and there. Not to mention your name came up in the article about Thomas' wife."

"How long have you doing this?"

"You mean the P.I. gig?"

She nodded.

"It's been two years. After high school, I went for a degree in political science. By the time I graduated, I no longer knew what I wanted to do. I totally changed course and brought my mother a lot of anxiety by joining the Marine Corps. After a couple of tours in Afghanistan, I realized I could no longer stomach seeing my friends getting blown up day after day. I got out, went back home to New York, considered going to the police academy, become a cop like my old man and my grandfather before him. Keep up the old Irish tradition. Then a P.I. friend down here offered me a job as his partner and I thought, why not? My very first case was a missing kid, a little three-year-old boy, abducted by his father. The mother was so distraught she couldn't think straight. Her ex-husband was a real mental case. She was terrified he would harm their son rather than give him back. The cops were dragging their feet and weren't getting anywhere.

"She came to us. I was able to trace the father after a couple of days. He was holed up in a motel with the boy and was threatening to kill himself and the child. I calmed him down, told him if he released the child to my care, I would talk to the mother about not filing charges. It took about three hours, and he finally turned him loose. The poor kid was scared stiff. Then the cops got there. They had me talk to the father some more and I persuaded him to come out. They cuffed him and I took the boy back to his mom. It was one of the most satisfying things I ever did. I was hooked and I haven't looked back since."

Jessie nodded. "Must have been incredibly stressful."

"It was. Of course, most days are pretty routine. There's the usual stuff, background checks for employers and real estate agents, property owners worried about potential renters. Then you have spouses checking on each other, divorce cases and lawsuits. And with all those online dating sites, people want to make sure they're not being conned. Unfortunately, it happens more often than you think. There is no lack of crooks out there."

"How is it working out with your partner?"

"He passed away last year. An aneurism to the brain. He was a nice guy and we got along great. After some thought, I decided to go on solo. I don't think I could ever find another partner like him," he said softly.

"I'm sorry. It had to be rough."

"Yeah. He left behind a wife and two great kids. Two boys, teenagers. For the longest time none of us could get past it, like a raw wound refusing to heal. You try to ignore it, yet you know it's there. It aches, and when you touch it, you want to scream your bloody head off. They're doing better now. I see them every couple of weeks. The boys play baseball, so I usually go to some of their games. Sometimes we do pizza and the movies."

Lilly came to her mind and she nodded. "And the wife?"

He shrugged. "The kids keep her going. She went back to school. She has a couple more years before she gets her nursing degree. She tries to be tough. You can tell it's still hard for her." His voice caught in his throat for a moment. "Those two, they loved each other very much."

After a couple more miles, he switched over to Federal Highway and pulled into a shopping plaza in front of a restaurant. The sign above the door read Casa d'Angelo. "Heard good things about this place," he said eyeing her cautiously.

"Always glad to try someplace new," Jessie said.

He let out a long breath and she laughed. From its sleek appearance to the soft lighting and music, the atmosphere was meant to appeal. A smiling maître d' greeted them and led them to a table in an alcove.

The menu choices were numerous, and Jessie selected the jumbo prawns in white wine, garlic, fresh tomatoes and olives. Liam chose veal Scaloppini with wild mushrooms, fresh tomato, and oregano. They agreed on a bottle of Chardonnay.

After the waiter had poured their wine, they sat quietly for a moment, sipping from their glass, until Jessie leaned forward.

"Now, tell me exactly how you got involved with Courtel."

"I thought we weren't going to talk about the diamonds," he protested.

"No, you said you weren't going to bring them up," she pointed out.

"So, you don't mind talking about it?" he asked.

"Isn't that's why we're really here?"

He frowned. "No, not at all. I wanted to have dinner with you, pure and simple."

She scrutinized his face to see if he was telling the truth. He stared back at her with those unflinching eyes, and she decided he was. "Okay, I believe you. But we are going to discuss it anyway. Otherwise it's going to hang there between us. So tell me all about it."

"One of my cousins is something or other at the U.S. embassy in Paris. It's one of those lengthy titles no one remembers. Anyway, he is good friends with Marcel Lebon, the Courtel CEO. They see each other socially and they play golf together. So during their last game, Marcel told him about the heist and mentioned seeking someone in the U.S. to represent Courtel. My cousin brought up my name. Marcel contacted me, we talked, he offered me the job and here we are," he explained.

The waiter brought their entrees and poured more wine.

"'So now you have the unenviable task of locating the diamonds. Good luck," Jessie exclaimed.

"There has to be a trail somewhere. It's just a matter of figuring out where to start."

She shook her head. "Right now it's a dead end. Dariel is gone and so is his wife. He could have hidden the diamonds just about anywhere."

"True. It's going to take some luck."

Jessie raised her eyebrows. "Some luck?"

He laughed. "Okay then, a lot of luck. We have to try. We could start by retracing his steps starting with the theft at the airport up to the time of his arrest. It's not a very lengthy time frame."

"When you say 'we have to try', do you mean you and me?" she asked.

He grinned. "I was hoping that's what it meant. Are you okay with working together?"

She hesitated. Her preferred method of investigating was to work alone. She liked the freedom of making split second decisions without having to consult anyone else. But the odds of finding the diamonds were slim to none, and having Liam helping her might turn out to be beneficial. Besides, he wasn't a reporter, so she didn't have to worry about him competing for the story. Finally, she agreed, but not before adding that they had to lay certain ground rules.

His eyebrows rose. "Sounds serious."

She nodded. "It is. We don't keep secrets from each other. If you have a lead, you share. Same with me. Any new ideas along the way? We tell each other. No lone-ranger stuff. Understood?"

His eyes crinkled with a smile. "You're tough. I'm fine with all of the above. Are we good now or do we need to shake hands on this?" he teased.

She laughed. "No shaking hands. Let's say I trust you to remember those conditions."

He signaled the waiter. "Good. Let's celebrate this historic agreement. How about some espresso and tiramisu?"

She grinned. "Espresso yes, tiramisu, no. I don't need a sugar overload right now."

The waiter took away their dishes. Jessie pushed aside a few crumbs and with her finger, she traced an imaginary line on the white tablecloth.

"Let's start with Dariel's timeline. Point A: The airport. On Monday afternoon he took the briefcase. My guess is he hightailed it out of there and didn't check the contents until he reached a safe spot. Then he got a glimpse at his prize and, lo and behold, there it was, lots of money and precious stones.

"Point B. According to what he told me, he stopped at a jeweler to check on the value of the diamonds. We have to find the jeweler. From what Dariel told me, he didn't pawn them. But the man might be able to give us an idea of what he planned on doing with them. Point C: The police arrested him at his house on Tuesday evening—"

The waiter arrived with the coffees. Jessie took a sip of the espresso and inhaled deeply.

"Mm…very good. End of the line."

Liam looked puzzled. "What do you mean, end of the line?"

She scoffed. "It means we have nothing else. He had Monday night and most all of Tuesday to hide the gems."

"Maybe we should start by taking the drive from the airport to his house, see if any place catches our attention," Liam suggested.

Jessie shook her head. "That's just too broad an area. Who knows which route he chose? Plus, I think he may have picked up Lilly from school."

"Lilly is Thomas' child?" he asked.

Jessie nodded, smiling sadly. "Yes. She is an adorable little girl. She doesn't know yet both her parents are dead."

"No one told her?" Liam asked.

"Right now, she's in foster care. Her aunt is scheduled to come and take her back to Minnesota in a couple of weeks. The social worker wanted to wait until then to tell her. So, if I want to keep on spending time with Lilly, I have to abide by her rules."

Liam smiled. "You like her."

"Actually, even though I've only known her a short time, it's more than that," Jessie conceded.

He reached for her hand. "I get it. I feel the same way about my partner's boys. These children don't deserve to go through the heartache of losing parents. All we can do is try to make life bearable for them at this time. Let them know they're loved."

When they left the restaurant, Liam headed back south on A1A. With the windows rolled down they could hear the waves gently washing on shore. Liam suggested a stroll on the beach and Jessie agreed. Parking was not a problem at this late hour. They walked for a couple miles, two dark silhouettes against a sky teeming with stars. The air was brisk and the breeze refreshing. Surprisingly, she enjoyed talking to him and found him to be a good listener. It was close to midnight when he dropped her off at the cottage.

"I had a great time, Jessie."

She nodded. "Me too."

"Do we want to start searching for the gems tomorrow?"

"I have a few things to wrap up first. I'll call you," she said.

He leaned over and brushed her lips with a kiss. "See you soon then?"

She smiled and he left.

When she went to bed later, she lay awake for a long time, images of diamonds dancing in her head, and intermingled with them, a set of amazing green eyes.

Chapter Fourteen

Leaning on the hood of his car, Hakim stared at the façade of the building, musing over the events of the past few months. When Abboud first mentioned using sarin as a weapon of choice for an attack, Hakim was stunned. Nerve gas was not something he had ever considered. To start with, he had no idea on how to obtain it, and the thought of handling the extremely volatile gas made him uneasy.

But as his uncle laid out his plan, he became convinced they could pull it off. Besides, the concept of shaking up the U.S. and its disdainful complacency became more and more appealing to him. After all, it was doubtful the American intelligence agencies would expect such an attack and most likely they would be unprepared. Abboud was extremely careful. He avoided any kind of chatter on the social networks or the usual Internet sites under surveillance by the CIA, the NSA, Homeland Security, or any other shadowy U.S. agencies. Communications between members of the cell were limited to throw-away phones replaced after just a few calls. So far, they had managed to stay completely under the radar.

He told his uncle he would do it.

"Good. You understand how important this will be to our cause. It's time to show them we will not be defeated," the man assured him.

"Where do we start?" Hakim asked.

"Keep your eyes open for a possible target. We want to bring about maximum casualties. In the meantime, find an empty building for sale in an area with little traffic. Then get back to me."

Hakim began his search, spending days on end driving around. It took several weeks of checking various neighborhoods, as far north as Pompano and all the way south to Davie, without much success, until he finally found what he considered a good location.

By chance he had taken a turn onto a side street off Oakland Park Blvd, a short distance west of I-95. After a couple of miles, of driving past dingy warehouses and empty lots overgrown with weeds, the street suddenly came to a dead end. With a sigh he turned around and started back when he noticed an offshoot he'd missed on his way in. A dirt trail partially hidden by a clump of shrubs. He hesitated for a moment, then took it. Narrow and marred by potholes, it was a challenge to navigate.

He was beginning to regret his decision, when he saw it. Just past a junkyard, an unoccupied two-story building with a yellowing For Sale sign taped to a ground floor window. Right next to it was a ditch covered with dark green algae. A mild stench of rotten vegetation lingered in the air. He parked in front of the building and walked back to the junk yard. Littered with rusty carcasses of wrecked vehicles and surrounded by a sagging fence, it had a heavy padlock securing the gate. As he got closer, he noted with some satisfaction a boarded up shed at the center of the property. There would be no neighborly snooping going on from there.

On the way back to the building, he heard the

distant rumble of traffic from I-95. Somehow he found it reassuring. Although the highway was far enough, it was still easily accessible.

He eyed the property more closely, noting the peeling paint and the knee-high weeds. He peered in the windows. Although they were smudged with dirt and the interior was dark, he made out a large open space.

He dialed the number listed on the sign. While waiting for someone to answer, he assessed the open field directly across the street. Strewn with rocks and litter, it stretched for about five hundred feet before leading into a densely wooded area. It was perfect. There was plenty of parking all around and total privacy for their business.

Interrupting his musing, a woman picked up, listened to his request and put him on hold for a couple of minutes. When she came back on the line, she rattled off the information in a disinterested voice and he jotted it all down.

"I don't want you involved in the sale," Abboud stated, when he told him about his find. "Just sit tight. When it's time, I will get back to you."

"It needs quite a bit of work," Hakim said hesitantly.

"It doesn't matter. You will have to retrofit it anyway. Once the purchase is completed and I get a copy of the layout, I will provide you with a revised floor plan."

Three weeks later, Abboud called him back. The purchase had been made under the name of a foreign entity. The key to the property was in a lockbox on the front door. He gave Hakim the code to retrieve it.

Later that day, he brought Jamal along to check out

the place. Hot, dank air assailed them as soon as they opened the door. Wrapping paper and clothes hangers littered the floor along with an accumulation of dust and dirt. Bins with remnants of fabric and spools of thread were still stacked against the walls. A clothing factory maybe. No doubt the place had sat empty for a very long time.

On the bright side, the electricity and water were turned on. Hakim promptly tried the air conditioner. After emitting some suspicious noises and an initial wave of tepid air, it suddenly blasted cold air into the cavernous space.

A small area had been converted to a kitchen. It consisted of a dirty sink, a couple of cabinets with missing doors, a stained Formica countertop and a rusty old refrigerator. Jamal cautiously opened the door. A coke can sat on the top shelf. He reached out and took a hold of it. It was cold. He turned to Hakim. "Hey, believe it or not, this piece of shit still works," he declared with a grin.

On the opposite end of the first floor, they found a closet sized bathroom with a sink and a toilet, both of them filled with vile brownish water.

A narrow stairway led to the second floor. It was bare except for a couple of old metal desks and office chairs. Another bathroom had a filthy shower, and a hole in the floor where the toilet once stood.

"Man, this place is a fucking mess," Jamal said.

Hakim nodded in agreement. "It'll keep us busy for a while."

"What the hell are we going to do here anyway?"

"Whenever we're done with the remodeling, Abboud will let us know what comes next. Then we'll go over everything. In the meantime, we follow his plan and we don't ask questions," Hakim said.

Jamal gave him a strange look and shrugged. Later, the group met at the computer shop and Hakim informed them they had a new home. He sensed a buzz of excitement when he told them they would be moving in as soon as possible. When they joined the cell, he had made it clear they were preparing for an attack. Then time passed and they were growing impatient. Waiting was not their strong suit. Now at last, they were moving forward.

The following morning, a mail truck stopped at the computer store to deliver an express package. As promised, Abboud had sent the instructions for remodeling their new building.

An account had been set up for them at Home Depot. Hakim rented a large truck and picked up supplies. Over the next couple of weeks, the men replaced windows and toilets, repaired flooring, sawed plywood and drywall and erected walls to partition the first floor into basic living quarters. Every morning, they started early and worked late. Every night, covered with sweat and grime, they collapsed on their narrow cots, too exhausted to complain.

Once the remodeling was completed downstairs, Hakim went over Abboud's detailed instructions for the second floor. He quickly realized he did not have the expertise to handle the job by himself. Luckily, Mohamed had worked in the building trade for several years and he put him in charge of the project.

Abboud had made it quite clear. Building the lab would be a difficult and challenging task. The slightest variation from the plan could end up costing them their lives. For security purposes and in order to have an unobstructed view into the room, the plan required the installation of double pane glass panels on one of its two interior walls. The remainder of the walls had to be packed with double insulation and covered with thick sheets of heavy plastic.

All went well until one particular day turned out to be plagued by mistakes. They had to take down previous work, and start over. Tempers flared and a confrontation exploded between Jamal and Abdul. Mohamed intervened and they calmed down. But the rest of the day, discontent hung in the air like a smothering blanket of haze. It all came to a boil again later that evening. The men were seated around the table eating dinner when Hakim sensed Abdul's persistent stare.

"Is something wrong Abdul?" he asked.

"Yeah. Glad you asked. Finally. What are we doing all this for? Are we building a nuclear bomb here? We're entitled to know," the man barked angrily.

Hakim glanced around the table. Dark faces glared at him. They were no longer willing to wait for an answer. "Look, every one of you has worked really hard to transform this building. So be proud of this. We are the ones selected by the leaders of ISIS to inflict a deadly blow to the infidels."

Abdul shook his head vehemently. He was having none of it. "Then how come you keep us in the dark?" he shouted.

Hakim nodded. "I get your frustration. But right now, everything depends on getting back the diamonds we lost. We need them to finance our operation. Without them, our plans will have to change. It's the reason I haven't shared them with you yet. So let's concentrate on what we have to do. I swear, very soon I will have more information for you."

A moment of tense silence ensued. Then Abdul kicked his chair out of the way. It crashed against the wall and he stormed out of the room. Jamal followed. Even Mohamed, usually his staunchest supporter, gave him a stark look of disapproval.

Hakim knew he had to give them something. Soon.

Chapter Fifteen

The bell over the entrance of the computer store chimed softly. Expecting a delivery, Hakim went to the front of the shop and found a small balding man, with sallow skin, standing in the reception area. Wearing a beige uniform with "Port Everglades" embroidered on one pocket, and "Bobby" on the other, he clutched a laptop and stared at Hakim with washed-out blue eyes.

"Can I help you?" Hakim asked.

"I'm having problems with my computer."

Hakim nodded impatiently. "Usually that's what people come here for. I don't have much time but I'll take a quick look. If I can fix it right now, I will. If not, you'll have to leave it."

He reached for the laptop, set it on the reception desk. "All right, what's it doing?" he asked, his fingers flying on the keyboard.

"It freezes all the time. I have to keep turning it off and starting it up again."

"What's your name?"

"Bobby Metzer."

"You work at the Port?" Hakim asked.

Bobby nodded. "Yeah. Just got off a little while ago. I work nights."

"That's a big place. What do you do there?"

"I'm a janitor."

Hakim pointed to a chair in front of the window.

"Have a seat. I'll be back in a bit."

He took the computer into the shop and went to work. It only took about ten minutes before he stood staring at the picture on the screen. Then he slowly scrolled down.

"Bobby?" he called out.

"Yes?"

"Can you come back here?"

The man stuck his head around the corner. "Can you fix it?"

Hakim shook his head. "I don't think so."

"What's wrong?"

Hakim turned the screen in his direction. "This is what's wrong."

Bobby stared at the picture. His face turned even paler. His eyes went wild with panic. "No, no, that's not mine. I... don't know where this came from, but it's not mine," he shrieked.

Hakim pointed at the screen. "This little girl here, she's what? Six years old maybe?"

He scrolled further down. "All these kids, Bobby. You're looking at 8 to 10 years in prison. At the very least."

"No, no, please don't. I thought I took them off. Please don't call the police," Bobby begged, his voice quivering.

Hakim stared at him. "You thought you wiped out the hard drive, huh? Guess what? You didn't."

Tears ran down the man's cheeks. His chin trembled. "Can you take it off? Please? I'll give you whatever you want. I'll pay you. I can't go to jail. They'll kill me there."

Hakim sighed. "We might be able to work out

something, Bobby. Would you want to do that?"

Bobby nodded wildly. "Anything, I'll do anything."

"You know I'm sticking my neck out for you, so don't mess with me." Hakim warned.

"No! No! Whatever you want, you tell me. Just wipe it clean," he pleaded.

"Where do you work at the port?" Hakim asked.

Beads of sweat dripped off the man's brow and ran down his neck. "With the cruise ships and the terminals. I clean the terminals. I restock for the cruise ships, stuff like that."

Hakim nodded. "That's interesting work, isn't it?"

"I suppose," the man said faintly.

"How tight is the security to get on the cruise ships?"

Bobby shook his head. "It's really tight, just like the airport. What do you want to do?"

Hakim ignored his question. "What about the terminals?"

"You only have to show your boarding pass to get into the terminals."

"Which one is the biggest terminal?"

"Eighteen, it's the biggest. It's where the biggest cruise ships dock."

"Do you have access to it?"

Bobby nodded anxiously. "I can get the keys. On my shift there's nobody in the office."

"Draw me a map of the terminal," Hakim said.

"What, now?"

Hakim nodded. "Right now."

"Sure... But will you wipe the hard drive then?"

Hakim glared at him. He got a sheet of blank paper

from the copier and handed it to the man with a pen. Bobby drew the terminal and Hakim scrutinized the drawing.

"One entrance, one exit?"

Bobby nodded.

"Security check in the back?" Hakim asked.

"Yeah. Right before you go out onto the pier for boarding."

"Any recesses along the walls?"

"One over here and another over there," the man said, drawing a couple of recessed areas along the walls of the building.

Hakim considered the information. "If I wanted to have some items remain unnoticed, how would I go about it?"

Bobby shrugged. "I don't know. How big are they?"

"About the size of fire extinguishers."

Bobby's face regained a tinge of color. He smiled faintly. "If you let me know ahead of time, I could bring a couple of barrels from the supply storage. Position them along the wall. You could put your stuff in there. We usually keep some empty ones back there for the ships."

Hakim frowned. "Wouldn't anyone get suspicious?"

"Not if it's a day when passengers are boarding. At least not for quite a while. It gets pretty crazy around then. You have thousands of people packed in there. If anyone spots them, they'll probably think they're there to be picked up by the cruise ships."

Hakim rubbed his chin, going over the information. "Give me your phone number and your address. I'll let you know when the time is right."

Bobby shot a furtive look at his laptop. "So, does that mean we have a deal? You'll wipe it clean?"

"I'm keeping your hard drive, Bobby. You tell anyone about our conversation, you're a dead man. Got it?"

The man shook his head frantically. "I'm not telling anyone, I swear. Can't I have my computer?"

"You'll get it back after we're done."

Bobby nodded weakly. "What is your name?"

"My name is Nasir Hakim."

"When will you let me know?"

"Probably in a couple of weeks. You make sure you answer when I call you."

"I will. I promise," Bobby whispered.

On his way out he gave Hakim a look of despair. Not that Hakim cared. On the contrary, he felt really good. Bobby had just provided him with the perfect target for their attack.

****

The next day, the crew began construction of the man trap, an airlocked vestibule, leading to the lab. Once completed, each end would have a door hermetically sealed to prevent gas from escaping into the rest of the building. The door to the lab would need to be locked in order to open the door leading into the observation room. Both doors had to be special ordered. Despite Hakim's persistent phone calls to the manufacturer, it took two weeks before they were shipped.

To avoid any inquiries, Hakim had them delivered to the computer shop, then once again rented a bigger truck, and the men hauled them to the building in

Oakland Park. Although he had come to trust Mohamed's skills, Hakim went over each step of the construction carefully. Dying from nerve gas poisoning was not part of his plan.

Once the lab was fully sealed off, he bought a small air conditioning unit, and Jamal and Mohamed installed it in the lab's sole window. When it was in place and functional, they encased the rest of the opening with a layer of wood and foam. Keeping the room cooled with a unit detached from the rest of the building's air conditioning system eliminated any possibility of the sarin spreading throughout the building. Originally in liquid form, its high degree of volatility could easily turn it into a gas. It would only be a matter of seconds before the vapor concentration would penetrate the skin and result in death.

By the third week end of August, they were nearly done. There hadn't been any other outbursts from the men, but Hakim knew it was only because they had been too busy. He couldn't wait for it to happen again. He called them into the main living area after lunch, and they listened attentively as he explained they would soon have a guest, a scientist who would be working in the newly constructed lab on the second floor.

Abdul's brow creased. "A scientist? To make bombs?"

Hakim shook his head. "We're not making bombs. Are you familiar with sarin?"

With stunned looks on their faces, they sat silently for a moment. Then Mohamed spoke up. "It's a nerve gas. Saddam used it on the Kurds, and Assad used it in Syria."

Hakim smiled. "Exactly. We will be making our

own nerve gas. This is why this chamber you built, this lab, had to be totally secure. If not sealed properly, one slip could mean the death of each and every one of us."

"Making sarin can't be easy. This scientist, did he ever make it before?" Abdul asked.

Hakim smirked. "You could say he's an expert at it. At one time, he was one of Saddam Hussein's top chemical weapon specialists. His knowledge in the manufacture of nerve gas and its use is as good as it gets. Now, mind you, he's not a willing participant in this operation. Our brothers in Europe snatched him while he was attending a conference in Brussels. Right now, he is on his way and should be here in the next few days."

Jamal who had remained quiet until now, chimed in. "If he's uncooperative, how will you get him to make sarin?"

Hakim grinned. "We have the best possible guaranty. We are holding his family hostage in Syria. His wife, his kids, his mother. All of them. So I can assure you he's going to be quite eager to keep them alive."

The three men remained quiet, still stunned by Hakim's revelation. He continued. "Now, like I said before, this man will do as we ask and I don't see him attempting a getaway. But as an added precaution, we're adding a padlock on his room. To keep him safe. In case he has a sudden change of mind."

They were getting ready to go back to work, when Abdul pulled him aside. "You told us what we're making here. Why didn't you tell us the rest of your plan?"

Hakim patted the man's shoulder. "Everything still

hinges on getting back the diamonds."

"And if we don't find them?"

"We will still plan an attack. Only we'll have to wait until Abboud can arrange another source of funds for us."

Their eyes met and he could see Abdul wasn't satisfied with his answer. After a moment of hesitation, the man shrugged and walked away. He had told Abdul the truth. Without the diamonds, there would be no supplies to manufacture the nerve gas they needed for their attack. He desperately wanted to see it through. Time was of the essence. He had to find the diamonds.

Chapter Sixteen

Art called her into his office as soon as she got to work. Not one to waste time on niceties, he got right to the point. "What's going on with the diamond heist?"

She filled him in on the FBI agent's visit.

"So you're saying they're putting a lid on the story?" he huffed.

"Yep. We can't print it, Art. Not now anyway."

"And are they giving you the first shot at it when it can be printed?"

"Maybe."

He shook his head. "Well, in that case, I want you to stop wasting time chasing a story we can't print. I need your article about the Russian mobsters by the end of the week."

Jessie protested. "Let me stay on the Thomas story. It's not over yet—"

He cut her off abruptly. "No. Do as I say and concentrate on your assignment. If you want to go on, do it on your own time. Not mine."

Hardly able to contain her anger, Jessie stormed back to her desk. Lonnie was waiting for her. He raised his eyebrows. "What's going on?"

She shook her head in frustration. "Art doesn't want me to continue investigating the diamond theft."

She brought him up to date, then went on to tell him about Liam.

"Sounds to me like this could lead to more than a professional exchange of information."

She sighed. "It was only dinner, Lonnie. He's got a sense of humor and I like him, but seeing someone is not a priority right now."

"Really? How many years do you intend to wait before you start dating again? You might as well become a nun at this stage."

"Why is everybody so concerned about me having a relationship? It's not exactly something you put a time frame on," she protested.

"You should at least give it a chance. Maybe there is something there or maybe not. You'll never find out unless you go out with the guy, at least more than once," Lonnie pointed out.

"We'll see," she sighed before planting a kiss on his cheek.

After Lonnie left, Jessie glanced around to check if Art was still there. She didn't see him. She found Emily's number and dialed. After a few rings, she got a recording asking to leave a message for the Newhart family. She left her name and number then turned on the computer. She pulled up her unfinished story about the Russian mobsters and the white slave trade and went over her notes.

A few years earlier, a Russian Kingpin had her kidnapped and held prisoner on a freighter during her probe into a political plot to take over the U.S. presidency. There were some arrests made at the time, but it did little to stop the Russian mob from expanding their business. Although she was aware there was a major problem in the area, what she discovered stunned her. She quickly learned the sex slave trafficking was at an all-time high. While some mobsters were rounded up and arrested occasionally, there never seemed to be enough evidence to bring forth convictions. If any witnesses were even brave enough to come forward originally, by the time the cases came close to trial, they suddenly developed amnesia or disappeared altogether. After interviewing cops and district attorneys involved in the prosecution of the criminals, Jessie found it to be a constant source of frustration for them. A true case of revolving doors in the justice system.

It became even more apparent after she visited a couple of the strip clubs known to be mob owned, and tried to interview some of the young women working there. Everywhere she went, she met a wall of fear and silence. Once, when she approached a dancer at one of the clubs, a big thug grabbed her and threatened her life before he shoved her out on the sidewalk.

She leaned back in her chair, thinking about it for a while. There had to be a way to make contact with some of the girls without drawing the Russians' attention. No doubt it could be tricky or even dangerous, yet she was determined. She decided it was worth another shot.

After leaving work, she bought a sandwich and a bottle of water at a gas station, and drove out to a strip club known to be linked to the Russian mob. Located on 441 at the southern edge of Broward County, the one-story building was painted a stark black. Silhouettes of dancers, cut out of plywood, and painted pink, were nailed on the front. A huge neon sign on top of the flat roof flashed "The Doll House" in bright pink lights.

A narrow alley on the side of the building led to a

dirt parking lot in the back. She drove past a dozen vehicles and backed into a spot between two pick-up trucks. She now had a clear view of the back entrance to the club. She pulled out her sandwich and munched on it. Hopefully some of the girls working at the club would be coming out after their gig was over, and she would get a chance to talk to them.

Over the next half hour, she finished her lunch, balled up the paper wrapper, tossed it on the passenger floor and sipped her water while never losing sight of the door. So far, the only traffic consisted of men coming and going, some of them glancing at her curiously, while others pretended not to see her.

Another hour went by, and she was about to give up, when a young woman stepped out the backdoor carrying a large trash bag. She headed toward a dumpster located on the other side of the property. Jessie jumped out of her car and caught up with her. Startled, the woman turned toward her and for a moment, Jessie was taken aback. Facing her was a young girl, painted like a porcelain doll with large brown eyes and short black hair. Her ruby red mouth turned down at the corners as she stood staring at Jessie fearfully.

"Don't be afraid, I don't mean to harm you. My name is Jessie. Can we talk for a moment?"

The girl hesitated. "What do you want?" she asked with a heavy accent.

Jessie smiled at her encouragingly. "What is your name?"

She lowered her eyes and tried to walk around her. "I cannot talk to you."

Jessie blocked her way. "Why not? What are you

afraid of?"

The girl pushed her aside, dropped her bag into the dumpster, and rushed back toward the building with Jessie a couple of steps behind.

"Go away!" the girl said, her head cast down.

"Wait, I can help you."

The girl shook her head again. "No, you make trouble for me."

Jessie reached out and got hold of her arm. She tried to shrug her off.

"Let me go," she pleaded.

Her eyes were wide with fear now, and Jessie noticed the girl kept glancing up at the corner of the building. She looked up and caught the glare of a camera attached to the edge of the roof. It was angled in their direction. She let go of the girl's arm, positioned herself to have her back turned to the camera, and quickly pressed a business card in the girl's hand. She whispered in her ear. "Call me at this number. I will help you, I promise."

The girl turned away and ran into the building. Jessie went back to her car and decided to leave before some of the goons from the club came hunting for her. She had scant hope the girl would call her. From what she gathered, they were under surveillance all the time, and were often forced to live in houses owned by the Mob.

When Jessie got back to the office, she had a message on her phone. It was from Emily Newhart and it was dated about an hour ago. Afraid she was going to miss the woman again, she promptly called back.

"Hello?" The voice was soft and sounded tired.

"Hi, Ms. Newhart, this is Jessie Milner. I'm sorry I

missed your call."

"No problem. Can you tell me what this is about?"

"I'll be glad to. First I want to tell you how sorry I am about Dariel's death."

"Did you know my brother?"

Jessie told her how she had met Dariel and Lilly. "Did the police fill you in on everything?"

"Pretty much. I'm still in shock though. Dariel had a lot of problems, but I never stopped loving him. He was my little brother. Most of it wasn't really his fault. We didn't have what you would consider a normal family life. Our father had him pick pockets when he was still a child. It was the way we were brought up. I ran away at sixteen. Sometimes I have such guilt because I left Dariel behind. Maybe I should have helped him get away as well. It was hard just surviving on my own. I lived on the streets for a while. Really, my life was a mess until I met my husband. He saved me, you know," she said, her voice quivering.

"There probably wasn't a whole lot you could have done at the time. You were a child yourself. You'll be glad to know, though, he was a good dad, and his little girl adores him," Jessie assured her.

Emily hesitated. "How is she doing?"

"She doesn't know yet about her mom or her dad. The social worker said it would be best to wait until you get here. It's too much for her to deal with alone."

Jessie could hear her crying softly. "Oh my God, how am I going to tell her? She's just a baby."

"Giving her your love and your affection will help a lot, Emily. Lilly is a wonderful little girl, just full of life and energy." Jessie said.

"I wish I could come get her now. But I can't. Not

yet. Martin's blood pressure has been soaring and the doctor wants to run some more tests. They're putting off his surgery until next week. I feel so bad leaving her there."

"Listen, she's in a good home. I met her foster mom and I can assure you Lilly is okay. Also, I'm going to spend as much time as possible with her. So, right now, just concentrate on everything you have to contend with at home. Once your husband's surgery is over and he's well enough, it'll be time to come and get your little niece."

"Thank you so much for calling, Jessie. I can't wait to meet you."

"Same here, Emily."

Their conversation had been pleasant, better yet, reassuring. But here she was, still gripping the phone until her hand ached. Out of nowhere, a wave of emotions swept over her. She dreaded the emptiness Lilly's departure would leave in her life. To no longer hear her wonderful laughter, or watch her eyes light up in delight. To be unable to feel the warmth of her small arms around her neck or nudge against her cool cheek in a quiet moment.

Without realizing it, she was crying. Then she reminded herself she had no right to be selfish. Lilly deserved a good life with a real family who could offer her the warmth of a home, with a father, and a mother, and a big brother who would look after her. Jessie could see her now, playing in a big yard with the dog she longed for. She smiled through the tears. It was everything she could possibly wish for her sweet Lilly.

Chapter Seventeen

She had put off working on her human trafficking article all morning. Then, when she sat down to write, she was overwhelmed by a sense of exasperation. Countless young women were trapped and she couldn't do anything about it. If only she could tell their stories, maybe it would bring attention to what was going on. Her previous day's encounter with the Russian girl only magnified her frustration. It was all about fear and intimidation.

Sitting in front of her laptop, she sighed, trying to come up with something of importance. Nada, nothing. She leaned back in her chair, absentmindedly tapping her front teeth with her pen. Then suddenly, she had an idea.

Hoping Lonnie was still in the building, she raced upstairs, pushing through the stairwell door on the eighth floor, her chest heaving from the effort. Lonnie was sitting at his desk facing the entrance and he spotted her immediately. He frowned in concern at her appearance. As their eyes met, his expression changed to one of suspicion.

"Hey buddy," she said walking toward him, a friendly smile on her face.

"Buddy? Somehow, I have a feeling you're up to no good," he mumbled.

She waved away his doubts. "Nonsense." She

grabbed a chair nearby and pulled it up to his desk. "I was thinking—"

"That's what I'm afraid of," he protested.

She ignored him. "How about you coming with me for a visit to the Doll House?"

His face brightened. "A doll house? Is this for Lilly?"

Jessie laughed. "No. I mean the strip club down in Hollywood."

His eyebrows shot up. "Okay, now I'm really confused. We are talking about a strip club with women strippers, right?"

"Yeah, that's the one."

"Have you gone completely mad? What makes you think I would be interested—Wait a minute—is this an attempt to get me to switch teams?" he huffed.

"Of course not. It's for the article I'm writing about the Russian mobsters. I've tried to talk to some of the dancers. They're all afraid because there's always a couple of goons around to keep an eye on them. If you could distract them, just long enough, so I could have a few words with the girls, I may be able to get a phone number or a name," she said, trying to sound convincing.

Lonnie shook his head. "You are insane. Those goons, as you call them, probably will beat the shit out of both of us and throw us out of there. If they don't kill us first."

"No, Lonnie, listen. I have a plan. You tell them you are a journalist and you're there to sample their food because you are writing a special column on strip club foods."

He leaned forward getting close to her face.

"Jessie, hello, is that brain of yours working today? Do you really think anyone who goes to the Doll House gives a damn about their food?"

She shrugged. "Well they must serve some things, like burgers or hot dogs. So why not?"

He stared at her in disbelief.

"Please, Lonnie. I really need to finish the article for Art, and I can't, unless I get some interviews with the girls who work there. You should have seen the one I met by the dumpster yesterday. I bet she wasn't even sixteen. She was scared to death to talk to me."

"Jess, they will be scared to talk to you inside the club as well as outside," he argued.

"At least I can slip them my phone number. All it'll take is one of them to call me."

He shook his head and sighed. "I want you to know this is against my better judgment. I don't get paid enough to risk getting beat up by a bunch of mobsters."

Jessie hopped out of her chair before he could change his mind. "Let's go right now."

Lonnie followed her grudgingly. They reached the parking garage, and Jessie said she would drive. There was no way she was giving him a chance to back out, so she drove fast, weaving in and out of the traffic, until finally, Lonnie spoke up irritably and ordered her to slow down. She did. They still made it there in record time. The Doll House had a few more vehicles parked behind the building than during her earlier visit. She took it as a good sign. Hopefully it would lessen the odds of getting assailed if there were witnesses.

She pulled into a parking spot and they walked to the back entrance. Deafening music assaulted them as soon as they opened the door and stepped into the dank-smelling building. After a few seconds of getting used to the dimness, Jessie discerned two young women wearing G-strings slowly gyrating on the stage, their dance routine oddly out of synch with the harsh beat. Pulsating lights accentuated the pallor of their skin. To the left of the stage was a bar with a line of empty stools. As they walked up, the bartender shot them a disinterested look. Jessie ordered a *Cuba Libre,* and the man huffed scornfully when Lonnie asked for a glass of chardonnay, with ice, please. Jessie was annoyed. Lonnie, on the other hand, didn't seem to notice. They stood at the bar waiting for their drinks, checking their surroundings. She counted about a dozen customers, all of them males, most of them middle aged, with a fair share of balding heads and beer bellies among them. Seated alone at small tables dispersed throughout the room, they stared at the strippers grinding through their tired routine. Loneliness hung in the air, its presence every bit as strong as the yearning for sexual gratification. As her eyes got used to the darkness, Jessie spotted the young girl from the dumpster, picking up empty glasses and wiping tables. After a few moments, she noticed the girl chose to stay a safe distance from the tables occupied by customers, most likely in an attempt to keep from getting groped. Their eyes met and the girl quickly looked away. Jessie glanced at the bartender, who was playing around with his bottles and rearranging his glasses. She knew he decided to make them wait for their drinks as a sign of his contempt. He finally shoved a couple of glasses at them. Jessie balked at the price—thirty dollars for a measly glass of house wine and a rum and coke. She paid him, then reluctantly handed him a couple of dollars tip, only to have him give her the evil eye.

They walked to an empty table nearby and had barely taken a seat when a bald-headed man, shoulders and arms thick with muscle, emerged from a darkened hallway. He headed straight toward them.

His legs planted apart and arms folded tightly across his barrel chest, he glared at Lonnie with dark menacing eyes. Tattoos ran the full length of both his arms, and Jessie noticed an angry vein bulging in his neck. She tilted her head to get a better look at his tats, and he suddenly turned to her and barked in heavily accented English. "I know you?"

"Nope. First time here," she answered cheerfully.

"What do you want?"

Lonnie threw up his hands in protest. "Is this how you welcome new customers?"

The Russian leaned forward with an icy stare. "You no customers. Like I said, what do you want?"

Lonnie shrugged. "Well, actually, I'm a reporter for the *Broward News*. I'm doing an article on foods at nightclubs throughout the county. Can I see one of your menus?"

The man snickered. "Menus? What the hell you think this is, Olive Garden?"

Lonnie appeared nonplussed. "Okay, then what do you serve?"

The man eyed him sarcastically. "Nothing you would like."

Lonnie made a pout. "I'm sure you didn't mean it as an insult."

The Russian smirked. "Take it any way you want. We don't like pansies in here."

Jessie glanced at Lonnie. His face remained

expressionless.

She intervened. "I bet you have burgers or hot dogs, don't you?"

The bald man scoffed. "You want burger? Yeah, sure, I'll get you burger."

"My friend here certainly would, isn't that right Lonnie?" Jessie asked innocently.

Lonnie nodded solemnly. "Absolutely, I would love a burger. Oh, don't forget the onions and lettuce please. And I'll take fries with that."

The Russian stared at them, eyes clouded for a moment by indecision, then he turned to the young girl nearby. "Irina!" She came running and he shouted a few words to her in Russian. She nodded and left.

"You eat your burger and then you get the hell out of here. Got it?" the man growled.

"You bet," Lonnie said with a grin before taking a sip of his wine.

The Russian left after a couple more angry stares. Jessie waited until he disappeared, then got up.

"Where do you think you're going?" Lonnie asked over the din of the music.

"Restroom," she said.

"You be careful."

"Absolutely."

Jessie took off, gazing right and left, well aware of eyes following her along the way. A sign guided her down a dimly lit hallway where she spotted the women's restroom halfway down on the left. Before she reached it, there was another door with a handwritten sign marked "Stage Door". Without hesitating, she turned the knob and stepped inside. For a short moment, the brightness in the room nearly blinded her and she had to blink several times until her vision returned to normal. A step back to the seventies, the walls were covered with garish black and silver foil wallpaper. Gray shag carpeting was matted down by years of wear. Several chairs were lined up in a row in front of a large mirror surrounded by lights. Occupying two of the seats, a couple of women, wearing only pasties and a G-string, were applying make-up. Their skin had the unhealthy appearance of someone who never sets foot outdoors. Both of them stared at her, eyes wide with surprise. Jessie guessed she had very little time.

"My name is Jessie Milner. I'm a reporter, can I talk to you for a minute?"

The two girls looked at each other in confusion.

"Do you speak English?" Jessie asked.

One of them nodded.

"What's your name?"

The woman hesitated. "Oksana."

Reaching into her pocket, Jessie produce a couple of business cards and handed one to each of them. "Please call me if there's anything I can do to help, anything at all…"

"Like what?" Oksana asked.

"Like getting away from this."

Oksana nodded, glanced at the card and shoved it under a piece of clothing. The other girl sat staring at hers. Oksana shook her head, grabbed it out of the girl's hand and hid it as well.

"You must leave," she said urgently, her eyes straying anxiously toward the top of the door. Jessie turned and spotted the camera. She looked back at Oksana.

"Right now, or else it will be big trouble," the woman whispered softly.

"Okay, I'll go. Call me, please," Jessie said.

As she turned to open the door, the bald Russian burst into the room and glared at her angrily. "What you doing in here?"

"Took a wrong turn. I thought this was the ladies' room."

"Get out of here or I'll kick you out." He leaned in way too close.

Jessie shrugged. "Okay, okay. I'm sorry."

She glanced in Oksana's direction as she stepped out. The young woman was applying rouge to her cheeks. Her big brown eyes followed Jessie in the mirror.

Back at the table, Lonnie was waiting anxiously. "Where were you?"

She frowned, scanning the table. "Where's your burger?"

He stood up and grabbed her arm. A few feet away, the Russian leaned against a wall, leering at them threateningly.

"Never mind. Let's get the hell out of this joint."

"Wait a sec."

She reached for her *Cuba Libre*, took a drink and made a face. "Yuk, I can't believe I paid fifteen bucks for this crap. I should ask for my money back."

Lonnie shook his head emphatically. "Oh no, you don't. We're out of here."

At the back door, she stopped and exchanged one last icy stare with the Russian.

A frantic shout came from outside. "For Pete's sake, come on," Lonnie yelled, holding the door open.

"I'm coming," she protested before following him into the parking lot.

In the car, he let out a sigh of relief. "Man, I was scared shitless in there."

"You were rather impressive with the bald guy."

"That was just too dangerous."

"Mm… You have to admit, it was fun though."

He eyed her in disbelief. "You know you're crazy, right?"

She smiled triumphantly. "I made a contact in there, Lonnie."

"What? When?"

"A girl named Oksana. I gave her my card. I think she was interested."

"How do you know?"

She shrugged. "Just the way she reacted. I hope she calls me."

Lonnie gave her a concerned look. "Jess, you know you're playing with fire with those Russians goons. Just be careful, my love, okay?"

She patted him on the arm. "I know, I'll be careful, I promise. Oh, and I love you too."

They both laughed, but deep down, Jessie knew he was right.

When she got home, she had a message from Liam on her answering machine. She pulled out her cell phone and noticed there were two calls from him on there as well. She rang him back. "Hey."

"Hi Jessie. Tried to call you several times. Guess you must have been busy."

"I'm sorry. My boss ordered me off the Thomas case and I have to turn in the Russian mob story by the end of the week."

"So, you don't want to look for the diamonds anymore?"

His voice carried a note of disappointment, and somehow it pleased her. She hoped it was because he wanted to see her. On the other hand, maybe he just needed help in finding the gems.

"Oh, no way Jose. We're still going ahead. I just won't tell Art. Right now I have to work on the Russians. So maybe in a couple of days?" she suggested.

He hesitated.

"What?" she asked.

"I was hoping to see you before then."

She smiled broadly. "Okay, well, let's see how it goes tomorrow. I promise I'll call you back."

Chapter Eighteen

A bird tweeting persistently brought her out of a deep sleep. Her mind still in a fog, she groped the top of the nightstand for the phone. "Hello?"

Silence greeted her, followed by shallow breathing. Irritated, Jessie was ready to hang up when there was a whisper. "Jessie Milner?"

The accent sounded vaguely familiar.

"This is Jessie, who is this?"

"Irina, from the club. You remember?"

Jessie's heart skipped a beat. She sat up straight, recalling a set of dark frightened eyes. She glanced at the clock; it was ten after one.

"Of course, Irina. Yes, I remember you. Are you all right?"

"You say you help me. It is true?"

"Yes, I meant it. What can I do for you?" Jessie asked.

"Four o'clock, the bus come to Doll House and take us back to the house. I don't want to go no more."

Her voice quivered, and Jessie sensed she had been crying.

"I can come and get you," she said.

"Please," Irina cried.

"No problem, we have plenty of time. Will you be able to come outside without drawing their attention?"

"Every night I take trash out at two o'clock, you

come then?"

"I'll be there. Is there any place in the parking lot out of sight of the cameras?"

The girl hesitated a moment. "I think so, by the dumpster."

"I'll wait for you there. Don't be afraid. We can do this, okay?"

"You promise you come?" The young girl's fear was palpable.

"I promise, Irina. I will be there."

While she was getting dressed, disturbing questions suddenly raced through her mind. Where was the girl calling from? The caller ID had been blocked and she was pretty certain Irina had no cell phone. Next, suspicion took over. The Russians could have coerced her to call. To lure her to the Club, beat her up, or worse yet, make her disappear altogether. They were bound to know about her after her frequent inquiries and her snooping around.

Finally, she shrugged off her doubts. No matter what, a promise was a promise. She wasn't going to back down now. She made up her mind to go. Another glance at the clock assured her she had plenty of time. At this time of the night, it would take her less than a half hour to get to the strip club. She went to the closet and took out a shoe box wedged behind an old backpack. She sat it on the corner of her dresser and removed the lid. Carefully wrapped in a cloth was a .38 Smith and Wesson revolver. Although it mostly remained in the closet, every now and then, she took it out for a ride to the shooting range in Davie. A few years earlier, she learned how to use the weapon and now kept up the practice, just in case she needed it for self- defense. She kept cartridges in the box as well. She loaded the gun, closed the cylinder, clicked it back in place, and tucked it in her purse.

Twenty minutes later she was on her way to the Doll House. It was ten till two when she arrived at the club. Having plenty of time, she slowly circled the block twice while keeping an eye on her rearview mirror. She didn't notice anything suspicious. As she turned into the parking lot, she remembered seeing the dumpster during her previous visit. It sat next to a wooden fence separating the Doll House from a body shop. She drove up to it and scanned the surrounding area. There were no cameras. Somewhat reassured, she backed into a parking space next to the container, then noticed a big black pickup truck blocking her view to the building's back door. Even so, she decided to stay where she was out of precaution. If she moved elsewhere she might be visible on one of the cameras affixed on the building. Also, if Irina didn't spot her close to the dumpster, she might panic. She turned off the lights and the engine.

The thumping of loud music from the club shattered the quiet of the night, an unsettling mixture of serene darkness and throbbing sound. Two dim lamps in the back lot provided scant light as dark clouds hung low in the sky and humidity was thick as fog. After a few minutes of sitting in the stagnant heat, Jessie rolled down the windows, keeping a cautious eye on her surroundings. A short time later, the back door opened, followed by the sound of heavy footsteps. Quickly she reached into her handbag on the passenger seat and took hold of the gun. Just then, a burly man with a thick beard appeared at the front of the black truck, stumbling twice before he reached the driver's door, then cursed loudly as he fumbled with his keys. Finally, he managed to get the door open. As he did, he turned sideways and he caught sight of Jessie. He stopped dead in his tracks. She didn't move. The man leaned against his vehicle and lit a cigarette with an unsteady hand.

"Hey," he said drunkenly.

Jessie gave him a cold stare. After a minute or so, he seemed to make up his mind, threw away his cigarette, and staggered over to her car. He leaned in the window.

"Hey, Babe, looking for some action?" he asked in a raspy voice, his breath reeking of beer.

She shook her head. "Just waiting for my squeeze. She's getting off in a couple of minutes."

He hesitated, then spotted the gun in her lap. It was pointing in his direction. He pulled away like he was stung and went back to his truck. Before climbing in the cab, he leered at her in disgust. "Damn dyke," he muttered, as he took off in a cloud of dirt and dust.

Another fifteen minutes went by. Jessie was getting worried, wondering if something went wrong or if Irina got cold feet. With the pickup gone, she now had a clear view of the back entrance. She was still unsure about what to do next, when the door opened. A small silhouette wearing a hoodie stepped outside, carrying a trash bag nearly her size. The door snapped closed behind her, and she stood still for a moment scanning the lot. Jessie waved at her. As soon as she caught sight of her, the girl dropped the bag and dashed to the car. Without saying a word, she jumped in the passenger seat, and just as quickly, Jessie started the engine and took off. She waited until she was a full block away before turning on her headlights.

With the mixture of fear and excitement still intense, they drove in silence until they were several miles from the Club and Jessie deemed it safe to pull into the parking lot of a Denny's. The restaurant was well lit and despite the late hour, a number of customers were still coming in and out. She turned to Irina and smiled in relief. "We made it."

Irina quietly took off her hood and Jessie gasped at the sight of her face. Her forehead and cheek were bloodied. One of her eyes was swollen shut.

"Oh my god, who did this to you?"

"Ivan. I didn't want to do sex with customers anymore. They are mean and hurt me all the time, so he beat me. He say he will kill me if I say no again. I had to go," the girl said, crying softly.

Jessie reached over and took hold of her hand. "Oh Irina, I'm so sorry. You're safe now. He will never be able to hurt you again."

The girl nodded, drying her tears with her sleeve. "I waited until he went out for a while, then I sneak into office and use phone and call you."

Jessie gave her a reassuring smile. "You made the right decision. I'm taking you home and then we'll decide what to do next."

While driving east on 595, she realized how easily the Russians could figure out her involvement in Irina's disappearance. Her two recent visits to the club would certainly be suspicious, and since Irina's called her from Ivan's office, they could find out her name and where she lived. She slowed down. Just past the airport, she took the southbound exit on U.S.1 and drove to the nearest hotel. As they pulled in, Irina's eyes widened.

"This is your home?"

Jessie smiled. "For tonight, it's our home. Tomorrow, we'll see."

Once they were in their room, she took a closer look at the young girl's face. It appeared even worse under the bright lights. With a warm cloth, she gently dabbed at the wounds.

It was past three o'clock by the time they went to bed. Irina was still sleeping soundly when Jessie got up at eight o'clock. She went downstairs to the hotel's breakfast nook, had coffee and a bagel, and made some calls. She left a message for Sam Perrone, stressing it was urgent to call her back as soon as possible. Next she rang Art, told him about Irina, then listened to him rant and rave about her foolishness. As soon as she clicked off, Perrone called back. She told him about the girl and he listened quietly.

"Stay there," he said. "I'll be over shortly."

She got a refill on her coffee and waited. Perrone walked in twenty minutes later. He was thinner than the last time they met. His hair was streaked with gray and his suit had a well-worn shine to it. He gave her a tired smile, poured himself a cup of coffee, and took a seat across from her. He emptied a packet of sugar into his cup and stirred it slowly.

"Do you think she'll talk to me?" he ventured before taking a couple of careful sips of the hot beverage.

"I think so."

He nodded somberly and stood up. "Okay then, let's go."

Jessie grabbed a cup of orange juice and a bagel for Irina, and they went upstairs. The girl was awake. In broken English and between sobs, she told them her story. How she left Russia at fourteen, lured by the promise of a good job in America. Instead, the moment she arrived all her identification was confiscated. Then she was beaten, raped, and forced into prostitution by Ivan and his partner. That was her new life.

When Sam got ready to leave, Jessie walked him out. He shook his head. "Jessie, you have to realize, it's not just about Irina now. If she can identify this man Ivan and some of the other mobsters, they might finally be able to prosecute them. I have a contact at the FBI. We've worked together on several cases and he's a straight shooter. Let me give him a call."

It was midmorning when Perrone came back with the FBI agent. He introduced him as Special Agent Daryl Bellamy. He asked Irina for the names of the men who ran the strip club and jotted down the information. When he was done with his questions, he took Jessie and Sam aside and spoke softly. "As I suspected, these men are members of the Russian Mafia or the Bratva, as it is called. Ivan Zherdev and his associate Leonid Gorev are in the top tier, and we know they are deeply involved in human trafficking and drug distribution. They've also been linked to a series of mob related murders in South Florida. So far, we haven't been able to prove any of it. They are ruthless and rule by fear. No one dares come forward."

Jessie frowned. "What about the information Irina gave you? Isn't it enough to arrest these men?"

The agent sighed. "The moment she disappeared, I can tell you what happened. All the under aged and illegal girls were whisked out of there. They'll deny knowing Irina, and there will be no witnesses or records to confirm her story. Nonetheless, we'll see if we make anything stick. It's worth a shot."

Jessie couldn't believe where this conversation was going. "So what now?"

"When I leave here, I will arrange to have one of our female agents pick her up and take her to a safe house."

"And what about later?"

He peered at her glumly. "I can't make any promises. I can only say we'll have a good case in her favor, if her testimony helps us nail those guys. Some things are negotiable."

"I promised her she would be safe," Jessie said, frustration creeping into her voice.

"I will do whatever I can to protect her," Bellamy replied.

The two men left and Irina turned to Jessie. "I'm scared. I can stay with you?"

"Agent Bellamy is sending a lady agent who will take you to a safe place. After Ivan and his accomplices are arrested and go to jail, we will get together again and figure out what's the best for you," Jessie said weakly.

Irina nodded slowly, but the wounded look in her eyes told Jessie she had lost her trust. A couple of hours later, a female agent showed up. She was young and congenial, and Jessie hoped it would put Irina more at ease. They hugged before they left. With a void feeling in her chest, Jessie watched the slight girl walk away with the woman at her side. She gathered her belongings and checked out.

Art was still at his desk when she walked in the office. He frowned as soon as he saw her. "Where the hell have you been?"

She told him about the FBI's visit and Irina going to a safe house. When she was done, he shook his head, and Jessie wondered what was coming.

"I have to hand it to you, rescuing that kid middle of the night, you've got bigger balls than most of my guys out there. You could've gotten killed by those bastards." He frowned. "Now when the hell are you writing this up?"

"It'll be ready tomorrow. We can't mention Irina, not right now anyway."

He shrugged. "Take it as far as you can."

Although it was already five o'clock, she went back to her desk and started typing, words flying effortlessly on the pages, driven by her bitterness and anger.

Chapter Nineteen

Bellamy called as she was walking out the door on her way to work.

"I'm afraid I have some bad news, Jessie," he said somberly.

"What's wrong?"

"Irina is gone. She slipped out of the house while my agent was on the phone."

Jessie stopped in her tracks, dread tightening her chest. "How long ago?"

"Late last night. She probably got scared. Those girls often do."

"Where could she have gone?"

"She may have found her way back to the Club. Maybe she believes they'll forgive her. They won't. They would never trust her again."

"Can you please search for her?" she pleaded.

"Jessie, she's one of thousands of illegals in this country. We just don't have the resources to find them. Even assigning an agent to look after her in a safe house was more than I was supposed to do. I'm sorry."

She drove to work, focusing on the people in the streets, hoping somehow she would spot Irina on a sidewalk.

Liam called shortly after lunch. "What's wrong?" he asked as soon as heard her voice.

She told him and was greeted by silence. "Liam?"

"You shouldn't have gone to the Club by yourself. That was crazy."

"That's what I've been told. Several times as a matter of fact. So, I don't want to talk about it anymore," she said abruptly.

"Okay, I get it. Are you free this afternoon?" he asked.

"Why?"

"How about coming with me to the sheriff's office? In their infinite generosity, they agreed to give me access to the security video from the airport. It probably won't be helpful, but you never know. It's worth a try."

She thought it would help keep her mind off Irina. A half hour later they met at the Broward County Sheriff's building. At the front desk Liam asked for Boyd. They were directed to his office, a cramped windowless room with two desks facing each other. Boyd occupied one of them. Piles of folders were stacked unevenly on top. Two coffee mugs and a wire basket with more folders shared the remaining space. The other desk was neat and empty.

The detective looked surprised when he saw Jessie. "Liam, you didn't tell me you were bringing company."

Jessie smiled. "Don't worry, I can't publish anything related to the diamond theft, so my visit is totally off the record."

"What do you mean?"

"I had an FBI agent stop by and pay me a call. He informed me I couldn't publish any further information about the case. Said it was a matter of national security."

Boyd hesitated. "I don't know..."

"Jim, I don't see what harm there is for Jessie to see the video. Do you?" Liam said.

Although Boyd still didn't seem quite sure, he finally nodded in agreement. He retrieved a USB flash drive from a drawer and motioned for Liam to shut the door. Next he plugged the drive into the laptop on his desk. They waited for the screen to pop up.

"How did you get it on there?" Liam asked.

Boyd shrugged. "I'm far from technically savvy. I played with it for a bit and I managed somehow. This was patched together from the different cameras at the airport."

As the images came up, Jessie and Liam leaned over his shoulder to get a better view. He fast forwarded past the first few frames, then slowed down, pointing as he went along.

"Down there on the left, Thomas is entering the terminal. Check how he's scanning the place, searching for an easy mark. When he doesn't spot any, he heads for the new arrivals. Now over here, he slows down. He finds what he wants and he trails her for a while."

They followed Thomas walking a few paces behind a well-dressed woman.

"It looks like he's targeting her handbag. He's close enough, he's about ready to reach for it, then boom, there comes a bunch of kids fresh off the plane, swarming the area. She's surrounded and he can't get to her. They spoiled his game, so he drops back, probably wondering what to do next. Then shortly after, there's a commotion. It's the courier going down. He hits the floor, the briefcase goes flying, the crowd gathers and Thomas moves in, grabs the case, and takes off like flint—"

Suddenly Jessie gripped his shoulder.

"Hold on! Hold it right there," she shouted.

The two men looked at her in surprise and Boyd froze the picture.

Jessie leaned in closer. "The man, right there, pulling away from the crowd and going after Dariel, I've seen him before."

Boyd rolled back the film a few frames. The man appeared more clearly now, short, dark skinned and dark haired. "Are you sure?" Boyd asked.

"Yes, I'm sure. I just don't remember where." She shut her eyes tight, trying to recall, then shook her head in frustration. "Dariel told me a dark man chased him at the airport. He believed he was with the courier and he was sure he killed Mandy."

"So you think you saw him the night she died?"

"No, it was too dark and their car only stopped for a moment. It had to be someplace else."

"Why didn't you mention this before?" Boyd asked.

"I didn't really take it seriously. I thought it was just someone who saw him pick up the briefcase and chased him down for a while," Jessie said.

"Well, it doesn't matter now. I'm off the case," Boyd announced tersely.

"What do you mean? A couple of people have been murdered. How can you be off the case?" Liam asked.

Jessie jumped in. "Let me guess. The FBI told you to drop it. National security, right?"

"Yeah, whenever they want to take over, it's always for national security. That's why they confiscated the video from the airport." Boyd sneered.

Liam nodded. "You managed to get your own copy

anyway."

Boyd grinned sheepishly. "They told me they were coming to get it, so I stalled long enough to copy it."

"Do you think he's a terrorist?" Jessie asked.

"All I know is the FBI insisted on taking over the investigation. At first they focused solely on the German with the briefcase. Now, I think they're taking another look at this guy." The detective nodded toward the screen. "The two of them took the same flights to Newark and back on the same day. It seems to be too much of a coincidence, and let's face it, most of us in law enforcement don't believe in them."

"We need to find out who he is," Liam mused.

"Can you run him through your system?" Jessie asked.

Boyd paused, smiling.

"You already did, didn't you?" she asked.

Boyd nodded. "He made it pretty easy. Unlike the courier, he booked his flight under his real name, Nasir Hakim, born in the U.S. Parents are Iranian immigrants. One juvenile arrest for defamation of property, graffiti on a Jewish temple. He was fourteen. He was sentenced to community service for a year. No records otherwise. To all appearances, he went straight after that original incident."

"Can we get his picture?" Liam asked.

"Sure. But I didn't give it to you. Understand? At this point, my hands are tied. I can't stop you from snooping. Nonetheless, let me give you a few words of caution here," Boyd warned. "Don't get in the way of the Feds. They wouldn't like it."

As he was talking, he pushed a key on the computer and a humming sound rose from an ancient printer sitting on a small table nearby. A few seconds later it spit out a copy. The detective handed it to Liam with a shrug.

"Our equipment here is pretty old. This is the best I can do."

Jessie and Liam checked it out. Although it was somewhat blurry, it still gave them a fairly good image of the man.

Jessie rubbed the picture. "Is that a smudge on his cheek?" she asked.

Liam held it up to the light. "Maybe more like a scar," he said.

They thanked Boyd, and he waved them away. "You two are on your own now. I'm not at liberty to give you any more information. As a matter of fact, I shared too much already." He walked them out. "Good luck," he mumbled.

They stood on the sidewalk for a moment.

"What are your plans now?" Liam asked.

"I have to get back to the office, wrap up the Russian story so it can be published this Sunday."

He nodded. "Too bad you couldn't end it with the arrests of those scumbags."

Jessie sighed. "And Irina being safe and sound..."

"We can't change the past, only hope they'll pay for their crimes sometime soon. I have another case to work on this afternoon. When I'm done, I'll see what I can find out on this Nasir Hakim. Get an address. If so, we can go out tomorrow and check it out," Liam said.

"Call me when you have something."

"I have a better idea. How about I make you dinner tonight, at my place? Get your mind off this whole thing for a little while."

"What about your case?" Jessie asked.

"It'll only take me a couple of hours. So, are you interested?"

"Yeah, anytime someone is willing to cook for me, I'm interested," she said smiling.

"I don't know if I should feel hurt by the fact it's only the food enticing you to spend time with me."

"Wine and conversation work as well," she answered.

He laughed. "It's a deal. Let's say seven o'clock?"

She agreed and he gave her his address.

"Can I bring anything?"

"Only you," he exclaimed with a grin.

She took a few steps.

"Jessie, wait!"

She turned around.

"Do you like salmon?" Liam asked.

"Love it."

"Good, see you soon."

Chapter Twenty

On the way to Liam's, Jessie wondered if she made a mistake accepting his invitation. No doubt their initial encounter didn't start out so well. Now, however, she enjoyed his company and there was no denying she was attracted to him. She quickly dismissed her misgivings. After all, this was only a dinner, so why make a big deal out of it?

Although the eastern section of Pompano Beach was unfamiliar territory, Liam's street was wedged between Federal Highway and the Intracoastal and was easy to find. Expecting to see an apartment building, she was surprised to recognize his jeep parked in the driveway of a small home painted a pale peach color with bright green shutters. A gravel path led to the entrance. She knocked on the front door, and Liam appeared within seconds, greeting her with a big smile.

"For some reason I assumed you lived in a condo," Jessie said.

"Nope. This was actually my grandmother's home. After she passed away, my parents suggested I buy it, I agreed, and here I am. Come on in. I'll give you a tour."

Furnishings in the living room were limited to a tan leather couch, a television set and two matching chairs. Glass doors opened to a deck and a small grassy area with a spectacular view of the Intracoastal. A variety of boats lined both sides of the waterway.

A narrow kitchen with white cabinets had just enough room for a small round table and four chairs. Down a short hallway were two bedrooms and a bathroom tiled in vibrant pink and blue colors. Terrazzo covered all the floors throughout the house.

"It's not very big," he explained. "Works for me though. It could use sprucing up. Maybe you can give me some guidance. I'm not a very good decorator."

"I actually like older homes. They're a welcome change from the cookie cutters houses popping up in subdivisions all over the west side of town. Same floor plans, same granite countertops, same supersized bathrooms and monster closets. No one needs that much space for their stuff, do they? Take your terrazzo floor for example. It's made to last, it's beautiful, and it's getting popular again," Jessie said.

Liam grinned. "Great news. Since you like it, I won't have to spend an arm and a leg to change it."

He opened a bottle of wine and they sat on the deck as boats glided by. Like somber guardians of the deep, a couple of pelicans occupied the top of two deck posts. Soon the sun started its vanishing act beyond the horizon, and the sky took on dazzling shades of orange to bright red. A cool breeze, laced with salt, combined the scent of the sea and the smell of jasmines.

Jessie inhaled deeply. "This is as close to paradise as you're ever going to get."

Liam nodded. "I find I'm liking it more every day."

"What about your family. Do you miss them?" Jessie asked.

He grinned. "I do somewhat. I try to go back and see my parents as much as I can. I grew up in a two-story house in Queens. My grandparents moved here from Ireland. They lived on the ground floor. My parents, my brother, and I lived upstairs. Every Sunday, after Mass, it was dinner downstairs with my uncles and cousins in attendance. As a whole, it was fun to get together with the other kids. Sometimes there would be arguments, 'disagreements' as they called them, yet everybody always went home with a full stomach."

He paused for a moment. "Later on, my grandparents moved to Florida. Now they're both gone and my parents are getting older. They talk about retiring down here, but my brother is there and so are his kids. I think it's going to be hard for them to leave those grandchildren behind. What about you?"

"South Florida has always been home, so I've never been too far from my family. My mom still lives here. My dad passed away several years ago. I miss him a lot. He was a gentle soul. He never really liked to talk about his childhood. I know his family had to flee Nazi Germany during WWII. I imagine it was pretty rough for them and the memories must not have been pleasant. No brothers or sisters. I don't see how my mom could have dealt with more than one kid anyway."

He got up. "Now we know each other's familial history, let me check on dinner." He disappeared into the kitchen, rattled some pots and pans, was gone for a short while and came back out carrying two plates of food.

"You're okay with eating out here?" he asked.

"Sure. Let me help you." She took the plates and set them on the table, and Liam went back in to get more wine.

After Jessie took a few bites of her salmon she nodded enthusiastically. "This is really good. I'm not much of a cook myself."

"Well then, we can eliminate that as a possible source of conflict. I like to cook. Anything else I should know?" he asked.

"Let me see... I've never been married. I volunteer at the Wildlife Center out west whenever I can. Your turn," she announced.

"Had a girlfriend in college. She got married while I was in the Middle East. Last year she had triplets, no less." He grinned. "Nothing lasting since then. Having a job checking up on cheating spouses can make you cautious."

"You mean you're afraid it's the norm rather than the exception?" she asked.

"I hope not. I'm an optimist by nature." He shrugged and smiled. "But one has to be a realist just as well."

They sat quietly for a while and watched as the two pelicans flew off their posts and dove into the dark waters for their evening meal. After several successful attempts, they returned to the stands and resumed their quiet vigilance.

Liam laughed. "Their lives are pretty uncomplicated, aren't they? It should only be so simple for us. What is it you want out of your life, Jessie?"

She sighed. "In my job I come across a lot of ugliness, including corruption, infidelity, sometimes even murder or attempted murder. It's like peeling an onion. When you start probing you realize what you see is usually far from reality. Only after you remove many more layers of skin you may get to the actual truth. Ideally? If I could just eliminate a fraction of the bad out there, I would feel a lot better. I know, it's an impossible task. In the world we live in, all I can do is expose as much of it as I can. I do the research and write the articles. Readers can take the information I provide and sometimes they act upon it. Other times, they just brush it away, and go on as usual."

"To do your job can turn out to be dangerous as well," Liam mused.

Jessie shrugged. "Most of the time, it just gets me some pretty nasty comments from not so pleasant people. But speaking of danger, did you get any information on our Mr. Hakim?"

He shook his head. "I only have an address. Hopefully, it's still good."

"Let's check it out tomorrow," she suggested.

He nodded, letting his gaze linger on her face.

She tilted her head. "What are you thinking?"

"I think I should make you one of my famous Irish coffees."

She smiled. "Famous, eh? How can I resist."

He laughed and went into the kitchen. She heard a short flurry of activity, then he reappeared with two cups of coffee, generously topped with whipped cream.

Jessie took a sip. It was delicious and she nodded her approval. Liam grinned before leaning over close to her.

"May I?" he asked, gentling running a finger over her upper lip and holding up a tad of whipped cream. They both laughed. He reached for her hands and held them. Their eyes remained locked. The night breeze carried in the scent of salt and the faint sound of someone's radio playing a smooth jazz tune.

"Would you like to dance?" Liam asked softly.

"I would like that very much," Jessie answered.

He held her close, and they swayed to the music. He sought out her lips and they kissed, a long passionate kiss. A quiver ran up her spine, spurred by a yearning long ignored. Liam swept her up like a feather and carried her into the bedroom. She cried out in pleasure as he explored every curve of her body in a delight of discoveries. Nearby the sheer curtain danced in the breeze drifting in through the open window, and the cawing of sea gulls welcomed the night. They heard none of it, absorbed in their lovemaking, enjoying every moment, every touch. Later, as her head rested against his chest, listening to the comforting sound of his heartbeat, Jessie closed her eyes, letting herself drift away into a calmness she hadn't enjoyed in a long time. Eventually she thought she should go. As if he read her mind, Liam whispered in her ear. "Don't go. Stay, spend the night with me."

One glance into his deep green eyes and all resistance melted away. They made love once more, with less urgency this time, slowly with a newly discovered tenderness.

****

A distant sound jarred her awake. Her eyes opened in the darkness, and it took her a moment to realize where she was. She turned around. Sound asleep, Liam was breathing softly next to her, his head buried into the shadow of a pillow. She realized the sound came from another room, and she remembered leaving the phone in her purse.

She slid out of bed and made her way back into the living room, found her purse, and dug out her phone. The brightly lit screen revealed Perrone's number. Suddenly, she was wide awake. "Sam?"

"It's Irina..." He paused, "I'm sorry, Jessie, she's dead."

For a moment she was unable to grasp the words. Then pure, cold anger gripped her body. "They killed her, didn't they?"

"A delivery man found her in an alley. She was shot, execution style."

Jessie folded into one of the chairs, closed her eyes.

"Jessie, are you okay?" Perrone asked.

"Yeah, I'm okay," she said feebly.

"There's nothing you could have done. It was her decision to leave and they wasted no time finding her," the detective said.

She thanked him for calling and sat frozen in her seat until Liam walked in. He knelt beside her and took hold of her hands. "What happened?"

She shook her head. "Irina is dead."

He pulled her to him, held her tight. "I'm so sorry, Jessie."

"Those monsters killed her, and it's my fault."

"Stop," he said gently. "You can't blame yourself. The moment she left protective custody, she put herself in harm's way."

"She must have been so scared."

He lifted her chin, looked into her eyes. "She was confused, Jessie. The men who killed her are to blame, not you. They wanted to prove a point. To you, as well as to any of those girls who may get any ideas about escaping."

"You're right. They left her in an alley so she could be found," she said abruptly, getting up.

"Let me make you some coffee," he offered.

She stared at him glumly. "I need to go home. I

have things to do."

"Do you want me to check on Hakim today?" he asked.

"No, let's do it together, just not today."

He stroked her face. "Don't go yet. Let me make you some breakfast. We can talk about it if you want. Or we can just sit and eat and drink coffee."

She smiled sadly, held his hand against her cheek. "Thank you, Liam, I love you for this, but right now, I want to be alone."

He kissed her. "Will you call me later?"

She nodded.

"I'm really sorry," he repeated softly as he walked her out.

Once home, she took a shower, made a cup of coffee, then opened up her laptop and started typing. A couple of hours later she was done. She saved the text on an USB drive, put it in her purse and left. At eight thirty she walked past the empty desks on her floor and into Art's office. He was on the phone, but he put it down when she came in. He frowned. "Did you forget it was Saturday?"

She told him about Irina and his jaw dropped.

"I rewrote the whole article, Art," she said, handing him the flash drive. "It's different now. It includes Irina's story and what those people do to those young girls they enslave."

He started to speak, and she held up her hand. "No. Read it before you say anything." She got up. "I'll be busy for the rest of the day. If you need me, you know how to reach me."

When she got to the Wildlife Center, Doris took one glimpse at her and guided her to the kitchen table.

"Let's sit down a minute and talk."

Jessie told her everything and Doris listened attentively.

"What do you want to do now?" she asked.

"Whatever needs to be done."

Doris smiled. "Good, I can help you there."

She grabbed a pail loaded with diced fruit and handed it to Jessie. "I was about to feed our friends back there. So now, get to it girl."

The rest of the day was spent feeding the animals, cleaning cages and hosing down a couple of pigs caked in mud. Shortly after five o'clock, Daniel and Mike, Doris' two sons, showed up with take-out from *Pollo Tropicale*, chicken, rice, black beans and plantains. They all sat down together and ate, the guys joking and teasing as usual, and Jessie even managed to smile a few times. Exactly what she needed right now. When she got home, she called Liam and they talked a while, then she poured herself a glass of wine, turned on the TV, and stared at the screen. A comedian was doing a miserable job at being funny. She switched to another channel. A newscaster was talking. She could see his mouth moving, but she wasn't grasping any of it. At eleven o'clock, she went to bed. Tremendous fatigue weighed her down, yet she remained awake for a long time, staring into the darkness before finally dozing off.

Chapter Twenty-One

Although the sun was noticeably absent, the heat and humidity were not. A sky crowded with dark gray clouds threatened rain at any moment, yet Jessie paid scant attention to the clammy weather. Sunday had gone by in a fog. She caught up on emails, then distracted herself with housework and laundry, without picking up the phone even once.

Two consecutive nights of nightmares had left her body bone tired. Yet when she got out of bed on Monday morning, her mind was made up. She was going to intensify her probe into the Russian mob's involvement in sex trafficking, no matter how long it took, and she wouldn't stop until she found a way to bring them to justice. Then and only then would Irina's short life have some meaning.

Minutes after she reached her desk, Lonnie showed up.

"Did you have me under surveillance?" she asked, eyeing him suspiciously.

"You should know by now I have a network of spies working for me around the clock."

He told her he was sorry about Irina, and informed her the office was all abuzz about her article published in Sunday's paper. They were still talking when Art made his appearance, a somber look on his face.

"Great story, kid. I didn't change a thing. It went in

as is."

Jessie nodded. She deliberately had avoided reading the paper. She also wasn't going to inform him about her intention to pursue the mob story further. Not right now anyway. Art started walking away then stopped. Jessie glanced at him frowning. "What?"

"The other thing you were working on?"

"Dariel Thomas?"

He nodded. "I'll give you until next week to wrap it up."

"Great. All I have to do is find a couple of murderers, a few thieves, and some priceless diamonds. How hard can it be?" she said.

He patted her on the shoulder. "Glad we got our smart aleck back. I was worried there for a second."

After Lonnie left, she called Annabelle and set a date to pick up Lilly. Next she rang Liam. He answered right away, and she wondered if he had been waiting for her call.

"Are you free this afternoon?" she asked.

He said he was. They agreed to meet for lunch at Mario the Baker on University in Sunrise. She slowly drove up Sunset Strip, checking out the neighborhood. So much had changed since the days when she lived just west of the area, as a child. Back then, the old part of the city, east of University Blvd, was a retirement community, small houses with dime-sized yards. As the older people died off, it gradually became home to a more multicultural population. Once painted in uniform colors of plain white or tan, houses now wore colors ranging from deep blues to various shades of purples. An Italian butcher moved out, a Cuban restaurant moved in, and a little later, a Jamaican restaurant added to the diversity. Much had changed, but after all those years, Mario was still around.

Liam got there a few seconds after her, just in time for the sky to open up and monsoon-like rain pelted their vehicles. Parked next to each other, they waited for it to slow down. As was the norm in South Florida, five minutes later the downpour came to a halt and the sun reappeared, nature washed clean and ready for another splendid afternoon.

They went in. The server seated them and they ordered a pizza.

"When I was a kid, I used to come here quite often with my dad. It hasn't changed a bit. So many businesses in the area came and went since then. In South Florida, with its shifting population and varying tastes, it's a rare thing to have a restaurant last for more than ten years," she said, glancing around, recognizing the familiar surroundings.

They chatted until the waitress brought their pizza. Jessie took a bite of her slice and nodded. "Never mind the décor, their pizza is still as good as ever."

They finished eating and Liam produced Hakim's address. It was only a few miles away in west Sunrise, right off the strip.

"Actually, this is very close to where I grew up," she exclaimed.

He took Hakim's photo out of his pocket and pushed it in front of her.

"Take another look at him. Take your time. You mentioned you had seen him before. Do you think it may have been back then?"

She frowned at the photo and shook her head. "No. We moved to Plantation when I was a teenager and he's younger than me. He would have been a little kid back then. I'm sure I saw him much more recently. I just can't remember where it was."

He nodded pensively.

"What are you thinking?" she asked.

"We have to come up with a plausible story when we get to his house."

"If he's a possible terrorist, it better be a good one," she agreed.

"We're reporters checking on an airport theft."

Jessie raised an eyebrow. "Think about it. He didn't exactly contact the police, and we can't reveal having seen him on the airport cam. So how do we explain our visit?"

Liam groaned. "Yeah, I know, I know. Especially since he might be an accomplice to the courier. Do you have another idea?"

"Right now, our goal is to find out if he lives at this address. We have his photo. We know what he looks like. If he comes to the door, we apologize, say we have the wrong house, and then we get out of there."

"Do you really think he'll buy that?"

Jessie shrugged. "Doesn't matter. We just get going before he can give it a lot of thought."

Liam laughed. "All right. Let's go in my car."

She agreed and they left after finishing their lunch. After the earlier downpour, the air smoldered with dampness. The Hakim house was two streets over from Jessie's old house. Like most of the others in the neighborhood, it was a ranch style with a two- car garage. The grass needed cutting and the shrubs suffered from neglect. Liam pulled up in the driveway next to a small pickup. They walked to the door together and Jessie rang the bell. They stood waiting while no one answered. Muffled sounds of a television show drifted outside. Jessie rang the bell again and the door came slightly ajar. An older man, wearing a long white tunic, peered around the corner.

"Hi, we would like to speak to Nasir Hakim," Jessie said.

The man's eyes grew hostile. He shook his head vehemently. "Nasir is not here. He doesn't live here anymore for a long, long time. I already told the other agents," he shouted in accented English.

"The FBI agents?" Jessie asked.

"Yes. You must leave us alone. Go away," he yelled and slammed the door shut.

Jessie wasted no time ringing the bell again. After a couple of minutes went by, they realized no one would be coming back to greet them.

"That was fruitful," Liam mused.

"Well, at least we found out two things. The FBI is looking for him, and he doesn't live here anymore."

"You're right. It's more than we had before," Liam said.

They drove back to Mario's.

"What do we do now?" Liam pondered.

"Let's try to find Dariel's jeweler."

Liam made a face. "Considering how many jewelers are in the Broward county area, it could be difficult."

Jessie raised an eyebrow. "We're not going to let that stop us, are we?"

Liam laughed. "Absolutely not."

"Dariel told me his name. I think it was Sal."

"Okay, so we start calling jewelry stores and ask

for Sal. I mean, how many can there be?" Liam said.

They drove to Starbucks, got a couple of lattes, found an empty table and searched for jewelers in Broward County on their phones. Surprisingly, it was a pretty lengthy list. They split it between them and started calling. Lingering at their table for more than an hour, they were starting to get curious looks from the baristas, when Jessie finally had a hit. She sat up in her seat, poked at Liam and turned on the speaker. He put down his phone and listened.

"You mean Salomon Weintraub?" the woman on the other end asked.

Jessie took a chance. "Yes, of course. Mr. Weintraub. Do you have his address?"

"No, I don't." She hesitated. "Why you looking for him anyway?" she asked, suddenly sounding suspicious.

"My neighbor in Philly was an old customer of his. She was quite fond of him. I wanted to look him up, tell him she passed away."

She glanced at Liam and noticed his eyebrows shooting up. The woman's voice took on a note of sympathy.

"Oh, I'm sorry, honey. It's nice you want to tell him about your friend. Sal's a good man. His store is called 'Jewelry Paradise.' It's on the corner of Oakland Park and University. When you see him, tell him Shirley said hi."

"Sure will. Thanks a lot, Shirley."

Liam was shaking his head as she put her phone away. "Wow! You're a hell of a good liar. You spit that out real quick, too. I'm impressed."

She eyed him skeptically before deciding to take it

as a compliment. "Thanks. Now should we go find our pal Sal?"

They only had to drive a few miles north to get to the store. An old man eyed them for a moment before buzzing them in. The air smelled musty. The faded wallpaper had survived several decades, and the floor needed a good scrubbing. He limped out of a back room and peered at them from behind the counter. "Can I help you?"

A thought of her father ran through her mind; he had the same kind eyes. "Mr. Weintraub?"

He nodded.

"Do you know Dariel Thomas?" Jessie asked.

He frowned at her. "Dariel? Yes? Why do you want to know?"

"I'm sorry to tell you he's dead," she said.

Sal looked stunned. "What happened to him?"

Jessie told him. Sal bowed his head in sorrow. "I liked the boy. He had a good heart. A little foolish maybe. I was afraid it would get him in trouble someday. I don't understand, why are you here?"

"Dariel came to see you about some diamonds before he was arrested," Jessie stated.

Sal didn't react.

Jessie leaned toward him, resting her arms on the counter. "Mr. Weintraub, we're not the police. I'm a reporter and Liam is a private investigator. Dariel came to see you with the gems. You told him they were very valuable. Before he died, he shared that information with me. You can be honest with us."

"Okay. He came here. So what?" He shrugged.

"Were you going to buy the stones from him?" Jessie asked.

He shook his head. "No, no. They were very high quality, very expensive. Too rich for me. I told him maybe the Russians would be interested. They're the only ones who have that kind of money."

"How much money are we talking about?" Jessie asked.

"Close to a million dollars."

Jessie was stunned. "Indeed, that's a lot of money. Did you give him a name to contact?"

He shook his head. "I don't really know their names, only what I hear out there. You know, rumors."

"The Russian mob?" she asked.

He nodded somberly. "I warned him, though. These are dangerous people."

"We don't know if the Russians were involved. It certainly wouldn't be surprising. Right now, we're pretty sure Dariel died because of those diamonds," Jessie said.

Liam looked at him. "Mr. Weintraub, the diamonds are missing. If we find them, there could be some reward money from the insurance company for Dariel's little girl. Are you sure there's nothing else you can tell us?"

He shook his head. "The little girl, so sweet. He brought her in here once. He was a good daddy, you know. I wish I could help you. I just don't know anything else."

Jessie reached for his hand and squeezed it. "Okay, thank you. Stay well."

He shrugged. "How well can an old man be? They say each day is a gift, not always the one we want. At my age, I gladly would have given those years to a younger man, like Dariel, so he could have lived a nice long life and see his little girl grow up. The choice is not ours to make, is it?"

They thanked him again and left, standing near their cars for a short while.

"Did you know the diamonds were worth that much?" Jessie asked him.

"I had an idea it was in that range from the conversation I had with the CEO."

"Wow! I'm glad you told me," she scoffed.

"I wasn't sure, Jessie. Besides, what difference would it make? A million, half a million, it doesn't bring us any closer to finding them, does it?" he protested.

"And what about a reward for Lilly? Did you mean it?"

He nodded. "I'm going to bring it up with Marcel Lebon, the CEO of the insurance company. I think it's the least he could do. First, we have to find the diamonds."

"I know. Where do we go from here?"

He gave her a questioning look. "Maybe we can talk about it over dinner tonight?"

"As much as I would like to, I have to say no, Liam. If I don't go see my mother pretty soon, I'll have a real problem. How about a nightcap later?"

He agreed, and Jessie said she would call him. She drove to Sophie's condo in Sunrise Lakes. Her mother seemed pleased to see her. They went to the kitchen. Sophie loved to cook.

"How about some borscht and noodle pudding? I just made them."

Jessie didn't say no. They took their plates into the small dining area off the living room.

"How are you doing, Mom?"

"Terrible," Sophie said. "The Gestapo—"

"You mean the condo association?"

Sophie's condo, located in a huge senior citizen's complex, was a constant source of squabbling among its many elderly occupants and their board of directors.

"Who else? Like I said, the Gestapo. The dog of one of the women in the next building gained two pounds, and now he's over the weight limit. She promised to put him on a diet, it wasn't good enough for them, so now they want to expel her. Can you believe it? She's lived here for over twenty years." Sophie sighed. "I think the world is upside down, Jessie. Your father wouldn't believe it. Bless his heart."

She glanced at her daughter's plate. Anticipating her next move, Jessie held up a hand. "No, Mom, I can't eat another bite."

"You remember Mrs. Moorish's grandson? His bar mitzvah is next month. They invited me... I'm not going."

"Why not? She is a good friend of yours, and you know the family."

Sophie shook her head. "Nah. It's not right. I'm never gonna have grandkids, so..." she trailed off.

Jessie shot her an exasperated look, opened her mouth to argue, and decided against it. It was a hopeless cause. She stayed a while longer, listened to another litany of complaints, kissed her mother goodbye and left.

Drained, she drove straight home, poured herself a generous glass of wine, and sat outside to call Liam. He picked up right away.

"Sorry, I have to back out of that nightcap. I'm

having a large glass of wine right now. If I waited for you to come over, the bottle might be empty by then, and I would be very drunk."

He chuckled. "Your mom?"

"She knows how to push all my buttons and wring me dry."

"Let me guess, she gives you a guilt trip about marriage and grandkids?"

"You didn't tell me you knew her?"

He laughed. "Irish or Jewish, it doesn't matter, they know how to get to you. Every time I talk to my mother, I get the same thing."

"I'm twenty-eight years old, Liam, and she makes me feel like I'm fruit dying on the vine."

"Take it from me, you're the most luscious fruit I've ever seen."

"Thanks. What are you doing tomorrow?"

"I'm free. Do you have anything in mind?" he said.

"Maybe we could try the Sunrise mosque. If the Hakims are like the typical Muslim family, the Imam would surely know them. He might be able to give us some insights."

"Why not? It's worth a shot. I'll pick you up around ten o'clock," he said.

****

Jessie knew the location of the mosque, and she gave him directions.

Arriving after the mid-morning call for prayers, they stood near the entrance, and waited for the cleric to come out. A tall thin man with a dark beard and dark deep-set eyes, he looked on impassively as they walked up to him. Introductions were made and he said his name was Hanif El-Amin. Jessie held out Nasir

Hakim's grainy picture. He didn't reach for it.

"We're trying to find this man. His name is Nasir Hakim and he might be a member of your mosque. Do you know him?" she asked, holding it up close to his face. He barely glanced at it.

"Why are you looking for him?" he asked.

"He might have information about a theft," Jessie said.

The man stared at her coldly. "This sounds like a police matter. Are you with the police?"

Jessie held his stare. "No, but he might be able to help solve a crime. Do you know him?"

"Yes, and I already told the FBI the same thing. It seems they are looking for him as well. I haven't seen Nasir in quite some time, so I'm afraid I can't be of any help to you either."

"When was the last time you saw him?" Liam asked.

"A long time ago."

"Anything you can tell us about him?" Jessie asked.

He shrugged, his dark eyes unreadable. "Like I said, I haven't seen him for some time. He's a nice young man from a devout Muslim family."

"Do they worship at your mosque?" Jessie asked.

El-Amin shook his head. "This is not information I can share with you. Furthermore, you have no right to disturb Nasir's family. And finally, you're not welcome here with your questions. Do you understand?"

"Yes, you made this quite clear. Thank you," Jessie said and they turned to go.

The sound of his voice followed them as they walked out of the courtyard. "Whatever it is you're seeking, you won't find it here," he said.

When they got back to the car, they exchanged glances.

"He knows something," she said.

"You think so?"

Jessie nodded. "Definitively. The look he gave me, I could feel it."

"Maybe you're right, but he's not about to tell us."

While Liam was trying to back his car out of its parking space, a task complicated by a delivery truck partially blocking his exit, Jessie absentmindedly observed the cleric walking toward Pine Island Rd. He hadn't gone half a block, when a black SUV pulled away from the curb and trailed him at a very slow speed.

"I'll be damned!" Jessie exclaimed.

Liam slammed on the brakes. "What is it?"

"He's being followed. Watch that SUV trailing him. Let's see what happens," Jessie said.

They sat and waited.

"He did mention that the FBI questioned him," Jessie said.

"From the way he's dragging his feet, I would say he knows they're tailing him."

At the bus stop on the corner, the cleric took a seat on the bench, his eyes fixed straight ahead. The SUV pulled over and parked on the curb a mere hundred feet away from him.

Ten minutes later, a bus pulled up. El-Amin got on and the bus took off with the SUV right behind it.

Jessie shook her head. "It's amazing. They don't even try to be subtle about it."

"Maybe they're doing it on purpose," Liam

ventured.

"Why?"

"They want him to feel the pressure. If he knows anything at all, they may think they can intimidate him," Liam said.

The delivery truck was gone and Liam pulled out and drove away.

"What's next?" he asked.

"Would you like to see the Wildlife Center?"

He grinned. "Thought you'd never ask."

Chapter Twenty-Two

Right after lunch his father called. He was angry, shouting at him in Farsi. "What have you done, Nasir? Bringing shame to our family, like your mother's brother Haji?"

"What are you talking about?" he asked calmly.

"The FBI, they are looking for you."

He winced. "They came to the house?"

"This morning. You are a disgrace. Your mother is sick from crying. What have you done?"

"I have to go. I will call you later."

He disconnected abruptly, his heart thumping in his chest. How did they trace him? Then he realized. Yes, of course, the security cameras at the airport captured Thomas's theft. And at the same time, they also captured him chasing the thief. But how did they get his name?

They must have gone through all the names on the flight. Process of elimination. And what about the arrest years ago? He was a juvenile then. It was supposed to have been wiped clean. Of course, cops could still have access to those records. More likely it was enough to bring him under scrutiny. Standing in the reception area, he nervously scanned the parking lot. Could they be here already? Several cars were parked in front of the shop, none of them occupied and there was no foot traffic on the sidewalk, at least none he could see from his post.

The sound of the back door opening startled him and he rushed into the office. Two of his men were coming in. He shouted at them. "Abdul, Jamal."

They frowned at the urgency in his voice.

"We have to get out, right now. We're moving everything into the other building. We have to hurry. The FBI was at my house this morning. I don't know how much time we have left before they show up here. Abdul, back the truck up to the rear door. Jamal, pull all the paperwork from the file cabinets and put it into garbage bags."

The two men stared at him, a look of surprise on their faces.

"Come on, now. Let's go!" he yelled irritably.

They set off to follow his orders. While they were busy, he dumped the contents of the safe into a backpack, and they loaded everything onto the truck. Within ten minutes the two men were pulling out and Hakim was walking to his car. Suddenly, he stopped.

"Wait," he shouted.

Jamal slammed on the brakes and frowned. "What is it?"

"They can trace my car. We have to get rid of it," Hakim snapped.

"Let's torch it," Jamal suggested.

Hakim shook his head impatiently.

"No, no, I don't want to draw attention. I know a place out west. No one ever goes out there, except gator hunters. Follow me."

They drove away. Hakim's mind was racing the whole time. He should have anticipated the FBI would go over the airport film with a fine-toothed comb, looking for anything or anyone associated with the courier. Well, at least they would never be able to link him to the lab building. His uncle had arranged for foreign ownership and his name was nowhere to be found on the paperwork. Same with the old pickup. Purchased with cash and registered to a small business in Canada.

Now, he would have to be more cautious than ever to prepare for the attack. They were looking for him, and although this was an unexpected obstacle, he was determined to see it through, even more so, actually.

His hatred for this nation and its populace was growing deeper by the day. It ate at him, leaving a nasty taste of bile in his mouth. All those years when he had to contend with their snide superiority and see the barely veiled contempt in their eyes, just because he was Muslim, and his skin was darker than theirs. And struggling to keep quiet while they talked about murdering his brother jihadists. He sneered. Before he was done, they would find out what a real killing field looked like, and he would derive the utmost satisfaction in knowing many of them would die in agony.

Traffic moved at a snail's pace and he could hardly contain his impatience. They were slowly inching their way west on Griffin Road when the strident sound of sirens burst into the air. A glance in the rearview mirror revealed two police cars, lights flashing, weaving through traffic, racing in his direction. Vehicles pulled to the side of the road to get out of their way, and Hakim realized they would be right behind him shortly. He had to make a decision. Make a run for it or pull over? He glanced at the mirror again. Abdul and Jamal were still following him closely, waiting for him to make a move. Then the car in front of him drove onto the shoulder of the road and he did the same. As he came to a stop, he reached for the gun under his seat and wedged it next to his hip. His mind was made up. He would take down as many cops as he could. Determined, he gripped the handle of the gun. *Inshallah,* God willing, he was ready to die a martyr.

In the next moment, the police cars flew by at top speed, their momentum shaking his vehicle. A tinge of regret faded away quickly. After all, he had a much bigger mission ahead of him. He put the gun back under the seat and drove onto the road. Another look in the mirror confirmed Jamal did the same. The traffic didn't let up until they reached the western part of the county. After a few more miles, he finally spotted the dirt road he was looking for.

Years ago, he came here with a group of teenage boys seeking mischief. It was a time when he was still trying to fit in, be like the other kids in school. So he reluctantly joined them on their escapade, observing quietly while they smoked pot and drank beer on the edge of this deep canal snaking through the Everglades. Before long they were high as kites and one of them started a fight. Hakim tried to break it up. Someone had a knife. Next thing you know, blood was running down his chin and his neck.

Instinctively, he touched the scar on his cheek, a permanent reminder of that night. Looking back, he sneered, recalling how those fools thought they were invincible, splashing in the water while the bulging eyes of gators glowed eerily in the dark. It seemed like a lifetime ago. He shook his head. He never belonged with them and now, he wished he hadn't abased himself to their level. If he had the opportunity today, he would squash them all, like the nasty cockroaches they were.

As they moved on, grasses got higher, choking part of the trail, slowing them down. Twice he had to stop and remove tree limbs blocking the way. It didn't bother him as it assured him no one came this way recently. A few miles later, they pulled up to the right spot. The rope the boys had used back then, to swing into the water, still dangled from the big old oak tree on the bank. It was frayed and dirty now. He parked on the rise at the edge of the canal, and got out. Just a couple of feet away was a steep drop into the water.

Satisfied, he motioned for the men to get out of the truck.

"Right here," he said pointing down at the water covered with a layer of dark green algae.

"Is it deep enough?" Jamal wondered.

"Deep enough for gators and unwanted cars," Hakim said bluntly.

Reaching in the driver's side window, he put the gear in neutral. The three men got behind the vehicle and gave it a couple of good shoves. With little effort, it toppled over the ledge and headed straight down into the canal. As the water swallowed the car, it gurgled a few times, then within seconds, it was gone. Standing under the glaring sun, sweat running down their foreheads, they stared at the water, waiting, as if it would suddenly pop back up. The shriek of a black bird swooping down over their head brought them out of their trance.

"Let's get out of here," Hakim mumbled.

They squeezed into the cab of the truck and drove away. On the way back, the newspaper woman popped into his mind. With all the work and preparations at the building, he had neglected to keep up his surveillance on her. She was the only link to Thomas and therefore, the only link to the diamonds. And now more than ever they needed them to continue with their plan. He had to start tailing her again. The very last time he followed her, she didn't come home for the night. He suspected she had spent the night with the man she met. It angered him, but he had to let it go. Abdul brought him back to reality when he mentioned his father had bought a new car and wanted to sell the old one.

"What kind is it?" Hakim asked.

"A Chevy Malibu, the air conditioning will freeze your ass off and the tires are brand new. It's in great shape."

"Skip the sales pitch, Abdul, how much?"

Abdul shrugged. "It's only ten years old. Five thousand maybe?"

Hakim scoffed. "You're out of your mind. Tell him I'll pay two thousand."

Abdul gave him a wounded look. "All right. I don't think he'll like it."

Hakim knew he could probably drive the pickup, but frankly, it was a rough ride and he didn't particularly care for it. They pulled up to the building. Hakim went in, and the other two men started unloading the truck.

Seated at the table in the main room, Mohamed Salem was cleaning his weapon. Sporting a full beard and short cropped hair, he was lean and dark. It took four years of his life, and two tours in Afghanistan, to bring him at odds with the military. When he first met Hakim, he told him what he witnessed over there made him sick, and how he hated the way the Westerners treated Afghans.

Bitter and disillusioned, he got out, just barely avoiding getting kicked out for insubordination. He drifted all over the country for a while, working in construction and other odd jobs. He never found what he was seeking in his travels, so he came back to his home state of Florida and settled in Broward County. There he started attending the mosque and after a few months, he shared his feelings with the Imam who introduced him to Hakim. Finally, he had an outlet for his anger toward a country intent on destroying Islam and overtaking the Middle East. The U.S. might be where he was born, but it would never be his country.

A man of few words, he nodded briefly at Hakim then went back to his task. Hakim liked him, knowing he could count on him, no matter what. He went upstairs and peered into the lab. It hadn't been easy. Construction was finally completed and it was ready to become operational. Although it was a satisfying sight, it also was a painful reminder he still didn't have the diamonds to continue with their plan. With the deadline just weeks away, and without the chemicals for the sarin or the scientist to make it, it was only a pipe dream.

Reluctantly, he went to his office, got a phone out of his desk drawer and dialed Abboud's number. Once again, he had bad news. Having to vacate the computer store was a minor glitch. On the other hand, the fact the FBI knew about him could become a problem. His uncle listened attentively as he went over everything once again and Hakim sensed the anger coursing through the man's veins.

"What about the Thomas child?" Abboud asked, after an agonizing silence.

"The girl?"

"Yes, of course. It is my experience children often observe more than you know."

"It's possible, but she's only about five or six years old," Hakim said.

"That is of no importance, Nasir. She still might know something. You have to get to her."

"I will find a way to get her."

"Stop wasting time, make a move now. Get her and question her. Then get rid of her," Abboud ordered.

Hakim brought up the scientist. "Yes, uncle. And what about our package?"

"It will be there in the next few days. Is everything ready?"

"We're all set," he affirmed.

"Then let's hope you get the goods before it's too late," Abboud snapped before hanging up.

Hakim turned to find Abdul standing next to him. "What?"

"The Malibu?" Abdul said.

"Yes, yes. Did you talk to your father?"

Abdul grinned. "Good news. He said he would take three thousand."

Hakim scoffed. "I said two thousand. Tell him take it or leave it."

Abdul looked dejected. "He'll take it."

"Good. Have Jamal drive you there to pick it up."

"And the money?"

Hakim retrieved the backpack from his closet and dumped the money on his desk. He was counting out two thousand dollars when he glanced up. Abdul stood in the doorway, transfixed by the pile of money. Their eyes met. Hakim held his gaze until Abdul squirmed and looked away. Hakim continued counting, gave him the money and put the rest back in the closet.

Later, lying in bed on his back, he stared up at the open rafters. He wondered how far he could trust Abdul. He hadn't noticed it before, yet today, it was greed he spotted in the man's eyes, and it could spell trouble for their operation.

Of the three men he had recruited, Abdul was the one he wasn't sure about. The son of an older Lebanese couple, he grew up spoiled, lazy, and lacking direction. Got in trouble with the law a couple of times, carjacking at fifteen, burglary at sixteen. Both instances were wiped off his record as a juvenile. Now at twenty-one, he wanted to join the war on the infidels, make a name for himself. Hakim took him on reluctantly, hoping he could shape him into a jihadist. He still had his doubts. For right now, he would put them aside. He considered Abboud's orders. Tomorrow was Sunday and with any luck, the reporter would go get the child. If so, he would be ready and if the girl knew anything at all, he was going to find out. Yes, hopefully it would be a day of success. *InshAllah*!

Chapter Twenty-Three

With the morning sky bloated with rain clouds, Jessie thought it would be a good day to take Lilly to the movies. She called Annabelle and they agreed on a one o'clock pick up time. She had barely put down the phone, when Liam called.

"Is your date book full for the day?"

"As a matter of fact, I'm booked all through the afternoon. My date and I are seeing a new movie, and I can't wait."

"Who's the fortunate fellow?" Liam asked.

"Actually, it's a she," Jessie answered.

"Aha! Let me guess, little Miss Lilly?"

"You guessed right," she said.

"Lucky girl."

"I'll call you later, maybe we can catch a bite out this evening."

"Yeah, I really miss you," Liam said.

Jessie laughed. "We saw each other yesterday."

"And I'd love to see you every day," he said softly.

"Here you go, going all mushy on me."

"Mush is my forte," he said.

"I noticed."

It was his turn to laugh. "See you later then."

When she pulled into Annabelle's driveway a few minutes early, Lilly was already glued to the front window, anxiously waiting for her arrival. As soon as she spotted her, the child's eyes grew wide with excitement. Seeing her bright little face, so full of eagerness and energy, nearly made her heart melt. She smiled and waved at her, then ran inside, grabbed her in her arms, twirled her around while Lilly shrieked in delight.

The movie was everything they hoped for—drama, laughter, tears and, of course, all of it ending on a happy note. It was a children's movie, after all. After a couple of hours sitting in the dark, sharing a container of popcorn and two candy bars, Jessie decided they needed some fresh air. The rain had come and gone while they were in the theater, and a bright sunshine greeted them when they stepped outside.

She squeezed Lillian's hand and smiled. "Want to go for a walk?"

The child nodded enthusiastically. "Can we go to Smalley Park?"

Jessie remembered the park. She had been there once for a birthday party. It was on the other side of town. She raised her eyebrows. "You know the park?"

The little girl nodded again. "Daddy takes me there sometimes."

Sadness tugged at Jessie's heart. "Well then, that settles it. Smalley Park it is."

After a forty-minute drive, they pulled into the parking lot. Only one other car occupied a spot. They stepped around the puddles and stopped at the playground, where a young father was pushing a toddler on a swing.

Lilly used the slide for a while then pulled Jessie away toward the duck pond.

"Oh no," Lilly said, stopping in her tracts.

Jessie was alarmed. "What's the matter, sweetie?"

"Mommy duck only has two baby ducks left now."

"How many did she have before?"

"When Daddy and I came here, she had six babies. They were really cute."

"Maybe the others grew up, moved away to have their own families, and now Mommy has a couple of new babies. Do you remember how long ago it was when you came here with your dad?"

"Right before the police took him away."

Jessie frowned. "Are you sure?"

Lilly nodded. "After he picked me up from school."

Jessie peered at her. "Did you go anywhere else that day?"

The child pointed toward the trail. "We went back there."

"How far did you go?"

Lilly shrugged. "I don't know."

"Well, I think we both could use a little exercise, don't you agree?"

"Sure," Lilly said and scampered away.

Jessie smiled at her boundless energy. She hurried to keep up. Soon they reached a wooden boardwalk overlooking a small stream. Perched on top of flat rocks along the edge of the water, turtles basked in the sunshine. They watched them for a while, then Lilly took her hand.

"Come on. I'll show you my favorite place."

Soon the boardwalk ended and they were back on a narrow dirt trail shaded by scrub oak. Dense green foliage grew on both sides of the path with occasional bursts of color from purple beauty berries and scarlet

Jatropha blooms. Then, to Jessie's surprise, the trail widened into a clearing. In its midst sat an old wooden gazebo surrounded by patches of delicate blue wild flowers.

"This is beautiful, Lilly, I really like it."

The child smiled. "Me and Daddy, we like it, too. It's where he has a secret place."

"What do you mean?" Jessie asked.

The child's brow creased in concern. "I promised him I wouldn't tell."

Jessie reached for her hands reassuringly. "You trust me right?"

Lilly nodded.

"I understand you don't want to break the promise you made to your Daddy. So, if instead of telling me, you just show me where it is?"

Lilly thought about it for a moment, hesitating, then she smiled.

"I know Daddy will like you. He won't mind."

She ran to the back of the gazebo and Jessie followed. Lilly pointed at the wooden lattice covering the bottom of the structure. Jessie leaned in and noticed one piece was broken, seemingly propped up with dirt and some mulch. The child squatted down and pulled off the slat, revealing a small opening. Jessie knelt down beside her. She squinted and peered into the darkness. All she saw was a possible home for snakes or other dangerous critters. She could think of at least a half dozen that gave her pause. She hesitated.

"Are you sure, Lilly?"

The little girl nodded. Putting caution aside, Jessie pushed away some of the dirt until her fingers could fit into the hole. Slowly, she reached inside. Her heart took a leap when she touched something unusual. She glanced at Lilly. The child gave her an encouraging look. It was no time to chicken out. Resisting the urge to yank her hand back out, she let her fingertips linger on the object. It was damp and slick, but it didn't bite, nor was it moving. A good sign indeed. She took a deep breath, took a hold of it, and pulled it out. It was a tightly wrapped plastic bag. She held it up and grinned at Lilly.

"Don't move!"

Jessie nearly jumped out of her skin. A few feet away, a man with eyes as cold as they were dark, pointed a gun at them. A small scar was visible on his left cheek. She had no problem recognizing him. A chill crept up her spine. Lilly let out a soft cry. Taking the child's hand, she gently guided her behind her.

"It's all right, Lilly. Just stay right there," she whispered. She started to get up.

"I said don't move!" he barked.

She knelt back down in the dirt. "What do you want?"

His chin pointed at the bag. "You know what I want. It's right there in front of you. Open it, slowly. You try anything, I'll shoot. First the kid, then you."

Willing her fingers to stop trembling, Jessie untied the knot and the plastic bag opened, revealing a dark velvet bag tied with a black cord. Lilly whimpered behind her.

"It's okay, baby, it's okay," Jessie said soothingly. She glared at him.

"Open it!" he ordered impatiently.

It was a tight double knot and she struggled to loosen it. Finally, it gave way and Jessie gasped.

Glistening against the velvet fabric, were the biggest, most translucent diamonds she had ever seen. She took hold of a gem and held it up for him to see.

"Is this what you're looking for?" she asked.

His eyes narrowed. "Put it back and tie the bag, hurry."

She obeyed, retied the knot and offered him the bag. "It's all yours."

He snatched it out of her hand, all the while keeping his gun pointed at her. She caught hesitation in his eyes.

"Look, you have the gems, there is no sense in harming us now," she said softly.

He stared at her for a moment.

"Give me your phone," he ordered.

"It's in my bag."

"Then dump your bag," he said impatiently.

She turned her purse upside down. Everything came tumbling down and settled on the grass. Lipstick, comb, a pack of chewing gum, some tissues, a small note book, and her phone.

She picked it up and held it out to him. He grabbed it and shoved it into a back pocket.

"Stay here, don't leave for a half hour. If you try to follow me, I will shoot both of you," he threatened waving the gun.

"We won't follow you," she said.

As soon as Nasir Hakim left, Jessie reached for Lilly. Folding her arms around the child, she pulled her small trembling body close to hers.

"Don't worry, Lilly, he went away, and he won't be coming back. He's gone for good. But I'm really tired. If it's okay with you, we'll rest here for a little while."

Lilly nodded. They sat in the gazebo and the child put her head in her lap. Jessie stroked her hair. The little girl relaxed, and Jessie managed to calm her own pounding heart.

Fifteen minutes later they walked back to the parking lot. To Jessie's relief, there was no sign of Hakim. A woman and two small children were getting out of an SUV. Jessie went over to her and asked if she could borrow her phone. The woman hesitated before glancing at Lilly's ashen face. She quickly pulled out her phone and handed it to Jessie. "Of course. Are you okay?"

Jessie nodded before stepping away to make a call. Her mind in a daze, she could only think of one phone number at the moment. She dialed it and uttered a sigh of relief when Sam Perrone answered on the first ring. He listened without interrupting as she told him about Hakim.

"Sam, he took my phone and I don't have the FBI's number. Can you call Williams and let him know?"

"I will. Don't go anywhere. I'll be there in a few minutes," he said quietly.

She returned the phone to the woman and related an abbreviated version of the holdup at the gazebo. As Jessie talked, the mother's eyebrows shot up in concern and she promptly loaded up her children and left.

Jessie held Lilly while they waited on a bench at the edge of the parking lot. Suddenly the child sat up.

"Jessie, will Daddy be mad at me?"

"Oh, no, no, Lilly. You were very brave. He will be so proud of you."

"It was the same man who came to the house."

"Yes, I know. Now, the police will get him and you won't need to worry about him ever again."

"When can I see Mommy, Jessie?" the child cried.

Jessie closed her eyes, deceit gnawing at her. "Not yet, sweetie."

Lilly broke out in sobs. Tears welled in Jessie's eyes. It was all she could do to keep her own emotions in check but she had to, for Lilly's sake.

A half hour later, Perrone drove into the parking lot with Boyd in the passenger seat. Sam parked on the grass next to them, and the two men jumped out of the vehicle.

"Are you all right?" Perrone asked, his brow creased with concern.

Jessie shook her head, tilting her head toward the child.

"Lilly, we have to talk to Jessie for a little while. Is that okay?" Perrone said.

Her frightened eyes said no. Jessie knelt down, gently took her chin in her hands. "Don't worry baby, we'll be just be a couple of steps away. We want the detectives to have all the information about the bad guy so they can arrest him, and take him to jail. You will see me the whole time."

Lilly nodded and they stepped away.

"I'm worried about her, Sam. This really shook her up," Jessie said.

He nodded. "I'm just glad he didn't harm either of you."

"I think the gun frightened her the most, especially when he kept threatening to use it. It was pretty damn scary. Were you able to get a hold of the FBI?" she asked.

"I left a message for Williams."

"Now tell us exactly what happened," Boyd said.

They listened somberly as Jessie related their frightful encounter.

"Dariel decided it was safer to hide the gems out here than to keep them in his house," Boyd concluded.

"He was right. No one would have ever thought of looking in this park. If Lilly hadn't shown you the spot, the diamonds could have been there as long as the gazebo would be standing," Perrone stated.

"How the hell did Hakim find you?" Boyd asked.

"He must have been following us for quite some time. The moment he showed up in the clearing, I remembered where I'd seen him before. Last Sunday I took Lilly to the beach. When we left, we stopped at the ice cream shop. While we ate at the outside patio, I saw this man sitting in his car in the parking lot. The place was busy. At the time I thought he was waiting for his wife and kids. But it was him. It was Hakim."

Perrone nodded. "It sounds like he hoped Thomas told you or Lilly where the gems were."

"How would he even know I went to see Dariel in jail?" Jessie wondered.

Boyd frowned. "Nothing surprises me anymore. After all, they managed to get to him in his locked cell. Obviously, the man has accomplices inside the jail."

Jessie glanced over at the child, seated on the bench, waiting patiently.

"Lilly is asking for her Mom again. How much longer are we going to lie to her?" she said.

Boyd shook his head. "I don't know. Mary Gilmore wants to wait for the aunt. Poor woman. Meet the child for the first time and have to give her the bad news. It's going to be hard on both of them."

"She's a smart little girl. Pretty soon she's going to suspect something is wrong," Jessie said, her voice breaking.

Boyd leaned in, speaking softly. "Jessie, at least she still has family willing to take her in. Do you know how many kids we see who end up in the system for years after tragedy strikes?"

She nodded. "You're right. I just don't want her to experience the heartache."

While they were talking, a police car entered the parking lot and two deputies got out. Boyd greeted them, talked to them briefly, and they returned to their car and waited.

"They'll stay with Lilly while we walk back to the gazebo," Boyd told Jessie.

"Good, I don't want to take her back there again. Not after what she just went through," Jessie said.

"Was there anyone else around when you got here?"

"Only one car. A man and his little boy. They were still on the playground when Lilly and I left on the trail. When we came back from the gazebo, there was a woman with two children in the parking lot. They were just getting out of their car. I borrowed her phone to call you. When I told her we were approached by a man with a gun, she hightailed it out of here," Jessie explained.

At that moment, a dark sedan pulled into the parking lot. Special Agent Bruce Williams got out, then stood by the side of the car. Within seconds, a middle aged woman with short cropped hair and a dark complexion stepped out of the passenger side.

Together, they headed toward them. Once again Williams wore an impeccable suit with matching tie and kerchief, looking like he just walked out of a GQ photo shoot. His companion wore a navy jacket and skirt over a white blouse and dark low heels.

Jessie couldn't help but smile as she noticed Perrone glancing down at his cheap suit. He would never be a beacon of stylishness. Williams introduced the woman as Special Agent Sonia Estrada. She seemed intense and Jessie guessed she was not one for idle chit chat.

The next hour was spent going over every detail of Hakim's appearance, what he said, how he said it, and finally, the description of the diamonds. The two police officers came to sit with Lilly while the rest of the group walked to the gazebo. Jessie showed them where the gems had been hidden. Williams almost knelt down and she wondered if he would risk getting his knees dirty. As if he read her mind, he straightened and brushed some imaginary dirt off his pant legs. In the meantime, Estrada threw in a question here and there. Mostly, she took notes on a small pad she carried.

After returning to the parking lot, Boyd and Perrone stood by while Williams talked to Lilly. He asked the little girl questions about the bag, its contents, and the day she came to the park with her father. Holding on to Jessie's hand for support, the child answered clearly and without hesitating. After a few minutes, it was evident she didn't know what the bag contained, or where it came from. Finally, they were done. Williams said he would be in touch. He turned to leave and Sonia Estrada followed him for a short jaunt before swiveling around and coming back. She handed

Jessie a business card.

"Please call me if you remember anything else," she said before rushing off to catch up with Williams.

Boyd turned to Perrone, raising his eyebrows. "Not even a thank you for bringing them in on this. Makes me feel like shit. Sorry Jessie," he added, looking contrite.

She smiled and Perrone shook his head.

"It's the way it goes with the Feds, Jim. They take over and you're left out in the cold."

Jessie had pulled Lilly to the side so the child couldn't hear their conversation. She crouched down and looked her in the eyes. "Are you okay, baby?"

Lilly nodded and Jessie hugged her. "You must be tired. I'm going to take you home."

Lilly's blue eyes teared up. "Jessie, home is with Mommy and Daddy."

"You're right. But Annabelle is a nice lady and she does her best to make you comfortable at her house, doesn't she?"

The child's little head bopped up and down. "I like her a lot."

"And you know what? She really, really cares about you." Jessie reached for her hand. "Come on, sweet girl, let's go say goodbye to the detectives."

Boyd and Perrone stood talking to the two cops, no doubt answering some of their questions about the day's events. When Jessie and Lilly approached, they stopped their conversation. They walked them back to Jessie's car. Boyd helped Lilly into her seat while Perrone held the driver's door open for Jessie. As they got ready to leave, he leaned in and whispered into her ear.

"Hakim got what he wanted. I don't think you'll have to worry about him anymore, but do me a favor, keep an eye out anyway. Just to be sure."

She smiled at him in silent agreement and drove away.

Chapter Twenty-Four

He could hardly believe it. Finally, the diamonds were his. Now at last, the preparations for the attack could resume. Exhilarated, Hakim noticed he was driving too fast. He promptly slowed down. Now was not the time to get stopped for speeding.

His mind drifted back to the encounter in the park. He had followed the reporter and the kid on the trail, keeping a safe distance, planning on cornering them at some point and interrogate them. When they stopped to watch the turtles, he hid behind some shrubs. He was ready to make his move when they took off again and kept walking, until they reached the gazebo. He saw the girl lead the woman behind the gazebo. Puzzled, he decided to wait. Straining to see through the bushes, he watched as she kneeled on the ground and peered under the wooden structure. Then she reached inside and took out a bag. Suddenly there was no doubt in his mind. This was Thomas' hiding place for the diamonds. He pulled out his gun and jumped out. After making sure the gems were in the bag, he had every intention of killing the child and the woman, just as Abboud had ordered. Yet standing there, ever so close to the woman, he couldn't bring himself to do it. Even while she glared at him with those hazel eyes full of defiance, he was aroused by her fierceness. A lioness defending her cub. He walked away.

At last, he arrived at their building. He raced inside, tightly holding onto the bag. Jamal was alone downstairs, with the television blaring, absorbed in some reality show Hakim despised. He shrugged. Nothing could spoil his mood right now.

He headed for his room, closed the door, walked to his desk and opened the second to last drawer. He groped underneath and pulled off a piece of paper taped to the bottom. It was blank except for a phone number. Wasting no time, he dialed. The phone rang and rang, until finally, aggravated, Hakim gave up. A few minutes later, his cell phone chimed.

"Yes?" said a heavily accented voice.

"I have the gems."

"It's about time," the man growled.

Hakim chose to ignore the comment. "The list you have, is everything ready?"

"Some things, very hard to get—"

Hakim interrupted angrily. "What do you mean? I was told there would be no problem."

The man laughed. "Calm down. You don't let me finish."

"Okay then. Can you get them or not?" Hakim asked impatiently.

"Yes, yes! You too worried."

"When will everything be ready?"

"Already have some. Maybe two more days to get rest," the man said.

"And the passports?" Hakim asked.

"You bring me photos and information, I guarantee you the best."

Hakim held back a sigh of relief. Things finally moving forward. "Good, call me back as soon as you have all the merchandise. We have a deadline."

The man at the other end scoffed. "Deadline? You late, not me."

After talking to him, Hakim retrieved another new throwaway from his desk drawer. He dialed and there was no answer, but he knew Abboud would ring him back shortly.

He sat staring at the wall, his mind racing. Two weeks was all the time they had left to produce the sarin and finalize the plan of attack on his chosen target.

The phone brought him back to the present.

"I have the stones," Hakim said, hardly able to keep the excitement out of his voice.

"Good. Did you make contact?" Abboud asked abruptly.

Hakim was disappointed. At least he could have offered him a few encouraging words after all he'd done. He didn't even ask how he got them back. "Yes, he said he would have everything ready in two days."

"Excellent. I just had word the Iraqi will be there tomorrow. It's not a good idea to have his transporter come to you and know your location. I gave new instructions. The driver will call you when he arrives and you arrange the pickup. Select a safe place to meet him."

Hakim had waited patiently until this moment, when everything was finally falling into place for him. He almost told Abboud his news several times before, but each time he held back as their plan could still fall apart. Not anymore. He had the money, the diamonds, the lab and soon, the scientist to produce the sarin.

"Uncle, I have more good news," he said his voice brimming with excitement.

Abboud waited.

"We have a target for the attack and it's perfect," Hakim announced.

"Yes, tell me," Abboud said.

Hakim went on to tell him about Bobby Metzer and Terminal Eighteen at Port Everglades.

"Are you sure you can count on this pedophile?" Abboud asked in a doubtful tone.

"I'm sure. He is terrified of being arrested and going to prison. He will do anything I ask him to do."

"Do you have a target date?" Abboud asked.

"I checked the cruise schedules. There is a new big cruise ship, *The Wonder of the Seas,* scheduled for its maiden voyage out of Port Everglades on Saturday, September third. There will be five thousand four hundred passengers going through Terminal Eighteen that morning. Peak time will be somewhere around eleven o'clock in the morning. We'll plan for the attack to take place at that time. It's the perfect place to release the sarin. Do you agree, Uncle?"

Abboud remained silent for a moment. "What about the cruise ship? Wouldn't it make a better target?" he asked tersely.

"Yes, Uncle, it would be a great target. But to gain access to the ship is nearly impossible. Security is much too tight. I believe this is our best choice for the success of our attack."

"It is agreed then, Nasir. Everything is in your hands now, Nephew. You must see this through to the end. For ISIS, for the Caliphate. *Inshallah!*"

"*Inshallah!*" Hakim repeated.

After their conversation ended, it was clear to him, no matter what, their attack had to be carried out. They could not fail.

****

On the way to Annabelle's, Lilly dozed off. Jessie hoped it was a good sign, maybe indicating she was getting over their frightful encounter. When they got to the house, she stayed for a while, sitting in the kitchen with Annabelle, talking in a hushed tone, not to draw the children's attention. The foster mom's eyes grew big as saucers when Jessie recounted the events at the park. Concerned, she peered in the living room. Lilly had already settled in on the family room couch with the other little girls, watching a movie and giggling at the antics of a pig named Babe.

Annabelle turned back to Jessie. "Are you going to be safe?"

"Yes, don't worry. He got what he wanted, so there's no reason for him to come after us anymore."

Annabelle offered her some lemonade. Jessie declined, eager to get back home. Before she left, she hugged Lilly once more and promised to pick her up again soon.

Although she had been the picture of calm in Lilly's presence, it was a different story now as the scene at the park replayed in her mind. Not until she realized how tightly she was gripping the steering wheel did she understand how much it had affected her. She took a deep breath and eased her hold. She was not going to let Hakim instill fear in her heart.

On the way home, she thought of calling Liam, then remembered she had no phone. She made a U-turn and went to Best Buy. There were plenty of phones to pick from. She winced at the prices. However, after the young clerk keyed her information into his computer, he gave her a cheerful grin. "Good news. You have theft coverage, so your bill will only be for the hundred dollars deductible."

"So I get a replacement phone and give you a hundred bucks?"

"Unless you pick a more expensive model, then you pay the difference."

"No, no. Just give me the same phone."

Fifteen minutes later she left the store with her new phone. With her emotions settled down, she realized her stomach was growling. She made a stop at Publix and selected a bourbon roasted chicken, some salad ingredients, a baguette and a bottle of merlot. Walking through the parking lot to her car, Liam's phone number popped back into her mind. She dialed it while driving home. He answered on the first ring.

"Did you eat already?" she asked.

"No, I was waiting to hear from you."

"Haven't had a chance to call till now. Listen, I just left the market, do you want to come over and have dinner?"

He hesitated.

"What?" she asked.

"You're actually cooking?"

"What's so amazing about that?"

"Nothing, I'm just surprised. You said you didn't like to cook."

"I don't. But occasionally, I make an exception."

His tone changed to one of anticipation. "I'll be right over."

"Hold on. Give me a little time here," she protested.

She pulled into her driveway, relieved to see Liam

wasn't there yet.

In the kitchen, she cut up the chicken, put it on a platter, and then mixed the lettuce, cucumber, and tomato in a bowl with a bottled vinaigrette. She sliced the bread and was uncorking the wine when the doorbell rang.

He kissed her lightly on the lips and followed her into the kitchen. "Wow, you're a quick cook," he ventured, examining the food on the table.

"Anything over ten minutes is a waste of my time," she said.

"I see that."

She frowned. "What did you expect? I told you I was on my way home."

He held up his hands in protest and smiled. "No, baby, it's great. I don't really like a lot of competition in the kitchen, so believe me, I'm thrilled."

She snuggled up to him. "Good. You can be sure I will never, ever try to beat you on that score."

He pulled her into his arms. "Mm... this feels better than anything I can imagine."

"Really? Nothing?" she asked, raising her eyebrows.

He smiled enticingly. "Well, maybe something..."

"Now or later?" she asked.

"Will the chicken complain if it has to wait?"

She shook her head. "It wouldn't dare."

"Good," he whispered in her ear, then picked her up and whisked her into the bedroom.

It was after eight when they sat down to eat dinner, and it wasn't until they were almost done that Jessie told him about Nasir Hakim and the diamonds. Liam nearly chocked on his food, his eyes wide with disbelief.

"You waited until now to tell me this?"

She shook her head. "I wasn't ready to talk about it earlier. I really couldn't. I needed this, this time, just us, in the bedroom." She smiled. "Brought me back into a healthier frame of mind."

He nodded soberly, reached for her hands, his green eyes locked into hers.

"It scares the hell out of me to think of the danger you were in. I just found you, I don't want to lose you, Jessie. Not now, not ever."

She smiled. "I'm still here and I'm not going anywhere soon."

"Good, keep it that way, will you?"

They finished their wine.

"Okay, how about dessert? I bought double fudge and almonds ice cream," she said.

"I know we had an incredibly luscious appetizer earlier, but I had a different vision for after dinner," he said with a mischievous grin.

She laughed. "Okay, Mister, let's go, I want to make sure you're not all talk."

As she slowly walked to the bedroom, she left a trail of clothes until he caught up with her, then turned, and they exchanged a passionate kiss. They made love, slowly, tenderly, as if time was forever theirs before they went to sleep in each other's arms.

The next moment, Nasir Hakim was standing over her, stone faced, his eyes black as sin. His gun was pointed at her and this time, there was no hesitation. Slowly and deliberately, he brought down the cold muzzle of the weapon to her forehead and gave her an evil grin just before he pulled the trigger. The deafening sound of the gunshot echoed through the night. Her screams were lost in silence. Her eyes flew open to the pounding of her heart. She was drenched in sweat. Her eyes probed the darkness, the dial of the clock on the nightstand glowing at half past two. She made out the shadow of Liam's body next to her, sleeping soundly, his breathing soft and steady. She took a deep breath, closed her eyes. He was here with her and she was safe. She snuggled close to him, his warmth melting the cold fear, and drifted back to sleep.

Chapter Twenty-Five

"What are you doing today?" Jessie asked.

Liam gently rubbed her back. "Going down to Hollywood, to get in touch with a guy I know. Those diamonds are bound to surface any day now. If the old jeweler was right, it could be with one of those Russians fences. Maybe I can get ahead of the curve... Want to come?"

"I have to stop at the office this morning, share the latest with Art. Can you wait for me?"

"No problem, gives me a chance to get caught up with some paperwork. Call me when you're done and we'll meet up."

Reluctantly they got up and shared a breakfast of cereal and fruit before Liam headed out. Jessie showered then left for the office. Lonnie was loitering near her desk and he peered at her inquisitively as she approached.

"What?" she asked defensively.

"Huh-huh. What did you do last night?" he asked arching an eyebrow.

"None of your business."

He laughed. "Oh yes, I knew it. It's written all over you. Is it what's his name...Liam?"

She shrugged. "You don't know half of it."

"Well, let's hear it then," he huffed.

Jessie told him about the diamonds and Hakim. His

eyes nearly popped out of his head.

"Oh my God! Thank goodness you're okay. He had a gun pointed at you?" he sputtered.

"Yeah. And now they have the stones to do God knows what with them," she sighed.

"Did you tell Art?"

"No, of course not. I just got in."

"And what about Liam?" Lonnie asked.

"He knows. He came over last night."

Lonnie managed a wicked smile. "I knew it. Hence the glow today."

The elevator doors opened and discharged Art, along with several reporters. As he walked through the glass doors, he frowned and glared at them. "What's going on?"

Jessie glanced at the other journalists who were heading for their desks nearby. She wasn't about to let them in on her story. "Let's go into your office and I'll tell you."

Art nodded, then led the way. Jessie sat in the chair facing him. Lonnie stood in the doorway. Art gave him a look of dismissal.

"He already knows, so he might as well stay," Jessie said with a shrug.

Lonnie smirked and took the other chair across from Art's desk.

"Okay, so let's have it," Art said.

Once again, Jessie related the events, noticing how Art's face changed gradually from one of boredom to being fully attentive.

"He held a gun on you?" he gasped.

"Yeah, and he walked away with the diamonds."

Art shook his head. "Holy shit. What did the cops

say?"

Jessie sighed. "The FBI is running the show now, and they're not talking. By putting two and two together, this is what I got so far: the stolen diamonds were intended for terrorists here in the U.S. I have no clue what they plan on doing with them. But it can't be good. Dariel and Mandy got in their way and they're dead. We know the Feds are looking for Nasir Hakim. We don't know how many others are involved. The odds are, he's not doing this alone."

She paused.

"And?" Art asked impatiently.

"The two detectives I talked to, Perrone and Boyd, are pissed off. They wanted to continue their own investigation of the Thomas' murders. But since it involves the same individuals that the FBI has on their list, they've been taken off the case."

"So, where does that leave us?" the old man asked.

Jessie stifled a smile. She liked the fact he said *us*. There was no way he would deny her this story now. She leaned in. "Art, we have to keep our investigation going as well. I hooked up—" she glanced at Lonnie, who made a funny face. She turned back to the editor and continued, "I'm working with this private investigator who was hired by the insurance company to find the diamonds. So we have a couple of different sources now. We'll have a hell of a story here. That's if we keep digging, of course."

The old man sighed. "If the FBI doesn't let us publish, what good will it do?"

"They won't be able to keep us from publishing once they get their guys. At that point, we'll be ready. We'll have the full story from A to Z, way ahead of any other news organizations. And we already have the details, from yours truly of course, about where the gems were hidden and how Nasir Hakim held me up at gun point," Jessie pointed out.

He moaned. "Fine. Go ahead. Just make sure you keep me posted. And young lady, do not put yourself in harm's way again. I don't want to lose one of my best reporters."

Jessie grinned. "Why, thank you, Art. That's a compliment."

The old man looked over at Lonnie then back to her. "No, no, it's not what I meant. Just stay the hell out of trouble."

Jessie wasn't having it. "You heard him, Lonnie. He said 'one of my best reporters, right?"

Lonnie nodded solemnly. "He did."

"Whatever. Get out of here, both of you. I have work to do," the old man growled.

Back at her desk, Jessie called Annabelle, who assured her Lilly was at school and she seemed fine. Jessie recalled her own nightmare of the previous night.

"Do you think she just buried the whole dreadful episode? She's already had the trauma of the car chase and her parents disappearing from her life."

"I know. First thing this morning, I called the social worker. I told her about the hold-up in the park and she agreed Lilly needed some counseling. So she's arranging some sessions with a child psychologist for her. She's going to call me back with the information," Annabelle said.

"Good. Let's hope sharing her emotions with a professional will help her."

"It's a good thing indeed. In all my years as a

foster mom, I've discovered just how resilient some children can be. They'll go through some hellish situations and manage to come out of it unscathed. I'm hoping this will be the case for Lilly," the woman stated.

Hopefully Annabelle was right, Jessie thought as she gathered her notes and started typing on her laptop. She had a lot of catching up to do while waiting to hear from Liam.

Chapter Twenty-Six

Two days had gone by since he got back the diamonds, and still nothing. Hakim hated waiting. He was getting more and more impatient. The Russian hadn't called back about the supplies, and he hadn't heard anything about the scientist's arrival. However, he decided it was time to inform his crew of their plan. Remodeling was completed, meaning they had too much idle time on their hands. Their patience was wearing thin. A couple of scuffles had to be broken up between Jamal and Abdul. He also had put a restriction on their trips outside the building, for security purposes, he had explained, but that didn't seem to appease them. When conversations ended suddenly when he entered a room, it was a sure sign the situation was getting precarious.

On this morning, he had asked the two women to join them for the meeting. Both Maggie Randall, their newest member, and Jenna Morales remained on the fringe of the group and therefore continued to live in their respective homes. Jenna's job at the sheriff's department was too important to jeopardize. Having her keep her distance simply made sense. On the other hand, Maggie would be a distraction to the crew. Not something he wanted to deal with at this time.

The men were already in the meeting room when Maggie walked in. After taking a seat next to Jamal, she turned to look at him. They locked eyes, she smiled, and he forced himself to smile back. Ever since they met, he couldn't think of a jihadist with more deceiving looks than Maggie. A few months earlier, Jamal attended a frat house party where the main attractions consisted of sex, drugs and booze. Hakim hadn't wanted him to go. Jamal argued it might be a good place to find recruits for the jihad, and he reluctantly agreed.

Students sat around, drinking beer and smoking pot, except for one small group who was gathered around a young woman. She was railing loudly about the American presence in the Middle East and how she was ready to take up the fight with ISIS. Jamal listened to her rants, thinking she was drunk. Later he offered her a ride home and she accepted. She lived in a grubby studio apartment above a gym. She told him she worked there occasionally as a personal trainer.

That night they slept together, and after seeing each other for a while, he realized her anger with life wasn't fueled by alcohol. She fully intended to join ISIS. He told Hakim about her and they set up a meeting. To be on the safe side, they arranged for it to take place at the ball park on Sunset Strip. Having arrived a half hour early, Hakim sat on the bleachers and surveyed the area. It was deserted. He looked on as Jamal parked the car and his passenger got out.

He couldn't have been more surprised. Petite with a slight build, long blond hair and deep blue eyes, Maggie was a life-sized Barbie doll. Immediately upon laying eyes on her, he realized she could be an asset, the least likely person to be stopped at a checkpoint, a definite advantage. According to their plan, Jamal would remain in the vehicle until Hakim gave him a signal. Without hesitating, the young woman walked toward him. She stopped just short of the bleacher and stood in a defensive posture, her arms folded across her chest.

"So you're Nasir?"

He nodded and indicated the seat next to him. "Sit, please."

She sat down next to him, and he immediately fired off a relentless barrage of questions. Asked her why did she want to become a Jihadist? Was this a fad? A way to put some excitement in her life? After all, he pointed out tersely, she wasn't even a Muslim.

She glared at him, fire smoldering in her eyes. "This is absolutely not a fad. I plan on converting to Islam. Ask Jamal, I read the Koran every day. It's America and all of Europe who are the aggressors. They want to invade the Middle East and kill all Muslims, just like the Crusaders did in the name of Christianity back in the Middle Ages."

"So, what do you think you can do about it?" he retorted.

She smirked. "You don't take me seriously, do you? You wait and see. I am going to the Middle East. I will join the fight for ISIS and do my part, while you and Jamal are sitting around here, talking a good game and doing nothing."

Hakim looked at her soberly. "What if you could join the fight right here?"

Maggie frowned. "What do you mean?"

"We will show this country what we can do. We are bringing the war to them."

She squinted at him. "How?"

He shook his head. "First you must answer my question. Are you ready for jihad?"

She hesitated, and he leaned in closer to her face. "You say you want to go to Syria. Once you do, let me tell you what will happen. More likely you will die. The worst part is, you will die in obscurity. No one will even remember you. If you stay here, if you take part in our attack, they will never forget you. Which do you prefer, Maggie?"

She eyed him carefully. "If I join your group, what do I have to do?"

"Take part in our plan. I can't tell you what it is yet. Right now, you have to trust me."

After a short moment, she nodded solemnly.

"Good, you won't regret it," he assured her.

He came back to the present. Everyone was seated. He stood at the head of the table, his hands on the back of a chair and his eyes roaming the room. This was his moment.

"As you know, our brothers in ISIS have entrusted us with a mission to bring this country to its knees once again, *Inshallah.*" Hakim tightened his grip. He could sense their eagerness.

"Saturday, September third, the *Wonder of the Seas*, the biggest new cruise ship in the world, is scheduled to sail out of Port Everglades for its maiden voyage with five thousand four hundred passengers…"

He paused a moment. "But that ship is not our target."

The silence was palpable. He went on. "Our target is the ship's terminal. Number Eighteen."

Surprise was written on their faces. Hakim waited again, giving them time to process the information.

"You see, in order to board the ship, every single cruise passenger must go through this terminal. This is where they check their luggage. This is where they get screened. Boarding starts at eleven am. In less than an hour, this terminal will be jam packed with excited travelers waiting to be processed so they can start partying. They don't know it yet, but they won't be going on this cruise. As a matter of fact, they will be on their way to hell."

Jamal spoke up. "If this nerve gas is our weapon, isn't it going to be a suicide mission?"

Hakim shot him an annoyed look. The man was interrupting his flow. "No, Jamal. Even though we will use a very strong grade of gas, our plan limits our exposure. And we will have the protection of an antidote."

Jenna scoffed. "Where do we get sarin? You can't just smuggle it in, like guns."

Hakim remembered she wasn't present during their previous talk about the nerve gas. "You're right, Jenna. One of Saddam's top scientists is set to arrive here any time now. He will manufacture the sarin in our lab. He's had lots of experience"—he grinned—"and hundreds of dead Kurds are proof of the potency of his product."

She nodded and he continued. "The port has three entrances and each one has a checkpoint. To get past them, we'll need two things, a valid passport and a cruise ticket. We'll have both. Ticket information will show Jamal and Maggie are a married couple. The same will apply to Jenna and myself. Abdul and Mohamed are booked as single passengers. The two married couples will have rental cars. One of the single men will arrive by cab, the other by hotel shuttle. We will allow fifteen minutes between our arrivals and we will use different entrances."

"Tell us more about the operation," said Mohamed softly.

Hakim smiled at the man he knew he could count on to retain a level head. "Each one of us will have a backpack with sarin containers."

He paused as all eyes were riveted on him. "Gaining entrance to the terminal is easy. Once again, you will only be required to show your ticket and ID. The pre-boarding security check, which includes luggage, is inside the building. It's located at the very back of the terminal, before the exit to the pier and admission to the ship. But our attack will take place long before that point. Our goal is to set up all the cylinders to release the sarin inside the terminal. Then we get out of there."

"And if our path to the exit is blocked?' Jamal asked.

"With the element of surprise and the confusion to follow we should be okay. There's always a possibility we will have to fight our way out," Hakim said.

"So we'll have weapons?"

"Yes, we'll go over it later."

"You mentioned new passports?" Abdul asked.

"Everyone will have a new identity. When you leave here today, go to a drugstore or a UPS store and get your passport photos taken. I will turn them over to our supplier along with our new names and he will provide us with new passports."

A shrill sound interrupted him. Hakim reached into his jeans pocket and fished out a phone.

"Is this Nasir Hakim?" a terse voice asked.

"Yes?"

"I have your merchandise. But there's a problem."

"What do you mean?" Hakim asked.

"I will explain later. Where do we meet?" the man said abruptly.

"Where are you right now?"

"On I-95, going through Deerfield."

"Keep going on I-95, when you get to Cypress Creek Road, take the exit and head west for about a mile. The Sheraton Suites will be on your right. Turn in and go around to the back."

"Okay," the man said.

"What are you driving?"

"A delivery truck with 'Canadian Imports' on the side. What about you?" the man asked.

"A dark blue Ford Taurus. I'll be there in a half hour."

The conversation ended there, leaving him to wonder about the potential problem the transporter alluded to. In the meantime, most of the group had dispersed. A couple of the men remained seated.

"If you have any more questions, it'll have to wait, I have to go. The Iraqi is here. Abdul, let's go pick him up."

Chapter Twenty-Seven

It took twenty-five minutes to get to the Sheraton. A line of cars weaved through the parking lot waiting to load or unload luggage at the main entrance. Hakim navigated around them, then made his way to the back of the building until he reached an area with only a couple of cars. He parked and killed the engine.

A few minutes later, a small truck came around the corner of the building, driving slowly before stopping at a back entrance. A man got out, stacked some boxes on a dolly and wheeled them inside. Hakim hesitated and was about to drive around the front once more, when the man came back out, jumped into his cab, and left. Another five minutes went by before a larger truck appeared and drove toward them. The driver flashed his headlights twice, then parked next to a tall hedge. On the side, big bold lettering read "Canadian Imports". Hakim and Abdul remained seated, waiting while a short bulky man got out and walked over to them. He eyed them cautiously.

Hakim frowned. "You said something was wrong. What is it?"

"It's the package. He's sick. Been throwing up all over my truck, and now he's passed out."

"How did you get him into Canada?"

The man shrugged. "Came in on a freighter three days ago. We have a couple of men working at the port.

Got him in easy. Lucky for us, the Canadians aren't too concerned about security, not yet anyway."

"And getting him across the border?" Hakim asked.

"I have a regular delivery run every week to New York. So the customs guys are used to seeing me. Of course, for the kind of merchandise I carry, we had to make special provisions," he smirked. "There's a false bottom in the truck. We use it a lot. I had him in there. They told me to warn him if he made as much as a peep, his family would be dead. I didn't have to. He was out most of the time."

Hakim didn't ask what sort of merchandise the man smuggled in. His guess was it would be either weapons or drugs, maybe both. None of it mattered to him. His only concern right now was to get the nerve gas production going. He nodded his approval and the driver raised the back door of his truck. He pointed to stacks of boxes.

"I put him back in the hold after I checked on him last time and let him take a piss. Then he started getting sicker. I didn't want to keep him in there, but I had to. In case I got stopped. Had to move all those damn boxes by myself, so now you two are going to do it."

Hakim was fuming at the man's lack of cooperation but knew better than to put up an argument and attract attention. He ordered Abdul to get in and hand him the boxes. Fueled by his anger, he quickly stacked them on the pavement as the driver watched impassively. Once they were done, they waited while the driver hopped in the back and pulled on a latch in the floor of the truck. It was barely visible. As soon as he opened it, they were greeted by a revolting smell.

They instinctively stepped back, hands over their noses.

"Damn. He puked again," the driver growled.

Hakim fought off the stench and glanced into the opening. With the box too short to hold someone as tall as he was, the man was drawn up into a fetal position. His body was gaunt. His clothes were stained with vomit. His pasty complexion stood in stark contrast with the greasy black hair stuck to his skull. Shielding his eyes from the brightness of the light, he moaned weakly.

"Well, at least he's not passed out anymore," said the driver curtly.

Hakim leaned in. "Rasul Ahmad?"

The Iraqi nodded and Hakim reached down and took a hold of his arm. He motioned to Abdul to grab his other arm. "Come on," he ordered.

They pulled the man out of the box only to have him collapse on the floor, too weak to stand. Hakim laid his hand on his forehead. He was burning up.

"How long have you been sick?" he asked.

"A week maybe, I don't remember. Since the ship."

"You're a doctor. What's wrong with you?" Hakim barked.

"Pneumonia, I think. I'm not sure," he answered, so softly they could barely make out the words.

"He needs medicine," the driver said.

"If he was sick when he got off the boat, why didn't your people get him some meds?" Hakim asked angrily.

"They were too much in a hurry to ship him here. I told them he wasn't well. They decided to send him anyway."

"Bringing us a dead man wouldn't do us any good, now would it?" Hakim scoffed.

They hefted the Iraqi off the truck and shoved him into the back seat of the car, where he immediately collapsed. Hakim got in the car and Abdul climbed into the passenger seat. The driver frowned, motioning to the boxes sitting on the pavement;

"Hey, you're gonna help me load these?"

Nasir didn't answer. He started the engine and pulled away. Glancing at the rear view mirror as he drove off he smirked at the sight of the angry driver standing by his truck, cursing at them.

"What are we going to do about him?" Abdul asked glancing at their sick passenger in the back seat.

Hakim didn't answer. He was assessing his situation and he didn't like the results. They only had a limited time to get ready for the attack. Now, instead of being able to start making the nerve gas right away, he had a man who could be dying. If Ahmad had pneumonia, he would need antibiotics as soon as possible. To take him to a doctor would be risky at best. In his present condition, they might insist on admitting him to the hospital. Obviously, that was not an option.

"We have to get our hands on some antibiotics," he said.

Abdul creased his brow and Hakim glanced at him.

"What? You have any ideas?"

"I may know where to get some pills."

Hakim shot him a doubtful look. "Okay, let's hear it."

"I know this guy Tony, he's from the old neighborhood. He works at a pharmacy in Tamarac. Every time I see him, he bitches about it being a shit job and how rotten his pay is. With a little incentive, I think I can talk him into giving me some pills."

"Think he's there today?" Hakim asked.

"Man, the guy is there every day. Like he said, it's a shit job and he needs the money. You got to come up with it, though. I only have a twenty."

Following Abdul's directions, Hakim got off 95 at Commercial and went west. The pharmacy was tucked away in a strip shopping center. There were several available parking spaces in front of the store, yet Hakim kept going until he found a spot in an area devoid of traffic.

Abdul stared at him. "What the hell? You could have parked right over there. Now I have to walk through the whole damn parking lot."

"It's better here. I don't want anybody to worry about him back there."

Hakim took out his wallet, pulled out a wad of cash, counted out a hundred and handed it to Abdul, who eyed the money skeptically.

"Not enough, man."

"How much?" Hakim said, impatiently.

"You want him to turn me down? It's not easy, you know, they have cameras in there watching them. He gets caught, he gets fired."

Hakim sighed and peeled off another sixty. Abdul grabbed it. "That should do it. After all, generic antibiotics shouldn't be more than a few bucks."

Grumbling, Abdul got out and took off toward the store. After waiting a half hour, Hakim was getting nervous. From his seat, he could hear the Iraqi wheezing as he struggled to take short shallow breaths, followed by violent bouts of cough. The man might not make it if they didn't get the medicine, and he couldn't leave him to go check on Abdul. So he kept on waiting, ready to take off in a hurry if he heard sirens or noticed a cop pull up to the pharmacy.

Finally, Abdul came out of the store. As he approached the car, he raised his arm and held up a small bag he was carrying.

"You got it?" Hakim asked anxiously.

"You bet your ass."

"What took so damn long?" Hakim asked.

Abdul snarled. "Geez, relax, will you? First I had to wait till there were no more customers around so I could talk to Tony. I told him it was for my grandmother. I said she was sick with the flu and refused to go to the doctor. Then I slipped him the money. For a minute he was confused, and I wondered if he was gonna rat on me. Then he nodded he was okay with it. But he had to wait until the pharmacist got a phone call, so he could go and get the pills off the shelf without him noticing." He shoved the bag at him. "Here, it's all yours."

Hakim opened it and grabbed the pill bottle. It was Levofloxacin. The name was familiar to him. Inside were a dozen pills. He turned to Abdul with a nod of approval.

"Good work, man. Now let's get out of here."

Ahmad was passed out again in the backseat. When they got to the house, they picked him up and carried him upstairs to his cell. Once he was lying on the cot, Hakim touched his forehead and nearly recoiled. The man was burning with fever.

"Bring me the pills and a glass of water," he told Abdul.

"How you gonna get him to take a pill when he's out?"

"Never mind, just get the stuff," Hakim snapped.

A few minutes later, he pried open the man's mouth, inserted a pill, pushing it as far back as he could with his finger, then carefully poured a trickle of water in the corner of his lips.

"You don't think he's going to puke again?" Abdul asked.

"We'll soon find out."

It took a couple of days before Ahmad showed any sign of improvement. Although Hakim managed to get him to swallow the antibiotics, he couldn't get him to eat, and he barely drank anything at all. Finally, his fever broke, and he was awake more often. Each time Hakim walked into his cell, the Iraqi's dark eyes stared at the ceiling, ignoring his presence. He reeked of vomit and rancid sweat.

"Time to take a shower, Rasul," Hakim told him one morning. The man didn't react. "Look, you may not like your situation right now. I understand. You know what your purpose is here. And as soon as you're done, you'll be on your way home. So, try to make the best of it."

"You really plan on letting me go?" the man asked, his eyes reflecting doubt.

"Yes, of course, why not? We won't need you after you get us the sarin. Now come on, let's get you cleaned up. You'll feel a lot better. You'll see. Can you stand up by yourself?"

Ahmad nodded, pushed himself off the cot and Hakim led him to the bathroom. He handed him a towel, a bar of soap, and a set of clothes.

"These should fit you," he told him.

As he sat waiting for the Iraqi, he pondered his next move. The man had been sick for four days, which meant they were further behind than ever. Now he would have to push him to produce the sarin in half the time they planned.

Ahmad still retained his pallor when he came out of the bathroom. At least now he was clean. And better yet, the stench was gone.

Hakim grinned in approval. "Good. Are you hungry?"

Ahmad shook his head. "What do you want me to do?" he asked in a resigned voice.

"Follow me."

Hakim took him to the lab.

"We built this for you. It's going to be your workplace. Your home until you're done."

The Iraqi didn't answer.

"They told you what you'll be doing, right?" Hakim asked, his voice reflecting his annoyance.

"I have a pretty good idea."

"You will be manufacturing sarin for us. I ordered all the items you need and I should get them by tomorrow. There is a list in the lab. Check it, make sure it's correct. If anything is missing, you must let me know immediately."

"Do you realize what you're doing?" the man asked.

"What do you mean?"

"Sarin is very volatile, dangerous. Are you aware of what can happen if it's mishandled?"

"Of course. This is why we built this lab, to protect you and us as well."

Ahmad looked at him. "So what exactly are you planning to do with it?"

Hakim gave him a cold stare. "None of your concern. Your only duty is to provide us with a potent strain of sarin. We will take care of the rest."

"And when I'm done, you'll let my family go?"

Hakim shrugged. "As long as you provide us with the gas, there's no problem."

"How do I know you will stick to your promises?" Ahmad asked.

"You don't. But then, what choice do you have, right?" Hakim said. He turned away and went into the lab. The Iraqi hesitated for a moment, then followed him.

"Here is the list," Hakim said, picking up a paper on the worktable. "As I said before, anything else you need, let me know now. We have a very limited time frame to get this done, so don't waste any time, and don't try to drag things out. Got it?"

Ahmad's eyes lingered on the list for some time before making eye contact. "Pressurized cylinders. Is this how you plan on transporting the gas?"

"Are you familiar with this method?"

Ahmad's face darkened. "I am. Although bombs were the preferred method for my previous employers."

"Like the ones Saddam used on the Kurds?"

"Yes, just like that," the man answered, a note of sadness in his voice.

"So we'll put a new spin on it," Hakim said.

"You'll be killing people all the same."

Hakim sneered. "Only those who deserve to die."

Ahmad shook his head, and Hakim flew into a rage.

"Don't think you can show contempt for us. You killed those Kurds with your bombs, so you have blood on your hands, no matter what you say."

Despite Hakim's anger, the scientist remained calm. "I agree. I have their blood on my hands. Back then, just as now, I did it so I could keep my family alive."

Hakim sighed. "Let's not discuss it any further. Check the rest of the list."

"What size storage tank are you getting?" Ahmad asked.

"Hundred gallons."

Ahmad nodded. "It's imperative to have it equipped with the correct circuits to control fill and pressure build up."

Hakim jotted down the information.

"Anything else?" he asked.

"The transfer line, it's not listed here. Without it, I can't put the gas into the cylinders."

"I will make sure you get it. And as soon as I take delivery, you get started."

After he took Ahmad back to his cell, he realized he shouldn't have lost his temper. In order to get their prisoner to do the work, he had to remain level-headed, or this man could be a problem. If Ahmad even doubted for a moment his family wouldn't be released, Hakim sensed he wouldn't hesitate to sabotage his work. He had to make him truly believe he would be reunited with his family. He smiled as he remembered the only teacher he didn't despise in high school. Use the carrot, the man often emphasized, and you will never need a stick.

Chapter Twenty-Eight

Liam was waiting on the sidewalk when she pulled into the Starbucks parking lot.

"You want me to drive?" he asked, leaning in.

Jessie shook her head. "No, get in and tell me where we're going."

"Hollywood Beach."

She took the ramp to I-95 and headed south. It was one o'clock and surprisingly, traffic flowed pretty smoothly. Liam had her get off at Sheridan and go east. After a hopeless sweep trying to find a space on the street, she gave up and opted for the parking garage at the corner of Hollywood Blvd and A1A. On this day, the ocean glistened under the bright afternoon sun as waves lapped gently on the sand. A wooden boardwalk ran alongside the beach for two and a half miles starting at Hollywood Blvd. Hordes of skaters, pedestrians, runners and bicyclists somehow managed to maneuver around each other without colliding. They joined the crowd, strolling past souvenir shops and restaurants for about a mile, before Liam stopped in front of a pizza joint. He squinted into the dark interior. Standing in the bright sunlight, Jessie only saw shadows when she gazed in the same direction. Liam, however, smiled and motioned for her to follow him as he headed inside the restaurant. Sitting at a high top, two customers were hanging on to beer mugs and sharing a pizza. A waitress behind the register was busy counting out some change. She glanced up as they came in, then went back to her task.

Sprawled over a small metal chair, his body overlapping on both sides, a very fat man eyed them wearily as they approached. On the table in front of him Jessie made out a deck of cards, a box of CDs and a pack of cigarettes.

"Liam, you sly dog, haven't seen you for a while," he said, his deep set eyes carefully appraising Jessie.

"Been busy. Meet my friend Jessie. We need a bit of information and hoped you can help us."

The man cackled, motioning them forward. "Ah, yes. Come, have a seat. Let's see what Big Daddy can do for you today."

He grinned at Jessie. "Liam here may not have told you this, but I am a depthless fountain of knowledge."

Liam pulled out a chair for Jessie and grabbed another one for himself. He turned back to the fat man.

"Depthless? I don't know, Big Daddy, that's a hell of a lot of knowledge."

"Let's hear it," the man said.

"We're trying to find someone who could fence some very expensive diamonds."

Big Daddy leaned forward, breathing heavily from the effort. "Let me guess, it has something to do with a diamond heist in Paris?"

Liam nodded. "Pretty much everything. What did you hear?"

The fat man shrugged. "It's all the talk around here. No one knows who has them."

"How about a Russian fence in Hollywood?"

Big Daddy snickered. "If you want Russians, you

have to go south of here, Sunny Isles beach in particular. It's not for nothing they call it 'Little Moscow'."

"Anything more specific?" Liam urged.

Big Daddy leered at him for a moment. "What's it worth to you?"

Liam laughed and reached for his wallet. "How much?"

"Well, you know, a man's got to make a living. Besides, those Russians, they're dangerous dudes, man. They don't like it when someone mentions their names. I'm taking my life in my hands by helping you out here…" He shook his head in what appeared to be intense apprehension.

"Uh-huh," Liam said, doubt reflecting in his eyes as he fished a couple of twenties out of his wallet and put them on the table.

Big Daddy stared at him in disbelief. Liam sighed and pulled out two more twenties. "All I got, man. Let's have it."

With amazing speed for a man of his size, Big Daddy reached over with one fat paw, scooped up the money and shoved it into his pants pockets. "Sasha's Kebab House down on Collins Avenue. Just don't say I sent you," he warned.

"Anybody else?" Jessie asked.

Big Daddy shifted his gaze to her and he grinned, revealing an upper rack of gold teeth. "A mighty fine-looking lass you got yourself, Liam. Honey cake, if you get tired of him, you let me know, 'cause I'll always be available for you."

"She asked you a question. Just answer it," Liam said tersely.

The man shrugged. "Of course, there's always someone else. Those bastards have their greedy hands in almost everything these days. I just don't know who they are."

They got up.

"You have my number. If you find out anymore, give me a ring," Liam said.

Big Daddy nodded. "You got it man. Bye, darlin'. Don't forget what I said."

Jessie ignored him and walked out. They headed back on the boardwalk. "Where did you find this winner?" she asked.

Liam grinned. "Yeah, I know, he's a piece of work. Believe it or not, he comes up with some pretty good information on occasion."

"Is this all he does?"

Liam shook his head. "He sells weed and a few other substances I don't ask about."

They reached the parking garage and got in the car. "Do you know how to get there?" Liam asked.

"I think so. Collins Avenue is over on the barrier island between the beach and the Intracoastal."

"Okay, then let's go."

Jessie got back on I-95, headed south, then took the off ramp onto Hallandale Beach Blvd and went east until they reached Collins Avenue. Condos and hotels occupied the more expensive properties along the beachside. Stores and restaurants lined the other side. She drove slowly as they looked for the restaurant Big Daddy had mentioned. They found it wedged between a high-end shoe store and a smoothie shop. Jessie had to circle the area several times before finding a parking space.

She had a bad feeling as soon as they entered Sasha's Kebab House. Dark and narrow, the restaurant had a small bar tucked in the back with just a few tables in the front. Two men stood leaning on the bar talking and they turned to watch them come in.

"We closed for the day," one of them said with a strong Russian accent.

"The door wasn't locked," Jessie retorted.

The man pulled himself away from the bar. Tall, muscular and bald headed, he looked intimidating. "Don't matter if door open. I say, we closed."

Jessie nodded. "No problem, we don't want to eat. We just want to ask you a few questions."

The other man seemed much older. Short with a square jaw and dark eyes he spoke up next. "What questions?"

"Did anyone approach you today and try to sell you some diamonds?" Jessie asked.

The man frowned, looking back to his companion.

"Who the hell are you?" Baldy asked.

"I'm a reporter for the *Broward News* and my friend is a private detective. A few weeks ago, there was a diamond heist in Paris. Now it seems the gems are here, in South Florida. Actually, they may even be in this area. A French insurance company is rather anxious to get those diamonds back, so they hired my friend to find them. There may be a reward involved for their recovery."

The older Russian came toward them, stopping just a foot away from Jessie, before motioning to his cohort.

"Dimitri, the door," he barked.

The younger man nodded, locked the front door, and then stood in front of it.

"Are you Sasha?" Jessie asked.

The older man sneered. "No Sasha here. Now, I want to hear why you think we have anything to do with heist?"

"Like I said, it's because we're pretty sure the man who stole the diamonds will try to fence them in this area," Jessie said.

"And why the hell he come here? To kebab place, huh?"

She shrugged. "I think maybe you know why."

Suddenly he reached to his back and pulled a gun out of his waistband. He waved it in the air a couple of times, before directing it at Jessie, anger boiling over in his eyes.

Liam stepped in front of Jessie. "Hey, hey, no need to get upset. We're not here to make you mad."

The man pushed him out of the way, his face inches from Jessie.

"Boris!" the one named Dimitri called out, adding a few words in Russian.

Boris waved him off, still glaring at Jessie. "You reporter, you have a smart mouth, you know? You come here with crazy story about diamonds. You say we have them. Is that what you say?"

Liam shook his head. "No, not at all. We're simply trying to find out if someone contacted you to try and sell you the diamonds."

Boris stared at him. "You make big mistake coming here. You know?"

Liam raised his hands in defense. "We're just asking around. If you haven't heard anything, we'll be on our way."

The Russian wasn't going to let them off that easy.

He scoffed. "So you go to shoe store next door now, right? Ask if they have stolen diamonds?"

"No, I think we'll go back and check with the police. See what they found out. Sorry we bothered you," Liam said.

Boris stood still, his eyes going from Jessie to Liam, not saying anything, his gun still pointed in their direction. Liam firmly grabbed Jessie's arm, pulling her away. "Come on, Jessie, we're leaving."

They turned to go. Dimitri was still blocking the door, eyeing them coldly. After an anxious minute, Boris spoke a few words in Russian.

Dimitri snorted. Finally he unlocked the door. As they walked out, he warned in a low voice, "Don't come back."

Standing outside on the sidewalk in the bright sunshine, Liam let out a sigh of relief. "Those Russians sure have a nasty disposition. Let's get out of here."

They hurried off. Jessie was still fuming. "I can't believe I had a gun pulled on me twice in two days, and we still don't know where the diamonds are."

Liam shook his head. "I don't think they have them. Boris seemed genuinely surprised when you brought it up."

"So we're back to square one. I'm pretty sure Hakim wanted the diamonds so he could sell them. If he didn't sell them to those guys, where do we go from here?"

"It could be he hasn't made a move yet. We can tell the cops about the kebab place. They could always place them under surveillance. See if he shows up."

Jessie nodded. It sounded like a good idea. She called Boyd. The detective listened carefully as she told him about their encounter with the Russians at the restaurant and their reaction.

"Even if we were still on the case, Jessie, Sunny Isles Beach is out of our jurisdiction. We would have to get their police force involved. But I'll get in touch with Williams, let him know about the kebab place. It'll be the FBI's decision whether or not they want to check on those guys. They haven't exactly kept us in the loop as far as their investigation goes. It's typical of federal agencies. They think they're way above the local yokels." Boyd scoffed.

She sighed. "Okay, thanks."

"Jessie?"

"Yeah?"

I don't think your visit to the Russians was a smart move. You know you could have gotten shot by those bastards?" Boyd said.

"Well, I know now."

"All I got to say, is you be careful who you deal with down there. The reputation these guys have is well earned," Boyd warned.

They disconnected and Jessie drove back to Starbucks to drop off Liam so he could get his car. She was on her way back to work when her phone rang.

"Ms. Milner?"

It was a woman and Jessie didn't recognize the voice. "Yes."

"This is special agent Sonia Estrada. We met at the park yesterday," she said.

"Yes, I remember you. What can I do for you, Special Agent?"

"You paid a visit to Sasha's Kabob House in Sunny Isles Beach this afternoon."

Jessie was surprised. "Yes, I called Detective Boyd and told him about it. We thought they may be the fence for the diamonds, but they didn't seem to know anything about it. Maybe you could place them under surveillance to see if Nasir Hakim shows—"

The woman interrupted her abruptly. "Ms. Milner, I don't want to know about the Kabob House. I'm calling to tell you to stop pursuing your very own agenda. I believe Special Agent Williams expressly asked you to keep out of this."

"No. Agent Williams asked me to refrain from printing my story. I agreed. But I didn't say I would stop working on it. My intention is to follow his request. Once you've got your man and the diamonds are recovered, we are going to publish this story."

She was greeted by silence. "Agent Estrada?"

"Your refusal to follow our orders will end up landing you in hot water. We may have a serious terrorist threat here and your interference can endanger not only our investigation, but our nation as well, Ms. Milner."

"I'm not interfering, I'm contributing. If it hadn't been for Lilly and me, the diamonds would have stayed buried under the gazebo. Although they were taken by Hakim, at least now you have a thread to follow," Jessie protested.

"You have no idea what you're getting into," the woman warned.

"Did Williams tell you to call me and threaten me?"

"Ms. Milner, Special Agent Williams is not my boss and he did not ask me to call you. We work as a team and we both know what should or shouldn't be done to solve our case. As he told you before, and as I'm telling you now, stay out of it. Good bye," she said curtly.

Jessie was annoyed. Although she was at a dead end right now, if something new came up, she wasn't about to let it slip away, no matter how much the FBI wanted to keep her quiet.

Chapter Twenty-Nine

Heat waves rose from the asphalt parking lot as Hakim opened the truck door. *This must be what it feels like in the desert of Syria. Sand and intense heat.* Despite it all, he yearned to join his uncle someday soon to expand their Islamic Caliphate. Until now, Abboud had insisted on keeping him here, in this vile country. Hopefully, once their mission was successfully completed, he would let him go to the Middle East, or even Africa.

He grabbed a small black pouch from under his seat and told Abdul to wait. He stepped out of the vehicle. Eying the back door of the Doll House, he hesitated. Unconsciously, he gripped the bag and took a deep breath. Being in possession of the diamonds gave him the upper hand right now, but he had little trust in the Russians. Once he turned the stones over to them, they could easily double cross him. Yet the arrangement had been made through his uncle and there was no other way, so he opened the door and stepped into the darkness.

Blaring music assaulted his every sense. His eyes adjusted to his surroundings and he spotted a naked young woman slowly gyrating on a stripper pole. While she started swaying faster to keep up with the tempo of the music, her pale face withheld any trace of emotion. A few customers sat at tables in front of the stage. They followed her routine with slack jaws. A couple of men leaned on a bar nearby nursing their drinks. The bartender glanced at him briefly. No one else paid attention to his entrance. Hakim stood waiting, wondering what to do next, when a young man with the shoulders of someone who devoted his life to the gym appeared out of nowhere. He stopped in front of Hakim and eyed him silently.

"Ivan is expecting me," Hakim said, not sure the man would hear him over the din of the music. He nodded, turned on his heels, and Hakim followed him down a narrow corridor. At the end, he led him into a drab windowless room.

"Wait here," he said before disappearing.

Hakim glanced around. There was very little furniture in the office besides a weathered wooden desk and a couple of chairs with stained seats. A large safe in the corner briefly caught his attention before his eyes landed on a storage tank and a stack of boxes nudged against a wall. The top box was open, and partially visible was a yellow hazmat suit. His clenched jaw relaxed. This was part of his order, and he was ready to talk business. He sat in one of the chairs and waited. Ten minutes went by and no one showed up. Irritated, Hakim considered returning to the bar when a door he hadn't noticed previously was thrown open. A burly man with a bare torso and a tattoo of a bear on his shoulder entered the office. On the way to his desk, he zipped up his fly and glanced at Hakim with a sly grin. His eyes appeared glazed over and Hakim wondered if he was drunk. "Ivan Zherdev?" he asked.

"Da. You bring my package today?"

Hakim nodded. "And you have a list of items for

me. Are they ready?"

The man plopped down into his chair and groaned.

"Did you get everything we requested?" Hakim said impatiently.

Zherdev nodded. "Of course. Except for one chemical substitute."

Hakim frowned, and Zherdev waved his hand in dismissal. "Don't worry, it works the same. Original is no longer available in America."

"Are you sure?"

The Russian sneered. "Government think they smart. They don't know, what is this called again?" He tapped his forehead impatiently, then smacked it with a victorious grin. "Ingenuity, it's right word? Da? We always find a way. Trust me, you use new ingredient, you get even better product."

Hakim still looked uncertain. "It'd better work."

Zherdev sounded annoyed. "If I tell you it works, then it works."

"And the weapons?"

"Da, I show you."

"Are those my hazmat suits?" Hakim asked, tilting his head toward the boxes.

With a sigh, the Russian got up and went over to the boxes. He pulled on the yellow suit and it billowed out. Ivan turned to him, raising his index finger to emphasize his words. "This is very best, Level A. Excellent protection, at least thirty minutes, plus light weight, only five pounds each."

"And the self-contained breathing apparatus?" Hakim asked.

Zherdev shook his head. Disappointment spread in his dark eyes. "You worry too much my friend. It's all here, SCABs, portable tank, top grade lightweight aluminum cylinders, and enough chemicals to kill half the population of Miami."

Hakim stiffened and the man scoffed. "What you think? You ask for all this and I don't know what for?"

Hakim's eyes narrowed.

The Russian shook his head. "No, no. I'm with you. Americans, they shit on us. You kill as many as you want. Means nothing to me. But why only three suits?"

"No concern of yours," Hakim said tersely.

The Russian shrugged. "Okay, okay. Your business, not mine."

Hakim eyed him for a moment, wondering if he should be concerned, then deciding to let it go. "Is there a transfer line for the tank?"

Zherdev smiled. "Of course."

Hakim remembered the scientist's request. "And the tank has circuits to control pressure?"

Zherdev sighed. "Da. I go all over this with your Commander. We have good understanding. Believe me when I say to you it is taken care of."

Hakim was surprised. "You know him?"

The man smirked. "Da, Afghanistan. Abboud and me, we go back long way. We make bond. Like Americans like to say, he rub my back, I rub his."

"What about the passports?" Hakim asked.

"No problem. You bring information?"

Hakim reached into his pouch, grabbed an envelope and laid it on the desk. "It's all here, photos and names we want to use. When will they be ready?"

"Two days, I call you."

"The guns?" Hakim asked.

Zherdev got up, moved the top box out of the way and opened the next one. He pulled out a pistol and held it up. "Two 9mm Glock, good, yes?"

"What else?"

The Russian sneered. "You too impatient. Two Remington and one Sig Sauer, nine millimeters. Guns like new."

"Ammo?"

The man nodded on his way back to his desk. He sat down and rubbed his hands in anticipation. "Now, your turn."

Hakim reached into his pouch again, pulled out a small velvet bag, and set it on the desk. The Russian stared at it for a moment, his eyes glowing with anticipation, then he slowly untied the cord and pried the bag open. He gently shook the diamonds onto his desk. His face lit up. Almost delicately, he picked up a stone, held it up to the light and eyed it with fascination. "Beautiful," he breathed.

Hakim nodded in agreement. "The best there is. Now if you give me my supplies and the money, I'll be on my way."

Zherdev smirked. "Why hurry? In Russia, we celebrate good transaction with drink," he said, pulling a bottle of vodka out of a desk drawer.

"I don't drink," said Hakim.

The man shrugged then looked like he had an idea and grinned. "I think of better way. Oksana, come here!" he yelled.

Startled, Hakim frowned at him. "What is this?"

"Just wait my friend," the man said, then shouted louder.

"Oksana! Now dammit!"

A young woman wearing a silk kimono stepped into the room. Zherdev glared at her. "Take off that piece of shit!"

She untied the kimono and dropped it on the floor.

"This, my friend, is gift to you. She the best I have. She do whatever you want. She knows to please. Yes, Oksana?"

The woman didn't answer, staring straight ahead with vacant eyes. Hakim, who had avoided looking her way until now, turned his attention toward her. Standing naked in front of him, the slender young woman had long brown hair falling over her shoulder. Her skin was pale, her features delicate, her breasts small yet appealing, with dark nipples. A warm rush spread in his groin. He hesitated then glanced at the Russian. The man was eyeing him with a wicked grin.

"She good as she looks. Trust me, I know," he snickered.

Hakim gave him a small, almost imperceptible nod.

"Good, you will like, believe me," Zherdev said as he gathered the diamonds, gently dropping them back into the bag. Next, he opened his safe, tucked the bag away and pulled out several bundles of money. He handed them to Hakim. "It's all there. You can count it."

Hakim shook his head and put the money into his pouch.

Zherdev grinned. "Good, good," he said before turning to the girl.

"Oksana, take my friend to back and don't disappoint him or you know what I do," he warned, raising his arm and making a fist.

The girl bent down to pick up her discarded

kimono, exposing a smooth pink bottom, and Hakim lost all sense of reluctance. He quickly followed her into the other room and shut the door behind him. It was nearly an hour later, after an alarmed Abdul came looking for him, that Hakim emerged from the back room looking disheveled. The Russian was still sitting at his desk. He chortled. "No complaints?"

Hakim ran his hand through his hair, avoiding Abdul's stare. He shook his head.

Zherdev nodded in satisfaction. "Very good. I want my friends happy."

Hakim turned to Abdul, motioning to the tank and the boxes sitting along the wall.

"All this has to go to the truck."

"You help him. Get dolly for tank. Go," the Russian said to the bouncer who came in with Abdul.

The two men grabbed some boxes and left.

"You will call me when the passports are ready?" Hakim asked.

"Da. And you come back to visit Oksana again. On the house for you and your friends. You tell Abboud I treat you well. We stay partners for anything you need," the Russian said.

Hakim didn't answer. He waited until the two men finished carrying everything out, then left hurriedly.

The whole time he stood there, he regretted having given in to his urges. Although the woman gave him intense pleasure and obeyed his every request, he was angry with her for tempting him and even angrier for letting this Russian mobster exploit his weakness. He couldn't wait to get out and swore to himself this was the last time he would set foot in this building. He thought of the reporter again and realized the whole time he was with the girl, he was imagining it was her under him. He shrugged it off, and rushed out of the building. With a sigh of relief, he stepped out of the darkness and into the sun.

****

Slumped on a stool in the lab, Rasul listened indifferently while Hakim showed him the items the Russian had provided.

"According to my supplier, one of the chemicals you requested was unavailable in this country. He substituted another and assured me it would work as well. I need you to check and make sure. Do you understand?" Hakim asked, annoyed at the scientist's lack of interest.

Rasul nodded.

"Good. You are to start working on the product right away. We only have a little more than a week to get ready. Let me know if you need anything else. If I'm not here, let one of my men know. We will make sure you get whatever you need," Hakim said.

He eyed the man pensively, noting once again his pale skin and his demeanor. He had an idea. "If you complete the process ahead of time, I will arrange a phone conversation with your family. You can assure them you will soon be home and be reunited with them."

Sure enough, the Iraqi sat up straight and a glimmer of hope appeared in his eyes. "Do you swear?" he asked in a trembling voice.

Hakim nodded. "I swear."

The man got off his stool and walked to the table with the ingredients. "Okay. I will start right now."

Hakim pulled a hazmat suit out of one box. "Here,

put this on. Don't want to lose you before you even get going." He grabbed the other suits and walked out, locking the lab door behind him.

Chapter Thirty

The call came in a couple of hours after Jessie got to the Wildlife Center. A property owner who noticed her horses acting strangely had walked to the back of her pasture and found a small goat tied to a fence by a short length of rope. With barely enough room to move, he was unable to reach the nearby grassy area to feed. She gave directions to her ranch in western Davie. Doris and Jessie headed out right away.

"I usually come in the front entrance by the barn, so I don't know how long he's been tied up back here," the woman said when they got there.

Doris nodded. "I'm glad you found him. I don't think he would have lasted much longer. This was just plain meanness, to leave him like this to die."

The poor animal was so emaciated, they wondered if he would make it, but his eyes were still full of life, giving them hope he would survive his ordeal. Back at the center, Jessie coaxed him out of the car and after a few moments of hesitation, he jumped out. They brought him to an empty pen and he trotted in without further ado.

"Let's give him water and a small amount of food. I don't think he could handle a whole lot right now," Doris ventured.

"I can run to the feed store and get some more alfalfa hay, maybe some pellets," Jessie offered.

Doris shook her head. "No need for you to go. Let me call Mike, he's on his way here and he can stop and pick it up. In the meantime, I still have some vegetables bits I cut up earlier. I bet he would like that."

They went back to the kitchen and gathered some apple and celery pieces, and Jessie took them back to the pen. The goat eagerly ran up to her and started eating. As she stood quietly keeping an eye on him, her phone beeped. She had missed its familiar chirp earlier. Now there was a message. As she listened to the recording, her face changed.

"This message is for Jessie..." There was a slight pause, probably while she was reading her last name off the business card. "...Milner. This is Oksana, from the Doll House. Please don't call this number. It is not my number. I will call you back when I can, bye."

She sounded anxious, in a hurry.

"Damn!" Jessie muttered, upset about missing the call.

She remembered the name. The pretty girl in the dressing room, the one who took her card and quickly shoved it under her clothes. When she went back into the house Doris noticed her frown.

"What's wrong?"

"Remember when I told you about Irina, the young Russian girl?" Jessie asked.

Doris shook her head. "Yeah, poor child. It's unbelievable, in this day and age, this is still going on."

"Another girl from the strip club just called me. I gave her a card when I went there with Lonnie. She left a message on my phone but she said I can't call her back. What if she's in trouble? Should I go to the club to see if she's okay?" Jessie fretted.

"By yourself? I don't think so. Besides, if they realize she talked to you, it could put both of you in jeopardy. No…" Doris stressed. "She's being careful and you should wait for her to call you back."

"And what if she can't get to a phone again?"

"Just give her time. If she doesn't call you back within the next twenty-four hours, then call Sam," Doris cautioned.

Jessie sighed deeply. "You're right. I just don't want another girl to lose her life. Especially if I can do something to prevent it."

Doris patted her hand. "I know. If she calls back and tells you she needs help, then you take it from there. In the meantime, keep your phone at hand at all times."

A few minutes later Mike arrived with supplies for the goat. They went back to the pen. All the food scraps were gone and the little guy was resting.

"Just give him a couple of handfuls of pellets. We'll increase the quantity tomorrow," Doris said, still looking concerned.

Mike smiled. "He's eating. He'll be just fine, Mom."

Jessie stayed at the Center another couple of hours, cleaning cages and checking on the animals in various stages of recovery. A blue heron with a broken wing was mending nicely, while a bunch of baby raccoons were learning to get on without their mother, lost in a vicious attack by a pit bull. On her next stop, a beautiful mallard duck eagerly limped toward her and she was glad to see he would soon be ready for release. During the whole time she kept her phone nearby. Oksana never called back.

****

It was six am when her phone chirped on the nightstand. All night Jessie was in a state of semi-alertness, worried about missing a call from the Russian girl. She jumped up and answered. The voice at the other end was but a whisper. "Jessie Milner?"

"Yes?"

"This is Oksana. You came to the club."

Jessie gripped the phone tighter. "Yes, I remember you. Are you all right?"

"I can't talk very long. I'm downstairs in the house. Maybe I have to hang up, you know. You helped Irina."

"I wanted to help her, Oksana. I failed," Jessie said softly.

"No. She was a silly little girl and she made big mistake. Not your fault. It's Ivan who killed her."

"Do you want to leave?" Jessie asked.

Oksana ignored her question. "Listen, I have information. I tell you quickly. Okay?"

"Okay." Jessie said.

"A man come to club, Arab man. He brings diamonds for Ivan, and I hear them talk. Ivan, he gets him chemical things to make some dangerous stuff, kills thousands people. He also gets him outfits to wear, like er... like Chernobyl."

Jessie gasped. "Hazmat suits for radiation?"

Oksana whispered impatiently. "Yes, yes. Like that."

"Did you see the man?"

Oksana paused for a second. "I see him."

Her voice had changed and Jessie detected a thread of anger.

"Can you describe him?"

"Short man, dark hair, curly, dark eyes, mean eyes. He has small scar on left cheek."

Jessie nodded. *Nasir Hakim.*

"And the diamonds, where are they?"

"Ivan put them in safe," the girl said quietly.

"When did all this take place?"

"Yesterday. I have to go," Oksana said.

"I understand. Listen, are you going to try and get away?"

Jessie was surprised at her reaction.

"No. I stay. You call police. Get Ivan and Leonid arrested. Put them in jail. Then I take the girls and we go."

Jessie realized she was being protective of the other girls, didn't want to leave them to suffer the same fate as Irina. Yet, she was concerned. "Where will you go?" she asked.

"Don't worry. I have contact," the girl said.

"If you need help, you call me, and let me know. I'll do everything I possibly can, Oksana."

"Yes, you tell police the Arab is coming back for passports."

Jessie's heart took a leap. "Passports? When is he coming back?"

"I don't know, A couple days, maybe. I must go now."

"Okay, yes, please be careful, Oksana. Don't take any more chances."

Jessie clicked off and sat on the edge of her bed, going over their conversation. What was Nasir Hakim up to? Was he planning some sort of chemical attack? Suddenly frightened, she rang Liam.

He answered in a voice thick with sleep. "Jessie?

Are you all right?"

"I know where the diamonds are," she said.

"What? How did you find out?" he shouted into the phone.

She told him about Oksana's call.

"No problem. All we have to do is figure out how to get in there and break into his safe." Liam scoffed.

"Liam, this is about much more than the diamonds right now," she chided.

He sounded contrite. "Sorry love, I know. This is no time to make jokes. What are you going to do?"

"I'm calling Sonia Estrada."

"She won't be happy. They told you to back off and stay out of it," he warned.

"Not this time. Not with Oksana's information."

"Call me back after you talk to her," he said.

She dialed Estrada and the call went straight to voice mail. She left a message, asking the agent to call back, and telling her it was urgent.

She went to the kitchen, turned on the coffee pot. She needed a jolt this morning. She barely had time to have a sip when her phone rang. It was Estrada and she didn't sound happy.

"Don't tell me you're still looking into the diamond case," she said curtly.

"I have information coming to me, and I don't think you want to ignore it," Jessie retorted.

"What is it now?" the woman asked harshly.

Jessie relayed her conversation with Oksana. When she finished, there was a pause on the line.

"Agent Estrada?"

"And all this happened this morning?" the woman finally asked.

"She called me around six o'clock. Hakim showed up at the Club yesterday."

"And this woman is sure it was him?"

"She described him to a tee, including the scar on his cheek. And he had the diamonds. Who else would it be?" Jessie said, her voice rising angrily.

"Calm down, I believe you. I just have to make sure I have all the facts."

"Oksana said Ivan Zherdev was getting passports for Hakim and he would be back to pick them up in a couple of days. This will be your chance to nab the guy. You need to put surveillance on the strip Club right now, before it's too late," Jessie stressed.

"We will take care of it. You know this needs to remain out of your paper, understood?"

Jessie sighed. "Of course. You have to get this man before he attempts something terrible."

"I know. We'll do everything we can to stop him." Estrada's voice softened. "And Jessie, thank you for calling."

Sharing Oksana's information with the agent didn't do much to allay her fear. The more she thought about it, the more she was concerned. She took a quick shower and left for work.

Art stopped short when he got off the elevator and spotted her seated at her desk. "What's going on? Is there some sort of imminent disaster brewing to bring you in here today?" he asked, planted on his short legs in front of her desk.

She nodded sullenly. "It's going to be a disaster all right, unless it can be stopped."

He frowned at her. "What do you mean?"

She told him, then shook her head. "I don't know

what to do, Art. I just hope Agent Estrada takes it seriously. I wonder if she even believed me."

Art set his briefcase on the floor, grabbed a nearby chair and plopped down.

"Judging from my experience with the Bureau, they never are very forthcoming. More likely it won't be any different this time around. But it would be foolish for them to ignore the kind of information you had. And believe me, they're no fools." He mused pensively for a moment. "You can be sure they'll check it out."

Jessie looked at him and they held each other's eyes.

"Damn, that is some scoop, kid. Too bad we can't publish it."

She sighed. "I know."

Suddenly she had an awful thought. "Oh God! I hope they don't go in and confront Zherdev. He would probably guess it was Oksana who ratted him out. She was there when he put the diamonds in the safe. Even if they arrest him, he could still get back at her."

Art shook his head. "Above all else, I wager they want to get this terrorist. The Russian and the diamonds...I think that's all secondary to them. I bet they'll watch the strip joint and arrest him when he shows up for the passports. Once they get him, then they'll haul in the Russians."

"I hope so," Jessie said.

He went to his office and Jessie absorbed herself in her notes. It was midmorning when the phone rang. "Jessie? This is Annabelle, can you come over?" The foster mom said in a shaky voice.

"Is Lilly okay?" Jessie asked, frowning in concern.

"No, no, she's not— I mean physically she's okay— I really need for you to come to the house, talk to her…"

"I'm at the office. I'm leaving right now, and I'll be there as soon as I can." Jessie assured her. She signaled to Art she had to go and he nodded.

"Don't get into any more trouble," he shouted as she rushed out. She drove over the speed limit all the way to the foster home and pulled in behind Annabelle's car. She must have been watching for her. She opened the door before Jessie even rang the bell.

"What's wrong?" Jessie asked in a low voice.

"Lilly knows," Annabelle whispered, looking crushed. "She overheard me on the phone talking to my sister. I was telling her about Lilly's parents." Her lower lip quivered. "I had no idea she was there. I believed she was upstairs playing with the girls. I turned around and there she stood. Oh, her eyes, her eyes…"

Tears streamed down her cheeks.

Jessie threw her arms around her. "Annabelle, you didn't know."

The woman shook her head. "No, no. I should have been more careful. It's unforgivable for her to find out like this."

"Where is she now?"

"She ran upstairs, went into the bathroom. She won't come out, Jessie. I begged and pleaded, but she won't say a word."

Jessie nodded and guided the woman to a chair in the kitchen. She poured a glass of water and set it in front of her. Annabelle kept shaking her head in despair. "What did I do? That poor child."

Jessie rubbed her shoulder gently. "She's upset right now. I'll go talk to her."

Jessie went upstairs and peered into the first bedroom. Two little girls sat next to each other on the bed, staring at her with big, frightened eyes. The bathroom door was closed. She knew it was a Jack and Jill set up, accessible from both sides. She went to the second bedroom and gently knocked on the other door.

"Lilly? It's Jessie, can I come in?"

Silence.

"Lilly, I know you're upset. Can we please talk?" she said softly.

Another moment of silence, followed by the sound of the door being unlocked. She waited a second, then reached for the knob and opened it. The child sat on the tile floor with her eyes closed, her face wet with tears.

"Is it okay if I sit down next to you?" Jessie asked.

Lilly nodded and Jessie lowered herself to the floor. "Baby, I'm so sorry you had to find out about your mom and dad this way. I know how much you love them and miss them."

Lilly opened her eyes, tears running down her cheeks. "Why did everybody lie to me, Jessie?" she asked softly.

"We didn't want to. We just didn't know how to tell you."

"I miss Mommy and Daddy," the child said between sobs.

Jessie shook with grief. "Oh, Lilly, I'm so sorry. I wish I could make everything better for you. I really do."

"I don't want to stay here anymore. I want to go home."

"Your aunt Emily will be here soon. She is your daddy's sister, and she loved him very much. I talked to her on the phone. She is really nice and she can't wait to meet you. She would like for you to come live with her family."

Lilly frowned. "Do I have to go live with them?"

"I think you'll really like it there. They live on a big farm with cows and chickens and goats. Maybe even rabbits. They will love having you."

Lilly looked at her, a ray of hope in her eyes. "Do they have a dog?"

Jessie smiled. "I'm pretty sure they do."

"Mommy is allergic to dogs, so I couldn't have one."

"Your mom would be very happy for you to have a dog."

Lilly was quiet for a moment. "I heard Annabelle tell her sister about Mommy and Daddy."

"I know. She really feels bad about it. She didn't want you to find out this way. Can you forgive her and can you forgive me, Lilly?"

The child nodded. Her blue eyes were drenched in sorrow. "Why did they die?"

"Because there are some very bad people in this world. They will harm others, whether they did anything wrong or not."

"Where do you go when you die, Jessie?"

Jessie hesitated. "I'm not sure. A lot of people think we go to heaven to be with God. Other people have different beliefs."

"Like what?"

"It's complicated, baby."

"So I won't see them ever again?"

Jessie remembered her father, and her own uncertainties about religion and death. "You know late at night, when you look at the sky and see all those beautiful stars?"

Lilly nodded.

"What if the people we lost turn into stars? Then they can shine ever so brightly at us to let us know they love us and watch over us. So when it's really, really dark, look up there, and your heart will tell you which ones they are."

Lilly inched closer and then rested her head against Jessie's shoulder. "I miss them so much," the child said softly.

Jessie gently ran her fingers through the silky blond hair. "I know you do, sweetheart."

They sat together on the bathroom floor for nearly an hour, sometimes talking, sometimes just listening to the quiet around them. Finally, the child sat up and turned to Jessie. "You want to go see Annabelle?" she asked.

"Do you?"

Lilly nodded. "I don't want her to cry anymore."

"Then let's go."

They went downstairs where Annabelle was still sitting in the kitchen staring at the walls. She looked at Lilly anxiously and nearly started crying again.

Lilly ran to her and hugged her. "It's okay, Annabelle. I'm not mad at you."

"Oh, Lilly. You are the sweetest little girl."

At Annabelle's insistence and after a passionate plea from Lilly, Jessie agreed to stay for lunch. The other two youngsters joined them for chicken and salad, and everything seemed fine on the surface. But an occasional glance at the little girl revealed the lingering sadness she tried hard to hide.

****

She was only home a very short time when Nina, her landlady, appeared at her patio door, wearing a purple saree, bangles on her arm and beads in her hair. She was bare footed and wore a toe ring. Instead of her usual martini glass, she was carrying a tiny cup.

Jessie eyebrows shot up. "Hey, Nina. No martini today?"

The woman smiled and raised her cup to Jessie's nose. "Mint tea."

"Does it have anything to do with the cool new outfit?"

"I turned a new leaf last week. Hello new life. I joined a meditation group and now I do mental purification. I am ten years younger, you see it, yes? You should try."

Jessie scrutinized her face, but didn't notice anything different. Nonetheless, she nodded. "Yeah, you look great, but I'm not much of a tea drinker."

The woman shrugged. "Well, you should try it anyway. You get way too much stress with your job. By the way, you had visitors again."

Jessie frowned. "Who was it?"

"Same man, tall, good looking, dress real nice. He had a woman with him this time." Nina shook her head in disapproval. "She is not dressed so nice, though."

Jessie nodded. Sonia Estrada and her cohort, Bruce Williams.

"They looked very annoyed you weren't here."

"They'll get over it."

"Anyway, they said they would be back later. So,

fair warning."

"Thanks Nina. Got to go now, I have to make some phone calls."

The woman nodded, a look of disappointment on her face. "All right then. See you later."

She turned to leave, then stopped abruptly and bowed. "Oh, and Jessie, *Namaste.*"

Jessie grinned, bowing as well, "And *Namaste* to you too."

She sighed and closed her patio door. Nina and Hinduism? That was a very strange mixture indeed. Guess the woman had to find a new way to define her life. Better than downing a half a dozen martinis every day.

She was in her bedroom, changing clothes, when her doorbell rang. The two FBI agents were standing at her door, wearing long faces.

"Can we come in?" Estrada asked.

"I was just getting ready to go for a walk. Sure, yeah, come in."

She ushered them into the living room and they sat next to each other on the couch.

"What can I do for you?" she asked.

"We wanted to go over everything we talked about on the phone, make sure we didn't miss anything," Estrada said, glancing at her partner.

"Okay, what do you need to know?" Jessie asked.

"You said you met this young woman during a previous visit to the Doll House strip club in South Broward County. When did the encounter take place?"

Jessie nodded. "A week ago, when my friend Lonnie McKenzie and I went there around lunch time. I wanted to talk to some of the young women who are forced to work there. It's a really sad situation. Once before, I met one of the girls, Irina. She later contacted me and I helped her get away—"

"Yes, we know about Irina Chekov. Let's get back to this woman, Oksana," Estrada said abruptly, then made a face. "Sorry, we may not have a whole lot of time with this."

"I understand. I gave her my card. Asked her to call me. Then a Russian goon came in and chased me away."

"So, she called you, out of the blue, this morning at six am?" Williams asked.

Jessie nodded. "Yes."

"And somehow, she knows this Russian, Ivan, has the diamonds. He gave Hakim money and boxes of chemicals to make a radioactive bomb of some kind," Estrada recited.

"Oksana didn't know what he's planning to make, but she was sure it was something meant to kill a lot of people."

"Why was she so sure?" Estrada asked.

"She overheard their conversation," Jessie exclaimed.

"Was she in the room with them?"

"At some point she had to be. She saw the Russian put the diamonds in the safe."

Williams leaned in, his eyes probing hers. "Ms. Milner, what did she say about a bomb?"

Jessie glared at him. "I told you. She was concerned when she spotted the outfits Ivan got for Hakim. They were similar to those worn by the rescuers at Chernobyl, the nuclear site, where all those people died from radiation—"

This time it was Williams who cut her off. "Ms. Milner, we know what Chernobyl is."

Jessie was annoyed. "Very well then. With this information, you can assume they are planning an attack of some kind."

"What did she say about the passports?" Williams asked.

"Hakim is getting new passports from the Russian. He's supposed to pick them up in a few days." Frustration got the best of her. "Instead of going over this whole thing again, maybe you should be watching the strip club so you can catch Hakim when he comes back for his passports."

"Don't worry, Miss Milner, that's exactly what we're doing," Williams said.

"No, you're not, you're here talking to me."

Estrada smirked. "Be assured we're not the only two agents working on this case."

"So, you have the club under surveillance?"

Williams nodded. "Around the clock."

"You won't arrest Zherdev before you get Hakim, right?"

"Why do you ask?"

"Because I'm worried he would find out it was Oksana who turned him in. Even if he's in jail, he could still have her killed."

"No, we're getting Hakim first," Williams assured her.

"I'm glad to hear it."

"One more thing Ms. Milner, did Oksana, request any money, help or favors?" he asked.

"Nothing. When I asked her if I could help her in any way, she turned me down."

"Did you wonder if she might be setting you up?" Estrada chimed in.

"No, not at all. On the contrary, she risked her life to call me with this information."

Estrada shrugged. "She could have been coerced into calling you."

"First of all, she didn't ask to meet me. If the Russians intended to get me, they could easily do so at any time, or any place. It's no big secret where I live. And why would they tell me Ivan has the stolen diamonds in his safe, and that he sold Hakim boxes of chemicals and hazmat suits? Makes absolutely no sense, does it?" Jessie said, not bothering to hide her annoyance.

The two agents didn't answer.

Jessie shrugged. "The reason Oksana gave me all this information is because she wants those men in jail. She plans to escape with the other girls they forced into prostitution. They want to get away as far as they can from the Russian mob."

Estrada nodded. "Anything else you can recall from your conversation with her?"

Jessie shook her head. "I have a question for you now. Will you let me know when you capture Hakim?"

They didn't react.

"I'm the one who brought you this information. At least give me the courtesy to get the first stab at the story," Jessie insisted.

The two agents exchanged glances and Estrada nodded.

Jessie smiled. "Thank you."

They left. Jessie walked to the patio door and glanced out. The sun was shining, the sky was a deep blue. There was not a cloud in sight. It crossed her mind again how disaster could be just around the corner, yet nature went on uninterrupted in its pattern, regardless of the turmoil surrounding it. Suddenly she was very tired, feeling the full weight of the knowledge she had acquired just hours ago.

She called Liam.

"Hey love, you sound tired," he said.

"I feel like I've been through the wringer today. Want to go to the beach?"

"Sure thing, when?"

"How does right now sound?" she asked.

"I'll be right there." he said.

Chapter Thirty-One

He parked down the block from the Doll House, and sat in the car as Maggie Randall scampered down the sidewalk. Suddenly she stopped, swiveled on her high heels and gave him the finger, then resumed her walk as if nothing happened. Seething with anger, Hakim shook his head. A couple of times in the past, he had considered getting rid of the two women after the attack. Neither Maggie nor Jenna knew their place in the new Islamic world, showing their disrespect almost on a daily basis. Now Maggie's behavior confirmed it once again. However, for the time being, he had to exercise patience. He still needed them.

This morning, after Zherdev called to tell him the passports were ready, Hakim decided he was going to send Maggie to pick them up. Exposing his weakness to the Russian had left him feeling dirty. He wasn't going to give him the pleasure of humiliating him again.

At first Maggie acted flattered when he said he had a job for her. Then, when he picked her up in front of her apartment building and told her about getting the passports at the Doll House, she suddenly got mad. "You're kidding right? A damn strip joint? They treat women like dirt in those," she spat out.

"Do you want to be a part of this operation or not?" Hakim shot back.

"Yeah, I do. If you make me go in there, I'm not

letting those filthy Russians grope me."

"No one will touch you," Hakim assured her, trying to keep his voice calm. "It's business. When you go in, you tell them you're there to see Ivan Zherdev. They'll take you to him. You say I sent you to pick up the passports, he'll give them to you and you leave. I'm telling you, it's easy."

"Then why don't you do it?" she riposted.

Hakim waited until she was out of sight, then got out and glanced around. Other than a white van parked on the other side of the Strip Club, there was very little going on. It was a fairly quiet area, a mixture of residential and a few businesses. It was still early, and the traffic was scarce. On his side was a boarded up two-story red brick building. A barely legible sign indicated it was a gym at one time. He leaned against the building and checked out the empty soccer field across the street, right next to a huge old oak tree and a Baptist church. A lone kid was kicking a soccer ball in the dirt, raising dust clouds all around him. Nearly an hour went by. He was getting anxious. He went back to the car and sat glaring through the windshield, thinking maybe he should go check on the damn woman. The white van hadn't moved, but now there was a man stepping out of the back. He stretched his legs a couple of times, and Hakim could see he was talking on the phone. Pretty soon, another man got out of the passenger side of the van, then the driver joined them as well. They stood looking around for a while, then they all climbed back inside. Hakim stiffened. He had a bad feeling. His mouth was dry and he swallowed hard, not knowing if he should leave or wait for Maggie. Then suddenly, she appeared, walking toward him, her long blond hair flowing behind her. She barely had a chance to get in. He was already backing up into the driveway next to him.

"Hey, hey, wait a minute!" she yelled at him.

"What took you so long?" he muttered.

She pulled out a packet from her handbag, shoved it at him. "Here. First, the son of a bitch tried to talk me into stripping for him, then when I told him to go to hell, he kept me waiting forever."

Hakim slowly drove away, his sight fixated on the rear-view mirror. The white van wasn't moving. He turned at the next street.

"Is it all here?" he asked.

She shrugged. "How should I know? I only picked them up, you can check them. If you're not happy with them, I'm not going back. You can tell him yourself."

"Did he say anything else?" Hakim asked.

She glared at him. "He asked why you didn't come."

Hakim didn't answer. He drove on and kept checking the mirror. Still no one behind him. Just ahead was the access ramp to I-95. He accelerated.

Chapter Thirty-Two

"So did they put on a surveillance team on the strip joint?" Sam Perrone asked Jessie, seated next to his desk. She had dropped in unexpectedly, hoping he would be able to give her some insight.

"As far I know they did. It's been five days now, and when they say no news is good news, I don't think it applies here," Jessie answered.

Perrone shook his head. "Things are different with the FBI."

"Have you heard anything?" she asked.

"Nada. Not that they would share with us, mind you. But if they had nabbed Hakim, they would have arrested Zherdev as well, and we would have found out. To my knowledge, the club is still up and running."

"I left a couple of messages on Agent Estrada's phone. So far, she hasn't called me back. I wonder if I should try calling Williams," Jessie said.

"I don't know. They're probably just ignoring you and will continue to do so until they get their man."

"I could go back to the club, see if Oksana is there," she pondered.

"Not a good idea, Jessie. It's too dangerous for both of you. One of these days, you'll have to learn to be more patient."

She sighed deeply. "I don't think I was born with that gene." She glanced at him sideways, and noticed he was suddenly focused elsewhere. Jessie turned to see what was holding his attention. A young woman stood at a desk nearby going through some paperwork. She was short, a few pounds overweight, and had curly black hair.

"Excuse me for a moment." Perrone got up and headed toward the desk. "Jenna. Can I help you with something?" he asked.

The women nearly jumped out of her skin, her face suddenly flushed. "Oh, you startled me. I thought I left a piece of paper here earlier," she stammered.

"Were you working on this computer?" Perrone asked.

"I was, this morning. I'm done now."

"What was it? Maybe I can help you find it," Perrone said.

She shook her head. "No, no. I already checked. I must have left it somewhere else."

Perrone smiled. "Okay then, good luck."

"Thank you, Detective," she said.

He waved at her as he walked back to his desk. "No problem."

Grinning at Jessie, he sat back down. "Sorry. Jenna works in the I.T. Department."

"Where is Boyd today?" Jessie asked.

"Had to go to court this morning. An old case of his is being retried. He has to go back to testify. Some of those retrials are a real pain in the ass."

"I'm sure it happens more often than you like," Jessie said.

He shrugged. "Yeah, we have to try to keep the bad guys in jail, right?"

He checked his watch. "Hey, it's lunch time. You

want to go get a bite?"

Jessie hesitated.

"Come on. How can you say no to a Cuban sandwich, plantains and Cuban coffee? I'll even share a flan with you. Deal?"

"Where?" she asked.

"I'm thinking Las Vegas in Plantation."

"Sounds good." She got up. "I'll meet you there. I want to go see Lilly afterwards."

"How is she doing?"

"It's hard to say, Sam. She's just a little girl trying to cope with the loss of her parents. How can that be easy?"

On the way out, they walked past the young woman. Jessie waved at her and the girl waved back.

They were half way through the flan when Perrone's phone rang. He answered and Jessie noticed his face changing. Listening to the one-sided conversation, she soon became excited. She could hardly wait for him to disconnect.

"I got some of it. They arrested the Russians?" she said anxiously.

Perrone nodded. "That was my contact at the Hollywood Police Department. I had talked to him about the Russians and their possible involvement with Hakim. Seems the FBI swooped into the Doll House late last night, arrested Zherdev and his associate, Leonid Gorev. They had a search warrant, turned the place upside down. Not only did they get the diamonds in the safe, there was a gun as well. And guess what? It's the same caliber used to kill Irina Chekov. With a little luck, the forensic ballistics should confirm it's the same gun."

"What about Hakim?" Jessie asked.

Perrone shrugged. "Nothing on him as far as I know. Either they got him and are keeping him under wraps, or they gave up on him coming back to the strip joint."

"If they got Hakim, they were supposed to let me know," Jessie said.

"Come on, Jessie, you know better. Keeping you in the loop, or us for that matter, is not part of their strategy."

"And if they didn't get him?"

"They have the Russians. If the gun pans out, there's enough evidence to go for a murder conviction. Should be sufficient to persuade at least one of them to try and make a deal." Perrone ventured.

"What kind of deal?" Jessie asked.

"My guess is taking the death penalty off the table for one." He leaned in. "Now, Jessie, this is just me talking. Plain speculation, none of it on record."

She frowned at him. "Sam, you know me better by now. I appreciate you telling me what's going on. I would never get you in trouble." She tapped her head. "The information is going to stay right here until I'm given the go ahead to print it."

He nodded, somewhat embarrassed. "I know, I know, just have to say it."

All of a sudden, Jessie's eyes widened. "What about Oksana and the other girls? Did your friend mention them?"

He shook his head. "Nothing."

"I hope she got away. You know they would have her killed if they suspected she gave them up."

He patted her hand. "It sounds like she's a pretty

smart girl. She had a plan and you were part of it. She told you about Hakim and the diamonds, hoping it would lead to the Russians' arrest. I'm guessing she was actually counting on it. I bet she took off with the other girls as soon as she could, and they're somewhere safe right now. At least that's my opinion."

Jessie nodded. "You're right. It makes sense that she was laying the groundwork for their escape."

They parted in the parking lot and Jessie drove to Annabelle's house. The woman greeted her with a warm smile.

"Jessie, I didn't expect you. Mary Gilmore took Lilly for her session."

"With a psychologist?"

Annabelle nodded. "Her second one. So far, so good."

"Does she talk about it?" Jessie asked anxiously.

"Not really. She's a little more relaxed, playing with the girls again. For a while she wouldn't have anything to do with anyone. Hardly came out of her room."

"She had to find out sooner or later. I don't think it ever gets easier to learn your parents are gone. She loved them so much, and I'm sure they reciprocated her love tenfold. It must be awful to deal with the emptiness. Hopefully the therapist will help her cope with it."

"Do you want to stay for a cup of coffee or tea?" Annabelle offered.

"No thanks. I just had Cuban coffee with my lunch. I'm still wired. Tell Lilly I came by. If it's okay with you and with her, I'll come and get her this weekend, take her to the beach."

Annabelle smiled. "She'll love it. You are the one person who means the most to her right now."

"Did you hear from her Aunt Emily?" Jessie asked.

"I talked to her yesterday. Unfortunately, her husband is still in the hospital, so she probably won't be here for another couple of weeks."

"In a way it might be better for Lilly. It will give her a little more time to adjust. Too many drastic changes in a short period of time could even be harder on her."

They hugged and Jessie left. On her way out, she phoned Liam. "Where are you?" she asked.

"I'm doing a surveillance on an errant spouse. Would you like to join me?"

"A tryst of some kind?"

"A seedy Motel *Rendez-Vous*. This guy's not a big spender either. The girl friend should be offended," he snickered.

He gave her the address, and twenty-five minutes later she pulled up next to his car at the Windy Pines Motel on 441 north of Commercial Blvd. The building desperately needed a facelift and a new coat of paint. A few scrawny shrubs dotted the landscape, with no pines in sight, windy or otherwise. Weeds thrived everywhere. Jessie jumped into Liam's passenger seat. "Lordy, you're right. This is more like a place to make a drug buy than a love nest."

He grinned wickedly. "Well, something must be going right. They've been in there for more than two hours."

"Maybe it took a while to check out the linens and root out the bed bugs. Did you check the register?"

He raised an eyebrow. "For what? I followed him

here and she was waiting in front of the motel door with the key card. They couldn't hold off a minute longer, so they groped outside for a while, gave me a chance to snap some pretty telling pictures. Then finally they went in to pursue their passionate encounter."

"Wow, you should have been a romance writer," Jessie said.

"His wife will feel less than romantic when I give her the prints," he scoffed.

"Can't be pleasant to be the bearer of bad news, especially when it concerns someone the person loves." Jessie shook her head.

"I don't think love is a factor here, Jessie. From what I've seen so far, it's more about money."

"If they have money, what the heck is he doing bringing his squeeze to this place?"

"I told you, he's a cheapskate. He also believed he was being smart when he asked his wife to sign a pre-nup. Guess what? This little caper will nullify it, so wifey will walk away with a pretty tidy nest egg."

Jessie sighed. "What a world."

He leaned over and planted a kiss on her cheek. "I've missed you."

Jessie arched an eyebrow. "We were together last night."

"I know. I missed you since then."

She smiled. "I'm amazed. Even after witnessing such relationship betrayals, you're still a dreamer at heart."

"What can I say? Told you I was an optimist. Plus I grew up in a home where there was plenty of love, so I believe in it."

"Well, that announcement deserves some good

news," she said, patting his hand.

"What?" Liam asked.

"The FBI is now officially in possession of the diamonds."

His eyes widened. "What? When?"

She told him about her conversation with Perrone.

"Heck, as soon as I'm done here with Mr. Infidelity, I'm going to see them," Liam exclaimed.

"No, I don't think it's a good idea right now."

"Why not? I have a right to claim the diamonds for my client," he protested.

"If you contact them, I doubt if they'll even admit having them."

"So what do you suggest?" he asked.

"First let me see how forthcoming they are."

"You mean Estrada and Williams?"

She nodded.

"Okay, I'll wait—" The love birds emerged from their room, looking flushed and somewhat exhausted. The man was lean and tall with an elaborate comb-over to hide creeping baldness. The woman was a redhead, short and pudgy, wearing a too-tight dress and dangerously high heels.

"Poor darlings, this little encounter must have zapped all their energy," Jessie whispered.

The couple descended the stairs and after another passionate embrace headed for their separate vehicles, without as much as a glance in their direction.

"Lost in love," Liam sighed.

"Are you still going to follow him?" Jessie asked.

"No, I think I have enough to sink the bugger. I'm meeting the wife in a couple of hours. Then I'll be free for the rest of the day. Can I tempt you with dinner at my house, spaghetti ala carbonara? Seven o'clock?"

She laughed. "I don't know what carbonara is, but I trust you, and when it comes to food, I can easily be persuaded."

****

She didn't have to call the FBI. Her phone chirped as she pulled into her driveway. "Agent Estrada, so good to hear from you," Jessie said.

The woman didn't seem to share her good humor. "Ms. Milner, has Oksana called you back?" she asked tersely.

"Why do you think she would?"

Estrada paused for a moment, and Jessie held her breath, hoping she would tell her about the raid.

"Last night we arrested Zherdev and his accomplice Gorev at the Doll House. Several women were rounded up as well. Oksana Yudin was not among them. One of them led us to the house where they lived. It was empty. We think they probably got a phone call warning them about the raid and took off. We hoped she would get in touch with you."

Jessie closed her eyes, relief sweeping over her. "No, I didn't hear from her."

"If she does call, you must emphasize she should turn herself in. Let her know in exchange for her testimony, we will provide her with protection and a new identity. As long as she remains out there, the Russian mob will be after her," the woman said.

"Did you get the diamonds?" Jessie asked.

Silence on the line.

"Agent Estrada?" Jessie repeated.

Finally she spoke. "We did. Once again, this information must remain unpublished, understood?"

"Yes, I'm aware. However, Liam Donovan was tasked with their recovery by the insurance company, so when will he be able to get them?"

"Not at this time. Frankly, it might take a while but they will get them back."

"What about Hakim? Did you arrest him?"

"No. We did not."

"So he never came back for the passports?" Jessie asked.

"There were no passports."

Jessie frowned. "Do you think Oksana was wrong about them?"

"I don't know. This is one of the reasons we need to talk to her. Frankly, I can't discuss this case with you any further."

Jessie bristled. "What can you tell me, Agent Estrada?"

"Only what I told you so far."

Somehow, Jessie managed to contain her impatience. "Okay. So I'll be waiting to hear more from you soon."

Chapter Thirty-Three

Rasul Ahmad was in the man trap, stepping out of his hazmat suit, when Hakim walked into the observation room with Jamal trailing him. A few seconds later the scientist joined them.

"Done?" Hakim asked.

Ahmad nodded.

Hakim eyed him suspiciously. "How do I know you did it right?"

"The reason you brought me here is because I've done this more times than I like to recount. It's the right formula," the man said wearily. He pointed to a series of containers lined up on a shelf in the lab. "You have twelve pressurized cylinders with release valves, and two smaller glass containers filled with sarin, all of them ready to go. Exactly as you requested. What more do you want from me?"

Hakim stared at the containers. They appeared harmless. He shrugged. "I want to be sure it's the right potency."

"It is the highest, most powerful grade of nerve gas you can get, twenty-five times more deadly than cyanide. It's also under pressure, extremely volatile, and has to be handled with caution," the man warned.

"Tell me how it works," Hakim said.

"Within seconds of exposure, the subject will drool, vomit, and defecate himself. The lung muscles will be paralyzed, causing respiratory arrest. Sarin has no smell or taste, so he has no idea what's going on. Death will follow in less than ten minutes," Ahmad said in a voice barely above a whisper.

Jamal laughed nervously. "Man, that's some mean shit. We'll make the front page of the paper for sure with this stuff."

Hakim was still not persuaded. Suddenly he turned to Jamal. "We're going to test it."

Jamal's eyes widened. "How?"

Hakim didn't answer, glancing back at the Iraqi.

"Did you check the antidote the Russian got us? When and how is it to be administered?"

This time Ahmad pointed to a pile of small packets stacked on a table inside the lab. "It's the most recent version. You have two kits per person. The first one is the antidote. The second kit is an anticonvulsant. Both of them are to be injected in the outer thigh or buttocks as soon as possible after exposure to sarin."

"Will they work if they're administered prior to exposure?"

Ahmad shrugged. "I don't see why not."

Hakim nodded pensively, then turned to Jamal. "Bring the gas cylinders out of the lab."

Ahmad shook his head vehemently.

Hakim shot him an annoyed look. "What is it?"

"I would leave them in the lab until you're ready to use them."

"Why?"

"As I said before, when you're dealing with a very volatile product, there's always the possibility of leakage," the man said.

Hakim glared at him, stiffening at the scorn

reflected in the man's eyes. In a sudden burst of anger, he grabbed his arm. "Okay, they stay in the lab, and you're going back to your cell."

Ahmad resisted, pulling away from him. "I would like to talk to my family now. You assured me I could when I was finished."

"Right now is not a good time. Besides, I don't have their number yet."

The scientist took a step forward and glowered at him. "You said I would be freed when I was done. You gave me your word."

He didn't see it coming. Hakim's first punch landed on his jaw, the second one in his gut. Ahmad doubled over, moaning with pain. Hakim stood back, rubbed his knuckles. "You asked for it," he hissed.

Ahmad's shoulders slumped in defeat. "Please, I just want to see my family," he said plaintively.

Hakim took a deep breath. "Let me work on it. Just don't push me again," he warned.

He led him back to his cell, locked the door and motioned to Jamal to follow him.

"You really letting him go?" Jamal asked after they left the building.

"Of course not. The first thing he would do is go to the cops."

"He wouldn't do that with his family still held hostage, would he?" Jamal asked.

"We don't have them anymore."

"What do you mean?" Jamal asked.

"They got rid of them a long time ago."

"They killed them?"

Hakim leered. "Yeah. He just doesn't know it yet." He glanced at Jamal to check his reaction. The man's face remained impassive and Hakim wasn't a bit surprised. Jamal was twenty-two, yet looked much older. A deep scar ran from the corner of his eye down to his chin, a reminder of a knife fight to protect his turf when he was only twelve years old. His eyes were dark and deep set, having seen too much, and reflected a life of hardship growing up in the streets. When Hakim met him, the only emotions Jamal still had left in him were anger and hatred, making him a prime recruit for his mission. Becoming a jihadist was the ultimate revenge for the way the world had treated him until now.

They got in Hakim's car. "Where we going?" Jamal asked.

"To make sure the gas will do what we want it to do."

"How?" Jamal asked, looking perplexed.

"With a guinea pig."

Jamal shrieked in laughter. "A real guinea pig?"

Hakim gave him a scornful look. "Of course not, Jamal. I'm talking about a human guinea pig, like a volunteer."

"A volunteer?" Jamal repeated.

"Why not?"

Jamal raised a doubtful eyebrow. "Who the hell would volunteer to be gassed to death?"

"You don't tell them that part."

"Yeah, how are you going about it?"

Hakim grinned. "I have a pretty good idea."

"You're doing this today?"

Hakim nodded. "We only have until Saturday to get it right. If something is wrong, then it gives us a couple more days to have the Iraqi fix it."

Jamal shook his head. "I still don't see how you're

getting any one to go along with this."

Hakim shot him a knowing look and grinned.

It was nearly four o'clock and the traffic on I-95 was building up. All of a sudden, the skies opened up, delivering a torrential downpour. They moved along at a crawl until they reached Sunrise Blvd and Hakim took the eastbound ramp. A couple of miles down the road, the rain had stopped, the clouds dissipated, and swirls of steam rose from the pavement. Hakim turned in at Holiday Park, one of the oldest parks in Ft Lauderdale.

He remembered this place well. When he was a child, his mother often brought him here with his sister. He also recalled it was a frequent hang-out for the homeless. He drove past the playground. It hadn't changed a whole lot since those early days of his childhood. Right now, no children played on the aging swings. He went on a bit further before stopping in a parking space under the shade of an ancient oak tree.

"What are we doing here?" Jamal asked.

Hakim smiled. "You'll see."

They remained in the car for a while, sitting in silence, checking out the surrounding area. After a few minutes, an old man, groaning from the effort of pushing a heaping grocery cart, headed in their direction. Oblivious to their presence, he stopped a few feet away from their car and rummaged through his cart. Mumbling to himself the whole time, he finally pulled out something wrapped in wrinkled paper. Looking satisfied at last, he sat on a nearby bench and peeled back the wrapping, tossing it on the ground. Eagerly, he chewed on what appeared to be the remains of a sandwich.

Hakim motioned to Jamal and they got out of the

car. As soon as he spotted them, the old man drew in his hand to hide his food, all the while eyeing them suspiciously.

Hakim stopped in front of him and smiled. "Hi there."

"What do you want?" the man asked.

"How is your day going so far?"

"Why the hell do you care?" The old man scoffed before taking a cautious bite of his food.

Hakim laughed. "Because I'm a caring person, and I'm here to make you the best offer you've had in a long time."

"Oh Yeah? What?"

"My friend and I run a marketing company," Hakim explained. "We test new products before they are released for sale and we need people to try them out. Right now, we have a brand-new item. It's an ointment for minor pain. All it requires is for you to rub on a few dabs of the ointment and give us your opinion."

The man shook his head. "I don't have no pain,"

Hakim shrugged. "Sure you do, everybody does. But you can just pretend. It doesn't matter. The pay is the same either way."

"That's all you have to do?"

Hakim threw up his hands. "That's all."

The old man frowned. "How much you paying?"

"That's the best part. We give you five hundred dollars for just a few hours of your day."

The old man's eyes lit up. "Five hundred? In advance?"

"As soon as you get in my car, I'll hand you half the money. We go do the test, then I bring you back here and give you the other half. Takes an hour, maybe two, tops. What do you say?"

The homeless man hesitated. He glanced at his cart. "What about my stuff?"

"Don't worry about it. You stash it over there behind the dumpster, no one will get it," Hakim assured him.

The old man shook his head. "No, no, I can't just leave my stuff. Everybody is always trying to steal it from me. This is my stuff. You don't know. It's everything I got," he mumbled.

Taking out his wallet, Hakim pulled out several hundred-dollar bills, waving them in front of the man. "What if I give you a thousand dollars? Look, I'm giving five hundred right now, right this minute. You can buy a whole new cart full of stuff," he promised.

The man wasn't budging. His eyes were wild. He appeared terrified.

He started screaming. "Leave me alone. You just want to take my cart, I know it. Leave me alone!"

The two men backed away, glancing around. A young couple was walking toward them, pushing a baby in a stroller. "Never mind," Hakim said, motioning to Jamal.

They jumped back into the car and Hakim drove away. He was fuming. So close, they almost had that stupid crazy old man.

"Wow, old bastard sure is fucked up," Jamal pondered.

Hakim nodded, anger darkening his brow. He got back out on Sunrise Blvd, turned east.

"Now what?" Jamal asked.

"Let me think," Hakim answered impatiently.

Suddenly Jamal burst out laughing.

Hakim shot him an angry look. "What's so funny?"

"That was a really good story you cooked up back there with the old creep."

Hakim smiled. He had to agree. It was a good story. But now they had to start all over. He drove south for a while, then remembered the homeless liked to congregate near the Greyhound bus station on Third Street, near Broward Blvd and Federal Hwy.

Sure enough, as they neared the station, the sidewalks were noticeably more crowded. Men hung out on benches, others drifted around, none in a hurry. After all, they had nowhere else to go. The trick now was to find a loner, someone they could approach without drawing attention to themselves. Hakim drove another block and parked the car on a side street. They got out and took off toward the bus station. He was still trying to figure out what to do, when Jamal tugged at his sleeve and pointed behind them. Hakim glanced over his shoulder. A solitary man with a backpack was ambling down the sidewalk, heading in their direction.

"Where the hell did he come from?" Hakim wondered.

"Maybe from one of the alleys back there," answered Jamal.

They stopped and waited for him. As he got closer, he slowed down and eyed them cautiously.

"Hi there," Hakim said.

The man didn't answer.

"Are you taking the bus?" Jamal asked.

He shook his head. "Nope. At six o'clock some of the Mission people bring food down here. Usually it's not bad, you know, and it's free, so if you're interested…One decent meal a day can make a hell of a difference in how good life is, right?"

He was tall, with a gray beard, bloodshot eyes and thinning hair tied back in a long ponytail.

Hakim smiled. "Actually, we're here with an offer for you."

The man took a step back, shaking his head vigorously. "Hey man, wait a minute, you got the wrong guy here. I'm not in the game. If you want sex, you're gonna have to go elsewhere."

Hakim laughed. "No, no, nothing like that. It's a marketing offer. We're testing a new product at our lab and we need a volunteer. All you have to do is dab on a cream to treat aches and pain, then wait a few minutes to see if there's a reaction."

"You mean, like an allergic reaction?" the man asked.

"Yeah, exactly. It pays really well, and it's quick and painless."

"How much?"

"One thousand dollars for two hours' work. How does that sound?" Hakim said.

The man's eyes lit up in surprise. "One thousand bucks?"

Hakim nodded. "A couple of hours and you're back down here with a huge wad of money in your pocket."

He hesitated and Hakim shrugged. "If you don't want to take this once-in-a-lifetime opportunity, we're going to the station. Plenty of guys down there will jump at the offer. Heck, we'll probably have to fight them off with a stick. So, make up your mind, right now. You will never get another chance like this."

The man squinted, giving them a once over. It was obvious he was debating, maybe wondering why they had to take to the street to find a volunteer for that kind of money. More likely, he thought this was just his lucky day.

"No more than two hours?"

Hakim nodded. "Max two hours, bro."

"When do I get the money?"

Hakim took out his wallet, peeled off five hundred-dollar bills, and handed them to him. "When the testing is done, you get the other five hundred."

He stood eyeing the money for a moment, his thumb rubbing over the crisp bills before he shoved them into his pants pocket.

"Okay. When do you want to do this?"

"Right now. Tonight. The sooner we turn in our results, the sooner the company can start using their product." At least that part was truthful.

"Where do I have to go?" the man asked.

"We'll take you. Our car is parked close by. The lab is not far," Hakim assured him.

The man followed them and they retrieved the car. Hakim turned up the volume on the radio to discourage further conversation, then took off for the house.

When they pulled up to the building the man looked around, frowning. "What kind of business is this?" he asked.

"It's a temporary testing site. After they confirm the product is ready for the market, it will be closed down," Hakim said.

"There's no danger with whatever it is you're testing, right?" the man asked.

"None. The Federal Drug Administration would

never allow us to go on with tests if there was any risk whatsoever," Hakim assured him.

The man took a deep breath and Hakim took him into the lab. "What's your name?"

"Harry."

"You take a seat right here, Harry." Hakim pointed to a bar stool. "I'm going to get the product, you will rub it on your skin and we wait twenty minutes. If you don't break out, all's well."

"And if I break out, then what? You said it wouldn't affect me."

"Don't worry. It's a very mild irritant. If you happened to break out, which is highly unlikely, we have a pill to stop it. So it's not a problem, buddy."

The man sat on the stool reluctantly. He crossed his arms and glanced nervously around the room. "I don't know... I don't feel good. Maybe I should go."

"Look man, you're here now and that's a lot of dough, right? Let's just do the test and you get the money. Then we take you back downtown. Unless you want us to drop you off somewhere else. With a thousand dollars in your pocket, you may want to change your plans. You think about it, then let us know, okay?" Hakim said, smiling reassuringly.

Mention of the money brought a grin to the man's face. "You're right. Maybe I get myself a really good steak dinner, and dessert. I like pecan pie with whipped cream on it and a cup of coffee. Then I'll get a nice motel room to stay for the night, with a real bed for a change."

"Sure. Listen, I'll be right back," Hakim said. He went into the observation room and locked the lab door behind him. "Jamal, go get Mohamed and Abdul. I want them to see this. Then you know what to do." He went to the cell to get Ahmad. "Come, we have a volunteer."

The Iraqi's eyes widened. "What do you mean? Who would volunteer for this?"

Hakim roared with laughter. "See? You're doubting my powers of persuasion. Believe me, this man volunteered."

"What did he volunteer for? Surely not to be killed by sarin nerve gas. You must have lied to him."

Hakim was no longer amused. "Yes, I did. Now, enough of this, we are going to do the test and make sure it works exactly as you promised."

Ahmad shook his head. "You are a monster. You probably lied to me too, didn't you? You have no intention of letting me go."

"Why do you think we want nerve gas? We plan on using it. Anymore squeamishness on your part stops right now. If you intend to keep your family alive, you will do as I say." Hakim threatened, his voice cold as ice. He grabbed the man's arm and pushed him forward. "Now."

When they got to the observation room, Jamal was standing in the man trap between the two pressurized doors leading into the lab. He wore one of the hazmat suits and held a glass container. Mohamed and Abdul watched cautiously from a distance.

Hakim approached them. He spoke softly so the homeless man couldn't hear him. "Don't worry, we got this. Jamal is only wearing the protective gear as an added precaution. This is how it's going to work. Jamal will open the door to the lab just enough to toss in the glass container with the sarin. By the time it hits the floor and breaks, he will already have the door closed and be safe in the man trap. In the meantime, the gas will have been released and then we wait for the show to begin."

Abdul and Mohamed nodded, but they weren't moving any closer. Amused by their fear, Hakim glanced at the scientist. Standing still as a statue, he stared at the man in the lab. His face looked ashen. Hakim realized he had probably seen this trial performed previously. Ahmad must have sensed him nearby. He turned in his direction and their eyes met.

"Don't do this," the Iraqi pleaded softly.

Hakim ignored him. A commotion inside the lab brought his attention back to the homeless man. He had run to the door and was yanking on the handle without success. Panic was spreading on his face.

"Hey, what's going on here? Why is the door locked?" he shouted, his voice quivering with anxiety.

Hakim stepped up to the glass and spoke to him soothingly. "Don't worry, Harry. The door locks automatically when someone comes in or goes out. The testing has to be done in a sterile environment. That's why you're in there and we're out here. My assistant is getting the cream right now, then we can test it and we'll be done. And remember our deal, a thousand bucks for a few minutes of your time. So, have a seat, relax. It won't take long, I promise."

"Why are all of you watching me out there?" he asked with a frown.

Hakim smiled reassuringly. "The company wants multiple observers for veracity of the results. If we don't do this, no moolah for us."

Harry nodded and hesitantly went back to his seat.

Hakim gave a slight nod to Jamal. He grabbed the door handle, twisted it quietly, pulled the door open slightly, and quickly tossed the vial into the lab. The door was closed and locked again before the vial hit the floor. It shattered near the homeless man, splashing liquid all over his skin and clothing. Startled, he jumped off the stool, tripped over one leg, lost his balance and landed on all fours, cutting his hands on shards of glass from the broken container. In the meantime, separated by the door and unable to see what was happening in the lab, Jamal remained in the man trap, waiting for Hakim's signal to make his exit.

Inside the lab, the man was rubbing his face with a bloody hand in an effort to wipe off the sarin, while doing his best to pull himself to his knees with the other. Finally, he was able to get up and stumbled toward the door.

"Let me out, dammit!" he growled.

When no one responded, he turned, climbed over the stool and onto the work bench. As he raised his fist to pound the glass, his nose started running, his muscles twitched, tears streamed down his cheeks, and his face contorted.

"Please, let me out. You don't have to pay me anything else. Just let me go. I didn't do anything," he begged, his mouth twisting. Drool ran down his chin.

Hakim stepped closer to the glass, fascinated by the spectacle. Suddenly, Harry let out a horrendous shriek and a wall of vomit hit the glass, startling all of them. He shook once, then rolled off the table onto the floor, convulsing, twisting and moaning.

Ahmad had turned away with his head down. Mohamed and Abdul stood back, shock reflected in their eyes.

Soon there was only silence. The man's body twitched and shuddered a few more times, then stopped moving altogether. Hakim turned to his crew, noticed the dismay on their faces, and grimaced in annoyance. "What the hell did you expect? This is good news. It means we're ready for the attack."

Abdul shook his head. "I've never seen anything like it."

Hakim smirked. "Exactly. That's why we're using it."

Jamal was still waiting in the mantrap. Hakim told him to stay there, then he ordered Abdul to get some large trash bags. "Put on a hazmat suit, help him bag the body, then take it out to the truck."

He turned around and found himself locking eyes again with the Iraqi. Not liking what he saw, he quickly looked away and motioned to Mohamed.

"Take him back to his cell, then call the women. Tell them to get here as soon as possible. We have to talk."

A couple of hours later, they all filed into the room and Hakim savored the moment. This was his cell, his attack, and it was closer to getting accomplished than ever before.

Gone was the fear of failure. He was going to strike a deadly blow to this evil nation and no one would ever be able to take that away from him. The hatred consuming him would finally be soothed. He took a deep breath and started.

"Earlier, most of you witnessed our sarin trial. There is no doubt we are ready for the attack on Saturday. Let's go over every detail once more. Our destination is terminal eighteen in Port Everglades. To keep from drawing attention, we will get there separately. He looked around the room and his gaze stopped on Mohamed. "No beards, short hair only. Everybody must be clean shaven. Good old American boys off to have a good time, right? As I mentioned before, we'll be entering the Port from different directions. Mohamed, you start out from a hotel van bringing the passengers to the Port. Abdul, you take a cab."

The two men nodded. Hakim continued, "Jenna and I, we'll be coming in on Eller Drive. Jamal and Maggie, you use the Eisenhower Blvd entrance. Boarding is set to start at eleven. The terminal should be jammed packed by eleven thirty. This is when we strike."

Holding up a paper, he continued. "This is a drawing of the inside of the terminal. Notice the three different areas marked with an X along the walls," he pointed out, "Saturday morning, there will be a couple of large storage barrels or trash bins near each one of those sites. Jenna and I will go to the west wall site behind the restrooms. Jamal and Maggie will head to the east side containers, and Mohamed and Abdul to the north site. Each one of us will carry a large backpack with two pressurized cylinders. You've seen them in the lab. They look like fire extinguishers. Close enough to fool anyone at a glance. When you reach your designated area, you open the pressure valves on the cylinders, drop the backpacks either in the barrels or behind them if necessary. The gas will start releasing right then and there, and you get the hell out of there."

He waited a moment, checked their faces, tried to

read them. "Any questions?"

"Yeah. Who is placing those containers?" Abdul asked.

"He's not one of us. But he knows the terminal inside out."

"If he's not one of us, how do you know you can trust him?" Abdul scoffed.

Hakim glared at him. "I can assure you he will do as told."

"And our getaway?" Maggie asked.

"A driver with a van will be waiting for us on 14th Avenue."

"Same person?" Abdul asked.

"Yes. We won't have much time or we risk getting caught. If your access is blocked, there are a number of places you could hold out at the port. The container yard is one of them. Friday night we'll go over the different options to exit the area."

Hakim observed them as they reacted to the information with a mixture of excitement and anxiety. This was real now.

"What about the antidote?"

"In your pocket, you will have two syringes. Inject them into your thigh or buttocks right before you enter the terminal."

"Do we really know they work?" Jenna questioned.

"They were issued by the military for their soldiers in the Middle East. So yes, they were tested."

Hakim's eyes lingered on Jenna. "Is there any doubt in your mind, Jenna?"

She didn't flinch. "No. I'm ready."

"Good. Because we are committed to this attack. From the beginning it was understood, if needed, every one of us is willing to die a martyr for the Jihad."

A moment of silence ensued while they took in the information.

"When are we getting the guns?" Jamal asked.

"Tonight. We don't use them unless there is no other choice. Got it?"

They nodded and Abdul spoke up. "If everything goes off as planned, what will be our next move?"

"Abboud has arranged for us to leave the country. We can't stay here. You can be sure they'll be turning over every rock looking for us."

"Where will we go?" Maggie asked.

"Some place safe. I should find out by the end of the day."

****

With the meeting over, Hakim went back to his room and called Abboud. As usual, the phone rang several times with no response. And as usual, he hung up, sat and waited. Five minutes later his phone rang.

"Give me good news, Nephew."

"We are all set to go, Uncle." Hakim told him about the sarin test on the homeless man. Abboud grunted his approval.

"Did you get rid of the Iraqi?" he asked.

"Not yet." He hesitated. "What if we still need him?"

"No, it's time, Nasir. Do it," Abboud ordered.

"The men want to know what comes next."

"After the attack, call the number I sent you last month. They will give you an exact pick up point. Soon you will be home."

Hakim frowned. "Home?"

"Somalia. Our new home, Nephew."

Hakim smiled. "Thank you, Uncle."

"We won't speak again before then. *Inshallah!*

"*Inshallah!*" Hakim said.

He found Mohamed in the living area and they went into his bedroom. He closed the door behind them. "Do you have your gun?" he asked.

Mohamed nodded.

"We have to kill the Iraqi," Hakim said.

"Now?"

"Yeah. We don't need him anymore."

"Do you want me to do it?" Mohamed asked.

Hakim nodded. " Take him out by the walled area in the courtyard and shoot him. When you're done, bag him, load him on the truck. Abdul and Jamal will dispose of both bodies later tonight."

Chapter Thirty-Four

"So, you're going to write a follow up on the Russian arrests?" Art asked after Jessie relayed her conversation with the FBI agent. They were sitting in his office and she was about to respond when Susan Blandish, her cheeks flushed, poked her head in.

"Do you have a minute?"

"What is it?" Art asked curtly.

Everybody knew the old man hated to be interrupted when he was busy. Jessie started doodling on her note pad.

"Just heard from my contact at the Sheriff's office. They found two bodies in the Glades this morning—"

Art cut in impatiently. "So what else is new?"

Bodies in the Everglades were as common as alligators. As a matter of fact, they often were the first ones to find them. Susan ignored him and went on. "A couple of kids were out there fishing when they stumbled across them. They were partially out of the water. Supposedly, they still had a few pieces of trash bags tied to them. This is where it gets interesting. My contact said one of them was really weird, looking like one of those zombies on Walking Dead."

Jessie's head shot up. "What do you mean?"

"He wasn't sure. The lab guys showed up in hazmat suits. They set up a tent and a shower. Everybody who had any contact with the bodies was isolated and had to get some kind of treatment. He said they whisked the kids away, rushed them to the hospital and they're being kept in quarantine. It was all very hush hush, then the next thing you know, the FBI shows up," Susan added excitedly.

Jessie glanced over at Art and their eyes met.

"Nerve gas?" he ventured.

She nodded. "Could be."

Susan gasped. "You knew about this?"

"No, not about these men. We were aware there was a possibility someone was planning to make nerve gas."

The woman's eyes grew bigger. "You mean sarin, like what Saddam Hussein used on the Kurds in the Middle East?"

"I'm afraid so," Jessie replied soberly.

"Damn, that's pretty terrifying."

Jessie got up. "Any chance your friend gave you the location of the bodies?"

Susan shook her head. "He could already be in trouble for telling me as much as he did. But he likes me. He asked me out for a date. The sheriff warned all his guys to keep this under wrap."

"If this man was killed by nerve gas and the word spreads, it could create a major panic," Art stated somberly.

He turned back to Susan. "Maybe you should call back this fellow, tell him you're good for a date."

Susan made a face. "I don't think so, Art. He's nice but he's old,"

"How old?"

"I don't know, like you maybe."

Art moaned. "Oh geez."

Jessie could hardly stifle a laugh as she headed for the door. "I'm going to call Perrone, see what he knows."

She went back to her desk, dialed the detective, and got his messaging. "Hey Sam. It's Jessie. I need to talk to you. Call me as soon as you can."

Next she phoned Liam. He answered right away.

"Remember Oksana mentioned the Russian gave chemicals and hazmat suits to Hakim?"

"Yeah?"

"Two bodies just turned up in the Everglades and from the information we have so far, it seems at least one of them was exposed to a deadly chemical. According to our source, he's like a zombie. I think Hakim either got his hands on some sort of nerve gas or he's making it himself."

"How the hell would he know how to make such a thing?"

"Are you kidding? It wouldn't surprise me for a minute if the instructions were on the internet."

"And you think they made a trial run?" Liam asked.

"Possibly. Or the guy got poisoned while handling it."

He considered the information for a moment. "Can you find out more about it?"

"I called Sam, left a message. I'm hoping he'll call me back soon."

"Let me know when he does," Liam said.

At noon, when she hadn't heard back from Perrone, Jessie was chomping at the bit. She had to find out something. So she called Boyd and got his recording. Out of desperation, she located Sonia

Estrada's business card in her purse and dialed her cell phone. After a couple of rings, the Agent answered.

"Agent Estrada, this is Jessie Milner. I'm sure you're busy, so I'll cut right to the chase. The two bodies found in the Everglades this morning, did they die of exposure to nerve gas?"

"Where did you get this information?" the woman asked coldly.

"We have our sources. Can you please answer my question? The public has the right to know if their lives are endangered by a deadly chemical."

"Ms. Milner, we have not yet determined the exact cause of death of those individuals, so do not speculate on something you don't know. Everything we are doing at this point is done out of precaution."

Jessie sighed in frustration. "So, you're not going to deny or confirm they were killed by some sort of chemical exposure?"

"We do not deal in vagueness. Once we have the facts, we will pass on the information. Trust me, if we find out the public is at risk, we will let them know. Now, you'll excuse me. I happen to be very busy."

She was gone before Jessie could retort. She hadn't expected much and got even less. Still, she was upset. She had to find out what was going on.

She called Perrone back again and this time, he answered. He sounded tired and testy.

"It's about the bodies found in the Glades this morning. We hear they may have been exposed to some deadly chemical. What do you know, Sam?"

He sighed, and she worried he was going to brush her off. "Jessie, you can't publish any of this, not now anyway, okay?"

"I got it. You know you can trust me," she promised.

"The word just came in. It was sarin."

"The same sarin they are using in the Middle East to kill thousands of innocent people?"

"Not exactly."

She was taken aback. "Then what was it?"

"It wasn't the same sarin. They tell us it was a much stronger strain."

"Oh my God. Do you think it's Hakim?"

"They're pretty sure it's him."

"Did they get an I.D. on the bodies?"

"Not yet. One of them looked like he was gassed. But it seems like a gator got to him first. The lower half of his body was gone. The other man didn't die of sarin exposure. He was shot to death. It was lucky those kids found them when they did or both bodies would have disappeared in the next few hours. Gators are always on the prowl. They don't waste time."

"How long do you think they were out there?" she asked cautiously.

"According to the coroner, just a few hours. It's serious enough for the FBI to call a meeting with all the South Florida law enforcement agencies this afternoon. I would say they're worried. Now Hakim has proof the sarin is working. It could mean something is about to happen real soon and we've got to get ready for it."

"An attack?"

"Exactly. The trouble is how to try and narrow it down to a time and a target. There are just too many possibilities."

"Like a mall or a theater? My God, it is really frightening when you think of it. And they still aren't getting any closer on finding Hakim?" she asked.

"Everybody is looking for him. So far, no luck."

"What time is the meeting?" Jessie asked.

"Three o'clock."

"Where?"

"Jessie, you can't be there."

She sighed in exasperation. "I know. Will you call me when you find out something?"

He hesitated.

"Please, Sam. I'm partially responsible."

"Why?"

"If I hadn't led Hakim to the diamonds, he might not have had the means to get the nerve gas."

"Trust me, he would have found a way. I'm sure he's not in this alone. During the Russian's interrogation, the FBI found out he provided him with six passports. And the diamond heist proves there is overseas involvement as well. Looks like we're all going to be busy."

All afternoon, she kept an eye on the clock. Four o'clock came and went and her phone didn't ring. Unable to sit at her desk any longer, she signaled to Art she was leaving. She went home, changed into a tank top and shorts, and took off for the beach.

Usually the sight of the ocean was a calming force. Not today. Her mind wouldn't let her relax. Thoughts of a sarin attack taking place anywhere, anytime, were terrifying. After walking for a couple of miles, she stopped, sat down, took some deep breaths, and stared ahead. Small sand pipers ran along the edge of the water, chasing the waves and the tiny insects left in their wake.

For them life was only a matter of getting the next

bite of food, surviving one moment at a time. For humanity, it was somewhat more complicated. Knowing something evil was about to happen tied her stomach in knots.

Her phone rang and she answered anxiously.

"The meeting is at the FBI building in Plantation," Liam whispered.

"Where are you?"

"I'm there now. I don't want anyone to hear me."

"How did you find out where it was?"

"A friend on the Plantation Police force told me. It's not like they could hide it. There are so many cops here right now, it looks they are having a convention."

"So what are you doing?"

"I'm hanging around in the lobby. Trying to glean some information from some of the uniforms I know. Not too successful at this point. They're not exactly in the loop either."

"Is the meeting still going on?" she asked anxiously.

"I believe so. Let's put it this way, no one has left so far."

Jessie glanced at her watch. It was six o'clock. "This is really dragging on."

"Three hours is a long time. My instincts tell me it should be over soon—"

He stopped talking abruptly.

"Liam?"

"Here they come. I'll call you right back," he said softly before hanging up.

She went back to eyeing the ocean and the birds, wondering if Liam would be able to find out anything. It seemed like an eternity before he called back.

"How did you do?" she asked.

"I caught Sam on the way out. We talked about five minutes."

"And?"

"How about we catch some dinner and I'll tell you?"

"You're making me wait till then?"

"Only a short while, I promise," he assured her.

Jessie glanced over at the sandpipers and sighed. "We might as well eat. I've been watching the birds feasting on their meager food source for the past hour now. It seems like a whole lot of work for so little reward. They must be exhausted at the end of the day."

He laughed. "Where are you?"

"At the beach. Thought I could find some peace here. It's not happening, so I'm heading home."

An hour later Liam picked her up and they were on their way to Olé Olé Mexican Grill on West Broward Boulevard. He stubbornly insisted on waiting to talk about the meeting until they were seated in a booth. The waiter hovered, and they placed orders for margaritas and a platter of super nachos. As soon as he left, Jessie glared at him.

"Okay, enough waiting. Tell me what you know, right now."

He shook his head. "It's not very encouraging. With no more to go on than what they have presently, they are flying blind on this one. Sam said they tossed around a number of possible targets. They agreed one site clearly stood out."

"Which is?"

He glanced around the room carefully. There was no one within earshot. "The Hard Rock Stadium."

Jessie frowned. "Why the Stadium?"

"There is a big concert scheduled for Saturday night. It's sold out and the Stadium holds over 65,000 people. It would be a devastating attack."

Leaning back in her seat, Jessie considered the possibility. The stadium, located in Miami Gardens, south of Ft Lauderdale and west of I-95, had undergone a five hundred million dollar renovation just the year before. Now boasting a new canopy, all new seating, and four giant, high-definition scoreboards at the top of each corner of the stadium, it was a beautiful arena.

The waiter brought their food and drinks and Jessie stared silently at her glass, still trying to absorb this information. "What is their plan?"

Liam shrugged. "Sam didn't say. He just wanted to remind us we are both bound to secrecy on this for now."

Jessie creased her brow. "So they're going to pool all their resources to make the stadium safe. Still, how can they be sure that's the target?"

"They're not. They just don't have many other options."

Jessie shook her head in doubt. "I don't know. With a venue that big, security would be tight anyway. Getting past them would seem impossible."

"You think they may have a different target in mind?"

"According to Sam, Hakim got fake passports from the Russian. In my opinion, it means he's planning to get away. Even under normal circumstances, the stadium has a big police presence. An attack there would be nothing short of a suicide mission."

"So, where else?"

"The concert is Saturday night's big event. Of course, it could be any other place or any other day for that matter," she said. With little appetite left, Jessie paid scant attention to their food, unable to keep her mind off a possible sarin attack. "What can we do?" she asked.

"Not much, Jessie, other than hope they catch Hakim before any of this comes to pass."

They left the restaurant soon after and she asked him to drop her off at the cottage.

"Are you sure you're okay?" he asked, frowning in concern.

"Not really."

"Do you want me to stay?" he asked, pulling up in front of her home.

She shook her head. "I have to give this some more thought. It's best if I'm alone for a while."

He reached over, pulled her forward and kissed her forehead. "I understand. Try not to fret too much. With every cop in a hundred-mile radius looking for Hakim, maybe they'll get lucky and catch him before anything happens."

Chapter Thirty-Five

"Bobby, this is Nasir Hakim. Do you remember our encounter at the computer shop?"

"I remember," the man stammered.

"Good. And you also remember our conversation about those containers? Or barrels as you called them."

"Uh-huh."

"I'm glad you have a good memory. After all, we wouldn't want those naughty pictures to get out. Years in prison can really take their toll on a man, especially a pedophile. Don't you agree?"

Bobby didn't answer but Hakim heard his labored breathing. He smiled. "Of course you do. So, this is what you will do. After you get to work tomorrow night, place two of those barrels in each recess you marked on the map of Terminal Eighteen, and an additional two on the other wall. Six barrels all together. Got it?"

The man's panting got frantic.

"Bobby? Calm down. Do not get excited. Do you hear me?" Hakim snapped

"Yes. Tomorrow night, Friday. Six barrels. I'll do it," he whimpered. "Will you get rid of the pictures then?"

"Sure, Bobby. There is one more thing. When you get off work tomorrow morning, go to the car rental at the corner of 441 and Broward Blvd. I arranged for you to pick up a passenger van. It's all paid for, and it's being held under your name. Drive it home and leave it there. Call me after you place the barrels and I'll give you the rest of the instructions."

"And then you'll give me back my laptop?" Bobby asked plaintively.

"Call me after you place the barrels in Terminal Eighteen," Hakim said tersely."

****

Bobby made an effort to pull himself out of his chair but his legs shook. After a couple of tries, he finally stood up. His head was spinning, and he thought he was going to faint. Holding on to the wall, he slowly made his way to the kitchen. He opened the door of the cabinet under the sink. The bottle of vodka stood in the back behind a box of dishwashing powder and a can of bug spray. He pushed them aside and reached for the bottle with a trembling hand. Gripping it close to his chest, he made it back into the living room and collapsed into his chair. Unscrewed the cap and took a swig. Then another. He did this until the bottle was nearly empty. But all the vodka in the world couldn't erase the conversation he had with Hakim. *Put the barrels in Terminal Eighteen on Friday night.* He knew only too well what Saturday was. The maiden cruise for the *Wonder of the Seas.* Departure terminal, Number Eighteen. Number of passengers, five thousand four hundred.

Suddenly Bobby was terrified. He threw the vodka bottle across the room and it shattered against the wall, glass flying in every direction. A small shard lodged in his forehead and a trickle of blood ran down his face. He didn't even notice. His chin dropped on his chest and he sobbed.

****

"Did you get it done?" Hakim asked.

"I just left the terminal. The barrels are in there. I put them the way you wanted," Bobby answered in a feeble voice.

It was two a.m., but Hakim picked up the phone as soon as he called and he wondered if the Arab had been waiting for it to ring. Bobby climbed back into the maintenance cart.

"And you picked up the van, right?"

"It's at my house," Bobby said.

"At eleven fifteen tomorrow morning, you drive it over to 14th Street, inside the port, and you wait for us."

"Us? What do you mean us?" Bobby stammered.

"There will be six of us."

"You didn't say that before," the man whined.

"It makes no difference to you, understand? If you want to stay out of jail, you'll do as you're told," Hakim growled.

"Okay, okay. Don't get mad," Bobby whimpered.

"Tomorrow, Bobby. Be there."

Bobby didn't answer. He didn't have to. The man knew he would do as asked. He was weak and despicable, and Hakim knew that as well.

As he tucked his phone in his pocket, a fiery bolt of lightning lit up the sky. Thunder rumbled all around him. Bobby cringed. It started raining and he shrugged. What did it matter? Maybe it would be best if he got struck tonight and died. That way he would never have to find out what horrible thing he was a part of. He started the engine and drove away from the terminal.

Chapter Thirty-Six

The rain pounding on the roof brought her out of a restless slumber. The bright dial of the clock on the night stand read four a.m. Troubling thoughts were quick to spring up in her mind. There would be no more sleep on this night. Wide awake now, she probed the shadows in the room, looking for nonexistent answers.

If the FBI was right, this could be the day they would face a horrific disaster. Unable to stay in bed any longer, Jessie got up and went to the kitchen. She made a cup of coffee and peered out the window. It was a gloomy sight. Puddles stood on the patio cement and the wet outdoor furniture glistened in the dark. Although the rain had stopped for the moment, an ominous sky, swollen with rain clouds, stared back at her, threatening more of the same.

Back at the kitchen table, she turned on her laptop and sipped the hot brew, hoping the sameness of a Saturday morning routine would somehow allay the fear of the unknown. Scanning the local news online, she saw no mention of the possibility of an attack. So far, the police had managed to keep the information under wrap. Checking the weather report next, she found out there was a fifty percent chance of rain and wondered if it could be bad enough to cancel the concert. In that case, it might give the FBI and the police more time to find Hakim before he could carry out his deadly mission.

Five o'clock rolled around and she considered calling Liam, then decided against it. There was no sense in waking him so early. Instead she caught up her notes on the Dariel Thomas story. Lilly crept into her mind and she sighed. Her time with the child was limited now as her aunt's arrival was scheduled for the following week. Her sole consolation was knowing Lilly would live on a farm with a loving family and lots of pets to share her affection.

Having trouble concentrating, Jessie stopped typing, and went to the patio door. A look at the sky revealed tinges of daylight filtering through the clouds. While she stood there, the rain returned with a new-found fury. Violent gusts pelted the windows in angry waves. She went back to the kitchen and had another cup of coffee.

Finally, a little after six thirty, as if a gloomy curtain had been lifted, the rain stopped and the sky cleared. It turned into a brilliant blue as the sun emerged on the horizon, bringing brightness and hope with it once again.

Jessie threw on shorts and a tank top, grabbed her sandals on the way out, and headed to the beach. A formation of pelicans glided past, high above the beachline, and she followed their flight until they disappeared. After a few miles, Jessie took a seat under a slender palm, enjoying the briny morning air. She gazed south and noticed an oil tanker on its way to the port. A short distance behind it, the gleaming white silhouette of a cruise ship came into view. As it got nearer, she was amazed at its sheer size, then realized it was the *Wonder of the Seas* the newest, biggest cruise ship ever built. Unease crept into her every nerve cell. The ship was scheduled to leave Ft. Lauderdale today for its maiden voyage to the Western Caribbean.

All at once, a devastating image ran through her mind. What better target than a ship at sea with five thousand four hundred passengers aboard and no way for them to escape? What better place to release sarin gas? By the time the police could reach it, it would be too late. She sighed. Was paranoia finally getting the best of her? Her feeling of dread increased as the ship glided elegantly into the port.

She glanced at her watch. It was seven thirty. She reached for her phone and realized she left it on the kitchen counter. She got up and headed back. As soon as she got home, she would call Liam, share her concern with him. As she walked, different scenarios played out in her mind. It was overwhelming.

No matter what, she had to talk to someone, even if it meant appearing crazy. Without realizing it, she had broken into a run, her body's alarm taking control. She made it back to the cottage in a half hour. Still out of breath, she dialed Liam's phone and got his answering machine. Maybe he was in the shower. She left a brief message for him to call before remembering he had mentioned a meeting in Coconut Creek this morning. Unable to sit still, she dialed Sam Perrone. He picked up after a couple of rings.

"Hey, Jessie, what's up?" he asked sounding apprehensive.

"Sam…" she said, hesitating, anxiety mounting in her chest.

A note of concern crept into his voice. "What's wrong?"

"You may think this sounds far-fetched, but I just went for a walk on the beach and the new cruise ship was coming into the port. Today is its maiden voyage and by this afternoon there will be more than five thousand passengers aboard, plus all the employees, another two thousand people or so. What if that's their target?"

He was silent for a moment and her heart sank. Nonetheless, she persisted. "Sam, just think about it. They could release the gas in the whole interior of the ship before the passengers would even know what was happening. It's possible, isn't it?"

"It's possible, but not really feasible. First they would have to get the gas aboard the ship. Their security is really tight prior to boarding. I can't imagine they would get past it."

"But it could happen," she insisted.

"Frankly, I don't see it," he said bluntly.

She saw there was no point in pushing any further. "Is the FBI getting things under control for the concert tonight?"

He sighed. "It's total chaos right now. By this afternoon, though, we should be better organized. We've mobilized all the surrounding areas police forces, Palm Beach, Dade, and Broward. Everybody entering the arena tonight is going to be scrutinized, and then scrutinized some more. Also, we'll have a no fly zone for five miles around. And the parking lot will be under heavy surveillance as well. If this is their intended target, they're going to have a nasty surprise."

She gasped. "You're already there?"

He chortled. "Everybody is already here."

"I hope you nab them and this will be the end of

it."

"Jessie, I don't know if the end of terror attacks will ever come about. We put out one fire just to see another one start."

"I wish you luck."

"Thanks. We need it," he said.

Jessie sat staring at her phone. Sam was right. Getting the nerve gas aboard the ship would be next to impossible, yet she couldn't quite let the idea go, wondering how good the security actually would be at the port. What if she checked it out herself? She had no plans for the day, and Liam hadn't called back yet.

She mused over the idea while eating a bowl of cereal. After a quick shower, she slipped on a pair of jeans and a T-shirt, pulled her hair up into a pony tail, grabbed her hand bag, and was ready to head out the door when Liam called back.

"Sorry, love, I was next door helping my neighbor. He's a nice old man, a widower. Unfortunately, he's nearly blind as a bat, and has two left hands to boot. While he went for a stroll early this morning, his dishwasher went on the fritz and flooded his kitchen. We pulled it out, cleaned up the mess and turned off the water until the plumber gets there. Just got back in and listened to your message. Is everything okay?"

Jessie filled him in on her suspicions. "Do you think it's a foolish idea?" she asked.

"Actually, I don't. It could be a target as much as the arena, or a mall or a supermarket. There are multiple possibilities."

"I was just leaving. I'm going there to get a look at the security myself."

"Do you want me to come along?" he asked.

"What about your appointment?"

"I could reschedule," Liam said.

"No, don't. Like you said, it's just one of many possible sites. I'm only going there to see from myself, satisfy my curiosity. You go ahead and we'll meet somewhere later."

"Are you sure?"

"Positive," she announced.

"Okay, keep me posted. I'm going to get cleaned up now. I'm pretty scuzzy at this point."

After talking to him, she wondered once more if her idea was just a waste of time. Nonetheless, she got in her car and left.

Traffic was dense this Saturday morning, and Jessie suspected the arrival of the ship had something to do with it. After all, more than five thousand people would soon be pouring into the port to start their cruise on the new ship. It was ten forty-five before she reached the port entrance and turned onto Eller Drive to join a long snaking line moving at a crawl pace. Each car had to stop at the security gate to present tickets and boarding passes to the guard on duty.

When it was her turn, Jessie showed him her press pass and told him she was writing a story on the new cruise ship. He glanced at it for a moment then handed it back with a grin. "Did you see it yet? It's pretty awesome. Me and the Mrs., we're planning on a cruise. Not this time though, it's too expensive yet for our budget."

"Yeah, it's quite impressive," Jessie said before thanking him and slowly driving away.

The signs ahead indicated the ship was docked at Terminal Eighteen located on the left, while the parking garage entrance was on the right. All cars were directed to the garage, and she would have to switch from the left lane to the right shortly.

Glancing at the rear-view mirror to watch for an opportunity to move over, she nearly froze when she caught sight of the driver of the car coming up on her right. It was Nasir Hakim, and he wasn't alone. Seated next to him was a young woman. Jessie slowed down, to give him the opportunity to pass her. When he was nearly even with her car, she tilted her head slightly sideways to shield her face. She needn't have worried. His attention was focused straight ahead. As he drove past, Jessie got a better look at his passenger, and the sight struck her like a lightning bolt. It was the IT tech from the Broward Sheriff's office. She couldn't remember her name, but there was no mistaking the face. Suddenly her heart was racing, her head spinning. This had to be the place. Why else would Hakim be here on this particular day? And now one thing was clear to her. During the whole investigation, the woman at his side fed him information from the police, keeping him one step ahead at all times. Jessie recalled the day Perrone caught her going through a desk. There was no more doubt in her mind—the terrorist plot involved the cruise ship, not the stadium. She had to get hold of the police quickly. But first, she had to remain calm. Taking a couple of deep breaths, she reached for her phone. As she did, the driver in the car behind her honked his horn impatiently and she hoped the sound hadn't alerted Hakim. She picked up her speed slightly while still avoiding moving up next to him.

They neared the parking garage and he took the lane on the right leading to the ramp. Jessie didn't want to go to the garage. Hakim could see her there and keep her from alerting the authorities. Instead, she veered to the left toward the terminal. She drove a short distance, pulled over and dialed Perrone. The phone rang and rang before going to voice mail. Frustrated, she called Liam, with the same result. He had mentioned taking a shower. Realizing she still hadn't entered the FBI's numbers into her new phone, she started dialing 911.

"Hey, miss, you got to move, this ain't no parking area."

Jessie nearly jumped out of her seat. She hadn't seen the security guard pull up next to her on his golf cart. Arms crossed tightly over his chest, he wore a stern frown on his long narrow face.

"I'm sorry, this is a real emergency. I have to make a phone call right away," Jessie exclaimed.

"Yeah, well, it's gonna have to wait. You can't stay here. You just turn around and go back to the parking garage. You drove right by it, you know. I don't see how you could have missed it," he scoffed.

"Look, I need to call the police," Jessie insisted.

His eyebrows shot up. "The police? Really? What the hell for?"

"It's a matter of national security. I have to reach the FBI."

He sat back and shook his head in obvious disgust. "I can't believe what some people will do and say when they want to get their way. This is your last chance, Missy. If you don't get out of here, I'm going to have you arrested."

"Good," Jessie shouted angrily. "Call the police, right now. Tell them to patch you through to the FBI. Ask for Agent Williams, tell them it's Jessie Milner and tell them Nasir Hakim is at Port Everglades. Hurry up, or there's going to be a terrorist attack on the *Wonder of the Seas*, and you'll be responsible."

Suddenly the man seemed taken aback by her tone of urgency. "This better be true..." he grumbled wearily as he dialed a number. "I have a woman here who says there's going to be a terrorist attack right here at Port Everglades. Yeah, yeah, she says it's gonna be on the *Wonder of the Seas*. She wants us to contact an FBI agent, Williams..."

He paused. "What?"

Nodding, he listened to the other party on the line, then looked at Jessie. "What's his first name?"

"Bruce. Special Agent Bruce Williams. Tell them to hurry."

He relayed the information, listened for a moment and turned back to her. "And your name again?"

"Jessie Milner."

He repeated her name, then waited for a response before he continued. "Yeah, boarding is at Terminal Eighteen."

With a frightened look in his eyes now, he listened some more and waited. A moment went by and it seemed like an eternity. Jessie sighed, irritated.

"What's going on? We're wasting time here, are they getting the FBI?"

The old man opened his mouth to answer, then glanced back at Jessie, nodding. "Yeah, she's here. Hold on."

He handed her the phone. "They want to talk to you."

Jessie nearly ripped it out of his hand. "This is Jessie Milner. I'm a reporter for the *Broward News*.

Who am I speaking to?"

"My name is Special Agent George Palmer. I know who you are. Are you certain the man you saw was Nasir Hakim?"

She could hardly contain her exasperation. "Listen to me, there is no doubt it was him. I am absolutely positive. You must hurry and get here before it's too late. We're talking sarin. There will be more than five thousand people on that ship and if he gets on board, lots of them are going to die. Did you get hold of Agent Williams?"

"Calm down, we're trying to reach him as we speak. Pretty much everybody is at the stadium. But agents will be there shortly. In the meantime, you stay put. Don't attempt to do anything, do you hear me?"

Jessie handed the phone back to the security guard.

"What did he say?" the man asked.

Jessie looked at Terminal Eighteen, a short distance away. "They're on their way. I'm supposed to meet them at the Terminal."

The guard frowned suspiciously. "I don't think that's a good idea. And you can't just leave your car here."

Jessie grabbed her handbag and jumped out. "Then you move it. I already told you this is an emergency, damn it!" she shouted over her shoulder and briskly took off toward the terminal.

On her way, she dialed Sam Perrone again, but got no answer. This time, she left a message. "Sam, it's Jessie. Nasir Hakim is at Port Everglades with the IT Tech who works at the Sheriff's department. I don't remember her name, but it was her. I saw them, Sam. They drove into the parking garage near Terminal

Eighteen. I'm going there now to see if I can find them. The target is not the stadium, it's the cruise ship. Call me back."

As she got closer, she saw people pouring out of the parking garage and heading toward the terminal to join the long line already waiting to get inside. A buzz of excitement rose from the crowd when they got a better look at the huge ship docked alongside the pier, the source of their enjoyment for the next seven days. Chatter and laughter echoed through the air, and Jessie shuddered. If she was right, this could all turn into a horrifying scene at any moment.

Stationed at the entrance to the terminal, two cruise line employees, both of them senior citizens, scanned tickets before sending passengers into two separate lines. Since most of them were directed left, Jessie guessed the passengers guided to the right were repeat customers with special passes for an accelerated boarding. Jessie stepped closer to glance inside the building and was met by angry stares from the crowd, a clear warning about jumping the line. Slowly she made her way toward the exit from the parking garage, scrutinizing everybody as she walked past them. She didn't see Hakim or the woman among them. Guessing they already were in the building, Jessie rushed back to the entrance and approached the attendant closest to her. "Excuse me."

Busy examining the ticket he was holding, the old man peered at her with watery eyes and frowned in annoyance. "Yes?" He glowered.

"I have to get inside, it's an emergency," she said urgently.

Glancing at the waiting passengers, he shook his

head and pointed at the line. "Miss, all these people were here first. You'll have to wait for your turn."

"No, I can't. I have to get in right now," she said, brushing past him. There was no more time for explanations or guilt.

"Call the police," she shouted over her shoulder. "There is a terrorist inside the terminal. Call now!"

Chapter Thirty-Seven

"Over there," Jenna said, pointing at a parking space.

Hakim nodded, drove around the corner to the fourth floor, and pulled into the available spot. The garage was filling up fast, with a long line of cars still lined up on the ramp behind him. They got out, retrieved their backpacks from the trunk, walked past the elevators, and took the stairs to the ground floor.

A few minutes later they were in line at the entrance of the terminal. When their turn came, the old man glanced at their tickets and waved them to the left. So far, so good, everything was going as planned. The cavernous room was already crowded, passengers moving slowly inside the cordoned off area toward the security check point. He guessed close to a thousand people were waiting for their turn at the security check, with more coming in all the time.

Turning his attention to the west wall, he spotted two large yellow barrels in a recessed area and grinned. Bobby had done his job. Weaving their way through the crowds they reached the restrooms where they had a good view of the entrance. Hakim glanced at his watch. It was eleven twenty and no sign of the others.

"Where are they?" Jenna's question reflected his own concerns.

"I don't know. They should be here anytime. Keep

an eye on the entrance. We can't miss them."

"And if they don't make it?" she asked.

He looked at her for a moment, hesitating. Her face was set in a dark scowl.

"If they don't, we should go ahead anyway," she said abruptly.

"Our cylinders won't be enough to—"

"I don't care. We should take out as many as we can," she said abruptly.

Surprised by her sudden determination, he was about to respond when he tensed up.

Jenna stared at him. "What's wrong?"

He didn't answer, instead, he grabbed her arm and pulled her in the direction of the barrels. Luckily Bobby had left enough room between them and the wall so they could slide behind them. Ignoring Jenna's frowning face, he took off his backpack, propped it against the wall and motioned for her to do the same. Despite the ice-cold air in the terminal, heavy beads of sweat clustered on his forehead. He crouched down further. Puzzled by his behavior, Jenna just stood there.

"Get down," he growled.

She lowered herself beside him. "What is it? What did you see?"

"It's that damn reporter."

"Jessie Milner?"

He nodded.

Jenna peered around the side of the container. "Are you sure? I don't see her."

Hakim ignored her. His mind was reeling. What was the woman doing here? Could it be a coincidence? There was no way she could have known about his plan. He leaned to the side and watched as Jessie moved through the crowd. All at once, she turned in their direction and he quickly pulled back. He waited a few anxious seconds, then looked again. She was walking toward the restrooms. She entered the men's room, came back out shortly before disappearing into the women's restroom. There was no doubt in his mind now; she was looking for someone. He checked his watch again, eleven twenty-five. The team should have been here by now. Hakim wiped his brow. A rush of apprehension tightened his throat. He forced himself to take a deep breath and turned his attention to the line in the cordoned off area. It was getting shorter and for some reason no one else was entering the terminal. More passengers were waiting out there, so what was going on?

Then, out of the corner of his eye, he saw the reporter step out of the women's restroom. The door closed behind her and she hesitated, turned to look in their direction... and stood staring at the barrels. He pulled Jenna closer but the damned woman set out in their direction anyway. Suddenly, the unmistakable screech of sirens blasted through the air, and his heart pounded with rage. That bitch! It was all her doing. He had a chance to kill her at the gazebo and instead, he let his feelings interfere with his decision. How could he have been so damn weak? He glanced at the cylinders, quickly running through his remaining options. With fewer passengers still waiting in the terminal, releasing the gas right now would guarantee few casualties while assuring his death. Not at all what he had in mind. No, that was pointless. For a brief moment he considered making a run for it. Then he got a glimpse of the SWAT team moving to block both the entrance and the exit, and knew how that scenario would play out. And last, staying put would leave them trapped against the wall with no recourse but to give up or be shot to death. So, with none of these options acceptable, he had to find another way and fast. Jessie was nearly upon them. He reached for the gun tucked in his jeans.

Chapter Thirty-Eight

Frustrated, Jessie stood thinking. After spending all that time scrutinizing the long lines of people waiting in the terminal, there had been no sign of Hakim or the woman. Could she have been wrong after all? Had she mobilized the police and the FBI for nothing? Pulled them away from the stadium where they truly might be needed?

No, it was no mistake. She saw Hakim. She was sure it was him. Could he have figured out a way to board the ship? She glanced around once more, her eyes lingering on the baggage checks area, the imaging portals, the metal detectors and all those security guards manning the access ramps. How on earth would he get past all that while transporting nerve gas? She shook her head. It was seemingly impossible. So what then?

Suddenly, she had another thought. What if Hakim only came to scope the area on this busy day? There was no better time to do so than during an actual boarding. And so far, nothing had indicated his attack would take place today. She stood still for a moment while doubt crept further into her mind. She glanced around the terminal once more and realized she had yet to check the restrooms. Walking quickly, she pushed open the door to the men's room. An older man was standing at one of the urinals. He turned to look at her and his face took on a shocked expression. Jessie glanced around. He was alone.

"Sorry," she said sheepishly as she exited.

The women's restroom was twenty feet away. Two women stood at the sinks, one busy washing her hands, the other one carefully applying make-up. Neither one looked up when she entered. There was a flush from one of the stalls and a teenager stepped out, flinging her long hair behind her. She looked at Jessie and smiled. It wasn't Hakim's companion. The other stalls were unoccupied.

She sighed and walked out. There was no sign of a police presence inside the terminal and she wondered if her requests to the FBI and the police had been ignored. At least she wouldn't have to go through a lengthy list of excuses and apologies about her theory. At that moment she heard sirens blaring, their shrieks echoing loudly throughout the terminal. Jessie groaned. Within seconds, members of a SWAT team, wearing body armor, protective helmets and gas masks, appeared in both doorways, pointing assault rifles and high caliber guns at the crowd. Passengers huddled in the terminal, staring at them in fear and confusion. One of the men held a bull horn.

"Please do not be alarmed. For everybody's safety, we will be evacuating the building at this time. We ask you to slowly come forward, in a single file, with your hands raised above your head. Once we clear you, you will be escorted to a waiting area until boarding resumes."

As passengers regrouped to form a line facing the exit, Jessie waited near the restrooms. There was no rush to get out there and try to explain. She was still looking around when her eyes landed on two yellow barrels sitting along the wall nearby. Intrigued, she headed in their direction. Half way there, she caught a slight movement from behind one of the barrels. Frowning, she stepped closer and found herself face to face with Nasir Hakim. Before she could emit a sound, he grabbed her, spun her around and put her neck in a choke hold. In the next moment, the cold metal of a gun pressed against her temple and fear rushed through her like a train out of control.

"Don't move," he growled. She barely heard him over the sound of her own blood pulsing in her ears.

"Drop the bag."

She let her purse slip to the floor and stood still. At first no one noticed. The passengers were still inching toward the doors, nervously waiting to exit the building. Then suddenly a deafening sound went off by Jessie's head. Pain surged in her ears. She cried out and the crowd stared at her with terrified eyes. Hakim held up his gun.

"No one moves, no one else leaves the building. This shot went to the ceiling. The next one will be for anyone disobeying my orders."

He tightened his grip on Jessie's throat. "And that includes you," he whispered in her ear.

"Please, I can't breathe," she pleaded.

Hakim relaxed his hold, just barely, and she sensed his tenseness. Despite the turmoil in her mind, she had to remain calm. She closed her eyes, took a deep breath and reopened them, determined to see this through. With her lips and mouth dry as sandpaper, she tried to hold back a cough, moving her head ever so slightly. As she did, Hakim brutally pulled her closer again, and pain shot into her neck.

Two large groups of passengers remained in the terminal. Their anxiety was almost palpable as they stood huddled against the wall. All at once, a man and a woman sprang away and ran toward the door. Hakim was on them immediately, aiming his gun in their direction.

"Stop or I'll take you down right now!" he shouted.

The couple froze. "Get back over there," Hakim ordered, motioning in the direction of the other passengers.

They promptly headed back and melded into their group. From the corner of her eye, Jessie caught sight of the bulky figure of Bruce Williams stepping cautiously into the terminal.

Hakim stiffened. "You take one more step and I'll put a bullet in her head," he warned, his gun back at Jessie's temple.

The FBI agent stopped and held up both hands in defense.

"No problem. I'm not armed," he said calmly. "I'm Special Agent Williams. Who am I speaking to?"

"You know who I am," Hakim retorted.

"Indeed, I believe I do. Nasir Hakim. May I call you Nasir?'

Hakim didn't answer and Williams went on. "Good, I take it you don't mind. I'm here to talk. Work things out together. But first, Nasir, I must ask you to release Ms. Milner and the rest of the passengers."

Hakim sneered. "Do you think I'm a fool? As soon as I turn them loose, you'll kill me."

Williams nodded soberly. "I understand your concern. So let me take their place and you can be assured nothing will happen to you."

"Do you really believe I would trust you?" Hakim said.

"Then let's work on coming to an agreement. You can start by telling me what your demands are and we will do whatever we can to accommodate them."

Hakim didn't hesitate. "A helicopter on the pier and $100,000 dollars in cash. Then I let the others go. The reporter stays with me until I reach my destination."

Williams shook his head. "No problem with the chopper and the money. However, Ms. Milner is not going with you."

Hakim's eyes flitted nervously around the room. Pulled tightly against his chest, Jessie shared the pounding of his heart, the tightening of his muscles. She sensed his desperation and knew this was not a man who wanted to die. She glanced at the Agent and hoped he realized it as well.

"Nasir, we will not do anything to endanger the life of our pilot. When you board this helicopter, you will be safe. You have my word," he stated calmly.

After a moment, Hakim nodded. "All right, I'll release her when I'm ready to take off."

Williams smiled. "Agreed. See, it's not difficult if we work together. But before we go on, we have to talk about the nerve gas. We know you had it with you. Where is it, Nasir?"

For a moment Hakim looked surprised. Williams smiled glumly. "Yes, we know all about it and unfortunately, we can't go any further in our negotiations unless you tell us where it is."

"If you try to trick me, I will release it. It's extremely potent and everyone here will die," Hakim threatened.

"No one has to die today, Nasir, including you, and I have no intention of tricking you. Tell me where it is and tell me where your friends are."

Hakim glanced over his shoulder. "Jenna is the only one here."

"Okay. Where is Jenna?"

Hakim opened his mouth to respond, but everyone's attention had shifted away from him. He turned to look. Emerging from behind the barrels, Jenna gripped a cylinder against her chest, one hand holding on to the release valve as she slowly walked toward the center of the terminal. When she got near Hakim, she came to a stop. Suddenly it seemed all sound had evaporated. A deadly silence ensued in the terminal. Jessie glanced her way. Standing perfectly still facing the entrance, the young woman was the picture of calm.

"What's in the cylinder, Jenna?" Williams asked quietly.

She sneered. "Death… for all of you."

The crowd gasped.

"If you release the gas, it will affect you as well," Williams warned.

Hakim scoffed. "No, it won't."

The agent nodded his understanding. "I see, you both took an antidote. But, let me remind you, there are SWAT teams armed to the teeth waiting out there for you. Antidote or not, you will not make it past them."

Hakim didn't answer.

"It doesn't have to come to that. We have an agreement, right? You get the money and a helicopter ride out of here, and you give us the sarin. Simple as that," Williams said.

Hakim nodded. "We do. But if you get any ideas about shooting us, you should remember I will have ample time to put a bullet through the reporter's brain. So, if I die, she dies as well."

Williams sighed. "Look, as I said before, we don't want anybody to die today. However, you have to surrender the sarin right now."

Hakim's breathing was getting shallower, and Jessie worried he would decide to release the gas after all. Finally he nodded.

"Jenna will hand it to you after we board the chopper."

"No, not acceptable. Do you have any other sarin containers?"

Hakim didn't respond.

"Unless you level with me, Nasir, we can't go on with our agreement." Williams said.

"There are three more cylinders behind the barrels," Hakim said.

"We need to get those out of here. First, Jenna, please put down the tank."

Hakim looked at the woman. "Jenna, do as he said."

She ignored him and started walking toward Williams.

"Stop and put it down Jenna!" the agent bellowed. She kept walking, her hand now moving closer to the release valve.

"Don't do this," the Agent warned.

"Jenna, no!" Hakim yelled.

The woman didn't answer, locked in a stare with the agent and getting closer.

All at once the roar of rotor blades resonated in the

clear sky and a deafening noise echoed throughout the building. Caught by surprise, Hakim released his hold ever so slightly. With every inch of energy left in her body, Jessie thrust her right elbow into his rib cage. He gasped in pain and loosened his grip some more. She struck again, harder, sharper, and this time he let go. Jessie pulled away, lost her balance and stumbled forward. There was only time for one thought on her way down to the hard cement floor, *guns*, then blackness took over.

When she opened her eyes, blurry faces were staring at her. A far away voice kept repeated the same refrain. "Jessie! Jessie! Are you okay?"

She answered. Her mouth felt full of cotton and only garbled words came out.

"Jessie?"

She closed her eyes, took one deep breath, then another. Opened them once more to see Liam anxiously gazing at her. "Are you okay?"

This time she nodded and smiled wanly. "What happened? Did I pass out?"

He grinned in relief. "Yeah. You scared the daylights out of me."

"Where's—" she stopped as she caught sight of the form sprawled on the floor next to her. Nasir Hakim's body was surrounded by a pool of blood. When she finally brought herself to look past him, she noticed another body a short distance away.

"Help me up, will you?" she said to Liam.

He pulled her to her feet and she walked over to take a look. Covered with blood, Jenna had been shot multiple times. Her thick black hair was sprawled around her, and her dark eyes were clouded by death.

"How—"

"They don't call them sharpshooters for nothing. The SWAT team stopped her. They had no choice. She was about to release the sarin. And the moment you pulled away from Hakim, they got him, too." Liam said.

Jessie sighed. "Is Sam here?"

"I'm right here."

She looked over her shoulder. The detective was standing behind her. He smiled at her.

"Did they secure all the sarin?" she asked.

"As far as we know, they got everything that was here. They carried backpacks. Each one of them had two cylinders with sarin. Besides the one Jenna had, they found three more behind the barrels."

"Was it just Hakim and Jenna?"

Sam shook his head.

"No, there were five more. After you alerted us, the FBI blocked all exits. No one was going anywhere. Four of them were caught in the lines between the entrances and the security gates. They also had backpacks with containers of nerve gas. Their plan was to release all of it inside the terminal at the same time. One of them, Abdul Malik, was shot and killed while making a run for it. Another individual, Bobby Metzer, was an employee of the Port Authority. Somehow, he got involved with Hakim. He was found sitting in a van on a nearby street, waiting to whisk them away after the attack. This was not meant to be a suicide mission. They clearly had planned a getaway, which was fortunate for us." What do you mean by fortunate?" Jessie asked.

"If Hakim had intended to die as a martyr, he

would not have hesitated to release the sarin, even after we showed up."

Jessie nodded. "And kill as many of us as he could."

"He was not quite the jihadist he imagined he was," Sam said.

"And now he's finding out there's no paradise or virgins waiting for him," Liam added.

"I think hell is a more appropriate place for him anyway," Sam said.

"How did you ever guess they were coming here?"

Jessie hadn't noticed Bruce Williams joining them. She shook her head. "I don't know exactly. I had a strange feeling when I saw the cruise ship pulling in the port this morning. I was wrong actually. I thought the attack was meant for the ship. Instead, it was obvious they planned on hitting the terminal all along."

"There was no way they could have gotten past the luggage check point with those backpacks, but the damage they would have done right here would have been horrific. An hour ago, there were nearly three thousand people in this building," Williams stated.

"Did you find out where they made the sarin?" Jessie asked.

The agent nodded. "According to one of them, Jamal Lufti, they set up their own lab, even brought in an Iraqi scientist to make the sarin. I guess they were holding his family hostage. Once he was done, they killed him. Lufti gave us the address, and a special terrorism task force unit is on their way there right now. We hope to get a lot more information once they get in there."

Jessie sighed. "Why?"

"There is no easy answer. According to what we know right now, they were all Americans. Yet the influence of the ISIS propaganda fed their hatred, and their discontent with real or perceived grievances. Unfortunately, there will be more like them. There always will be more," Williams said somberly.

Despite the fact that every part of her body ached from the ordeal, Jessie wanted nothing more than to get out of there. She had a job to do, and she had to do it quickly, before the rest of the media got hold of the story.

"I have to call Art, right now," she said, then realized she didn't have her phone. She checked her pockets, glanced around the floor.

"Is this what you're looking for?" Liam asked, waving it in front of her.

"Where was it?"

"Right over here, you must have dropped it when Hakim got ah—you know," he said hesitating.

She smiled. "Go ahead, you can say it. He had a choke hold on me. I had just pulled the phone out of my purse when he grabbed me. I also dropped my bag. It's got to be around here somewhere."

She reached for the phone impatiently and punched in Art's number.

"Jesus, Jessie, is that you?" he yelled.

She held the phone away from her ear.

"Yes, it's me, and you don't have to shout. My hearing is still sound."

"Well, I see you've still got the same mouth on you, so you must be all right. Perrone called and told me you were held hostage at the Port. How the hell did you get yourself into this situation?"

She went on to tell him a condensed version.

"Art, I'll be at the office in a half hour or so—" She glanced over at Williams who was shaking his head at her.

"Sorry, you're going to be tied up with us for a while," he said.

"Listen, the FBI won't let me leave yet. I'll be there as soon as I can. Don't go anywhere."

"Get everything you can from them. I'll have Susan come in and stick around until you get here."

"Okay. She gets to write the article, but I want a personal storyline on the front page. You owe me, Art."

"You got it."

"See you soon," she said with a grin of satisfaction before noticing Liam staring at her.

"What?" she asked.

"Ten minutes ago, this terrorist had you hostage, ready to kill you at the drop of a hat, and here you are, back in full reporter mode. I don't know how you do it. Aren't you the least bit shook up?"

She shrugged. "Of course I am. The idea of going home and taking a nap sounds great. But this is more important than my being tired and besides, there's no way I could sleep anyway. Not after all of this."

"Ms. Milner?"

Williams was standing at her elbow, Estrada at his side. Jessie was surprised to actually see a smile on her face.

"Is this yours?" she asked, holding up a handbag.

Jessie nodded. "Thanks."

"Agent Estrada is going to take you through the next few steps. Just outside the building there is a medic on standby who will be checking to make sure you are physically unharmed. When you're done, she will take your initial statement. Next, we'll go over it to make sure we didn't forget anything. And then you may go," Williams said.

Jessie sighed. "Fine. You have to give me some information as well."

Williams frowned. "About what?"

"About the terrorists."

"Ms. Milner, I told you as much as I can right now. We don't know if we have the whole cell yet."

"You promised me the full story when we first met."

"And you will get it. In due time. Right now, you'll have to content yourself with what you have."

She realized he wasn't going to relent at this point, and took off for the ambulance parked outside. The medic was a slim man with a goatee. He checked her over, noted the bruises on her neck and asked her a myriad of questions, to all of which she responded in the negative. After a while, he seemed satisfied, although he shook his head. "You're one lucky young woman. He could have easily crushed your larynx with this kind of hold."

"He didn't and I'm okay," she responded, thinking only of escaping this whole routine, and getting back to the office.

When they left the medic, they went back inside the terminal and found a couple of chairs away from the throng of policemen, FBI agents and SWAT teams, all of them still coming down from the tension of a near disaster. Jessie repeated her story and Estrada took notes.

A half hour later, Williams strolled over, read her

statement, asked a couple more questions, then gave her the go-ahead to leave, saying they would be in touch soon.

With a sigh of relief, Jessie started walking out, then stopped suddenly and took a last look around. The inside of the terminal was nearly empty now except for a team of investigators gathering evidence and a few FBI agents. All at once, anxiety gripped her chest and she had to leave. She found Liam and Perrone talking on the side of the building.

"I'm going to the office. Art is waiting for me," she announced abruptly.

From the looks on their faces, it was obvious they disagreed with her decision, but realized there was no point in trying to dissuade her.

"Call me later," Liam said as she walked away, and she nodded.

Her car was still parked where she'd left it. A couple of Ft Lauderdale cops were lingering nearby and walked up as soon as she approached. Politely, one of them asked for her driver's license, checked it and returned it with an apologetic grin. "Sorry. We have to check out everybody coming in or out, no exceptions."

She smiled back. "Believe me, I'm glad you are doing so."

"It was you, wasn't it?"

When she didn't respond, he continued. "It was you with the terrorist? I don't know how you kept your cool like you did. Then, how you made your move so the sniper could get him."

She shrugged. "It's over, thank goodness."

Driving past all the police vehicles parked along the sides of the road, she had to stop once more at the security gate for an ID check before finally reaching US1 and heading downtown. *It's over,* she told herself again, irritated at the tears streaming down her cheeks. She pulled into the parking garage and killed the engine. She sat there, suddenly choked by emotions. It was everything at once, knowing death had only been steps away, the tension tightening her chest through the morning's long and fearful hours, then seeing the lifeless bodies of Hakim and Jenna lying on the cold concrete. And now, finally letting herself acknowledge it was over indeed.

After a few more minutes, she wiped away the last of the tears, stepped out of the car and glanced up. High above, a solitary hawk, wings spread wide, glided by in a seamless blue sky. She kept her eyes on him for a while, and soon he was gone.

Chapter Thirty-Nine

Stepping out of the stairwell, she spotted them sitting at her desk, Art in her chair, Susan at his side. She pushed past the glass doors and they both turned to watch her walk toward them. As she approached, he shook his head at her. "Just this once, couldn't you have taken the elevator?"

"I take it all the time, Art. Today I needed the walk."

"Yeah, sure. Pull over a chair and sit down," he ordered.

Susan scrutinized her face, concern reflecting in her eyes. "We understand you had quite a morning. Are you okay?"

Art held up his hand. "Wait. Before you get started, I don't want to hear the abbreviated version of your adventure. Sue, you're going to record this, then you'll write the article. Jessie, you'll write your story in the first person."

"Front page," Jessie reiterated.

He nodded. "Absolutely. Tomorrow, Sunday edition."

Susan set up her phone and was ready to record by the time Jessie pulled over another chair. She plopped down and started talking. Surprisingly, Art didn't interrupt her once. When she was done, Susan grabbed her phone and went back to her desk. Art and Jessie stayed seated, their eyes met and he smiled, a rare sight on his normally dour face.

"You know, I never doubted I made a good decision when I hired you, but this"—he shook his head—"this is something else. You're a hell of a reporter, Jessie Milner, and I'm glad you made it out in one piece."

"Thanks, Art. Means a lot to me."

"Yeah, well, get busy. You have a story to write," he grumbled, pushing himself out of her chair. "Damn, this is the most uncomfortable chair I ever sat in."

"I agree. Does this mean I'm finally getting a new one?"

He scoffed. "Not hardly."

"I didn't think so," she sighed, watching him walk toward his office.

She turned on her laptop and started typing. It took her nearly an hour to complete her article, her mind somehow reluctant to go back to the morning's events once again. Finally she wrapped it up, printed out a copy and took it to Art. Standing in the entrance, leaning against the door jam, arms folded, she waited while he read it. When he was done, he dropped it on his desk and stared at her.

"Sit down," he said somberly.

She took a seat across from him, didn't say anything. She knew what was wrong.

"If this is your first-person narrative, why do I get the impression you're writing about someone else?" he asked.

Jessie shrugged and he leaned forward.

"Look, I understand this is difficult for you. You lived it and to relive it again for thousands to read about it can't be easy. So, go for a walk, take a stroll, whatever. Just get out of here for a while. Then try it again," he said almost softly.

"Okay."

Half an hour later she was sitting on a bench below the Broward Performing Art Center, gazing at the boats gliding by on the dark waters of the Intracoastal. A mother with two small children, a boy and a girl, strolled by and Lilly came to mind, bringing a smile to her face. For the first time today, a total sense of calm came over her. Although tragedy had brought this little girl into her life, it made it clear to her how love for a child can be gratifying. Up until the day she met her, her career had been her only purpose, her driving force. Now, she realized, it was different, her heart had room for so much more. And even though she was saddened about Lilly leaving soon to be with her new family miles away, one thing was sure—their brief time together had changed her life forever.

When she left to walk back to the office, the sun seemed just a bit brighter, the sky somewhat bluer. Life was not only about survival, it was also about hope, dreams, and finding happiness in those small moments coming one's way. A walk on a beach, a stroll in the park, the embrace of a child. It was all there; all she had to do was reach out and let it happen.

At the entrance of the building she took a long, deep breath, then attacked the stairs with renewed energy. Nothing was going to deter her. She was ready to write her story.

Chapter Forty

Three weeks later

"Jessie, get me some more burgers, will you?" Liam shouted over his shoulder, holding a bottle of beer in one hand while adeptly flipping a row of paddies on the grill with the other. Just coming out the patio door, Jessie turned around and stepped back into her small kitchen.

"Meat done?" asked Anita, Sam Perrone's wife, taking out bowls of coleslaw, potato salad and fruit salad from the fridge.

"First batch is done. He's ready for more."

"Here, let me help you," Sam said, walking in behind her.

"I'm fine, really," Jessie said.

"Well then," Anita hollered at her husband, "I could use a hand over here."

Laughter was drifting in from the patio where Doris and her two sons were being entertained by Lonnie McKenzie's husband, Tom, recalling the near disaster which was their wedding day.

Walking out with the burgers, Jessie caught the tail end of his story at the same time she noticed Nina had Jim Boyd trapped in a corner. He was shooting looks of distress in her direction. She grinned. "Nina, can I get you to lend a hand?"

Reluctantly, the woman pulled herself away. A look of relief spread over Boyd's face.

"He's single, yes?" she whispered as she walked past Jessie.

"He is…" Jessie shrugged, hesitating.

"What?" Nina asked, stopping abruptly.

"Remember he's a detective. Works long hours, has small paychecks, and his mother lives with him. He's a package deal."

Nina held up her hand. "Stop right there. No package deals for me, darling."

Jessie nodded and smiled as she walked away. They were sitting down to eat when the doorbell rang. Jessie opened the front door and stood facing Emily Newhart and Lilly. Her eyes lit up.

"I was afraid you wouldn't make it," she shouted, hugging both of them.

Lilly's aunt, a petite woman with short blond hair and warm blue eyes gave her a big smile. "We're leaving in the morning. I don't think Lilly would have forgiven me if we didn't come to say goodbye."

For the past week, Emily was a guest at Annabelle's house. Lilly's foster mom had insisted Emily should stay with them so she and the little girl could get better acquainted. To her relief, they were getting along just great, and Lilly could hardly wait to meet her cousin Benjamin.

"How is your husband?" Jessie asked.

Emily laughed. "He's doing very well. The surgery gave him a new lease on life. He said he has more energy now than ten years ago."

"Good," Jessie said, "because Lilly has lots of energy as well. She'll keep him busy, I'm sure."

"Aunt Emily said I could ride the horses and feed the chickens and the ducks. Will you come and see us, Jessie?"

Jessie smiled. "Don't be surprised if you see me standing at your front door one of these days."

She introduced Emily to the group and they gathered outside, eating and drinking, enjoying the evening breeze blowing in from the ocean.

At one point, Boyd inched up to Jessie, trying to be discreet and failing miserably.

"What the hell did you tell her so she finally left me alone?" he whispered in her ear.

"Who?" she asked innocently.

"Nina, your landlady. Didn't you see how she was all over me earlier and then, she talks to you, and suddenly she acts like I have the plague."

"I don't know. We just chatted."

"Well, let me tell you, whatever you said, I'm glad. That woman is way too much for me."

"I don't think you have to worry now, Detective."

"I think it's about time you call me Jim. Now, tell me why I shouldn't worry about Nina anymore."

Jessie shrugged. "I'm not sure." She started walking away, stopped and turned to look at him. "If by chance she asks about your mother, tell her she's doing well and it looks like she'll live another thirty years."

He stared at her. "What are you talking about? My mother has been gone for ten years, Jessie."

"I know, Jim. Trust me, it's best if you do as I say."

They rejoined the group. Jessie noticed Boyd's look of confusion didn't go away for some time. At least not until after he had another couple of beers.

Emily marveled at the beauty of the lush vegetation around the patio. Lilly sat on Jessie's lap, as they silently enjoyed each other's presence one last time. Much too soon, the evening came to an end and everybody left. Jessie held on to Lilly, willing herself not to cry.

"I will miss you so much, my sweet girl," she said.

"I love you, Jessie," the child said, crying softly.

"And I love you, I always will. Don't worry, we will see each other again," she promised.

Lilly nodded, they hugged once more and they left. Jessie stood by the door, unable to move, her heart suddenly gripped with a deep sadness. And despite all her best efforts, tears flowed down her cheeks as she watched the child she had grown to love so much walk out of her life.

****

Everyone was gone. Liam and Jessie sat quietly outside, listening to the happy chirps of a couple of birds nesting in a nearby oak tree.

"I talked to the CEO of Courtel this morning about the reward for Lilly," Liam said.

"What was his reaction?"

"He seemed receptive. According to the FBI, the diamonds should be released to them within the next few weeks. Anyway, he said they wouldn't wait until then and he proposes a sum of twenty thousand dollars. What do you think?"

"I'm thinking closer to thirty thousand. Invested the right way, it could pay for Lilly's college education."

"I'll call him back tomorrow and suggest your figure. I don't think it will be a problem. Did Perrone tell you if anything new came up with the captured terrorists?"

She shook her head. "It's all still very hush-hush. According to him, Hakim kept most of the information about his contacts in the Middle East to himself. When they raided the building, they found out it was where the scientist who made the gas was killed. And the homeless guy who served as a guinea pig for the sarin trial died there as well. Poor man. From what I read, it must have been a horrible death."

What she didn't share with him was the discovery of more nerve gas in the lab. It was quickly whisked out of there in a top, well, almost top-secret transfer. Of course, Jessie found out somehow, and was sworn to secrecy once more.

"So there are others still involved?" Liam asked.

Jessie nodded.

"They arrested the imam of the mosque we visited. According to Sam, he is refusing to talk. Apparently, he was involved to some degree. For one, they are linking him to the trustee who tortured and killed Dariel Thomas at the jail. On the other hand, Hakim's parents were much more cooperative. They mentioned a relative who is an ISIS commander in Syria. They did their best to discourage their son from having anything to do with him. Obviously, they didn't succeed. The FBI thinks this man was the ring leader and financier of their operation."

"So, not too likely they're going to get their hands on him?" Liam mused.

"Not in the short term," Jessie agreed, then after a moment, continued. "Then again, they're pretty good at finding those people using drones. So who knows?"

They fell into a comfortable silence, gazing up at a sky glowing with stars.

"Care to make a wish?" he asked.

Jessie smiled mysteriously. "I already did."

Liam grinned. They stood up and he pulled her close, covering her face with tender kisses. "I love you, Jessie Milner," he whispered in her ear.

She gazed in his eyes, those dazzling green eyes that drew her in from the start, and saw the reflection of her own passion. Reaching for his hand, she placed it on her heart. "Can you feel it?"

He nodded.

"Good, because it belongs to you," she said softly, before leading him into the house.

A word from the author...

Born in France, I grew up in the Alsace region with its picturesque vineyards and ancient villages. Florida is home now, where my husband and I enjoy life with a never-ending supply of sunshine and intrigue.

Thank you for purchasing
this publication of The Wild Rose Press, Inc.

For questions or more information
contact us at
info@thewildrosepress.com.

The Wild Rose Press, Inc.
www.thewildrosepress.com

To visit with authors of
The Wild Rose Press, Inc.
join our yahoo loop at
http://groups.yahoo.com/group/thewildrosepress/